D1018265

continued . . .

THE QUEEN'S KNIGHT

DEBORAH CHESTER

ACE BOOKS, NEW YORK

THE BERKLEY PUBLISHING GROUP
Published by the Penguin Group
Penguin Group (USA) Inc.
375 Hudson Street, New York, New York 10014, USA
Penguin Group (Canada), 10 Alcorn Avenue, Toronto, Ontario M4V 3B2, Canada
(a division of Pearson Penguin Canada Inc.)
Penguin Books Ltd., 80 Strand, London WC2R 0RL, England
Penguin Group Ireland, 25 St. Stephen's Green, Dublin 2, Ireland (a division of Penguin Books Ltd.)
Penguin Group (Australia), 250 Camberwell Road, Camberwell, Victoria 3124, Australia
(a division of Pearson Australia Group Pty. Ltd.)
Penguin Books India Pvt. Ltd., 11 Community Centre, Panchsheel Park, New Delhi—110 017, India
Penguin Group (NZ), Cnr Airborne and Rosedale Roads, Albany, Auckland 1310, New Zealand
(a division of Pearson New Zealand Ltd.)
Penguin Books (South Africa) (Pty.) Ltd., 24 Sturdee Avenue, Rosebank, Johannesburg 2196,
South Africa

Penguin Books Ltd., Registered Offices: 80 Strand, London WC2R 0RL, England

This is a work of fiction. Names, characters, places, and incidents either are the product of the author's imagination or are used fictitiously, and any resemblance to actual persons, living or dead, business establishments, events, or locales is entirely coincidental.

THE QUEEN'S KNIGHT

An Ace Book / published by arrangement with the author

PRINTING HISTORY
Ace mass market edition / December 2004

Copyright © 2004 by Deborah Chester.
Cover art by Michael Herring.
Cover design by Judith Murello.

ISBN: 0-441-01225-6

ACE
Ace Books are published by The Berkley Publishing Group,
a division of Penguin Group (USA) Inc.,
375 Hudson Street, New York, New York 10014.
ACE and the "A" design are trademarks belonging to Penguin Group (USA) Inc.

PRINTED IN THE UNITED STATES OF AMERICA

10 9 8 7 6 5 4 3 2 1

PART I

Chapter One

Coronation day.

In Savroix-en-Charva, the heart of the realm, church bells should have been pealing in honor of Mandria's newly crowned sovereign. It was a day intended for celebration and festivity. Country folk, nobles, merchants, beggars, and foreign visitors thronged the streets to witness the panoply and splendor of Mandria's grandest occasion.

On this cool spring day, however, the bells hung silent. The steps leading into the mighty cathedral ran with blood from the sprawled corpses of Duc Lervan, consort to the queen of Mandria and usurper of her throne, and his protector Sir Maltric.

Standing stunned and silent were the church and palace officials, much of the court, members of the palace guard, and as many of the citizenry as could be squeezed into the cathedral square. The Duc du Lindier, one of Mandria's most illustrious marechals, had just been arrested publicly for treason. Many of Lervan's supporters, including his chancellor Lord Fillem, were furtively melting into the crowd to avoid a similar fate.

In the great hush, Pheresa of Mandria, lawful queen and chosen successor of King Verence, stood rigid and trembling in the aftershock of having plunged a dagger into her husband's side. Despite her intense anger at his betrayal, she'd never dreamed their mutual enmity would end like this. She had slain him in self-defense, and had it not been for the patient training in weaponry given her by Talmor, 'twould be her corpse on the steps now.

The palace guard stood with her, and their allegiance had made all the difference thus far. Powerful Cardinal Theloi had abandoned his loyalty to Lervan publicly and acknowledged Pheresa as sovereign. But she did not trust him, could never trust him. As for the rest, Lindier, her own father, was still shouting Lervan's name as he was led away. Her gaze moved across the faces of her most powerful vassals, including the heads of the ducal houses of Gide, Clune, Roncel, and Meringare, seeking acceptance and support.

She saw only hostility or astonishment. Of course, she realized, when last her court had seen her, she'd been large with child. Her beauty and femininity evoked general admiration. Although she'd been the inspiration for many poems and ballads, she'd been an ineffectual ruler. Nay, how could these lords and courtiers know her for their Queen Pheresa, the sweet, gentle Lady of the Chalice? She hardly knew herself. Now she wore man's garb, splattered and stained from days of travel. Her hair hung wild and uncombed about her face. Like a harridan, she'd just shouted down the husband who had betrayed his marriage vows to her. When he'd tried to kill her, she managed to strike first. *No,* she thought, lifting her chin. *I am not the same.*

At the moment, her emotions were raging inside her in a chaotic mix, for she'd begun this day with expectations of disaster, and now there was all the hope in the world.

Only one thing remained clear to her: She must face her lords like a true sovereign and force them to respect her. If she did not regain their loyalty now, she would never have it.

It was strange, standing there in that frozen moment as though all history had stopped its slow unfurling from the spindle of time. The fact that she'd survived her conflict with Lervan and won filled her with heady exhilaration, yet she'd never been more afraid. She knew she was not safe yet, not until the crown rested on her brow. The throne, the very sovereignty of Mandria, presently teetered on the brink of disaster and chaos.

When I enter the church, they must follow, she thought. *If they do not witness my crowning, I am as much lost as if Lervan still lived.*

At the thought, her gaze strayed involuntarily back to the dead man at her feet. Lervan's sightless eyes stared at nothing. No charm remained in his slack features, no guile. Regret filled her, as sour as a luamin seed, before she pushed it away. *It did not have to be like this,* she thought, but he was gone to perdition, and she would not mourn him.

As she shuddered, Talmor stepped between her and the onlookers to shield her reaction from them.

"Stay strong," he whispered, his amber eyes keen with concern.

She glanced up at his handsome, bronzed face. He looked pinched about the mouth still, for he'd come with her to this place with the conviction that he was a puppet of the darkest forces and would slay her. Although his vision had been proven false, he carried the look of a man both haunted and reprieved.

As her eyes met his, her heart grew warm, for this man was the only one who mattered to her now. They had come through this ordeal together, and Talmor would never fail her.

A faint, wordless sound escaped her for all that she longed to say to him and could not at this time. He gave her a warning glance as he took her bloody dagger from her hand and wiped it clean on his leggings. His keen, always vigilant gaze shifted past her, and only then did she hear the scrape of footsteps.

She turned to find the commander of the palace guard bowing to her. Lord Nejel was a well-made man, sleek and aristocratic, with blond hair waving back from his brow. His rank insignia was embroidered on the front of his bright green cloak, and every bit of his armor and weaponry was polished to a blinding sheen. "May I escort your majesty inside?" he asked.

As he spoke, the guardsmen formed a double line up the steps.

Much heartened by their presence, she nodded to Lord Nejel. As she ascended the steps, she saw Cardinal Theloi watching her with so dour a look she warned herself to remain careful. Although she'd survived today's first danger, how many other obstacles remained between her and coronation? Would the church soldiers surround her the moment she entered the cathedral? Would she be spirited away to exile in a nuncery as Theloi had originally intended, or perhaps even to death? Although Theloi had appeared to accept her victory, she knew he was capable of great deceit. The question now was whether he would dare move against her inside the church or would he bide his time by plotting a new intrigue.

"Majesty?" Lord Nejel prompted.

Realizing she'd stopped, she made herself continue without glancing again at Theloi. On no account must she let herself appear uncertain. She must look and act assured, for her confidence would sway many of the undecided to her cause.

And so she smoothed the slight frown from her face and beckoned for Talmor to join her. "At my side," she said.

Talmor had never looked more serious. Tension radiated in the set of his broad shoulders, and his hand stayed close to his sword hilt. Only a few moments ago, there'd been a blaze of relief lighting up his face when he first realized he wasn't destined to betray her, but he wore the impassive mask he'd perfected while serving as her protector.

Bowing to her so that his unruly black curls flopped across his forehead, Talmor slung the saddlebags across his shoulder and took his customary place at her heels.

"No," Pheresa said. "At my side."

Talmor's eyes widened, and Lord Nejel drew an audible breath. Cardinal Theloi and some of the other dignitaries turned and headed rapidly inside the narthex. She felt suddenly too reckless to care how others regarded her public show of favor to Talmor. He was her most trusted ally and friend. He was her heart, her life. She wanted everyone to know what he meant to her.

"Come," she said, and Talmor obeyed her.

Walking with her head high, she passed the line of saluting guards to enter the shadowy interior of the vast cathedral as though she owned it, as though, minutes before, she had not been in imminent danger of arrest and disaster.

Instead, she walked to her destiny as Mandria's queen. The moment she saw the arching ceiling, burning candles, and coronation throne, her heart raced and thudded. Tremendous excitement suddenly took her breath.

Yet the solemnity of the clerics filling the narthex and the interior of the great church, so shadowy and quiet after the sunlight outdoors and filled with the scents of incense and candle wax, pressed down some of her elation and brought her a queer sense of uneasiness. She felt cold and newly worried, for her ambitions—such high ones, such large ones—suddenly overwhelmed her. How had she ever dared dream that she, so gentle and unsure a maid, could rise to the very pinnacle of power?

They halted in the narthex, for there were numerous officials milling about, all looking flustered by the changes in the planned proceedings. Longing to walk forward and anxious for the ceremony and ritual to be over, Pheresa could not stop herself from staring toward the throne, positioned at the opposite end of the nave.

The sight of it made her dizzy and breathless again.

"Soon," Talmor whispered to her. "You're nearly there."

She had to laugh beneath her breath. "Am I so anxious for it?"

Nodding, he let one corner of his lips curl ever so slightly in reassurance.

She drew several deep breaths, trying to steady herself.

Whatever problem was disrupting the officials, they seemed finally to have it sorted out. A cleric came bustling up and bowed to Pheresa. He was short and slightly plump, middle-aged with silvery hair drifting around his shaved tonsure. One of his pale pudgy hands pointed to the left. "If your majesty will consent to enter the robing room?"

Pheresa realized how dreadful her appearance must be. She'd never before appeared publicly in such dishevelment as this, garbed like a man and bare of jewels, quite unfit to appear. Yet for the first time in her life she was impatient with such vanity, for she'd learned the value of higher priorities than pretty clothes and courtly manners.

"No," she said, quite sharp. "Let us proceed as we are."

Everyone within earshot looked startled.

It was Talmor who said, "But your majesty's finery and jewels . . . and all the fuss about bringing them. Or will you be crowned wearing Lervan's blood?"

She shot him a penetrating look. "Are you a courtier already? How persuasively you appeal to my vanity, so that I will not mind that you dare to naysay me."

Talmor's brow puckered, but he held his tongue.

Already regretting her rebuke, she shot him a look of contrition and squelched her sense of impatience. She knew, after all, the discipline and demands of court life all too well.

"Of course," she said reluctantly. "I must at least don the coronation robes, even if the rest of my appearance cannot be remedied."

"If your majesty desires," the cleric piped up, "attendants have been summoned, to prepare for the ceremony."

She nodded coolly. "Very well. Lord Talmor, stay close. I—"

The cleric raised his hands. "This one must go no farther," he said shrilly. "Let the queen and her guard protector proceed, but this blasphemer may not pass."

Anger flashed in Talmor's golden eyes, and Pheresa turned on the cleric in outrage and suspicion. "What mean you?" she demanded sharply. "How dare—"

"By the lord cardinal's orders, your majesty. I dare not permit an evil doer, one tried and condemned, to cross into the holy spaces of the—"

The crashing cadence of booted feet in unison interrupted the cleric's explanation. With spurs jingling and chain mail clinking, a squad of church soldiers came marching up the steps from the warren of auxiliary rooms located below the sanctum. Shoulder to shoulder they strode into sight, their white-and-black surcoats all too distinctive, their hands on their weapons. Halting in front of Pheresa, so that they blocked her path, they saluted her.

She froze in place like a hare in danger.

Shoving the cleric aside, Talmor put himself between Pheresa and the church knights. Nejel joined him. Other members of the palace guard crowded up behind her. Boxed in on all sides by armed men ready to do battle, she felt her heart hammering her ribs while her blood ran cold. Certain now that this was indeed a trap sprung by Theloi's order—Theloi's *treason,* she thought angrily—she reached for the hilt of her dagger and vowed she would not let them take her alive.

"What mean you by this, Sir Brim?" Nejel was demanding angrily. "How dare you stand in the queen's way?"

"We stand not against the queen," one of the church knights replied gruffly, "but against the blasphemer with her. He cannot enter the holy places. He is forbidden here."

Swearing, Talmor reached for his sword, but Nejel gripped his wrist. "Draw no steel! Are you mad?" Nejel said in warning. "Think of where you are!"

"I am neither pagan nor blasphemer," Talmor said hotly, "and I will challenge any who call me so."

In that moment, Pheresa saw the trap laid for him. She tried to warn him, but it was too late. He'd already said too much.

Sir Brim drew in a satisfied breath. A bull of a man, he was thick through neck and shoulders, barrel-chested and long-armed. Now he glared at Talmor with a contemptuous smirk. "And I say you are both—"

"Silence, you fool!" Nejel commanded. "No challenge and no insult can be issued here on sacred ground, much less before the very queen. Sir Brim, you insult her majesty with this unseemly display. You cannot accept any challenge in these circumstances."

"Meddler! Who are you to dictate to me?" But as the

guardsmen at Lord Nejel's back closed in, Sir Brim raised his hand hastily. "All right," he said in sullen disappointment. "But I have orders to put the blasphemer out. And my orders will I obey."

Talmor drew breath, but Pheresa chose to intervene before he could repeat his challenge.

"Call you the queen a blasphemer, Sir Brim?" she asked.

The man turned to her aghast. "Nay, your majesty! I would not dare. 'Tis this pagan *sorcerel* that—"

"Lord Talmor is not a *sorcerel*." But even as she spoke, Pheresa knew that it was unseemly for her to be defending anyone, especially in public. She had been cornered into acting like a commoner, and such behavior would only cast more doubt about her ability to rule to those who witnessed this confrontation. Angry with herself, she glared at Lord Nejel. "Commander, clear the queen's path."

As Lord Nejel stepped forward resolutely, a priest in a white robe, a coif of pleated white silk framing his face, appeared before Talmor with a Circle held high in repudiation.

"Forbidden!" he cried. "Blasphemer, be driven out lest you defile these sacred proceedings!"

Talmor's face grew dark with anger, his eyes blazing. "Your majesty," he said, his voice hard and level. "With your permission, I shall withdraw."

"No!" Pheresa said in alarm. "I require your presence with me. I command it."

His eyes met hers in an unspoken message. "And I obey the queen in all things. But what need has your majesty of my service here? The guards and Lord Nejel can protect you. Permit me to withdraw, that no further delays hinder your majesty's coronation."

She understood him, but fear threatened the calm she was struggling to maintain. She was being neatly sundered from her most valiant and loyal protector. It infuriated her that Theloi dared dictate to her in this way, but at the moment she knew she must acquiesce if only to prevent bloodshed.

"Very well," she said, glaring at Sir Brim and the priest. "But the queen is most seriously displeased with this slander cast against Lord Talmor. He was exonerated from all charges cast against him. You do wrong here in seeking to resurrect what is past and finished."

"We knights of the church do but serve our orders, your majesty," Sir Brim replied.

She stiffened. "Clearly you serve no wishes of the queen."

Sir Brim glanced at the guardsmen and bowed to her without reply.

With her hands curling into fists, it was all Pheresa could do to keep control of her temper. *Please, Thod,* she prayed. *Let me take sovereignty quickly that I may teach these varlets their place.* She was tired of being underestimated because she was a woman, tired of being misjudged and patronized. Even if Theloi was not plotting to strike against her now, he had insulted her through this petty action against Talmor. She vowed she would not overlook it.

If she survived the rest of this day.

Fuming, she gestured permission for Talmor to go. It was not what she wanted, not what she had intended. He was being shamed and insulted unjustly. She hated it, and felt herself a coward because she did not continue his defense, however prudent it might be to wait.

He shrugged off the saddlebags, and for a horrified moment she feared he meant to hand them to her. Instead, he drew his dagger and swiftly sliced the stitching attaching the bags to their strapping. The bag containing her gown he held out to the cleric, who looked so confounded at being treated like a servant that he took it. The bag holding the precious seal of state and official documents of the realm, Talmor tied to his belt.

Relief swept Pheresa, for she could trust him to guard them with his life.

Talmor said, "I will await your majesty outside, if that is agreeable?"

"It is *not* agreeable!" she said sharply, but then managed to check her ire. "But . . . let it be done."

Talmor leaned close to Nejel's ear. "Stay close to her," he murmured. "Her life and safety depend on you."

"She is safe," Nejel replied, his eyes steady as they met Talmor's. "I swear it."

Talmor nodded and glanced at Pheresa with a last, quick frown. She glimpsed a flash of his rage and worry before he mastered his expression once more and strode away, moving fast with that catlike grace so distinctive in him.

The clerics and officials parted before him in haste. Some made furtive signs of the Circle as though to ward off evil, and Pheresa ached to see it. The bigotry of her subjects had never embarrassed her more.

"Is your majesty ready to proceed?" the cleric asked.

Despising the little toad, she turned and saw him pointing the way with an unctuous smile of satisfaction. Nejel and the other palace guards stayed alert, still ready for trouble, their hands close to their weapons.

The church soldiers parted smartly to line the passage, so that she was forced to walk between them to the steps. With her heart in her throat, Pheresa descended into the chambers below without knowing whether she walked to her destiny or her doom.

Chapter Two

No one spoke as Pheresa passed through a tiny side chapel, down the steps, and into the passageway beyond. She kept her gaze straight ahead, refusing to glance at Sir Brim at her side, or at the church knights following her. Lord Nejel stayed close, but the rest of the guards had been forced to remain behind. He alone served as her protector, and what good was he, outnumbered as he was?

Theloi has me in his power, she thought in near despair. *If these knights dare attack, I am lost.*

A small monk in somber habit was waiting to open a narrow door of heavily carved wood. Pheresa stepped into a square room of modest proportions, paneled with wood and bare of furnishings save for a cupboard and vestment chest in one corner, a simple chair, a prayer stool, and a small table. The latter held a wooden box of considerable age and wear, a reliquary, and an ebony scroll case carved with interlocking Circles. It was, Pheresa saw, a place for preparation. She glanced at the cupboard, wondering if the coronation robes were inside it, and dared not quite let herself believe she was going to wear them. *This room,* she told herself, *could also serve as a cell, for it was austere enough.*

Swallowing hard, she halted in the center of the room. "Where are the attendants I require?"

Theloi walked in, his robes pristine white, his yellow sash embroidered with holy symbols. His narrow gray goatee emphasized the crimped set of his mouth, but his green eyes were watching her astutely.

Sir Brim saluted him, and Theloi dismissed the knight with a casual wave before glancing at Lord Nejel. "See what's keeping the queen's attendants, will you, commander?"

Nejel snapped his fingers at the cleric who had sidled in to deliver the saddlebag. "You there," Nejel said sharply. "Jump to it."

Looking resentful, the cleric glanced at Theloi, who ignored him.

"Find out what delays the attendants," Lord Nejel said. "Go!"

With a huff, the cleric gathered up his robes and scuttled out.

"That will be all, Commander Nejel," Theloi said.

"I desire the commander to stay," Pheresa said quickly.

Both men turned to stare at her. Nejel's handsome face looked troubled and wary. She prayed she could depend on him to obey her.

Theloi's green eyes surveyed her coldly. "Will your majesty undergo confession and private mass before the ceremonies?" he asked. "Or will you carry the stain of Duc Lervan's blood on both conscience and heart to the throne?"

Pheresa stiffened. Had they been dueling with thinswords, that question would have been the mocking little tap and feint before the lunge.

"Does your majesty desire a witness to her confessional?" Theloi asked in his cold, spider-soft voice. "Or will the queen agree to dismiss Lord Nejel?"

Before she could reply, Nejel eased toward the door. "I shall await your majesty's commands outside," he murmured, and went out, shutting the door firmly behind him.

His departure was too hasty for her to feel anything but abandoned, especially since he had promised Talmor he would stay close by her. Pheresa found herself disappointed and fuming. Perhaps Lord Nejel considered her safe enough with this poisonous old man, but she did not.

Small, thin, elderly, there was nothing meek or holy about this cardinal. For years, he'd been one of her most determined enemies. He'd schemed and intrigued against her, and she had no doubt that Lervan had been his puppet.

Clearly he'd maneuvered her into his domain and isolated her as though he wanted to demonstrate the extent of his power.

But although she was tense and frightened, Pheresa refused to let him intimidate her. If she could not deal with the cardinal by herself, how could she prevail against the enemies of Mandria? If she could not get through this day by herself, how could she expect to rule the land? She would prove to Theloi that she was not a weak, spineless woman unworthy of the crown soon to be hers. She would prove it to all her subjects.

"Cardinal," she said briskly, "the queen acknowledges the value of your stated support today and hopes to see new accord between crown and church in the future."

His eyes narrowed, and she could feel such enmity radiating from him that she nearly reached for her dagger.

"Does your majesty mock me?" he whispered harshly.

"I would not presume. I take you very seriously indeed, lord cardinal."

"And it seems I have . . . underestimated your majesty."

Her chin lifted. "Most men do, at one time or another."

"I am not most men."

She shrugged and saw a tiny muscle twitch under his right eye.

"May I speak frankly?" he asked.

She nodded.

"Will I remain your majesty's spiritual adviser? Will I remain at Savroix?"

This was not what she expected him to ask. Startled by his

admission of uncertainty, she looked down to hide her surprise, but she did not know if she'd been quick enough to evade his sharp eyes. It had never occurred to her that Theloi might fear her in his turn, might be wondering and scheming how best to save himself in the ruin of Lervan's plans to seize the throne. She'd been so certain that Theloi was the supreme danger, and now her astonishment and relief were tremendous.

Such emotions nearly made her give herself away, but she managed to hold back a smile and quick answer. *Wait,* she thought. *Wait.*

"Will I, your majesty?"

When at last she looked up and met his eyes, she kept her face smooth of all expression. "I do not know," she replied.

The muscle twitched again beneath his eye. He leaned forward, his hand white-knuckled around his diamond-studded Circle. "Your majesty and I have seldom been in agreement, but I am loyal to the crown. My actions are always directed toward what is best for this realm."

Her anger returned. How pompous and self-righteous he was, she thought. Did he think her such a fool as to believe such lies?

Her stony silence seemed to fluster him. Theloi walked over to the table and stood staring down at its surface. "I can do a great deal on behalf of your majesty," he said, his voice soft and whispery, as delicate and evil as the swift scuttle of a spider across the back of someone's hand. "My range of influence is vast. My—"

Unable to bear more of this, she cut him off. "Are you pleading for a sinecure, lord cardinal?" she asked incredulously.

"No! I plead for my life. If you will have your own father arrested, who at court is safe now? How far do you intend to take your vengeance? How deep will you cut among the officials and ministers who remained behind when your majesty fled last year? You have wintered at Thirst and incited the upland chevards to violence, risking civil war with a reckless disregard of—"

"It is not your place to criticize me."

"I am permitted to ask your majesty to see reason. I am permitted to be concerned about the future well-being of Mandria. How far will your majesty go in tearing the court, and the realm, apart?"

There was a time when Pheresa would have answered him, earnestly, even sincerely. But she was no longer as naive and idealistic as when she'd left Savroix. She stared at him now, amazed by his plain speaking, and found herself increasingly suspicious of it.

"Will your majesty say nothing to me?" he demanded.

"I stand here in astonishment," she said finally, looking him over. "I did not realize you were such a fine actor, Cardinal Theloi. This display of distress and worry on your part is very well done."

He looked as though he'd bitten into something sour. "I assure your majesty that my concerns are real."

"No doubt. Only I'm not entirely sure what your concerns really are. Your informants will have told you how I fared in gathering support among those upland chevards. And 'tis your knights that stand outside this door, not my guards."

Impatience flashed in Theloi's eyes. "Must we feint and parry, your majesty? I seek only—"

"You are a supremely brilliant strategist," she broke in. "I do not think you fear for yourself, or your status, at all. Do you expect me to hasten to assure you that all will be well, or that all will go on as it did before?"

"Oh, I can see that little will go on as before," he said so coldly that her brows drew together. "Your majesty has changed considerably during your stay among the uplanders. Abandoning your people in their hour of greatest need. Jeopardizing the life of your unborn child. A *royal* child and potential heir to the throne."

"You—"

But he did not stop. "Consorting with a mongrel blasphemer without shame or decency, in violation of your marriage vows."

"Lord cardinal!"

"Showering favors on this acknowledged *sorcerel*, royal favors of land and privilege, making him a baron and setting him higher than his own father. Prancing him forth on this day before the assembly . . . has your majesty lost all sense of shame and modesty?"

"How dare you reprimand me!"

He came closer, his face tight and vicious, his eyes bright with contempt. "What spell has he laid on your majesty, to make you forget what is decent and moral? What control keeps he over you, that even now, here in this holy place, you defend him?"

So this was what Theloi had been up to, she realized furiously. Tricking her with his pretended meekness, making her feel victorious over him, even a little sorry for him, only to turn on her and plunge these accusations into her like dagger thrusts. And she, closeted with him in private, with not even a protector or an attendant to shut him up. She backed away from him, a little afraid of the ferocity in his eyes. If he'd gone mad, what was she to do with him?

"Killing Lervan . . ." Theloi's low voice went on relentlessly. "How could you do that, save through some working of a spell? You are no warrior, but a woman of weak and bendable spirit. I say this *sorcerel* has possessed your mind and soul, and trained you to do his bidding. I say your mind needs to be opened to an examination in order that exorcism can be—"

She approached him quickly and slapped him hard across the face.

He blinked, reeling back. His face turned stark white, save for the red finger marks across his cheek. A taut, furious silence fell between them.

"For a man worried about banishment," she said furiously, "you have surely sealed your fate. How dare you speak to the queen in such a way! Have you gone mad?"

"I am sworn to the glorious service of Tomias," he replied. "The office I uphold requires me to guard the spiritual well-being of this realm's sovereign. And your majesty is clearly under the—"

"Repeat not that vile slander," she broke in. "I'll have your tongue cut out for it!"

He dared smile thinly at her. "Ah, at last we have the Pheresa I recognize. A lady easily rendered distraught. A lady ready to threaten and bluster in silly, ill-thought ways." His smile abruptly vanished. "This is not Nether, your majesty, where such barbarism takes place. Under what law would you have my torture carried out?"

Her face burned from his mockery, his raw contempt. He dared too much, showed his hand too plainly. Did he have such power, she wondered, that he was not afraid of her at all?

"What mean you by all this?" she whispered.

"Your majesty possesses unaccountable luck," he said, lifting his hand in a small salute. "Today's events could not have been predicted to the slightest extent. Duc Lervan was at the very brink of taking the crown. Yet now he lies dead, and here is your majesty to take his place."

"Fiend!" she snapped. "He was the usurper, not I!"

"You have come here without an army, without supporters, with nothing save your *sorcerel* familiar, and you have prevailed."

Pheresa lifted her chin. "Thod is with me. My cause is just."

"Tell me this. Why want you the throne so intensely? Whence comes this ambition, this determination to have something you are so unsuited for?"

She hated him for making her defend herself. "I am Verence's chosen successor."

"That successor should be a man!"

"This is Mandria, not Nether!" she retorted. "Your mind is bound in the past."

He shook his head. "So dainty, so feminine . . . this new behavior *must* be magic. There can be no other explanation. You were a lovely princess, unspoiled, charming, the Lady of the Chalice. And now you are . . ." His gaze raked her up and down. "*This*. I counsel your majesty to surrender yourself to the ministrations of the church. Let us take this affliction from you and undo this spell."

"Oh, I see," Pheresa said harshly. "The last time we crossed wills, lord cardinal, you wanted to banish me to a nuncery so that I could be incarcerated into sainthood and kept isolated. Now you challenge my sanity and my soul. Why should I trust you, much less surrender my thoughts to your inquisitors?"

Theloi said nothing. His cold green eyes watched her the way a hawk might watch its prey.

Again, suspicions crawled through her. Why was he threatening her so openly? What meant he really to do?

She did not like the feeling of being maneuvered by a master hand, as though she had no more volition than a draught piece.

"There is something else," she said quietly. "You have been extremely bold today, lord cardinal, shifting your stance at every opportunity and doing all in your power to provoke me. Why? Isn't it time you uttered what you really came here to say?"

His smile never reached his eyes. "Your majesty has learned to be perceptive."

"Let's say that I've been forced to it. What are you really after?"

He bowed his head ever so slightly. "Your majesty is correct. These are all strategies I could try, were I opposed to your majesty's rule. But I have already assured your majesty of my continued loyalty to the crown."

"Go on."

"I have rule over the Reformed Church, as your majesty has rule over the land. I keep treasury from the tithes, and your majesty keeps treasury from the taxes."

"I don't need a lesson in civics," she snapped.

"Is not a truce to our mutual advantage?" he asked. "Let me suggest that your majesty not pursue inquiries into my past activities. After all, it is known that I encouraged Duc Lervan to come to court. I sponsored him, brought him to the notice of King Verence, and so forth."

"You also supported his false claim to my throne."

Theloi ignored her comment. "Let me suggest that your

majesty not inquire into my past activities, not persecute the church, and not attempt to undermine the very foundation of our realm. In return I shall—"

"Would you bargain with me?" she asked in astonishment. "Do you dare put yourself equal to me?"

"Your majesty's soul is in peril," he replied very softly indeed. "Mandria has already lost Prince Gavril to the horrors of evil. Will your majesty go that route as well?"

She gasped. "You threaten me, in very truth. You dare too much!"

"No, it is your majesty who does that," he said. "Making a baron of a bastard with mixed blood and magical powers forbidden to anyone shriven before Tomias! Killing your lawful husband. Leaving your child dead in a frozen Edonian grave. This is not what monarchs of Mandria do! We are not a land of barbarians, with tyrants who do as they please and repudiate the teachings of Thod!"

She found herself shaking. "Get out."

He stood his ground. "I warn your majesty not to make an enemy of the church. Take confession now and turn your soul back into my hands. Kneel on the prayer stool, and allow me to cleanse your mind and heart—"

She drew her dagger. It was not glowing white as it would have in the presence of Nonkind, but she knew there were other kinds of evil in this world, and Theloi's kind she could see for herself. "Get back from me," she commanded. "You'll not touch me. You'll not dare to whisper these untruths about me."

Lifting his hands, he assumed a look of false astonishment. "Your majesty surely cannot intend to refuse my benediction?"

She hissed, amazed that Thod did not strike him for his arrogance and blasphemy. *Truly*, she thought, *here is a despicable man.* "Do you really fear charges of treason, lord cardinal?" she asked. "Then go no further with these threats. As you have warned me, so do I now warn you. Turn not the church against me."

He used his diamond-studded Circle to make a sign of repudiation, then dared to smile. "We have spoken in private. Anything that leaves this room will be denied by me, and I'm sure your majesty will do the same. At the moment we have an impasse. But there will come a day when perhaps that will change."

Furiously, she sought a reply, but how could such arrogance, such blatant defiance be shamed? The sound of raised voices outside and a sudden knocking on the door made her jump. She sheathed her dagger.

"Enter!" she called, perhaps too shrilly.

Lord Salba, his gingery gold hair ruffled and his clothes disheveled, came bustling inside. As he saw her and Theloi standing on opposite sides of the room, he grunted to himself, bowed as low as his girth would permit, and clapped his hands smartly together.

"Your majesty!" he boomed genially, brown eyes atwinkle. "I am *delighted* to see you looking so well. I came as soon as the news of your—er—*triumphant* return reached me. How may I be of service?"

Relieved to see him, she stared to speak, but Theloi raised his hand. "If that is all, your majesty?"

"Quite all," she said coldly.

The cardinal coolly met her angry gaze. "Then I shall see that the necessary alterations for today's ceremony are in place. Do not keep your subjects waiting long, for your majesty knows all too well how swiftly fortunes can change."

The door closed behind him, and Pheresa released her bottled-up emotions by kicking the chair. "Thod smite that—"

"Your majesty, quickly, before we are interrupted," Salba said, dropping his bluff, hearty manner. "The seal of state, the documents . . . are they safe?"

She glared at him. "You might inquire about my well-being before theirs."

He brushed off this suggestion. "Your majesty looks extremely well. But these items of state are vital to securing your power. There's more to this business than putting the crown and scepter in royal hands." As he spoke, his gaze went to the saddlebag. "Is that it?"

"No," she said curtly. "The Baron of Edriel guards what you seek."

Salba's face grew pale, and he stared at her intently. She saw that he'd aged since she'd last seen him. Of course she knew that Lervan had removed him from the office of lord chancellor. No doubt Salba had had a difficult time surviving the recent political upheavals at court. She hoped that he'd remained as trustworthy and loyal as in the past. For his assistance in her escape from the Vvordsmen, she made herself now overlook his gruff discourtesy.

"Edriel," he said vaguely, as though he did not know who she meant, then his gaze sharpened. "Sir Talmor . . . your majesty's protector?"

"Lord Talmor," she corrected.

"Ah, yes. I'd heard rumors of this." He sighed and sent her an unhappy look. "Many rumors."

Her annoyance flared hotter. "Yes? Talmor saved my life at great personal cost. In the past it has been customary to reward men for their valor, but this court seems amazed that I want to do the same."

"It is not customary for valiant men to wield magic on their sovereign's behalf," Salba said, and knotted his heavy brows. "There will be trouble. Your majesty must expect it."

She sighed. "It has already begun."

"Ah. Is that why you and the cardinal were glaring at each other?"

"His eminence is quite mad. I want you to see that Lord Talmor is permitted to return inside this church. Theloi had no business driving him away, calling him a *sorcerel* and other—"

"Your majesty surely understands that there is a time and a place for everything," Salba said with a dismissive gesture. "And now is not—"

"I want Talmor present!"

Salba's bushy brows shot up. "So the rumors are more accurate than I thought. It would relieve me greatly to see that your majesty's sagacity and prudence have not entirely vanished."

At that moment she could have thrown something at him for daring to criticize her. Defiantly, she said, "I have been considering proclaiming Talmor my consort immediately after the coronation."

Although Salba blanched, she continued, "After all, my great-great-grandfather was married within minutes of putting on the crown. Is it not customary for some monarchs to announce their betrothals at such times?"

Glancing swiftly around as though to make sure no one was listening at the door, Salba edged closer to her. "Your majesty, I beg you to do nothing so rash. With your husband less than an hour dead, you must not supply authority to the slanderous charges of adultery and misconduct he laid against you."

Rage swept her so intensely it was as though a torch had been set to her garments, sending her up in flames. "I was forced to mourn Gavril," she said through her teeth. "I won't mourn Lervan!"

Salba opened his mouth, but she'd had enough. "No more of this!" she commanded. "If you will not assist me in this matter—"

"Your majesty, Lord Talmor's situation can be dealt with later. But at present, his reputation is such that people must wonder. Too much haste can only do your majesty harm, and right now—"

"I know what is required of me this day. How dare you think I do not?"

"Your majesty—"

"Enough!" Her voice was shaking from the effort she expended to keep it low and controlled. "Very well. I shan't offend my subjects today by pushing Lord Talmor before them, but at least permit him to enter the church. He is no pagan, no heretic. Thod above, after all his service and sacrifice on my behalf can he not be allowed to witness my coronation?"

"Your majesty," Salba said, looking troubled. "It speaks well of you to feel gratitude to such a man, but let not your kind and generous nature carry you into folly. If Theloi proclaims him a heretic, is it not better to allow matters to die down for a time? Let the man see to his new estates. Let the court become accustomed to—"

"You ask me to send him away," she said furiously. "My only friend and closest ally during exile. He stood true to me when others fled. He nearly died to save my life. He has been faithful as no one else has, and *this* is how I am to repay him?"

"Your majesty has many true and loyal subjects," Salba murmured. "Do not lose sight of that in your present infatuation."

She drew in a sharp breath. "Take care, Lord Salba. I have done nothing I need be ashamed for. And Lord Talmor is no heretic to be denied admittance to the cathedral. How can you support this injustice?"

"Your majesty is overwrought. Let us deal with matters one at a time, in order of their importance. What is vital now is to see your majesty safely and securely on the throne. After that, the rest can be handled in due process."

Despite her frustration, Pheresa recognized the soundness of his advice. She reminded herself that Lord Salba had always counseled her well. It did her no credit to lose her temper with him.

"I dislike this greatly," she said, sighing. "It is monstrously unfair."

"Many things in this world are unfair," he replied. "But we survive most of them. Lord Talmor is well able to endure a few insults, and I have no doubt that he will be happy for your majesty on this day, whether he witnesses the coronation or not."

When she nodded reluctantly, Salba rubbed his hands briskly together. "To other things. Am I reinstated as your majesty's lord chancellor?"

His effrontery made her brows rise, but she found herself nodding. "Yes, of course."

"Good. Then have I your majesty's permission to proceed as I deem fit?"

"At the moment, yes."

"Clearly you place uncommon reliance on this Talmor, since you have given him the very symbols of your power."

"*Lord* Talmor," she insisted. "Of course I trust him."

The chancellor turned away. "I must find the fellow without delay. The seal and documents of state must be secured and in the palace by the time your majesty arrives following the ceremony. For the signatures and other official reinstatements . . ." he added vaguely. "It was my only hope for this fiasco with Duc Lervan, that despite the coronation he would not be able to produce the seal or the rest of the—"

"Lord Salba," she interrupted impatiently, "Lervan is no longer a concern."

"Quite so!" His brown eyes suddenly twinkled. "Such a relief. Now, I ask your majesty to prepare as slowly as possible for your investiture."

"Why? Surely delay is only cause for—"

He held up his hand. "Forgive me. If I am to secure things swiftly and return, I must not tarry longer. Have I your majesty's permission to find Sir—um—the baron immediately?"

"Were Lord Talmor allowed on these premises," she said bitterly, "you would not have to search for him at all."

"Ah." Salba gave her a fleeting little smile. "May I withdraw?"

As she could hear the sounds of women's voices, high with excitement, approaching in the passageway, she felt suddenly unsure of Salba's motives, especially in light of his opposition to Talmor. She wanted time to think, for she disliked being rushed into hasty decisions. Moreover, she wanted someone she trusted to remain close by her.

As though he sensed her doubts, Salba dared take her hands in his age-knotted ones. "Pheresa of Mandria," he said proudly, "I have prayed long and hard that you would prevail. And now, despite tremendous odds, your hour of destiny has come. Seize it, and do not look back!"

"But, Lord Salba—"

"Courage, your majesty. I must hasten if I am to be in time. Thod keep you." And he was gone.

Pheresa wanted to call him back, but her attendants came rushing in, curtsying with glad little cries and excited chatter.

Barely pausing to ask her permission, they began unbuckling and unlacing her garments in a frenzy to make her ready. And as the door swung firmly closed, she glimpsed the church knights still on duty, as though to remind her of the church's strength and power, surrounding her on all sides.

Chapter Three

Talmor was halfway across the crowded narthex when four church knights closed in on him, crowding so tightly on all sides that before he could take action, a dagger was pricking his ribs.

"Say nothing," he was told. "Remain quiet and cause no trouble."

Already boiling with resentment, Talmor was in no mood to suffer additional insult. "Let me pass," he growled.

The dagger point jabbed him, making him wince, and he stilled his protests. A swift glance over his shoulder told him that the queen had already vanished from sight, no witness to this ambush. Around him the crowd of courtiers and nobles jostled in, accepting direction from the harried ushers. The guardsmen who were supposed to escort Pheresa seemed instead to be dispersing. Alarmed because they were not with her, Talmor tried to turn back but to no avail. Angrily he shrugged off a restraining hand, but they crowded him even closer.

One of his captors pointed at a narrow doorway on the opposite side of the narthex. "That door's for the likes of you, heretic."

"I'll leave the way I came in," Talmor said.

Again the dagger jabbed him. This time he felt the skin break and sting fiercely. He drew in a deep breath, forcing himself to hold his temper. He was in a church; it was a solemn state occasion; he was seriously outnumbered. Attacking these brutes would be futile, and instigating a public brawl would be an embarrassment for the queen. But he did not like how swiftly he'd been separated from her side. He did not like the fact that her guardsmen were no longer with her. And he did not like these ruffian church knights holding him captive at the point of a dagger.

"I was leaving the church," he said, trying to reason with them. "There is no need for this. Unhand me!"

The leader of the four knights, a thick-shouldered man just starting to run to fat, glared at him, standing so close that Talmor could smell the sourness of his sweat. "You'll leave as we want you to," he said. "Now curb that heathen tongue of yours and walk quietly, or Sir Gauve here will carve his initials on your ribs."

One of them shoved Talmor from behind, and, tight-lipped and fuming, he turned away from the main entrance and headed in the direction they wanted.

"See, men?" the leader said, smirking. "Nice and docile, ain't he? But then I guess being reduced to half a man has took the fight out of him."

Talmor's gaze narrowed, and he could feel his pulse beating hot and fast in his throat.

"Careful, Sir Nunn," one of the others muttered. "This heretic's dangerous."

Sir Nunn did not look worried. "We're protected from the likes of him. We've nothing to fear."

Certain he was heading for an alley to be beaten, Talmor lobbed the saddlebag into the arms of the closest guard. "Give that to Lord Salba, on the queen's orders," he called out.

The guard's mouth fell open.

"Here, you!" Sir Nunn shouted. "Hand that over!"

Talmor's heart nearly stopped, but the guard seemed to re-

gain his wits and backed away. "As the queen commands," he
said briskly, and strode away.

Sir Nunn shoved Talmor so hard he stumbled. "Very
clever," he growled. "Move!"

"Look!" someone said in excitement. "Isn't that the
queen's protector?"

"Is he under arrest?"

"He must be one of the traitors."

"No, he's a heretic. I saw a priest drive him back from the
queen."

"Keep back from the heretic!"

Louder and louder the voices buzzed. Talmor's heart
burned, but he kept his face stoic while the church knights
hastened him forward. The stately and very dignified Duc de
Gide, coming inside, paused to stare coldly at Talmor before
he walked into the nave with his retinue at his heels.

Some of the heart went out of Talmor. Was it only a year
past, he thought miserably, that the duc had honored him with
questions regarding the best way to start a young grandson's
training in swordplay? Why were courtiers so eager to believe
whatever slander the clerics were spreading?

Damn Theloi! he thought. For a copper piece he'd like to
give the crafty old cardinal a taste of fire and leave him
scorched around the edges.

Realizing the danger of what he was thinking, Talmor felt
horrified. He knew he must control himself as never before.

A priest with a shaved head and yellow robes met Talmor
and his captors in the shadows beyond the stone columns. By
his appearance clearly a member of the mysterious Rullien
Order, the priest stared at Talmor with a zealot's eyes and
made a gesture of repudiation.

Talmor glared at him, tired of being made a public scapegoat for the church's entertainment.

Officially the Rulliens were responsible for the archives
and preserving the old knowledge of the pre–Reformed
Church. They appeared seldom in public and performed no
rituals of ordinary worship. Talmor had heard it rumored that

Rulliens were masters of torture, and that they prepared the unfortunates destined for inquisition.

Unease slid along his spine.

"Enough of this," he said. "I demand my release, Sir Nunn. You've made sufficient display of me."

The Rullien priest opened the door ahead of Talmor. It did not lead to an exit outside, as he'd expected, but instead revealed a passageway lit by torches. Alarmed, Talmor dug in his heels, stiffening his body, but the church knights shoved him through the doorway. As soon as the door slammed shut, Talmor reached for his weapon, but a blow to the back of his head took him down before he could even draw steel. He sagged, desperately fighting not to lose consciousness, and only dimly was aware of being half-dragged, half-carried along the passageway and down a short flight of steps.

Someone kicked his feet out from under him, and he fell with a grunt. The world went gray and fuzzy, but then he was lifted upright and shaken until his teeth rattled. He blinked, trying to focus, just as a fist thudded into his midsection, doubling him over with a gasping cough.

"That's for Duc Lervan," Sir Nunn growled.

Another fist slammed into his low back. "And that's for Sir Maltric."

"Enough," the Rullien commanded. "Bring the fire-wielder this way."

Still stunned and dizzy, Talmor tried to gather his wits and break free, but found himself slammed against the wall.

Again the world went gray and indistinct. *Don't pass out,* he told himself urgently. He was furious at having been caught so easily, furious at not fighting back.

And then his vision blackened completely. Realizing someone had fitted a sack over his head, Talmor yanked it off only to be felled by a fist to his jaw.

He landed hard, his head thudding on the floor. Circling him like wolves, they kicked him repeatedly until he drew up his knees and moaned.

"Get up!" Sir Nunn said.

Talmor didn't obey. Again they dragged him upright and

shoved him forward. His vision cleared just as one of the men
opened the door to an austere room bare of any furnishings
save a stained table fitted with shackles. Beneath the table
stood a wooden pail filled with instruments of torture. Two
more Rulliens stood at the rear of the room, waiting, their
hands tucked inside the sleeves of their yellow robes. And
with them was the priest in the white coif who'd denounced
Talmor.

The sight of an Inquisitor waiting for him in that stark
chamber filled Talmor with near panic. He felt his captors'
hands tighten on him as though anticipating his struggles.
Breathing hard and fast, he swiftly wedged his foot against
the wall by the doorway to keep them from pushing him inside.

Sir Nunn kicked his foot to dislodge it. "I'll break your leg
if you try that again," he said, and put his hand in the middle
of Talmor's back to shove him forward.

Talmor, however, doubled over so that the momentum of
Sir Nunn's push staggered him off-balance. Twisting away
from him, Talmor drew his dagger and slashed at the leg of
the church knight on his other side.

Howling in pain, the man clutched his wound. Sir Gauve
was somewhere behind Talmor, swearing as he struck. Dodg-
ing the blow, Talmor spun around and surged upright, pro-
pelling himself at the man. Sir Gauve parried Talmor's dagger
with his own.

Talmor realized they must be under orders not to slay him,
or he'd already be dead. Using that as an advantage, he
slashed again with his dagger to keep the fourth man from
striking him and pivoted swiftly to keep an eye on both Sir
Nunn and Sir Gauve, who were charging him.

There came another blow to his head from behind. This
time his skull rang. The room went dark, and although Talmor
desperately tried not to pass out, he only found himself coming to as he was lifted onto the table. Although he tried to
struggle, they already had him shackled.

Fear coursed through his body, a fear he could not control,
for he was remembering how his brothers had tied him in

cruel ways, leaving him for hours until his young body was cramped and screaming with pain. He'd never forgotten that sick feeling of utter helplessness, or the craven desire to plead for their mercy. He'd sworn no one would ever do this to him again, and yet now—incredibly—it was happening.

"Look at him sweat," Sir Nunn said gleefully. "A month's pay says he'll piss himself."

"Silence!" the Inquisitor commanded sharply, and Sir Nunn obeyed.

"Will he throw fire at us?" Sir Gauve asked. "He's cornered, and likely to be—"

"Have faith in Tomias as your protection," the priest said, and pressed his palm against Talmor's face.

Pain pierced his skull, an agony worse than any headache. He felt as though his very thoughts were being shredded, and he could hear a queer, mumbling cacophony of voices echoing in his head, buzzing and babbling so crazily he wondered if he would be driven mad by it.

It was impossible to endure such pain. He screamed, his body twisting and thrashing against the table. Desperately he tried to recall the mental disciplines that Sanude had taught him long ago. But he could not force out the pain or resist the brutal violation of his mind.

Then it ended, as abruptly as it began. Shuddering, Talmor lay drenched with sweat, his heart hammering violently enough to burst. His wits seemed to have left him, and all he knew was an overwhelming sense of gratitude that the torment had stopped.

"So," the Inquisitor said softly, "he is not a *sorcerel* after all. Pity. Staking him publicly and burning his body would have given the townsfolk a spectacle guaranteed to bring new converts to the faith."

The disappointment in the man's voice made Talmor open his eyes briefly. But he saw only a blur hanging over him, and he closed his eyes without trying to speak.

Perhaps he blacked out again, for the thump of his head against something hard brought him back to consciousness. He found himself lying in a narrow alleyway at the base of a massive stone wall. The cold mud beneath his cheek helped revive him. He sat up slowly and tried to look around. It was a quiet, deserted little street, so narrow two men could not walk it abreast. He found himself to be intact, although bruised and feeling as though he might be sick at any moment.

The headache pounding behind his eyes began to ease. Drawing up his knees, he propped his head on them for a short while, then pulled himself together.

It was a struggle to regain his feet. His empty sleeve had nearly been ripped off at the shoulder. Tucking it back inside his belt, he did his best to remedy his appearance. He was grimy, disheveled, and battered, but alive. He supposed he should thank Thod that he wasn't lying in the gutter with his throat slit.

Sudden reaction gusted through him, making him reel back and prop his shoulders against the wall. Bowing his head, he breathed deeply until the trembling stopped.

What had the Inquisitor actually found in his mind? he wondered. What secrets had he been searching for? Feeling as though he'd been a pawn in a game he did not understand, Talmor started walking slowly back toward the cathedral square. Perhaps, he thought, it was better not to ask too many questions. He told himself to be grateful he'd survived this test and leave it be.

When he reached the square, still a bit unsteady, he found it milling with as much activity as before. Ushers in livery continued to try to organize the crowd waiting to get into the church. The bodies, Talmor noticed, had been cleared off the steps. Palace guards stood on duty, and from within the nave the sound of chantsong told him the ceremonies would soon begin.

While he had been put outside like a dog driven from the kitchen.

No sooner did that thought run through his mind than he rejected it. This ordeal had been far more than just a matter of humiliating him. Shivering, Talmor tried to disperse the lingering remnants of his fear. He'd never thought himself to be a coward, but nothing had ever hurt him quite as the Inquisitor had. Even now, he felt not entirely free of the priest's touch, as though something inside him had been branded.

Worst of all, he knew the Inquisitor could have destroyed his mind had he chosen to do so. Why hadn't he?

It made Etyne's old type of torture seem tame indeed.

Talmor turned his gaze toward the cathedral, taking care not to stand too close to the steps or bring attention to himself. It was hard to accept, but he knew he'd been taught a lesson today that no amount of new titles and position could erase. He was vulnerable, would always be vulnerable. If an animal in the palace inexplicably died, or if one of the scullery maids grew ill, Talmor knew he could be blamed for it. There would be more ambushes, more attempted beatings. He needed a protector, and that was another humiliating change he had to accept.

To distract himself from such miserable thoughts, he turned his mind to Pheresa. How was she faring in there? What had become of her? Was she being treated with proper respect? Was she safe? Would he be permitted to see or speak to her again? Or would scandal and rumor forever forbid him access to the queen's presence?

Talmor sighed. He had devoted himself to Pheresa's service for so long that now he did not quite know how to adapt to the reality of no longer keeping vigil over her safety. And all the self-reminders that no man was indispensable, all the pragmatism and stalwart acceptance of what could not be undone mattered little right now. He felt poleaxed and lost, unable to imagine what he should do with himself. Nothing in his life, no training or inclination, had prepared him to assume the role of an idle courtier, content to wait about for the monarch's whim like a lapdog hoping for its master's notice.

And, Thod's bones, not even to be allowed to see her crowned, after all they'd gone through . . . the bitterness of his disappointment was sour indeed. As for Lord Nejel serving today as Pheresa's protector, Talmor found himself neither relieved nor glad. He felt jealous and hot. He wanted to be near her in what was the greatest triumph of her life.

"Baron!"

The shout rose over the general buzz of excitement, but at first Talmor paid it no heed.

"Lord baron! Lord Talmor!"

Frowning, Talmor swung around and saw Lord Salba hastening down the steps at a speed unseemly for a man of his bulk and importance. Escorted by two guardsmen and trailed by a young clerk with shaggy hair and a cloak too short, the elderly chancellor pushed against the crowd until at last he reached Talmor's side.

"There you are!" he said, puffing hard. Red-faced from his exertions, he gripped the neck of his tunic as though it was constricting his breathing. "Morde a day, my good fellow! I've had no easy time finding you. Why aren't you where you're wanted?"

Alarm flowed over Talmor. "I sent a guardsman to find you, and—"

"Yes, yes. He did. I have it safe, no fear. All's well."

Relief made Talmor sag. He felt a hundred years old.

"Thod's bones, but you look rough."

"I've been—"

Salba raised one freckled hand to cut him off. "No doubt you're tough enough to withstand a simple beating."

Talmor blinked at him in dawning anger, but Salba gave him no chance to speak.

"Never mind that trouble inside. There's no time now to complain about a few rumors from your past. I've got to get to the palace without delay."

"But—"

"My thanks, baron, for your service in protecting so vital a treasure."

"Um, perhaps I'd better escort you, to keep it safe."

Salba glanced at the impassive guards behind him and snorted. "No need. I'm well protected."

"I've little else to do," Talmor insisted. "Now that I've been put out."

Salba's brown eyes assessed him without sympathy. "You're a courtier now, Lord Talmor. You'll wait on the queen, all day and longer if it pleases her. You cannot come and go as you choose."

"I—"

"There's a good fellow. Well done." And Salba was gone.

Talmor watched him go with his clerk and the guardsmen, and prayed that Lord Salba could still be trusted.

"Talmor!" came a shout.

Startled, he turned around just as Nejel and Sergeant Goddal joined him with merry grins and cordial backslapping. The weathered sergeant was smiling broadly. Lord Nejel, his blond hair waving back from his handsome brow, was actually beaming.

"Not long now until the event starts," he said with satisfaction. "I'll tell you straight, Talmor. I never thought this day would go as it has."

But Talmor was staring at the commander in such consternation it took him a moment to find his voice. "The queen! Where—"

With a laugh, Nejel winked at him. "Safe in the hands of her ladies-in-waiting. Stop worrying, Talmor, and come along. We've got a plan for smuggling you inside."

"Aye," Goddal said with a nod. "I missed all the earlier stir and fuss. Looks like ye had quite a tussle. Did they really drive ye forth with loud prayer and Circles?"

"Not quite," Talmor said wearily. "Lord Nejel, what about her majesty?"

"She's inside, where nothing can harm her. Look yon!" Nejel said, pointing. "See how many guards and church knights stand watch for trouble? There'll be none now."

"I gave you the charge for her safety," Talmor said in rising annoyance. "You swore you'd stay close to her."

Nejel frowned defensively for a moment, then shrugged. "Aye, so I did, but she's secure at present. Between the cardinal taking her private confession and her ladies-in-waiting swarming about, I tell you there was no room for a protector in that small chamber."

"But—"

Lord Nejel squeezed Talmor's arm. "Damne! Have you

lived so long on the knife's edge that you cannot relax now when danger is gone? She's well, I assure you. As long as she's inside the church, no harm can befall her. And when the coronation is done, and she emerges, I swear to you a full complement of guards will surround her every moment until she is back inside the walls of Savroix."

Frowning, Talmor nearly told Nejel what had happened to him, but held his tongue. He could prove none of it, and an accusation might bring even more trouble to him. But to leave the queen unprotected and wholly in the hands of the clergy . . . he did not like it.

Sir Pem came hurrying up and gave Talmor a wary nod of greeting. "I've brought the spare cloak."

"Good!" Nejel said. "Put it on, Talmor, and we'll take you inside as a guardsman. No one will notice you in this crush of folk."

The bold simplicity of the plan made Talmor catch his breath with sudden delight. He shot an eager look at Nejel, who was smiling.

"Well," the commander said breezily, "you were once a guardsman, were you not? You'll do it no dishonor. Besides, I know how much you want to see all the show and panoply."

Their kindness and high spirits balanced some of what Talmor had just suffered at the hands of the church. It was good to know he still had friends. His heart warmed, and with a smile he took the cloak.

Shortly thereafter, Talmor walked into the cathedral in the jostling amidst several officers of the guard, and, this time, although he feared recognition, no one stopped him or turned him back. They were crowded by the harassed ushers into a row of benches midway back behind wooden box pews enclosing the more august families and lords. Talmor found himself placed where he could see both the altar and coronation throne and did not mind the crushing heat of too many bodies crammed into too small a space.

Gazing around the shadowy expanse of the circular nave, he watched the priests coming and going from transepts to small chapels fitted into the perimeter of the nave. All was bustle and purpose; it seemed the ceremony was going to proceed as it should. And he was here in spite of everything, filled with glee at having defied Theloi after all.

From the choir stall came a new round of chantsong. Incense clouded the air, which reeked of too many bodies, sweat, candle wax, and warring pomanders and perfumes. People rustled constantly, whispering and gossiping, the buzz of conversation swelling ever louder in anticipation. The waiting went on for what seemed like forever. Some folks munched on refreshments supplied by their servants, and even Lord Salba—looking windblown—came rushing in to take his place.

Finally, Lord Nejel's elbow jabbed Talmor sharply in the ribs, catching him on a sore spot. "Look yon!" the commander said, as excited as a boy. "She's coming!"

Talmor's gaze shot to where Nejel was pointing. There, beyond the tide of heads craning to see, came the flag bearers. Pheresa's colors were borne side by side with the pennons of the realm. His heart swelled, and his throat choked up with pride. And swiftly he gave thanks to Thod for being here, against all odds, to see Pheresa crowned.

Chapter Four

Washed and gowned, with silk slippers on her feet, and jewels adorning her ears, throat, and fingers, Pheresa donned the coronation regalia. The thick velvet robe was so heavily embroidered with thread of spun gold it fitted over her gown like a stiff tent. Its sleeves, cut full and very wide, hung down over her hands and had to be pinned up. The folds were adjusted in order to shorten the sleeves, but the fabric was so thick and heavy that hemming it proved difficult for the harried seamstress.

The preparations were taking too long, Pheresa thought impatiently. Despite Salba's insistence that she dawdle, her instincts told her that every passing moment brought risk.

She wished there'd been time to say her prayers and make confession to a priest she trusted. Ideally, the monarch should arrive already prepared, so that it was necessary to be in this robing room only for the few minutes necessary to don the regalia.

Instead, there were these many delays, confusion, disorder, mistakes, and too much haste, with an excessive number of people crowding the small chamber. The air was hot and stifling. She'd been pinched and prodded and pricked whenever the seamstress grew too careless with her flashing needle.

Still, Pheresa knew she must go to her destiny attired worthy of the occasion, not for vanity's sake, but out of respect for the position as sovereign of the realm. She'd appeared before her people already this day as a wild, bedraggled hoyden in chain mail. Now she would appear before them as a queen.

Her wealth of long blond hair was braided with pearls and coiled into a heavy knot at the base of her neck. From the wooden box on the table, a Circle of plain gold, very old and worn, was placed in her hands. The scroll case of ebony with its carvings of interlocked Circles was opened, and a thin, yellowed curl of parchment was extracted for her to carry.

Aware of the value of these artifacts, Pheresa held them in awe. Although she tried to appear composed in the midst of so much bustle, inside she was a growing mass of apprehension and nerves.

Someone came to the door, and the general noise and chatter fell quiet. Turning, Pheresa saw the cathedral bishop standing on the threshold.

"I have come to give your majesty my blessing," he said.

The prayer stool was brought for her to kneel. The prayer he said over her was soothing. She felt herself grow calm and reassured. But when the bishop finished, she found the weight of her garments too heavy and could not rise unaided.

Seeing a quick exchange of frowns around the room, Pheresa knew that during the ceremony she would have to find sufficient strength to kneel and stand unaided. Nervous once more, she vowed to do it, for she would show her subjects no weakling.

The cloak, emblazoned with the colors of Mandria and trimmed lavishly with ermine, was placed across her shoulders. Tailored for Lervan, it was so long it dragged the ground.

"Leave it," Pheresa commanded. "I can walk in the cloak as it is."

"But your majesty—"

A young, rotund cleric appeared in the doorway. "It is time, your majesty."

Her mouth went dry; her heart started to pound. Lifting her chin, Pheresa held back her surging excitement and schooled her features into regal composure. "The queen is ready," she replied.

The women around her parted, and Pheresa emerged into the passageway, to find it lined with church knights at rigid attention. The bishop preceded her up the steps, which she found difficult indeed to negotiate in her heavy garments. Chancellor Salba, looking disheveled but triumphant, awaited her at the top. Lord Meaclan, her minister of finance, stood smiling beside him. The rest of her cabinet, with several notable absences, had assembled themselves there as well to honor her. Pausing before them, Pheresa let her gaze sweep the group as they bowed to her. Some of them had supported Lervan and stood sour and shifty-eyed before her. Several were beaming with undisguised relief. Others showed no expression at all.

Pleased by their attendance, Pheresa drew only partial reassurance from it. At least half, if not more, of them could not be trusted. She hoped their participation today did not lead them all to expect to remain in her privy council, for much was going to change.

Beyond these officials, she could see the narthex, empty now save for her guardsmen. The broad circular expanse of the nave was filled with people. Every part of the cathedral seemed to echo with sound, for people were craning to see her, whispering and rustling while the flag bearers solemnly positioned themselves to lead her procession. And although church knights stood at attention in each of the transepts, she saw a greater number of palace guards in evidence, their vivid green cloaks hanging in immaculate folds, their armor and weapons gleaming, their faces solemn. Even more green cloaks clustered in the center of the assembly. She supposed some of them were officers, and most, if not all, loyal to her.

In the distance, the voices of the choir lifted in chantsong, honoring Thod and Tomias. The crowd hushed abruptly, and a sense of anticipation filled the incense-thick air. At the altar, church officials, including the cathedral bishop and the esteemed Circle of Cardinals, filed into position. They wore magnificent vestments. Cardinal Atol spread his hands wide, and the assembly rose to its feet with a scrape and clatter.

Pheresa's heartbeat quickened anew. Emotions swelled her breast, and she trembled so violently she nearly dropped the scroll of holy Writ. Just in time she managed not to crumple it in her fist.

As a lone church bell began to toll the number of years King Verence had sat on the throne, the flag bearers moved forward. Holding her head high and shoulders erect, Pheresa stepped onto the runner of carpet stretching up the long aisle. Slowly and solemnly she walked, striving to remain graceful despite the heavy drag of her regalia. Faces swam past the corners of her vision, for she looked neither to the right or left. She heard little gasps of admiration, occasional nervous titters of laughter, and many whispers behind hands. Memories of other processions of state crowded her mind, especially the sad occasions such as Verence's funeral and the happy one when he'd crowned her Heir to the Realm.

The chanting of the choir rose and fell in strange cadence, echoing through the gloom beneath the solemn slow strike of the lone bell. She'd never heard the coronation recital before. It made her feel hollow inside, very conscious of the hand of destiny lying upon her now.

The bell stopped tolling. When she reached the altar, she paused and knelt, receiving a benediction from the bishop. The Circle of Cardinals, a body of five men at the pinnacle of power in church politics, stood shoulder to shoulder behind the altar, watching in silence as the bishop finished his prayers. The cardinals were convened only for the most extraordinary occasions, and seldom were they seen publicly in each other's company.

As the bishop stepped out of the way, Pheresa remained kneeling with her head bowed. From the edge of her vision, she could see the fabled Crown of Mandria on its velvet pillow, held by a round-eyed page. Such was the crown's magnificence that Verence had worn it only on state occasions, and this was the first time she'd seen it taken from the treas-

ury vaults since his death. Having believed it confiscated by
the barbarian looters, she found herself both surprised and relieved to see it here.

Had it been well and truly guarded, she wondered, or had
Lervan made some traitor's bargain with the Vvordsmen to
keep it? She supposed she would learn the truth soon enough.
There were long days to come, sifting through the full extent
and ramifications of Lervan's treachery.

But for the moment, it was the ceremony that occupied her
attention.

The scepter rested on the altar, along with the silver cup of
blessing, the sacraments, and a volume of holy Writ held between gilded wooden covers and bound with heavy chain.

She knelt for a long time while one by one the cardinals
came forward and spoke over her, sometimes uttering phrases
she understood, sometimes words so ancient she wondered if
anyone knew their meaning. She realized she was now a part
of Mandria's long history. Her name would never be forgotten. For good or ill, her reign would be recorded with the others, and by her deeds, honor, and decisions would she be
known throughout time. The third Queen Sovereign of Mandria's illustrious history, she wondered if she would be best
known as the woman who took the throne with blood on her
hands.

In her heart she prayed earnestly to Thod, asking for wis-
dom and courage, asking for support from the powerful ducs
and lords who would serve her as vassals, asking for the good
sense to remember the price she'd paid to wear this crown.
Never must she take her high estate for granted. Never must
she put her pleasure or vanity before the good of her subjects.
They depended on her. She felt their trust like a tremendous
weight pressing on her slim shoulders.

The first of Mandria's queens had been a fragile creature
who reigned for two years during a time of peace. The second
had been ambitious and fearless, pushing Mandria into trad-
ing with other realms, opening avenues of exploration in foreign lands, ever questing for gold to fill the royal treasury.
Because of Queen Maudine's industry—some said because of

her greed—Mandria had grown rich. *I will make it rich again,* Pheresa vowed. *I will find a way to rebuild all that Lervan has sullied and destroyed.*

Silence fell over her, and she pulled her wandering thoughts back to the ceremony. Cardinal Theloi stood at the altar while lesser priests unchained the book of Writ and opened the thick vellum pages to a place marked with tapes of silk. He began to read aloud, projecting his voice to be heard to the far reaches of the cathedral. The sonorous phrases of the ancient language rolled over Pheresa. They were incomprehensible, yet they carried a rhythmic cadence that almost lulled her into a half-mesmerized state. With a slight start, she realized he was injecting words of power into some of the phrasing, for every time he uttered one of the mysterious words, she felt a slight buzzing in her head.

Her suspicions renewed, for she did not understand what he was up to. These were not words of Writ, not even words of ancient Mandrian. These were words of magic, surely forbidden, yet did no one save she notice what he was doing?

Inside her pocket, the magicked dagger that went with her everywhere grew warm enough to be felt through her gown. That alarmed her even more, and she stealthily slipped her hand beneath her robes in an effort to reach the weapon.

Before she succeeded, however, Theloi abruptly stopped his reading. The book was closed and chained while Cardinal Atol served her sacrament. The taste of the sacred salt was extremely bitter, so much so that in surprise she nearly spat it out. With effort, she managed to hold it on her tongue in the correct manner until it melted. But even then, the bitterness lingered in her mouth, puckering her tongue unpleasantly. Someone, she thought with annoyance, had mixed the herbs and salt with too enthusiastic a hand.

After her, each of the cardinals took sacrament. She saw two of them grimace, and Cardinal Atol actually turned his back to the assembly and spat his out into his hand.

It was time for her to rise.

She hesitated a moment, gathering all her determination. A page edged forward under whispered instructions to assist her, but she motioned him away. Gritting her teeth, she pushed herself to her feet, realized she was hunching beneath the heavy weight of her garments, and forced herself to straighten. Perspiration beaded up along her hairline, and her knees and back trembled from the effort. For an instant, her temples swelled as though they would burst, and she had to take an unseemly gulp of air. But she stood erect and strong.

From behind her came a soft *ah* of approval from the crowd, and she found herself smiling with triumph.

The coronation throne was a battered, ancient relic of Mandria's earliest days, carved from a single piece of ironwood—no longer to be found in the realm—with a worn leather seat slung crudely between the crosspieces. It stood precisely positioned over a rectangular slab of limestone carved with the words of the allegiance pledge, the oath sworn by vassal lords to the king of Mandria since time had begun.

Carefully she turned around to face the assembly and waited while two pages gathered the heavy folds of her cloak before she sat down. With the skill of long feminine practice in managing wide, fashionable skirts, she succeeded in sitting without allowing her stiff robes to tilt upward.

Momentarily preoccupied with how the pages arranged the folds of the cloth of gold cloak around her, she drew a deep breath while she let herself take measure of this moment. She was enthroned, and no one had shouted in protest or come running up to interrupt what was transpiring.

A feeling of unreality filled her. Suddenly her ears were humming so much she heard the ceremony continue as though from far away. Although she stared straight ahead, her vision blurred and she found herself unable to focus on Lord Salba's face in one of the foremost pews.

It was relief, she supposed. Perhaps delayed shock. The ceremony was nearly over now, and thus far all was going smoothly. Another ancient rite was performed over her, but she made her answers with little conscious thought. It was as though her body belonged to someone else, and she was apart from it, observing what it said and did. In all her dreams of what it would feel like to be here, wondering whether she would cry or find herself grinning with delight, never had she imagined she would be so numb.

Too much has happened, she thought, feeling overwhelmed by all she'd undergone in the past several months.

It was time, she told herself, to forget the old hardships of the past. Time to look to the future, shining with hope and possibility. She had Lord Salba to advise her, Lord Meaclan to help restore the realm's finances, and Talmor to love her. In recent weeks, as she realized how deeply she loved him, it had been hard to hold to her marriage vows, but as of today she was married no longer. Soon—this night perhaps—she and Talmor would be together in the way she ached for.

The Crown of Mandria was brought forth, wobbling a little on the pillow borne by a nervous page. The sight of it scattered Pheresa's wayward thoughts, and she found herself unable to look away from this symbol of all that she'd become. Until she was crowned, she reminded herself, feeling suddenly chilled, nothing was secure or guaranteed. If her enemies meant to strike at her, now was the time. She shifted her gaze back to Theloi.

His thin, goateed face was expressionless as he concentrated on his task at the altar. She could detect nothing different about his manner than in any of the other cardinals.

Still, she shivered under her regalia, for the cold chills had not left her, and she could not seem to stop trembling. She felt clammy, her blood now pounding in her ears. Terrified that she was losing her nerve and would make some dreadful blunder that would botch the entire proceedings, she forced herself to concentrate.

Cardinal Varduel stood before her, holding the crown aloft and intoning something before handing the crown to Cardinal Tulaine, who said his part. The crown was handed next to Cardinal Ardminsil and so on to Theloi and finally to Atol, the last man to stand before her as the others encircled her.

Atol finished speaking and paused, letting his voice echo through the absolutely silent cathedral.

Although her heart was pounding, Pheresa forced herself

to keep breathing steadily. Why did he hesitate, she wondered. Was Cardinal Atol going to refuse to crown her?

She stared up at this portly, elderly man with the red spider veins of too much drink in his nose and cheeks. His gaze was kindly, and as their eyes met, a faint smile curved his fleshly lips. She saw then that he intended no protest or plot against her. Indeed, he looked confused, as though he'd forgotten what he was to say and do next.

Relief swept over her, and suddenly she had all the patience in the world. Theloi was whispering to Atol, prompting him, and Pheresa realized that the traditions of Mandria were heavy forces indeed. Whatever enemies she had among some of the churchmen, she saw that none of them quite dared to break the custom, law, and authority of her right to be crowned today. Not here, like this, out in the open before Thod and man.

She took heart, and her fright faded into renewed confidence.

Atol cleared his throat ever so faintly and lifted his brows in an unspoken question. At that moment, with a tiny start, she realized that he was now awaiting his cue from her. For this was when she must indicate whether she would submit her monarchy to the supreme authority of the church—a decision symbolized by waiting passively until Atol placed the crown on her head—or whether she would choose to take it from his hands and crown herself—thus accepting no supremacy above her own.

Indecision swept her. The silence remained acute, and everything seemed frozen. She gazed into Atol's rheumy eyes, unable to look away, and he continued to wait for her signal.

With irritation, she knew that she should have been prepared for this. She should have been advised by Lord Salba's assessment of current church politics and whether it was wise at this time to grant the churchmen enormous favor or rein them back. The entire tone of her reign could be affected by this decision; she should not be making it by guess.

But she had to. And she thought of the past, when Theloi

had schemed to cloister her in a nuncery for the rest of her days, of the intolerance and fanaticism that flourished in dark corners of some of the orders and sects, of the hypocrisy of the church knights who had withheld their support during the winter when she needed it so desperately. She thought of Theloi's scathing denunciation of Talmor only a short time ago, driving her beloved from this very cathedral.

And her heart grew hard.

The corners of Atol's eyes crinkled slightly at her long silence, and he looked pleased indeed as he exchanged a glance with Theloi and Tulaine. Some of the cardinals began to smile. The bishop actually beamed approval, and even Theloi's taut expression relaxed.

Atol lifted the crown above her head, but Pheresa reached up and took the crown from his grasp. He looked too astonished to resist, and, although Theloi uttered a swift, choked sound of protest, he was too late. Pheresa crowned herself.

The crown was surprisingly heavy and awkward. Her neck wobbled slightly beneath the weight, and although a rough edge of metal pressed painfully into her forehead, she did not care. The cardinals and bishop all looked thunderstruck. Atol's mouth hung open. Theloi's face whitened with rage. The assembly began to buzz as people turned to each other, some pointing at her with smiles, nodding, while others shook their heads in apparent shock. And in his pew, Lord Salba sat motionless, wearing a puckered, weary expression that she could not interpret at all.

Defiantly she faced her subjects, aware that she'd probably provoked the church to fresh enmity that might never be mended. But it was done, she thought with satisfaction. And whether her reasons were valid or petty, she did not care. It was done, and there could be no undoing it.

The crowd had risen to its feet, and as people shifted about, she saw farther back. There, in the midst of the officers of the palace guard, stood Talmor. Garbed in a green cloak, looking distinguished and handsome, he smiled broadly at her with complete approval.

Her heart warmed and gladdened. The world seemed to

have turned aright, and she knew she'd done the proper thing, no matter how much future trouble it might cause. She would be no puppet ruler, Pheresa vowed to herself. She would not be told what to do, or say, or think. Nay, she had her own plans for this realm, her own ideas for the changes to come. And, even if it took her a lifetime, she would curb some of the corrupted power of the church.

Glancing at the cardinals still ringed around her, she said softly, "Shall we continue?"

With a start, Atol broke loose from his astonishment and brought her the scepter. This, she allowed him to place in her hands with a show of meekness that surely fooled no one. The scepter was heavier than a broadsword, wrought of solid gold and engraved with symbols unfamiliar to her. A fist-sized emerald was affixed to its top, and the fabulous stone flashed blue-and-gold fire from its depths as she lifted the scepter vertically, her arm trembling from its weight.

She hung the chain of her Circle over the top of the scepter, and said, "Crown and church. Allied in the sight of Thod, to serve the realm."

The cardinals murmured the expected response, and several of her lords called out the response as well. Lord Salba began to look less worried, and Pheresa hid her smile. She felt confident and sure of herself now.

Having put the churchmen in their place for today, she intended no further show of defiance or rebellion.

Her heavy cloak of ermine and cloth of gold was removed, to be replaced with one of silk velvet dyed in the royal colors, embroidered with the most exquisite handiwork of gold thread, and studded with real diamonds that flashed and glittered so brilliantly the cloak seemed to be something alive. She had never seen any garment more beautiful, more breathtakingly splendid.

A rectangular box of very old wood was brought forth. From it came the chain of Maun, first king of Mandria. Its links were crudely wrought of solid gold, heavy but so soft the ravages of time had bent and even broken some of them. This was hung about her slender neck, while the carved ivory case containing the first written laws of the realm was placed beneath her feet.

She understood the symbols very well. She wore the crown and chain of Maun, and in so doing signified that she was descended from Mandria's royal line. She held the scepter, symbol of the sovereign's authority, hung with a Circle to represent her acknowledgment of the crown's alliance with the church. The cloak represented Mandria's wealth and sphere of influence among other realms. The laws beneath her feet indicated that she stood on the foundation of justice and due process. The vow of allegiance carved into the stone beneath her throne symbolized her authority over her vassals.

"So it is done," intoned Cardinal Atol. The second, third, and fourth cardinals repeated his words in turn.

Theloi stared down at Pheresa with his cold green eyes. "So let it begin," he said clearly.

Chanting from the choir swelled loudly for a few moments, then fresh silence fell over the cathedral. Pheresa rose carefully to her feet. It was difficult to stand beneath the weight of so many symbols. These objects had been wrought for a man's sturdy frame to bear, and well she knew it. But as a woman, Pheresa believed she'd been given the strength of will, strength of convictions, and the strength of intelligence in compensation for her lack of brawn. She intended to use all those qualities to the best of her ability.

Perspiring from her exertions and feeling smothered in the heavy garments of state, she kept her head high and allowed time to stretch as she gazed across the sea of faces. The bishop tried to prompt her, but Pheresa ignored him and waited until every face in the assembly was turned to her and every voice was stilled. A sense of anticipation grew and tightened, and she deliberately let it, wanting her subjects to pay attention. She ruled them now, and she had no intention of letting them forget it.

"My people," she began at last in a clear, steady voice, reciting the oath she had long ago memorized. "I, Pheresa of Mandria, do hereby accept the trust and responsibility placed upon me by Thod's will, the rights of succession, and the acquiescence of my subjects. I shall keep and defend the realm

against all enemies. I shall uphold the laws and customs of
our land. In all my duties and obligations shall I remember
Thod's will before my own, and in so doing preserve and
honor holy Writ. All this do I swear."

A cheer of acclamation rose from the throats of the assembly, and from the towers, the bells of the cathedral began to
ring in a joyous cascade of noise.

She faced the crowd without expression, although inside
her heart lifted and her spirits sang with triumph. Tremendous
relief rolled over her like a wave, and she found herself trembling as she hastily blinked back tears of emotion. *Queens do
not cry,* she told herself, firming her mouth to hold back the
smile that kept threatening to spread across her face. *Queens
do not laugh and jump for joy at state occasions.* But, oh, how
she wanted to skip and dance and clap her hands like a little
girl at that moment.

And then it happened.

From behind her came a boom of sound as though a door
had been slammed open. She heard the grating scrape of stone
sliding across stone, and a dank, warm gust of fetid, unwholesome air wafted past her nostrils as though the crypt had
been opened. Her heart jerked so hard it hurt beneath her
breast. As though pulled on strings, she turned partially
around and saw a mist boiling forth from the crypt, a mist
thick and red like the smoke of incense, only this was something unnatural. It spread toward her incredibly fast, while she
stood rooted in place, her mouth slightly open, her heart racing with the instinct to flee. Yet she did not move.

In seconds, she could no longer see the cardinals or the
bishop or attendants. Nor was there any evidence of guards or
church knights, who should have come rushing to her aid. She
was blinded and isolated in the mist.

Someone screamed, but there was a roaring in her ears that
made the shrill sound of terror seem faint and far away.
Pheresa dropped the scepter from fingers gone suddenly
numb and unresponsive. The jeweled end glanced off her
foot, and yet she felt the pain of it only vaguely, as though it
were happening to someone else.

The clammy chills returned, and her vision blurred as the roaring in her ears grew louder. The mist engulfed her, and although she had a dim awareness of a struggle happening near her and she heard Theloi shout in fear and Atol cry out sharply, she remained frozen and unable to move. She did not understand why she was so weak and dizzy, why she'd grown so helpless. The mist was icy cold, like the grave or something worse, and terrible memories of her ordeal after she accidentally swallowed eld poison swept through her mind.

In terror, she suddenly found her voice. "Talmor!" she screamed. "Talmor, help me!"

A shape appeared in the mist before her. It was not Talmor but a figure garbed in black, intangible and mysterious in her blurred sight. The harder she stared at it, the more ghostlike and difficult to see it became.

"Get back from me!" she snarled, fumbling with clumsy fingers for her Circle. Too late did she realize that she'd dropped it along with the scepter.

Gripped by the figure in black, she tried to struggle without success, for she remained too weak, as though a spell had been cast over her. As her jeweled cloak and regalia were stripped away, a hand as cold as death pressed against her face.

Fearing that she was going to be suffocated, she tried again to struggle, but the strange lassitude made her slow and clumsy. As she was lifted in her abductor's arms, she whispered, "In the name of Tomias I repudiate you."

A deep laugh issued from the figure in black. "You are ours, Pheresa of Mandria," its voice whispered to her in triumph. "Ours forever."

She could find no answer, for inside her grew the darkness and icy cold. She felt the heavy crown slip from her head and go rolling across the floor.

My reign is over, she thought vaguely, and knew no more as she was carried down the steps into the grave.

Chapter Five

When the mist first started pouring through the church, Talmor thought that the priests had lit additional incense burners with too much zeal.

Crammed on a hard wooden bench between Lord Nejel and Sir Pem, Talmor had spent the time before the start of the ceremony enduring the quick, sidelong glances of Sergeant Goddal, the sneers of Sir Lorne, the offensively curious fixation of Lord Avlon's gaze on his empty sleeve, and the whispered questions of Sir Carlemon in his ear. He knew all of these men, of course, for a protector worth his pay had better know every member of the palace guard from the commander to the lowliest sentry-rank knights.

"Patrols have been sweeping every road and every landing point on the river," Sir Carlemon was whispering, as pesky as a fly. "How'd you get her past 'em?"

"Are you asking a protector his professional secrets, Carlemon?" Lord Avlon drawled derisively. "Sir Talmor was always extremely dedicated."

Sir Pem snorted into his hand, and Sergeant Goddal's laugh changed hastily into a fierce coughing fit.

"Take heed," Nejel warned them quietly. "It's Lord Talmor now."

Lord Avlon, a younger son of a count, as was Nejel, frowned down his aristocratic nose at Talmor. "Why do you bother carrying a weapon at all?" he asked softly, his eyes cold. "Surely you don't use it."

Gritting his teeth, Talmor reminded himself that he was here as a spectator through the willingness of these men to take a risk on his behalf. But gratitude was a cold dish; he did not like it much.

"Used it on Sir Maltric, didn't he?" Sir Pem said.

"Did he?" Avlon shook his head. "I didn't see."

"Should have," Pem said gruffly, giving Talmor a nod of respect. "About as quick as he ever was. Form rougher and footwork not as good, but some hard work's been done of late to build strength into that other arm. For it was a blow as true as any, and well placed."

Sir Lorne scowled primly. "Protector killing protector . . . 'tis not—"

"No worse than husband killing wife," Sir Pem said.

"Or wife killing husband?" Avlon injected softly.

They all fell silent around Talmor, and he sat without moving, his hand clenched on his thigh. His jaw was clamped so tightly a muscle was twitching there.

A nobleman several rows ahead of them blew his nose with a great, honking gust, and Talmor nearly jumped from his skin.

"Steady," Lord Nejel said softly, with a restraining hand on his knee. "No one's noticed you, despite the chatter. Be at ease."

Talmor drew a breath, annoyed, but let Nejel's misunderstanding abide. He couldn't seem to relax, however, and his gaze kept going to the clusters of church soldiers standing at grim attention in the transepts. He watched the noblemen still filing into place, escorting wives and family dressed in finery. He took note of exactly how many guards were stationed where, whether the aisles were being kept cleared or allowed to fill with gossiping knots of courtiers, how often somber-robed clerics flitted like shadows along the perimeter of the great round nave. The officials and dignitaries, Lord Salba among them, stamped their feet and talked to each other behind their hands.

"What's it like, taking Nonkind venom?" Carlemon went on. As he bent even closer, his scented hair pomade sickened Talmor's nostrils. "Did they burn it or salt it out of you? I've heard that when you lose an arm you can still feel your fingers, and you itch like demon fire, even though there's nothing there to scratch. Is that true?"

The choir began to chant, distracting Carlemon's attention, much to Talmor's relief. Pheresa entered, walking solemnly in her regalia, her face a pale oval, her eyes dark and wide.

Standing with the rest, Talmor felt all the breath leave his body. She was the most beautiful creature he'd ever seen. For years, he'd been a slave to her beauty—the scent and grace and loveliness of her—but suddenly it was as though he'd never seen her before. Glittering and shimmering, the jewels and cloth of gold she wore set her alight with radiance. She dazzled him, and he wanted not to stand as she walked by, her robes rustling with every slow step, but to sink to his knees and worship her.

Theloi was right, he could not help but think while Nejel drew in a sharp breath, Pem leaned forward with his mouth agape, and even Avlon stared without his usual sneer. *I am a pagan, for 'tis her I worship today instead of Thod.*

She came to a halt before the altar, positioned beneath the occulus window high overhead, so that a shaft of sunlight stabbed down through the gloom to shine upon her. The ceremony and rituals began, and as he watched, engrossed in all that she said and did, he felt his chest begin to ache in a bittersweet mixture of pride and regret.

This was her destiny, and he could imagine her nowhere else, yet from this hour forward he would never again know the degree of friendship and privacy they'd shared during the past few months at Thirst Hold. Her star was ascending, and so was his to a lesser degree, but it meant a future in which Pheresa would become increasingly remote from him.

The idea of it robbed him of all sense, and for a moment he could do nothing save bow his head and try to master himself.

Be happy for her, he told himself sternly. *Be happy for yourself and grateful for all that is to come.*

Yet he was afraid of happiness, wary of it, distrustful of it. He could not relax, and the ache in his chest did not ease. Regret flooded him over all the time wasted, the opportunities lost during the winter, when he had lived so certain that he would kill her that he'd gone through the days in terrible strain. Terrified and anxious on her behalf, he'd been too worried to relax in her company, too fretful to let himself savor the sweetness of her shy friendship and trusting kisses. Every day during the hard journey to reach Savroix in time to stop Lervan's coronation, he'd felt himself teetering on the knife's edge, so afraid for her it was like being ripped apart.

But she was well. She was safe. He had to release his fears, let them flow behind him and be forgotten. She lived, and she was queen, crowning herself with an unexpected boldness that made the crowd gasp and murmur. A grin broke across his face, and he realized that Sir Pem was pounding him on the back.

"Morde a day!" the man was saying in amazement. "Look yon at her!"

"That's spit in the old cardinal's eye," Sergeant Goddal muttered.

"A stabbing and a crowning . . . the queen's not the helpless little damsel she used to be," Sir Pem went on. "Thod's bones, but I'll serve a woman like that. Damne, so I will!"

"You will because you're sworn to the duty," Avlon reminded him caustically, but Sir Pem ignored him.

Talmor paid little attention to their comments. He watched her hold aloft the scepter to the cheering crowd. The jewels of her crown glittered and flashed with every turn of her head. He had never seen her look more regal, and in his eyes she deserved every moment of her triumph. So slender and lovely was she that it was easy to underestimate her strong resilence, but Talmor knew her to be a survivor, a courageous one.

Happiness shone in her face. Her eyes searched across the crowd and met his, and he felt the darkness in him dropping away.

She said her vows, her voice clear and self-assured, while the incense fogged ever thicker from behind the altar. The bishop began to intone prayers, pausing at intervals for the response of the crowd.

Lord Nejel craned his neck, inadvertently bumping Talmor with his elbow. "I can barely see her for the smoke. What are the priests doing up there?"

The murky haze was beginning to curl around the hem of the queen's robes. Talmor frowned, for it seemed odd to him. Yet he told himself it was only more of the pomp and panoply.

Then he noticed that the smoke did not spread past Pheresa into the pews and benches. Instead, it swirled around her and the Circle of Cardinals, entwining foggy tendrils between the altar and coronation throne, and flowed not at all into the nave, as though some trick of the air kept it in place. Yet Talmor felt no breeze stirring in the stuffy interior of the church. He could not smell the acrid fragrance of so much incense, and it should have been overwhelming already.

Talmor looked swiftly at the guards. Nothing seemed amiss or out of place. The officials at the altar ignored the thick smoke swirling around them, as did Pheresa. Talmor could see the back of Lord Salba's gingery head in the foremost pew, but the lord chancellor stood quietly among the other dignitaries as though he perceived nothing peculiar happening either.

It must be part of the ceremony, Talmor assured himself again, but he no longer believed it.

"The queen," he said, and tried to push past Lord Nejel.

But they were all packed together too tightly, and Nejel would not budge.

Frustrated, Talmor poked the commander. "Stand aside. I must go to the queen."

Nejel shot him a look of exasperation. "Don't be a fool. You can't risk bringing attention to yourself."

Before Talmor could reply, the bishop's voice faltered in midsentence and fell silent. The odd break made Talmor look just as the bishop staggered and would have fallen had he not caught himself on the altar.

A sound came from the assembly as people pointed and pressed forward to see what was happening. Theloi stretched out his hand to the bishop, only to suddenly turn pale and sink to his knees out of sight. His collapse sent a clutch of church knights hastening from the west transept, but they stopped and glanced around uncertainly.

Talmor was already shoving against Nejel, and this time he jumped atop the bench with the intention of running along it behind the onlookers. Nejel yanked him down by the hem of his tunic and caught him roughly before he could go sprawling.

"Are you mad?" the commander was saying angrily. "I told you—"

"Something's wrong!" Talmor insisted, astonished that Nejel seemed oblivious to the danger. He twisted free of the commander's grip. "We've got to—"

"It's the stuffy heat," Nejel was saying calmly. "It's overcome the bishop, that's all. In Thod's name, you can't go up there!"

It was not smoke, Talmor suddenly realized, but instead some strange, spell-laden mist. He now felt the prickling sensation of magic in the air, along with a gathering heaviness like a stormy day when lightning is about to strike. At that moment the stuff turned a queer hue of red—like blood, he thought in alarm. It boiled up thicker than ever, and engulfed Pheresa entirely as though she'd been swallowed.

Talmor jumped and swore, and around him people cried out in fear.

He caught a whiff of damp, stale air as though the crypt had been opened, and overlying that came the stink of fire and bitterness. He'd smelled such an odor only once before, on the day he'd first met and rescued Pheresa from an attempted abduction just outside the palace walls. She'd been spell hit, and afterwards the air had smelled exactly like this. There had been thick fog on that day, too, he recalled.

His hand closed on Nejel's shoulder like a vise. "Move!" he shouted. "Get to the queen now!"

Nejel shouted back, but his voice was drowned out in the sudden commotion as people screamed and began milling in confusion. Only now—too late, Talmor thought furiously—did the guardsmen on duty hurry toward the altar. Again, Talmor tried to jump atop the bench, but with a crash it fell over. The people beyond Nejel and Sergeant Goddal shrieked and shoved in panic, some of them falling over the bench and knocking others down.

Pheresa screamed, her voice rising over the din. The sound of it pierced Talmor, and he went icy cold inside. Ignoring the tightly packed quarters, he drew his sword, swinging it high overhead to avoid taking off Nejel's ear.

The officer ducked to one side and swore, but he was also reaching for his weapon. "Men!" he rapped out. "To the queen! Now!"

Pem, Carlemon, Goddal, and Lorne closed ranks immediately around Talmor, hemming him in on all sides as together they moved forward in a block. Nejel and Avlon spread out, each forcing his way past the people pushing and jostling in the opposite direction. There was now a general panic among the assembly, with everyone frantic to get out.

Just as they reached the aisle, something happened near the altar that Talmor did not see. The choir scattered in all directions, and more people swept into the aisle, blocking Talmor and the men around him in an impasse.

Talmor took advantage of the confusion and managed to slip between Pem and Carlemon. The latter grabbed at him but caught only his empty sleeve, and Talmor pulled free. Knocking a courtier aside, Talmor was forced to jump sideways into a box pew to avoid being trampled in the jostling crush. He climbed atop the short wall of the pew, teetered a moment on the narrow surface with his sword flailing for balance, then jumped to the next pew wall.

A glance behind him showed that Sir Pem was following his example, as was Carlemon. The rest of his group remained bottlenecked in the aisle, struggling against the streaming crowd.

With every passing second and delay caused by the chaos and commotion, Talmor cursed Cardinal Theloi for having parted him from the queen's side.

"Fool!" he snarled to himself, barely controlling his impatient urge to knock a portly merchant aside with the flat of his blade.

No matter what anyone said, his proper place was protecting Pheresa from harm. He should have found a way despite the malice and complacency around him.

But there was scant time for self-recrimination. As he was about to leap again, a maiden in a rose-hued gown clutched at his leg, nearly toppling him off-balance as she cried out for help. He managed to get free of her and hurried on. By then, the mist was thicker than ever.

A substance neither fog nor smoke, and as red as fresh blood, it boiled around the altar and throne. So impenetrable was it that even standing atop the pew walls, Talmor could not see Pheresa or any of the churchmen who'd been with her when the attack began.

By now the church knights and guardsmen had converged on the altar site. Some waded valiantly into the mist, only to shout and retreat hastily. One ran deeper into it, then staggered out, clutching his throat. Talmor saw two church knights pulling a white-robed cardinal from the mist. The knights were coughing, and one of them slipped and went down on his knees. The cardinal—Talmor could not see which one—looked unconscious or dead. As others went cautiously to their aid, Talmor's despair rose.

For what hope had the queen of surviving this poisonous mist? Since her one cry for help, he thought frantically, there'd been no other sound from her. Was she abducted? Was she lying dead?

His entrails felt hot and loose, and fiercely he clamped down on such fears, refusing to think about anything except saving her.

Leaping down into the space between the foremost pews and the steps leading up to the altar, he pushed his way through the surge of hysterical courtiers and clerics. Someone collided with Talmor so hard he was knocked staggering, but he caught himself on the railing and scrambled over it to run up the steps to the guardsmen.

"Take heart, men!" he shouted. "Come on! To the queen!"

Looking surprised, they rallied to him and started forward.

"Guardsmen, stand where you are!" Nejel bellowed over the noise. The men halted, glancing back.

"To your queen, men!" Talmor shouted, waving his sword. "She needs you. Come! To the queen!"

"Talmor!" Nejel roared behind him, and Talmor could see the commander struggling through the crowd. "Don't be a fool, man! Get back from that unholy—"

Fury burst in Talmor's chest. What mattered caution when the queen's life was in peril? Growling, Talmor spun around and ran forward.

"Stop him!" Nejel roared.

Someone—Talmor saw not who—gripped his arm and nearly spun him off-balance, but Talmor yanked free and plunged headlong into the mist.

In two strides he was both half-blind and lost. He could not see ahead more than inches. Nor could he hear properly, for the red mist muffled and distorted sounds, further disorienting him as he blundered back and forth in his search.

"Pheresa!" he shouted, only to gasp and choke. Once he started coughing, he could not seem to catch his breath. Breathing in the mist was like inhaling frost, and it hurt to the very bottom of his lungs.

"Pheresa!"

She made no answer. Terrified of finding her collapsed or dead, Talmor blundered onward. The mist was cold, as cold as death, and already it had chilled him to the marrow. His fingers went numb around his sword hilt. Grimly, he tightened his grip to a stranglehold lest he lose the weapon, and forced himself onward.

But he was fast losing hope. No one could live in this stuff.

He felt as though he were smothering with every labored breath. His lungs burned, and now his eyes were tearing with irritation. Yet he had to find her. As he forced himself to take another step, and another, he suddenly doubled over in a violent coughing fit and sank to his knees.

The red mist smelled of magic, something dank and sour and evil. It choked the life from him, sapping his strength and breath; yet with gritted teeth, he forced himself upright. Dizzy and unable to draw sufficient air, he staggered another step or two and blundered into a solid object that he realized must be the altar. He gripped it with desperate fingers, his arm flung across it for support, heedless of the sacred items knocked asunder, then pushed himself onward until he stumbled into the coronation throne.

The throne went skidding across the polished stone floor, and Talmor stumbled upon a body.

Sinking beside it with a little groan, he put down his sword—cursing the hurlhound that had taken off his right arm—and swiftly patted his hand over the body. His fingers touched silk garments and a portly form. It was not the queen.

Something very near a sob escaped him. He picked up his sword and crawled forward awkwardly on his knees. "Pheresa!" he tried to call out, but he had so little breath it came out a croak.

His knuckles bumped into something hard and metallic.

Pausing, his breath wheezing laboriously, he picked up the object and held it close to his eyes, where he saw dimly that it was Pheresa's crown.

Loss and despair plunged through him, for at that moment he knew he would not find her in this evil mist no matter how long he searched. She was gone, taken, and whether she was still alive or already dead almost didn't matter. He had failed her. She had called out for him, and he had not reached her in time.

In all his years of service, he had never failed her before. He could not bear it now, and it was no excuse that he was no longer hale and whole, but instead a cripple with his instincts blunted and his reflexes too slow.

In self-disgust he flung the crown aside, picked up his sword, and staggered to his feet.

His knees would not support him, however, and he sank down again, gasping for air. The red mist was choking him. He could barely think now, could not remember why he was here, except he had to keep looking. *Crypt,* he thought dully. He had smelled it, could smell it still. Even if he had to crawl, he would try to head in that direction.

A shape came staggering through the mist, looming over him without warning, and ran into him. "Thod's bones!" the man shouted in fear, and swung his sword.

Still on his knees, Talmor lifted his own weapon just in the nick of time to parry a blow that might have beheaded him.

"Fool!" he shouted hoarsely. "I'm Mandrian, not Sebein!"

"What?" the other man said, coughing. "Thod's bones, are you friend or foe?"

"Friend, you fool! I'm for the queen."

"Sorry!" The stranger gripped Talmor's tunic and hauled him to his feet. "Are you Lord Talmor?"

Unable to speak for coughing, Talmor tried to fend him off. If Nejel had sent someone after him, Talmor had no intention of going tamely. He started off, intending to disappear into the mist where this stranger could not find him, but the man held him back.

"Come out of this, m'lord, before it kills us both."

Dizzy and half-conscious, Talmor pulled away.

"No, m'lord! Go not deeper into this red death!"

Trying to evade him, Talmor staggered and fell.

The thud of his head against the floor nearly knocked him out. He was so cold now, so weak he could barely move. Yet he reached out with his elbow and dragged himself a few inches forward.

The other man grasped his foot and would not let go. Angrily, Talmor wondered why the misguided fool couldn't understand he was only costing them precious time.

"Damn you," he whispered.

"Come . . . back," the man rasped out, coughing violently. Talmor tried to answer, tried to kick free, but he could do neither. Too weak to pull free of his assailant's grip, Talmor felt the mist pressing down, a smothering mass crushing him. And he was so cold, so numb, so witless, and so tired. It was too hard to keep fighting, too hard to keep breathing. Vows and determination, he realized in despair, were not enough to prevail.

And then the red mist turned black, and all he knew was darkness.

Chapter Six

Talmor awakened to find himself outside, being carried down the cathedral steps on a board. The sunlight dazzled him, making him squint. He raised his head, but it felt so heavy he let it fall back.

A shadowy figure leaned over him. "Be still if you value your life." And a cloth was flung across his face.

Angry and confused, Talmor wanted to shove the cloth away, but he lacked the strength. He fell unconscious again, and when next he awoke it was to find himself in a stark narrow room with brick walls and floor. Narrow windows set high near the ceiling let in the only illumination. The air smelled of puke and death. He saw two rows of barracks cots, perhaps twenty in all. Most were filled with men lying either unconscious or dead. Flies were buzzing, and now and then someone stirred or moaned.

In the distance Talmor heard the contentious murmur of masculine voices, too indistinct for him to understand.

Rolling his head to one side, he found himself staring into the sightless eyes of a dead man. The person on his other side shifted about weakly and coughed, but no one came to offer aid.

Sweating, Talmor tried hard to remember what had happened. Pain was throbbing through his chest and right shoulder; not exactly physical torment, but an uncomfortable sensation that he could not describe. He felt strange all over, peculiar, as though not quite tethered to his body. There was violence in him, not the usual coil of dangerous heat but something different, a dark, edgy sense of fury he did not understand. It reminded him of the Nonkind fever that had raged in his veins last winter, when he'd been wracked with hallucinations and visions most foul. Yet this was not like that; this was something originating inside him, natural, something he did not want to acknowledge. He felt afraid, wondering why he was here and what he'd done.

And somewhere, down in the most secretive part of him, he knew that he liked this strange hunger for violence. His hand moved restlessly beneath the rough blanket and curled around his sword hilt. Yes, he liked it. Just as he liked throwing fire . . .

Horrified by his thoughts, Talmor jerked himself up on his elbow. The room revolved around him slowly, forcing him to shut his eyes a moment before he managed to sit up. The effort awakened violent misery inside him, and he leaned over just in time to be sick. Afterwards, he straightened cautiously, blinking sore eyes against the light and favoring his aching head. His throat hurt with every swallow, and he hugged himself tightly, shivering and gulping in unsteady breaths.

One of his fellow sufferers stirred at the other end of the room and drew up his knees, coughing violently. Squinting, Talmor saw that it was Sergeant Goddal, but still no one came. There was nothing in the room save the cots and the afflicted. Not a table, not a pail of water.

Swallowing made him wince. His mouth felt puckered with thirst. Shakily, he wiped clammy sweat from his brow. When he stood up slowly, this time the room did not spin. Pleased, he rested a moment. He was resilient and quicker than most to recover from injury, but right now he felt newborn weak and decidedly queer.

The throbbing in his scar increased, and he put his hand to

his right shoulder, rubbing where his arm should have been. It hadn't hurt like this since the Thirst Hold knights had cauterized his wound with a magicked blade and purified him of the Nonkind fever. For a moment unreasoning fear swelled into his throat, but he managed to choke it down. He did not have the fever, he assured himself. It could not return unless he was bitten anew with Nonkind venom. Whatever afflicted him now had nothing to do with the past. Better he should put such fancies aside and cope with what lay at hand.

But as yet he could not quite remember what had happened.

"No!" shouted someone from the next room. "I tell you 'tis impossible. We'll never—"

Other angry voices drowned out the first.

Frowning, Talmor moved in that direction, picking his way slowly past the cots to the doorway. The door, fashioned of thick planks strapped with iron, stood ajar. Tired from walking even that short distance, still feeling weak and sore, Talmor propped himself there against the wall to listen a while, but the argument had died down momentarily. He heard someone muttering, a scrape of chair over hard floor, the faint jingle of spurs, and a heavy, frustrated sigh.

"Nejel, you're mad," drawled an aristocratic voice. "It was one thing to take the queen's side this morning when she stood bravely before all, but it's another to stay loyal now."

"I agree!" said someone else. "We can't risk fighting the church knights. They outnumber us three to one."

"Puny odds for guardsmen," Nejel said angrily. "You—"

"Have some sense, man, for Thod's sake! You'll get us hanged for treason."

"Or worse," muttered another.

By now Talmor had recognized the voices of Lord Avlon and Sir Lorne. His memory came flooding back, and he remembered what had happened in the church . . . and to the queen.

Staggering forward, he elbowed the door open with a bang and entered the adjoining room. It was long and open, with a battered table and exposed rafters, from which hung the banners of the palace guard. Talmor recognized the building as the guardhouse where, as a sentry, he'd spent his leisure hours sipping ale and listening to the good-natured joking of the men. The place was empty, save for a handful of worried-looking officers standing in belligerent poses. They sprang apart as he came in and turned to stare at him in either astonishment or consternation. Instead of their weapons, they reached for their Circles.

In three quick strides Talmor reached Lord Nejel and backhanded him across the mouth. As the commander staggered, Sir Pem drove his shoulder into Talmor, knocking the wind from him. Talmor collapsed like a man of straw, wheezing and coughing, unable to defend himself against Sir Pem's blows.

"Stop!" Lord Nejel commanded. "Let him up."

Sir Pem obeyed without protest, jumping to his feet and retreating with a promptness that surprised Talmor.

Choking, Talmor rolled onto his side and worked his way slowly upright. He leaned on the wall, cursing the weakness in his knees.

"Now is the time to take him, before he can regroup," Lord Avlon said.

Talmor sucked in more air and reached for his sword, but no one attacked. He frowned, lifting his head to look through the unruly curls that had fallen over his eyes, and found that the men had instead backed away.

Lord Nejel was probing his swelling lip gingerly. With dirt smeared across his cheek, his cloak torn, and his blond hair ruffled, the commander had lost his usual sleek air of assurance. Instead, he looked harassed and furious.

"Lord Talmor," he said now, "have you gone mad? Can you no longer tell friends from foes?"

"Tell me which you are," Talmor retorted. "I gave you charge of her majesty's safety, and you let her—"

A violent fit of coughing forced him to break off what he was saying. He doubled over, gasping for breath and pressing his fist to his mouth. When he lowered his hand he saw flecks of blood on it.

Something was said among the men, but he didn't listen.

He was too busy trying to hold off the gray blurring of his vision.

"No, m'lord!" Sir Pem said in a loud voice.

Roused, Talmor straightened in time to see Lord Nejel coming forward. Sir Pem tried to grab the commander's arm, but Lord Nejel evaded him.

"Take care!" Sir Pem said in alarm. "He's dangerous."

"If he meant to work his magic, he'd have done so by now," Nejel said. "I think I can survive a split lip."

Sir Pem looked everywhere except at Talmor. "M'lord, you don't know what he might do."

Lord Avlon moved to block Nejel's path. "Pem's right," he drawled to Nejel. "Talmor should be dead, or nearly so, not standing in our midst like a miracle performed."

Nejel halted, ran his tongue across his swollen lip with a wince, and looked at Talmor over Avlon's muscular shoulder. "What say you, Lord Talmor?" he called out. "Are they right? Are you drawing on the potent forces of evil to slay us with some new spell?"

Anger spread through Talmor. He could feel it gathering force, gathering heat. *By Thod,* he thought darkly, *if they want to fear me, I'll give them a good lesson in it.* But such thinking was wrong as well as dangerous, and he hastily struggled to master his temper. Sanude, he thought in shame, would be appalled with him for casting aside the teachings this way.

He noticed Sir Lorne stealthily backing toward the exit. Running to save himself, or to get help? Talmor wondered. He could see they were all afraid, despite their various shows of bravado. Even Lord Nejel kept flicking his gaze away from directly meeting Talmor's.

This curse will follow me to the end of my days, he thought bleakly. *The only thing they're willing to forget is that I was found blameless.*

"He doesn't answer," Sir Pem said nervously. "Maybe you shouldn't provoke him more, m'lord."

"And maybe he can't answer," Nejel said with a frown. "You will forgive us, Lord Talmor, for our surprise at your entry. You caught us unprepared for you."

Talmor's frown deepened. He dragged his gaze in turn to meet each of theirs and saw them go all shifty-eyed in response. "Damne!" he said hoarsely, coughing again. "I'm no *sorcerel!*"

Nejel cocked his head to one side. "Until now, I did not believe it, but you stayed in that filthy mist too long to be alive."

"Demon! Caster of magic!" Sir Lorne said rather wildly, making gestures of repudiation from a distance. "Everything the priests claim against you is true. You are in league with the darkness, or you could not be standing before us hale and—"

"Have done!" Lord Nejel said angrily.

"Consider, my lord!" Sir Lorne said, holding up his Circle. "How do you explain his appearance? The man who pulled him out of the mist died an hour past. Goddal is coughing up blood. Ames is dead, and so is Sufeau. We left Sir Talmor—"

"Lord Talmor," Nejel corrected him sternly.

"*Lord* Talmor," Sir Lorne said with scorn. "We left him lying in the sickroom, white as a shroud with almost no breath in him, and now he stands here—well."

"Hardly well," Lord Nejel said, frowning.

"I say we should call the priests to take him away before he casts evil over us. I'll fetch them—"

"Go out that door, and I'll see you die for it," Nejel said grimly.

Fear and defiance flashed across Sir Lorne's face. "My lord, take care, for I fear he is influencing you. We should have left him in the church to die."

"The way you left the queen?" Talmor shouted hoarsely. "I could have gone after her . . . I was nearly to the crypt when I was pulled back. Whose orders do you follow, Nejel? Whose, Avlon?" He let his gaze rake them. "For as Thod is my witness, I see no loyalty here to her majesty."

Shock whitened Nejel's face, and there was shame to be seen in Sir Pem and perhaps even Sir Lorne; but Talmor was coughing again, coughing so hard his knees buckled under him. He went down, and it was Sir Pem this time who rushed forward and caught him just before he hit the floor.

"Easy, sir," he muttered, tightening his hold while around Talmor the room dipped and whirled.

"Morde a day," the commander swore, coming to help. "He's really as ill as we first thought."

"Aye, he's bad," Sir Pem said grimly. "Made us think otherwise for a bit, though, eh? That's our Sir Talmor, valiant to the rattle."

Avlon kicked a stool to them, and together Sir Pem and Lord Nejel lowered Talmor onto it. He coughed until he retched.

Sir Pem held his shoulders, steadying him, and when Talmor finally managed to catch his breath and straighten, the knight gripped him hard to keep him from toppling off the stool.

"We'd better get him back to his bed," Lord Nejel was saying worriedly, but Talmor shook his head.

"Not that charnel house," he whispered.

They let him be, and he closed his eyes a moment, longing for Pears. His squire always knew how best to tend his hurts. He wondered where Pears was presently. Had he reached the city by now, or was he being held for questioning at some checkpoint on the road to Savroix?

Sir Pem gave Talmor a cloth, and he wiped his face and bloody mouth, longing for a drink of water.

"There's not much time left to save ourselves," Lord Avlon said quietly over his head, continuing the argument Talmor had interrupted. "Let us decide and have done. Nejel, you know I am right."

"I gave my oath—"

"Damne, so did we all," Avlon broke in harshly, "but circumstances have changed. As soon as he finds the strength, Cardinal Theloi will order us—"

Talmor drew in a breath. "Saw Theloi . . . go down."

"His eminence is alive," Nejel said quickly, giving Talmor a pat on the shoulder. "He is expected to recover."

The officers all drew the sign of the Circle. Talmor didn't. He felt no gladness at the news.

"His eminence's faith has protected him and the rest of the Circle of Cardinals," Sir Lorne said.

"Not Atol," Sir Pem spoke up. "He's dead enough."

"Perhaps Cardinal Atol's faith was not as strong as that of the others," Avlon drawled.

"That's blasphemous slander!" Sir Lorne said as though shocked. "My lord, you mustn't joke about it."

"I am not joking," Avlon retorted.

"Let us pronounce no judgments on any who are dead," Nejel intervened swiftly. "The guardsmen we've lost today were all valiant men of faith and courage."

"If Talmor here lives, he's the only one of the injured who will," Avlon said, eyeing Talmor suspiciously.

"Except for the cardinals," Sir Pem insisted.

"Well, of course, except for the cardinals." Avlon snorted. "They have their faith and the special protection of Thod. What say *you* regarding your own survival, Lord Talmor?"

"Leave him be," Nejel said. "He's sick enough to prove no magic saved him today."

Avlon shrugged. "You've evaded my question long enough, commander. When Cardinal Theloi orders us to produce the queen, what shall we do? I tell you we cannot keep up this pretense."

"Lord Salba has given us our orders," Nejel said stubbornly, "and we'll follow them to the last man."

"And if we die for treason?" Avlon asked.

"Then we die."

"There's treason here already," Talmor whispered. He tipped back his head to glare up at them. "When you talk of surrendering your oaths of loyalty to side with the church against the crown, you're no longer in the queen's service."

Lord Avlon's face darkened. "I'll take no reprimand from you—"

"Silence! Both of you!" Nejel commanded. "We have our orders, and we'll follow them."

"But—"

"No, Avlon. No vote! No discussion! We are pledged, and, by Thod, we'll stand for the queen to the last man."

"The lord chancellor has put us in an indefensible position," Avlon argued. "He is gambling with our lives."

"And his own. His head is as unsteady on his shoulders as ours."

With a quick glance at the other men, Avlon sneered. "That does not reassure me. Nejel, will you not think?"

"I *have* been thinking," Lord Nejel said. "All through the service I thought of Duc Lervan, and how the guard served him when he proclaimed himself king. I bent my conscience for that, but I'll not do it again. Not this time. Queen Pheresa was crowned today, and she is my sovereign."

"And if she is dead?"

Sir Lorne flinched, and Sir Pem swore under his breath, but Lord Nejel's gaze went to Talmor's for a moment before he turned back to face Avlon.

"If her majesty is dead," the commander replied, "then she must be proven so. Until then, I am pledged to her support. And so are you all. If that means lying to Cardinal Theloi, then we'll lie. If it means fighting church soldiers, then we'll die defending this palace against them." Nejel frowned as his hand closed on his sword hilt. "To the last man."

The muscles in Lord Avlon's heavy jaw bunched visibly. He swung his cold, derisive gaze to Talmor. "And you, lord baron, are you satisfied?"

Talmor was not entirely sure about the undercurrent running between Nejel and Avlon, but he'd been thinking rapidly while they argued, piecing together all that he'd heard since he came in. He did not like the conclusions he was reaching, for it was clear that Pheresa remained in mortal danger. She had not been rescued, or found. It did not even look as though any kind of search was being conducted. Certainly none of these men were out directing one, as they should be.

Resentment and frustration boiled inside him. He wanted to jump to his feet and call them to action. But since only a few minutes past they were ready to stake him as a heretic, he doubted any of them, even the commander, would obey his orders. That political games and intrigue were being played, with the queen's life at risk, infuriated him more than he could say.

"Well?" Avlon drawled. "Have you nothing to say, Lord Talmor?"

"Only this," Talmor replied. "What in the name of the Circle has befallen her majesty? If she is not yet found, what has been done? Why are you officers holed up in the guardhouse, doing nothing? Why have you left the city and retreated here to the palace? Has the cathedral been searched? The crypt? The passageways and offices there? What of the city? Have the gates been shut? Have the streets around the cathedral been cordoned off and searched? Have the city patrols been called out to assist in her majesty's rescue?"

None of them met his gaze, not even a flicker of a glance. A terrible silence fell over the room.

It was as though a vise squeezed Talmor's heart. He felt cold and hollow. Never, in all the years he'd known these men, had he believed them capable of retreat or cowardice. Slowly he rose to his feet.

"Lord Nejel," he said when no one spoke, "at least tell me that your men went into the crypt after her. At least tell me you tried your best and simply could not find her. I'll believe nothing less of her majesty's valiant guardsmen."

Nejel, white-faced, said nothing.

"We've done all we can," Sir Lorne said defensively. "Do you think we've been sitting at our ease all day while Lord Salba issues statements of reassurance? Seventeen men lie yon, injured and dying. Eleven more are outside in the lime pit, awaiting burial. All for having tried to go after her majesty. You—"

Lord Avlon laughed with harsh mockery. "Don't trouble to defend us," he said, silencing Sir Lorne. "This ill-bred mongrel offers us no thanks for saving his hide. Oh, no! Instead, we stand accused—we, the most elite fighting force in the realm—accused by this pagan of cowardice and dereliction. Most likely *he* is the one who drew the evil into the cathedral today. The priests are calling for his head, but we have shielded him in defiance of their edicts. All this we have done, and he turns on us, blames us, like the serpent he is."

Nejel flushed; his eyes were like granite. "Avlon, have a care what you say."

"Why? You've assured us we've nothing to fear from

him." Avlon turned his cold, heavy-lidded gaze on Talmor. Dropping his customary affectation of ennui and mockery, he said, "Have you not read our thoughts by now, lord baron? Know you not what we really think of you? Then I'll say it aloud."

"No, Avlon!" Nejel cried.

Ignoring him, Avlon went on glaring at Talmor. "How fiercely you judge us, Lord Talmor, standing here with your new rank shiny and bright. How you snap at us, as though you still hold a protector's authority. Well, you have none, sirrah! No say in what we decide for the queen's safety or best interests. You're nothing now but a plaything for her majesty's pleasure, you crippled whoreson, and as such you—"

In one swift motion Talmor drew his dagger and was on the man with his blade at Avlon's throat before the officer could react or defend himself. Ramming him backwards against the wall, Talmor held him pinned, ignoring what the others called out. Avlon's mouth was open, his eyes wide with surprise and dawning fury. Talmor's gaze was hot and fierce as he pressed the edge of his dagger to Avlon's skin, and the throbbing in his scar came back, keeping time with his rapid heartbeat. It pulsed in his head, urging him to kill.

Barely did he hold himself in check. "No longer her majesty's protector, no," he said in a low growl. "A cripple, yes. But not helpless. Not, I think, what you expected. You'll apologize for your insults, Avlon. And you, Nejel," he said, aware of the commander hovering behind him, "will start telling me the truth."

"We have told you the truth," Nejel said softly. "Talmor, let him go."

Talmor pressed his dagger harder on Avlon's throat. The man swallowed convulsively as beads of sweat trickled down his jowled face. But he kept his lips pressed tight and said nothing.

Someone moved behind Talmor, and he broke the skin on Avlon's throat, making the man flinch. Blood ran in a slow, narrow zigzag down his neck and soaked into the edge of his tunic. Talmor inhaled the warm scent of it, and the dark violence inside him raged and clawed like a caged beast, urging him to slice open Avlon's throat and drink the blood that spurted forth.

Somehow, Talmor fended off the temptation, but he was shaking with the effort to hold himself together. He turned his head slightly. "Don't be fools," he rasped out hoarsely. "I'll finish him if you take me from behind."

"Talmor," Nejel said in an unnaturally calm voice. He moved where Talmor could see him. Holding up his empty hands, he said, "We are your friends, your allies."

"No! You want to—"

"Talmor, we are loyal to the queen. We know you are likewise. If we fight among ourselves, we are surely lost. Let Avlon go."

Talmor's arm was trembling. His muscles were so tight they ached, and sweat was running into his eyes. Avlon pushed against him, but Talmor was well braced and nicked him again, making Avlon utter a choked cry.

"Do not move," Talmor whispered, fighting back the need to cough. He could see the grayness creeping up to the edges of his vision as it had before, and he blinked hard to keep his sight clear. Avlon was glaring at him with such hatred that Talmor knew the moment he lost concentration the guardsman would break free and retaliate without mercy.

"Talmor," Lord Nejel said, "you are not yourself. Let him go. Please."

Kill him now. Kill him now, chanted a dark little voice in the back of Talmor's skull.

He gritted his teeth, struggling not to plunge the dagger deep, and the weapon trembled in his hand. Avlon grew very still, wide-eyed, his nostrils flaring with every breath, as though he sensed how close he was to death.

"He has insulted the queen, and he's openly urged the rest of you to commit treason," Talmor said against the pounding in his head. Again he pressed his dagger a little harder, and again he fought himself to ease it back.

"Let him go," Nejel ordered. "He is no traitor, whatever you may think. So he lost his temper and insulted you, what of it? Put down your weapon, Lord Talmor, and release him. We are not enemies here."

Talmor felt his strength suddenly draining away. He needed to cough. He needed to sit down. The bricks on the wall behind Avlon were starting to crawl a little. He could sense Sir Pem and Sir Lorne hovering behind him, ready to strike the moment he released Avlon. *How,* he thought in sudden bewilderment, *did I come to be here with my knife at this man's throat?*

It was as though his memory was riddled with holes. He felt lost, a stranger to himself.

"Everyone, get where I can see you," he growled.

Nejel gestured, and Sir Pem and Sir Lorne moved reluctantly to the commander's side. Only then did Talmor lower his blade and step back.

Sir Lorne would have charged him, but Nejel flung his arm across the man's chest. "Stand," he ordered, and Sir Lorne obeyed.

Glaring in pure hatred, Lord Avlon whipped up his hand to touch his bloody neck and swore. "You'll pay for this, you—"

"Enough!" Nejel roared. "Both of you, have done! We've difficulties enough at present without challenges to honor being issued."

Avlon turned his furious gaze on Lord Nejel. "Challenges?" he echoed in a voice pitched high in disbelief. "Honor? Do you think I'll accept challenge from this bastard cur? He should be whipped at the post for his insolence."

"Barons are not whipped," Nejel replied. "And if you do not curb your tongue, you'll be confined. Now apologize."

Silence fell over them, broken only by Avlon's heavy panting. He glared at Talmor, who glared back, ready to fight if he had to, although in his present condition he knew he would lose.

Still pressing his hand to his wound, Avlon bowed his head slightly to Talmor. "I meant no ill toward the queen," he said in a voice both cold and cutting. "I retract any remark which might be considered insulting to her majesty. I am loyal to her cause. I serve her as I have sworn in my pledge."

But that was all he said, and Talmor realized he would not retract any insult he'd made to Talmor personally. Well, it was enough, Talmor decided wearily. He'd shown them he could still fight if necessary. He'd frightened Avlon for a short time, and if that made the man his mortal enemy Talmor did not much care.

"Well, Lord Talmor?" Nejel asked curtly. "Is that sufficient?"

It was not, and they all knew it.

"Aye," Talmor said, choking back a cough. He felt both hot and cold, as though fever raced in his veins. His throat was raw, burning with every swallow. But he made himself stand fierce and proud as he glared at Avlon. "Never speak of her majesty that way again."

Avlon's powerful hands curled into fists at his sides. He said nothing.

"Lord Avlon, you are dismissed to your quarters," Nejel said briskly. "Sir Lorne, go with him and make sure that cut's attended to at once."

Both men saluted the commander and headed for the exit, but at the door Avlon paused and looked back. "You'd better see that he's locked up and not just hidden," he said to Nejel. "Heretic or not, he's quite mad, and as such of no use to us at all."

Talmor stiffened. At that moment, if he'd still possessed his right arm, he would have hurled his dagger through Avlon's heart.

"I'll be the judge of that," Lord Nejel said angrily. "Go, Lord Avlon. You've done enough here."

Chapter Seven

Lord Avlon could not have said anything more piercingly cruel at that moment, for Talmor felt he was indeed going mad. Grinding the heel of his hand against his left eye, he dropped heavily onto the stool with an involuntary moan. For weeks he'd lived in torment, torn between abandoning Pheresa and staying with her. His worry had nearly driven him from his wits, wracking him night and day. Now all this had happened. He hardly knew whether he was conscious or dreaming, mad or sane, possessed or just ill, tired, and afraid. He did not know if or when his curse would stir to life and escape his control, as it did so often when he was hurt or exhausted. He did not understand why his scar burned and throbbed so intensely. Realizing he was rubbing it again, he frowned and dropped his hand to his lap.

"You're very ill," Lord Nejel said in concern, peering down at him. "Come, let Sir Pem take you back to your bed. You need rest."

The idea of returning to that room of horrors, possibly to be locked up with the dead and the dying, sent Talmor struggling to his feet in protest. Nejel, however, easily shoved him down again on the stool and held him there with a firm hand on his shoulder.

"Talmor," he said, shaking his head. "What are we to do with you? You strike me and nearly slice the throat of my ablest lieutenant. Are you so desperate to wreak vengeance in her majesty's name that you must attack your friends?"

Talmor stared up at him mutely and could find no words. He was shaking.

"Leave this in our hands," Nejel said persuasively. "I know you do not wish to hear it, but Lord Avlon was right in saying you are her majesty's protector no longer. Go and rest. Let yourself mend. We'll—"

"No," Talmor said, panting. "This is no time to rest. I have to help search for her."

Lord Nejel exchanged a look with Sir Pem. The pity in their faces infuriated Talmor.

"Why is nothing done?" he insisted. "Have you accepted her majesty's abduction? Condoned it? Is no action being taken at all? I do not understand."

"You'd better tell him all of it, m'lord," Sir Pem said. "He'll fret himself to pieces otherwise."

Nejel sighed and ran his fingers through his blond hair, sleeking it back from his brow. "Officially, her majesty is well and in residence in her palace. The abduction was thwarted. Officially, the church knights are questioning the townsfolk for the identity of those who attacked her majesty. Although the ruffians escaped, their capture and arrest is expected soon."

Talmor realized his mouth had dropped open. He closed it with a snap of his jaws. "What tale is this? Who can believe such nonsense?"

"The people believe what they are told," Lord Nejel said in a toneless voice.

"But it's a lie!"

Nejel met his eyes momentarily and nodded. "We have lost her. Thod's bones, but I blame myself bitterly for having abandoned the duty you gave me. I thought her safe in the cathedral, especially with so many guards stationed at all the exits. All save one," he said bitterly, and sighed. "I did not know there are catacombs beyond the crypt, secret passages known only to a few. Certainly not to me, the commander of the palace guard. Damne! I did not imagine such perfidy could reach her deep inside the holy sanctum!"

Talmor supposed he should absolve Nejel of blame and tell him it was no one's fault. But he could not do it. He *did* blame Nejel, blamed him for his ill-founded confidence and mistakes of judgment, blamed him for not comprehending just how much evil there was in the world, or how cruelly it could strike.

Frowning, the commander began to pace back and forth, absently fingering his swollen lip. "Just before the panic started in the church you said something about Sebeins. Do you truly suspect their hand in this?"

"Aye," Talmor said grimly. "I'd bet my sword on it."

"I asked the priests, but they confirm nothing. If they know—and surely they would recognize the presence of that cult—they are not saying."

"The priests always keep secrets," Talmor said, and began coughing again. He swallowed blood and grimaced. "I fought a Sebein once, years ago. His magic smelled like the spell used today. But I could be wrong."

"No, I value your instincts in these matters. You"—Nejel hesitated, suddenly looking uneasy—"have more experience with the ways of magic than most of us."

His delicacy did not appease the sense of insult Talmor felt. Resentfully, Talmor shook his head.

"We know the cult has no liking for her majesty," Nejel continued as though he had not noticed. "They must have been desperate to dare to penetrate the very cathedral, but such boldness served them well." His expression grew thoughtful. "However, there is another theory. The Lady Hedrina has been arrested and confined to her rooms in the palace."

"Lervan's mistress?"

"Aye. We suspect she has ties to Gant, but as yet that's not certain. If there is a connection, she could be behind this plot to abduct the queen."

"She moved fast, this lady," Talmor said, turning over the

possibility in his mind. "Could she have heard of Pheresa's return and laid her plans in time?"

"Um, perhaps not."

"But what is being done on the queen's behalf?" Talmor asked impatiently. "Morde! You prate of theories and intrigues, but we can establish blame later. The important thing is to rescue her majesty!"

"I know—"

"How much time has passed? If the queen was felled by the mist, she could be dying . . ."

"No!" Nejel gestured vehemently. "No, we will not think that. The cardinals are not seriously hurt, as we told you."

"Except for Atol," Sir Pem said gloomily.

"Yes, yes." Nejel glared at him impatiently. "And the bishop is recovering. You, Talmor, are alive. We must keep hope for her majesty. After all, had they intended to kill her, there are easier means of doing it. And we would have found her body. No, it was an abduction."

Talmor rose to his feet, knocking the stool back. He'd had enough of this chatter. The commander was purposely trying to distract him from the most important issue. He still did not understand why, but he was through trying. Without a word he headed for the door.

"Where are you going?" Nejel called out after him.

Talmor did not answer. His anger grew with every step.

"You must stay inside. You are not fit for action. Pem, stop him!"

Talmor reached for the door, but Sir Pem threw himself bodily against it, holding it shut.

"No, m'lord," he said, squinting at Talmor. "Not one foot will you set outside, and that's all there is to it."

Although he'd caught both Nejel and Avlon by surprise with quick, unexpected attacks, this time Talmor had no element of surprise on his side. He swung his fist, but Sir Pem caught his wrist grimly, twisting it, and punched him hard in the stomach.

Doubled over, Talmor dropped to his knees and struggled to breathe while gray-and-black worms filled his vision.

"Get him on his feet," Lord Nejel said from behind him.

Sir Pem reached down to grip Talmor by his tunic. Talmor drew his dagger, but Sir Pem was ready for that, too. He wrestled Talmor down and stamped on his wrist so that Talmor dropped the dagger. Sir Pem kicked the weapon away and hauled Talmor upright.

"Sorry about this, m'lord," he said matter-of-factly, "but you ain't going outside, not with a price on your head."

Held expertly with his arm bent behind him, Talmor found himself marched back to the stool and forced to sit down once more. They gave him water, and he gulped it thirstily without heed for his aching throat, and felt refreshed for it afterwards.

But all the same he burned with humiliation. There'd been a time when no man in the guard could have defeated him like this. He'd be damned before he wallowed in self-pity; but, merciful Tomias, he would give away his soul right now to still have his sword arm, to still be a warrior and not an object of pity and charity. Having lost the way of life he loved most, and, worse, perhaps having lost the woman he adored, he knew how easy it would be to fall into self-loathing, wretchedness, and despair. The dark side of him, the side that walked the edge of madness sometimes, could still claim him. In recent weeks, he'd had Pheresa to hold him steady and give him both hope and purpose. She'd made sure he remained useful. She'd given him love and trust and her steadfast reliance. But without her . . . if harm or death befell her . . . he could not bear to think about it.

"Why?" he asked hoarsely. "Why will you not let me search?"

"Because the moment you are seen, the church knights will arrest you," Nejel said wearily. "I've already told you the clergy intend to make you the scapegoat in this affair. Why won't you listen?"

"Aye," Sir Pem added. "You don't want them priests to get their hands on you. Not for interrogation, you don't."

Talmor thought about the inquisition chamber and the violation he'd already endured. A shudder passed through him.

"Aye," Sir Pem said, peering at him intently. "You don't

want to be burned in the public square for heresy and treason, do you?"

Talmor frowned. "If the queen is abandoned to—".

"She ain't abandoned!" Sir Pem shouted. "We're doing all we're allowed—"

"Sir Pem," Lord Nejel said sharply, and the knight fell silent.

Talmor eased himself into sitting straighter on his stool. "Commander," he said hoarsely, "stop tying me in cords of half-truths and hints. Stop delaying me from the action I need to take. I am a man of action, not intrigue. Political games are not for me. All I want is to help search for her majesty, not sit idle."

"Lord Talmor—"

"Please! I have been a guardsman. I served under you, took your orders. I—"

"Do not beg me!" Nejel shouted as though he could bear no more. Running his hands through his hair, he glared at Talmor. "In Thod's name, do not beg."

"Then tell me the truth. Why have you really called off the search? Why not enlist the aid of the church soldiers to rescue her? Why this elaborate pretense? What do you fear?"

Lord Nejel said nothing, but the pity in his eyes was not what Talmor wanted.

"Let me help," he said again. "Let me go in where you fear the spell still lingers. If I can get into the crypt, I am certain—"

"No! A thousand times no!" Nejel said explosively. "You cannot go near the church. We barely saved you as it is. I cannot let you risk yourself again."

"You are kind, but—"

"Kindness has nothing to do with it!" Lord Nejel said as though stung. "If the priests take you prisoner, and later the queen is found, how am I ever to explain to her majesty what we let happen to you?"

Talmor opened his mouth, but found himself with nothing to say. A tide of embarrassment rose up his neck. He realized he had mistaken Lord Nejel's concern and kindness for friendship; it was not and never would be. *Morde,* he thought angrily, *will I never learn the heartlessness of a courtier?*

"Have some more water, m'lord," Sir Pem said gruffly, shoving a brimming cup at him.

Talmor took it blindly but did not drink. At that moment he hated them for the care, hated them for letting him know the truth. He might as well be the queen's favorite hunting falcon or courser or lapdog, to be pampered, petted, and fed. What was wrong with them, he thought furiously, that they spent their time seeing to his welfare instead of the queen's?

Pacing back and forth, Nejel frowned at him worriedly. "Perhaps Avlon was right. We may have to lock you up for your own protection. Morde, this grows more impossible. Nothing I say to you calms you."

"Not when you are in the wrong!" Talmor whispered fiercely. He coughed, his chest aching, his throat on fire, and sipped at the water. This time, it did not help much. "Search," he croaked out. "Put every man to the task while she remains in danger."

"We follow the lord chancellor's orders."

"Damn his orders!" Talmor shouted. He hurled the cup at the wall. "I have given you *my* order."

Nejel's mouth set in a stubborn line, and he did not reply.

"Best tell him what he wants to know," Sir Pem replied.

"And have him do Thod knows what?"

"He ain't going to stand for anything less. Best tell him."

Nejel loosed a gusty sigh and turned to Talmor. "Very well, but give me your word you'll abide by Lord Salba's orders."

"I'll give no pledge until I know all you have to say," Talmor replied.

"Ah, damne! You stubborn—"

Talmor started to his feet. "I'd rather take action than talk. Let's—"

"No! All right. I'll tell you all of it, but you won't like it." Talmor sat down again.

Nejel stared at the floor between his boots. "I regret to say that the cathedral has been warded by priests skilled in countering magic. It is forbidden for anyone to approach the place, much less search its premises, until the magic inside it has dissipated."

"What?" Talmor asked in astonishment. "On whose authority has such an order been given?"

"Cardinal Theloi's."

Talmor drew a sharp breath, but Nejel was already holding up his hand to forestall him.

"That's church property, Talmor. We can't supersede the lord cardinal's orders regarding it."

"But if she was taken into the crypt—"

"We suspect that's what happened, but we don't know for certain. There was a great deal of confusion once the panic set in, and the assembly ran in all directions."

"There are other ways into the crypt besides through the church," Talmor said, frowning. "An outside entrance is but one, and—"

"We cannot search there. I have told you. We tried, but every man I sent in collapsed, before the church knights took over and forced us out."

"We had orders to go!" Sir Pem interjected fiercely. "Never think we retreated willingly."

"Salba's?"

"Who else?" Nejel said curtly.

"But why has he ordered the guard to make this lie about the queen being safe? What good does it do to keep the palace guard idle while her majesty remains in danger? Has he turned traitor?"

"Thod's bones, no!" Nejel said impatiently. "What think you the populace would do if they knew the truth? We have her not. We know not where she is or what's become of her. She was crowned by the scantest acclamation. Her throne wobbles as we speak. We barely hold order anywhere. Proclaim the truth of this disaster, and the entire city will be in riot. We'll lose control of it, and the palace, too, if we are not careful."

Feeling weary to his bones, Talmor drew in a long breath. There it was, the reason why they were so afraid. Complete anarchy faced the realm, and he realized that the lord chancellor had done the only thing possible as a stopgap measure. But Talmor wondered how long such a lie could be sustained.

Spies were bound to discover the truth very shortly. Such desperation at work would fool no one for long.

"But what is being done to find the queen?" He'd asked that question so often he was sick of hearing himself repeat it. "What?"

"We're searching," Nejel said grimly. "I swear to you we have not given up. But we must be discreet. We dare not betray our true purpose to the church knights. And you cannot join the hunt, because that would give everything away."

"Now that the church has forced you out, it will keep you out," Talmor said angrily. "This event has played right into Theloi's hands. He'll do nothing to save the queen's life. Instead, he'll be maneuvering a successor into place."

"That's a matter for Lord Salba and the other ministers to deal with. Meanwhile, we have to keep you out of sight. And preferably in bed. If you die—"

"I am not going to die," Talmor said fiercely, ignoring the taste of blood in his mouth. "The effects will pass, and I will not sit here, idle and safe, while she—"

"Aye, so you keep saying," Nejel broke in with a sweep of his hand. "But I tell you this is a matter for us, and we'll handle it as we see fit."

"But—"

"No, Lord Talmor! Enough! I've done my best to answer your questions and give you assurances, but you must be satisfied."

"Never!"

"Stop thinking like a lover and start using your head! She is gone, taken to whatever secret hiding place the Sebeins—if they're the villains—keep. Meanwhile, the city gates are closed. The streets surrounding the cathedral are barricaded and guarded by church knights. Agents are going from house to house, questioning any they suspect might know something behind the attack. The people have been told that the queen's abduction was unsuccessful. No one, most especially her majesty's cabinet and the church officials, must suspect otherwise." He held out his hands and dropped them wearily to his sides. "That is why even I can't be seen running to and fro in a frenzy, but must stay here, posting orders for the systematic search of the palace for Duc Lervan's supporters."

"The queen needs more help than this," Talmor insisted. "What good are your schemes to preserve her throne if she is lost?"

"She isn't lost," Nejel said. "As was said before, if they'd meant to kill her majesty, she'd be lying dead at the altar. No, Lord Talmor. She's alive, and if it's Vvordsmen who have her, or Sebeins, or even some conspiracy under Cardinal Theloi's influence, they'll surface soon enough with their demands."

"And so you are waiting?" Talmor asked in disbelief. "Just waiting for her ransom?"

"What else can we do?"

The blood pounded in Talmor's ears. Muttering a curse, he got unsteadily to his feet and began to pace back and forth until his strength gave out and he stopped abruptly, bracing himself on the table.

"Think on this," Nejel said. "Clune and Roncel are rumored to be joining forces with Cardinal Theloi. Gide won't do that, but 'tis believed he's angry about Lindier's arrest. If enough ducs are incited to wrath, they may well refuse to give their allegiance to the queen if—I mean—*when* she is found. Perhaps half of her cabinet ministers sided with Duc Lervan; on all sides stand her majesty's opponents. She surprised them today, and was crowned. But they are ready to strike back, to declare a new sovereign in an instant if we do not control the situation. Some of these men have no choice save to act swiftly against her if they are to avoid charges of treason, for they were in too deep with Lervan. This is the lord chancellor's thinking. And I concur with it."

Talmor was frowning.

"You see," Lord Nejel said very quietly, "if the palace guard stands for the queen, and she is not recovered at all, we'll lose our heads by order of whoever succeeds her. So our stake in this is as deep as anyone's."

"Yes," Talmor said coldly. "But if you switch allegiance to the church now and tell the cardinals the truth, you have a chance to survive."

Lord Nejel's face went white, and Sir Pem stiffened, muttering an oath beneath his breath.

"Lord Talmor," Nejel said angrily, "I have taken several insults from you today, but this is the last one I'll abide. How—"

"It's what Lord Avlon wants to do, is it not?" Talmor broke in. "Cut your losses, declare the queen lost, and side with the church? It's one way to survive, isn't it? Only you won't."

Nejel's fists were clenched at his sides. His gaze bored into Talmor's as though he'd forgotten his earlier superstitious fears. "Theloi would use us and discard us. He'd see us broken of rank, posted to the far corners of the realm, possibly assassinated."

Talmor nodded. "He would never trust you."

"Avlon and Lorne are not seriously contemplating mutiny," Lord Nejel said as though trying to reassure himself.

"How long do you think you can hold the guard together in this crisis?" Talmor asked.

"As long as necessary." Nejel straightened his shoulders. "We must if we're to get through this. The cardinal's spies are waiting for any sign of weakness. If we cannot stay united, we will destroy ourselves and perhaps the queen as well."

"Agreed. But united in purpose does not mean that I have to sit idle."

Fresh exasperation filled Nejel's face. "I will seek information on where the Sebein cult practices its blasphemy. They change their locations frequently, but we'll find a trail. As for you—"

"I know a way—a secret way—to the ruined church behind the palace." Talmor coughed, swallowed blood, and ran the back of his hand across his mouth. "I doubt her majesty is there, but a search of the tunnels might turn up something. I run little risk, for no one will see me there."

"But you're reeling on your feet," Sir Pem said worriedly, and shot a look of appeal at the commander. "M'lord, I can't advise it."

"I'll take a man with me," Talmor said.

Nejel frowned so fiercely that Talmor was certain he meant to refuse. "Are you well enough?" he asked.

"Does it matter?"

The commander shrugged and glanced at Sir Pem. "Go with him. Make sure he's not recognized. Put a hooded cloak on him."

Sir Pem's eyes were bulging, but he threw a salute. "Aye," he said briskly. "But Thod help us in this. Hiding him is one thing, but letting him prowl about—"

"Pem."

"Aye, m'lord. I'll find his lordship a cloak." Muttering under his breath, Sir Pem strode out, snapping the door firmly shut behind him.

Left alone with Nejel, Talmor sighed wearily. This was a small victory and hard-won. The fact that he'd had to plead and threaten for permission to search galled him. And the fact that he felt gratitude beneath his anger only worsened matters. He told himself he'd become no better than a mendicant dog, thankful for any scraps thrown his way.

"Thank you," he said, begrudging the courtesy.

But Nejel scowled. "Everything we've shared with you has been a waste of time. You're determined to thwart Lord Salba's judgment and go at this your own way, the consequences be damned."

Talmor saw no point in arguing. "Aye."

"Short of chaining you to a bed, I see few ways of keeping you quiet. I can only hope that when you collapse and Sir Pem has to drag you back, you won't have killed yourself."

Unwilling to answer those bitter remarks, Talmor told himself that he was not going to collapse. He meant to find the queen's trail, even if he had to elude Sir Pem and get back into the city to do so. He would need a horse for that short journey, and he wondered what had become of Canae and the queen's mount, left tethered at the back of the cathedral earlier today.

In the silence he could hear the faint moans and coughing in the sickroom. Compassion welled up inside him, and he pointed in that direction. "Will no one tend them or ease their suffering? As soon as I'm gone, will you let the physicians in?"

Nejel shook his head. "Those men are spell-sick, and the physicians won't go near them. Nothing can be done."

"Thod's bones, but you're a pitiless man," Talmor said in outrage. "At least send someone in to give them water. Let someone sit by them in kindness as they die."

"You could do that for them," Nejel retorted. "You do not fear magic as sensible men do. You could succor them in their last, wretched moments, and stay safely hidden from sight at the same time. I ask you to do this, Talmor. When my officers were present, I could not plead with you, but now I do. You served with many of these men. Will you not tend them?"

Guilt swept over Talmor, and he understood that Nejel had hoped for such a reaction. "'Tis their physicians and their priests they need now," he replied tersely, and suppressed a cough. "'Tis their commander they want to see in their affliction. Not me."

"You will waste your time and your strength," Nejel said with a sigh. "No matter what you pretend, you are in no condition to go out. This great show impresses no one, Talmor. The queen is not here to see how bravely you insist on coming to her aid. Why not get to your bed and be of use by causing us no more concern and trouble?"

"Oh, aye, bed," Talmor said bitterly, ignoring the other barbs. "Lie in there among the filth and flies while I wait to live or die?" He coughed and wiped away the blood. There seemed to be more of it each time instead of less. "I will live."

"I think you will not. And when the queen returns, we'll have her wrath for it."

"You've tried that argument before," Talmor said wearily. "It grows old."

"Even a protector is not sworn this far," Nejel said. "You are a fool."

"I love the lady."

Consternation puckered Lord Nejel's handsome face. He dropped his gaze as though he had no more to say.

"So should you all love her," Talmor said quietly. "She is a great lady, a queen to cherish. I would to Thod she could win the hearts of her people as King Verence did. She has his courage. She would rule us well—nay, better—were she given the chance."

Several changes of expression crossed Nejel's face, but he said nothing.

By then Sir Pem returned with a cloak thrown over his arm. "Ah, damne. I was hoping the commander had wrestled you back to the sickroom by now." He shrugged. "Ready, m'lord?"

Talmor took the cloak, but Sir Pem had to help him put it on. The knight shot another glance at Nejel, but the commander remained silent until Talmor was at the door.

"Thod speed," Lord Nejel whispered so quietly Talmor almost didn't hear him. "If—if your magic can find her, use it."

Astonished, Talmor looked back at him in time to see Nejel hastily touch his Circle as though in atonement for such a blasphemous remark. Although the commander had turned pale, he met Talmor's gaze without evasion.

"Use it," he repeated.

Giving him the sketch of a salute, Talmor pulled up his hood and stepped outdoors. He trudged across the busy ground, threading his way through the guardsmen being mustered or released from duty. It was duty change for the sentries on watch atop the walls. Commands rang out as they were relieved. A squadron marched by on its way to the stables. The men's faces looked grim and set within their mail coifs.

Sir Pem crowded close at Talmor's side, his eyes darting in all directions. "This way," he muttered. "Hurry."

As he turned down a narrow path between two barracks, Talmor was still amazed by what Nejel had said. Bleakly he wished he did have the special powers so many ascribed to him. But his curse existed only to destroy, not save.

He had nothing to help him locate Pheresa. Nothing at all, except raw determination, and that, he knew, was not enough.

Chapter Eight

Coming back slowly to her senses, Pheresa found herself lying on a tattered rug that smelled of mildew and rodent. In that instant, she knew that what she'd experienced was no dream, but reality. She sat upright with a jerk, her heart beating very fast, and pressed her hands to her face.

Do not cry. Do not be weak, she told herself, biting her lip in an effort to master her fear.

She remembered the ending of the coronation ceremony, the red mist, and the cardinals toppling one by one. She remembered feeling so terribly cold and peculiar. There had been a shadowy figure garbed in black who had seized her and carried her off into the crypt and catacombs beyond. After that, she had no clear recollection of anything save torchlight and whispers, rough fingers touching her face.

Now, as she sat up straighter and impatiently pushed her mass of golden hair out of her face, she had no idea where she was or how long she'd been here. It was time, she told herself, to stop moaning over her misfortune and find a way out.

Her surroundings were small, odious, and crude—not a room but in fact a cell, and a monstrous offensive one at that.

A simple torch made from a plait of straw soaked in pitch provided the only illumination. There was no window, not even a small peephole in the door. The pungent, smoky smell of burning pitch mingled with odors of animal, damp rushes, and something long dead. Stone walls, heavily cracked and uneven, and a floor of packed dirt were bare of ornamentation or furnishings, save for the tattered bit of carpet she sat on. She saw the floor littered with filth, including the tiny, picked-over bones of birds and lizards. Over in one corner, a rat den had been fashioned from rushes and chewed pieces of rug. The sound of muted squeaking came from inside the den, making her stiffen with alarm.

She saw a whiskered snout peer out, with two beady red eyes gleaming in the dark. With a choked cry, Pheresa jumped to her feet and retreated to the opposite wall, clutching her skirts tight against her legs.

The rat came out, a large black one with a long, naked tail. It paused to stare at her malevolently, then scuttled out of sight through a broken place at the bottom of the cell door.

Shuddering, Pheresa drew in a breath, waited until she felt sure the rat wasn't coming back, and went cautiously to push on the door. It did not budge. She tried kicking at the broken place with her heel, but only succeeded in bruising her foot. The wood planks were too stout for her to worsen the damage, much less make a hole big enough to crawl through.

She started to call out, then thought better of it and retreated to the corner farthest from the rat den. Her abductor clearly had no respect for her high estate, for she'd been incarcerated in a dungeon fit only for the vilest offenders. She was a queen, not a peasant, and her sense of insult helped her hold fear and despair at bay.

Her guardsmen, she assured herself, would not leave her here long before they came to her aid. She felt certain that Talmor was at this very moment leading men to her rescue, for he would not rest until he found her.

"Great Thod, in thy mercy guide him that he may come soon," she murmured, clutching her Circle.

But she knew she had to do more than pray and hope.

What could she do to stay alive and well, even to escape if she might contrive it? Again she glanced around the cell, but it had no egress save the door. She circled the small space, avoiding the rat den, testing the stones lowest to the floor in hopes of finding one loosened by a previous occupant. But there was no hidden passage of escape that she could find.

Hunger rumbled through her insides, and she found herself thirsty. Her throat felt sore and scratchy when she swallowed, but she did not know if that was from having breathed the foul mist or from lying on damp ground. She'd been stripped of her coronation regalia. Her crown, robes, and cloak were gone, as were her silk slippers. Her bare feet were filthy and cold. Her gown, sadly crumpled and streaked with dirt, was torn at the shoulder, and she had a deep, painful scratch there, clotted with dried blood.

Her earrings and the strands of pearls braided through her hair had been stolen, but she still wore the ring of state and her Circle. Sweeping her unbound hair back from her face, she reached into her pocket. The Saelutian dagger was gone.

Disappointment swept her, although she tried to tell herself that no abductor would be foolish enough to leave her armed. Still, it had been her talisman, her reassurance. Without it, she felt helpless indeed and very unsure of what was to happen to her.

Which of her enemies was responsible for this? she wondered angrily, pacing back and forth. Who dared carry off the queen of Mandria right under the noses of her guards, church soldiers, nobles, and courtiers?

Someone bold and cunning, she was forced to admit. Someone brave enough—or desperate enough—to attempt the unthinkable, and succeed. Just then, she would have wagered money that the blame lay with Cardinal Theloi. He was an extremely cunning and clever man, capable of plotting for years, possessing infinite patience, yet decisive and ruthless enough to strike hard when necessary. By returning to Savroix, she'd thwarted his plans to put Lervan permanently on the throne, and no doubt this was how the lord cardinal had retaliated.

The sound of approaching footsteps and a rattle at her door halted her speculation. She grabbed the torch from its iron ring. Holding it blazing before her as a weapon, she pressed herself deeper into her chosen corner and waited.

With a screech of its bolt, the door banged open on protesting hinges. Three men garbed in shapeless black robes stood on the threshold, staring in at her. She had never seen any of them before and found the sight of such gaunt, fiery-eyed creatures repellent. Clearly they were no rescuers.

The man on her left held aloft a torch. The man on her right carried a small iron kettle. The man in the middle leaned forward and bared his rotted teeth in what Pheresa supposed to be a smile.

"Ah . . . Pheresa," he said. "You are awake at last."

She drew herself erect, using anger to mask how much she was trembling. "You will address me as your majesty."

The spokesman laughed, displaying prominent, rather pointed teeth in front. Most of his jaw teeth were missing. Rotted out of his skull, she supposed, and averted her gaze. He was a beardless man, his face narrow at temple and chin, his cheekbones far too prominent. His hair had been cut so close to his bony skull it might as well have been shaved. His skin held an unhealthy pallor, as though he seldom ventured into the sunlight. His dark, deep-set eyes bored into her with an eager intensity that disturbed her, for his gaze made her aware that this man—whatever his identity—was a fanatic. She had met far too many zealots among the church knights, yet he had not the look of a man serving Tomias. He was not tall enough or muscular enough to be a church soldier. He wore no chain mail, no white surcoat with the distinctive black circles, and he was dirty. She discarded her initial theory about Cardinal Theloi's involvement, for these were not his eminence's usual sort of minions.

"Who are you?" she demanded. "What do you want?"

The man walked into her cell as though invited, leaving his companions to block the doorway. Pheresa caught a whiff of something acrid and unpleasant about him, as though he'd passed through a fire where something unwholesome had burned.

She had nowhere to retreat. Her chin went up. "The queen has not given her permission for you to enter," she said at her most regal. "Get out."

He stopped in the center of her small cell and went on staring at her for an offensive length of time. She had the impression that he was gloating over her, and her spine grew stiffer while her heart began to thump hard.

"I am afraid, *your majesty,*" the man said with mocking emphasis, "that what you want does not matter. But we will humor you . . . to a point."

She inhaled with such anger her nostrils flared, but held her tongue. She did not intend to bandy words with a mere ruffian.

He smiled. "To answer *your majesty's* question, you are the guest of the Sebeins of Valege."

"Sebeins!"

He bowed slightly. "Of Valege. This distinguishes us from other sects, but I suppose *your majesty* has not heard of Valege, or his teachings."

She felt as though she could not breathe, but to remain silent was to betray her fear. "I have not," she managed.

"You will learn more in time." He made a gesture such as a courtier might flourish. "What think you of your quarters? They are the best we have to offer. Are you not impressed by how well we live? Do you see what the official edict of persecution has driven us to? We live like rats in a sewer. But you, lovely queen, are going to change all that."

He took a step forward. Defiantly Pheresa brandished her torch, but when he lifted his hand the flames abruptly went out.

Her ears were roaring; her heart raced as though it would kill her. She stared at the smoking end of her only weapon, trying to stop the violent trembling of her hand, and vowed she'd use the hot pitch against him if she had to.

He gestured again, and the torch went completely cold and dead, as though it had been plunged into icy water.

She flung it away and pressed herself against the damp wall. Her gaze shot to his face, but she no longer dared meet his dark eyes. Great Thod's mercy, she thought, this man was using magic openly, with an arrogance that terrified her. Somehow, she forced herself to rally, and even managed to say in defiance, "So you can perform a few tricks for my amusement. Paltry tricks, sirrah. My court fool could do better."

Weak though it was, her insult made him scowl. "Your courage is false. Why pretend you have no fear? We both know better."

"Do not presume to know what lies in the mind of the queen," she retorted. "You cannot—"

"Are you not longing for a man named Talmor to rush in, behead my companions, and run his sword through my spine?"

She gasped for breath and dared not answer.

He came close enough to touch her but halted without doing so. "I am Bokune," he announced with sudden formality. "I have been chosen to initiate you."

"What mean you?"

"Long have we Sebeins waited for this momentous day when you, Pheresa, would be crowned sovereign. We rejoice in your good fortune, and we look forward to many long years of alliance."

"I'll have nothing to do with Sebeins!" she said quickly. "You tried years ago to coerce me, and failed!"

"Ah, that was Kolahl," Bokune said regretfully. "He was a fool, attempting to stalk your dreams before you had been initiated. But I am more skilled, I assure you. I will not fail, and once you have undergone the Rite of Blood, you will understand everything."

"I don't wish to understand. And I'll engage in none of your rites! Release me now, and I will consider not letting my guardsmen tear you to pieces."

He laughed so hard his dark eyes became slits. "Ah, great queen, how confident you are. Daring to negotiate when you have no position whatsoever except to grant our wishes."

"No one commands the queen!"

"Ah, but you are in our power. It has taken us years to capture you, but we are a patient people. We've had to be, to survive. No, great queen. Be sure of this: We will command you, and soon."

She'd stopped listening to his pompous speech. Her mind was spinning through alternatives. Even if she could somehow push past him, the other two men remained in the doorway, blocking the exit. Although she did not know what she could possibly do against a magic-wielding Sebein, she braced herself to resist whatever he meant to force upon her.

Bokune, however, simply lifted his hand and spoke a single word. The air rumbled in her ears, and her knees buckled beneath her. She collapsed without a sound, unable to move or cry out.

The other men came into the cell. One put his torch in the iron ring on the wall. The other set down his little kettle. They picked her up without a word, carrying her between them like a rolled-up carpet. Bokune stepped out into the passageway, and they followed with her.

Horrified, Pheresa could do nothing. She remained fully conscious, but her paralyzed body would not obey her desperate attempts to struggle. It was like being thrown back in time to when she'd drunk the eld poison by mistake and lay helpless for weeks, her body dying by slow degrees while her mind raged desperately for some means of survival.

Never had she imagined she would be put through another similar nightmare. Bokune glanced over his shoulder and smiled at her with a triumphant smirk, as though he knew he had incapacitated her in a manner she would fear most. It was the knowledge in his eyes, the quick, impudent wink he sent her that checked her rising panic and turned her thoughtful.

How could he know her secret fears? All Mandria presumably knew of her poisoning years ago when she was no one of consequence save Prince Gavril's betrothed. Mandria knew about the valiant quest to save her life that had sent Gavril, Faldain, and her on a hazardous journey all the way to Nether. Mandria knew she'd been cured miraculously by drinking from the Chalice of Eternal Life. But the people of Mandria did not know the true details of her nightmarish experience, the torment that wracked her body hourly, the terror that haunted her during those dark days in Nether when Gavril had descended into madness and the eld poison had crept through her body like a slow-burning fire. Rarely now did she have bad dreams from those evil days, but she recalled that there had been a time before her marriage when her sleep was sorely troubled with images and experiences from that time.

And the Sebein called Kolahl used to invade those dreams before Talmor killed him. Had Kolahl, she wondered, somehow invaded her memories as well and shared them with this cruel man? Why else would Bokune force her to reexperience an ordeal so terrifying and tragic?

Or was Bokune simply reading her mind at will, sifting through all her secrets? Even the idea of it outraged her.

She wanted to scream at her captors, but no sound issued from her throat. Inside, however, she flailed and shouted and struggled with all her might until Bokune abruptly halted in the passageway and turned to frown at her. He was sweating in the torchlight, his face paler than ever, his mouth clamped with strain.

Anger flashed in his dark eyes. He seemed about to speak to her, but then he simply glanced at his two henchmen. "Hurry," he said, and continued on.

Pheresa guessed that he did not find it easy to hold her incapacitated. She went back to struggling in her mind, calling up the worst curse words she'd ever heard on the tourney field, reviling Bokune inside her head, and imagining the pleasure of watching Talmor's sword disemboweling him. After all her struggles, effort, and tenacity, her coronation had been ruined by this vile dog spawn, this outcast, this—this would-be *sorcerel*.

She saw him stumble and reach out quickly to catch himself on the dirt wall. He glanced back at her with a grimace, breathing hard now, and hurried onward into a modest-sized chamber lit by several fires blazing in old iron tubs. Lined with deep shelves set between several entrances, the room was vaguely round in shape. The shelves were made of rotting boards, and on them rested skeletons. Some were placed neatly and surrounded with reliquaries and decayed scroll cases. Others obviously held the bones of multiple individuals crammed together in moldering heaps of rotted cloth and shrouds of cobwebs.

The air smelled so dank and stagnant Pheresa wondered how any of the chamber's living occupants could endure it. She felt as though she were breathing in decay and death, but she could not even cover her nose and mouth in defense.

Water dripped and trickled in the unseen distance. She'd heard rumors that the old catacombs beneath the city extended as far as the river. The Charva, according to legend, had once run thick with the blood of the dead in some of the ancient battles, battles so obscured in antiquity and legend that Pheresa did not even know their names or locations or outcomes. But she remembered that the Charva was said to hold the souls of the slain, and that was why the Nonkind monsters of Gant could not cross it. In the past, she'd paid scant attention to such old tales, but now, finding herself in this chamber of death, all sorts of imaginings filled her mind.

When her captors laid her on the floor, Pheresa saw that it was made of crumbling tiles layered with silt and dried mud as though in the past the river had flooded this chamber. Thoughts of people's bones floating about in muddy water horrified her so much that she returned her attention to struggling to move. So hard did she strain against the spell that she managed to wiggle two of her fingers.

Triumph gave her fresh strength. She kept moving her fingers although the effort made perspiration run into her eyes.

Bokune doubled over as though she'd hurt him. "Bind her!" he growled, his voice harsh with strain. "Then summon the viewers. Hurry!"

As soon as his companions had tied her wrists and ankles with cording, Bokune spoke a word that made Pheresa's ears pop, and the invisible force holding her prisoner fell away.

She dragged in a deep breath of relief and rolled onto her side to glare up at him.

"Be silent!" he snarled before she spoke. "Or I'll render you so."

"You can try," she retorted. "But you cannot hold me long. What weak magic you Sebeins command, compared to—"

"They're coming," one of the other men said.

Bokune knelt swiftly beside her and held up a dirty rag. "Stay quiet, or I'll use this to gag you."

The filthy cloth deterred her more than his threats of magic. She glared at him, saying nothing. With a grunt of satisfaction, he shot to his feet just as men and women garbed in shapeless black robes filed into the chamber. They took up places around the perimeter of the room, backs to the skeletons, the firelight casting harsh contrasts of light and shadow across their faces. Pheresa counted between a dozen and twenty of these individuals. Were they all the Sebeins that were left? she wondered. Had Verence's policy of intolerance winnowed them down to this tiny number? How she hoped it was so.

Yet she knew she must not grow arrogant and stupid. Certainly she did not intend to underestimate these ragged few. There were more than enough of them to inflict harm on her if they chose. She'd learned how dangerous fanatics could be. And, even more importantly, she was the one lying bound and helpless on the dirty floor, while they stood free. They could ransom her back to her kingdom and gain tremendous riches for themselves or safe passage to another land, whatever it was they sought. And she knew, although she loathed everything they stood for and despised them for the humiliation they'd dealt her, that she would gladly pay such a price just to be rid of them.

Bokune's two assistants carried in a crudely built table of scrubbed wood. It wobbled where they placed it, near the center of the chamber. Pheresa found herself lifted atop it and laid there, like a sacrifice on an altar.

Her fear came back, making her heart pound. She tried hard to hide it, tried hard to act like a queen despite the indignity of her present position. But when she saw the small knife gleaming in Bokune's dirty hands, she nearly cried out.

"Will you sacrifice me?" she asked, her voice no more than a choked whisper. "What is this wrong you intend to commit? What have I done against you?"

His free hand clamped across her mouth, cutting off her desperate questions. As he leaned down, his eyes held such satisfaction they were almost tender.

"Now," he whispered, raising the knife. "Let us begin."

Chapter Nine

"Bokune, I protest this!" A man stepped forward from among those lining the chamber. Gray-haired and bearing a terrible sword scar across his face, one that twisted the corner of his mouth and ran up through his left, blind-white eye, he spoke with a voice of authority and culture. "You are to *lead* her majesty through the Rite of Blood, not force her. You are to bring her will to yours, not break it. How can you command her properly when she is bound with ropes? She will remember your treatment of her, and it will taint the initiation."

Lying bound on the table, Pheresa looked at this unexpected champion with relief and gratitude.

Bokune scowled. "Her bonds are temporary, Kanth. She—"

"You have taken her weapon, too," Kanth continued, as though Bokune had not spoken. "And her shoes. You make a prisoner of her, and that is not the way of Valege!" Others in the group began to murmur. "If you cannot command her properly, let another perform the rite."

"No!" Bokune's voice rang out over everyone's, echoing through the chamber. "I was chosen among you all for this honor, and this will I do. I have the power to command her."

"I see that you fear her," the scarred man said, touching the cording around Pheresa's wrists. Someone in the group laughed briefly, and Bokune cast an angry look at the viewers.

"This is no occasion to be taken lightly," Kanth said in general rebuke, and the laughter stopped. "We have endured years of hardship, agony, and humiliation while waiting for this day to come. Our faith has been answered, for this queen crowned herself as Valege prophesied. She does not rule under authority of our greatest enemy, the Reformed Church. In this do we rejoice, for she is free to sweep away our persecution, free to honor the old favors that Verence forgot."

Pheresa listened to his speech with amazement. Had she been an unwitting puppet during the coronation, she wondered. Had she been influenced by the Sebeins to take the crown from Cardinal Atol's hands? Her bound hands curled into fists. No, she thought, she would not believe it. Kanth was just using demagoguery to sway his audience. In desperation, these people were clutching at anything for a favorable omen.

"Let our triumph not be spoiled with arrogance and conceit," Kanth went on, staring at Bokune. "Let the Rite of Blood be done properly, and under the authority of the old favors."

Bokune's dark eyes were blazing. "You were not chosen, old teacher. I was. Set aside your jealousy and let me perform the rite as I deem necessary."

"It must be done correctly," Kanth insisted. "She must not be bound with ropes, but with your mind. She must have her weapon in order to prove that she will not turn against us. She must be free of all constraint save yours. Can you command her, or are the rumors true? Do you fear that she possesses the power of the Chalice?"

Several people hissed, and even Bokune flinched.

"Say not that word!" he shouted, making a swift gesture of repudiation. "Call not to us the power of the unholy vessel."

"The Chalice is most holy," Pheresa said, trying to sit up. "Its name should be spoken with reverence."

Again there were uneasy outcries. Bokune glared furiously at her, but Pheresa would not meet his eyes lest he mesmerize her. Instead, she turned to Kanth. "You appear to be a man of reason. Do you and these people not realize that if harm befalls me, your kind will be scourged across all Mandria?"

Kanth eyed her stonily. "We are persecuted now."

"That will be nothing compared to the wrath of my subjects," she declared. "You know this to be true, or you would not urge Bokune to treat me gently."

Kanth drew his dagger and cut her bonds, ignoring Bokune's protest. Pheresa slid off the table in a hurry, aware that she was far from free, as the Sebeins encircled her. Their watchful, hostile eagerness reminded her of the starving mongrels that scavenge streets, daring sometimes to beg for food yet always prepared to flee.

She had never seen such people as these. Some, both men and women, wore their hair cropped as stubble-short as Bokune's. Others kept a more normal appearance. A few looked to be of peasant stock. Kanth, who was taller than the others, with the refined bone structure and long-fingered hands of aristocratic breeding, was not the only individual bearing horrific scars. Pheresa saw branded forearms, missing fingers or ears, crippled feet, and other signs of torture and punishment.

Although normally kindhearted, she felt no sympathy for these people. They surrounded her like wolves closing in on prey, and there was so strong a sense of anticipation in the chamber, such a *hunger,* that Pheresa felt it pressing against her.

"What do you people want of me?" she asked, trying not to sound afraid. "Why have you assaulted your queen? Why have you brought me here?"

"See?" Bokune said angrily. "She will not obey the strictures. She will not be silent. I warned you she would use her tongue in trickery and deceit."

"Bokune!" Kanth said in rebuke. "There is no deceit in her questions. Show her proper respect."

"She is to be silent! She is not to—"

"It does no harm to explain our intentions to her. You insult her with your rough manners. You are frightening her unduly."

"Let her be frightened," Bokune said sullenly. "And stop interfering, Kanth! I am no longer your pupil, and this woman does not need your chivalry. Were she free, she would order your throat cut in an instant. She is Verence's choice, not ours. She will refuse to honor the old favors just as he did."

"She must honor them!" Kanth said. He turned on Pheresa with such intensity she shrank back. "You will! You are a woman of honor. You will not compound the betrayal done to us."

"What betrayal?" Pheresa asked in bewilderment. "What favors?"

"Tell her, Bokune."

"I will explain nothing!" Bokune declared. "She wants no understanding. She's trying to delay the Rite of Blood."

"Please," Pheresa said to Kanth. "If you Sebeins want something, ask it without coercion and threats. We can at least discuss matters with common courtesy."

"No discussion!" Bokune shouted. "No explanation! She knows about the old favors. This pretense of ignorance is just more—"

"But I do not know," Pheresa broke in. "I have never heard of any—"

"Liar!" Bokune grabbed her roughly by her arms and shook her. "I told you to be silent!"

"Let the queen go!" Kanth ordered in a voice that caused the ceiling to rumble.

Bokune released Pheresa as though he'd been burned. "She delays us, hoping for rescue," he muttered. "You are a fool, Kanth, to pander to her."

Kanth stared at Pheresa with his single good eye. It was light brown, intelligent, and distrustful. "Your majesty," he said in his cultured way, making her wonder what he'd been before he turned to evil and darkness. "One monarch tells the next this secret. It has been passed through the royal successions since Valege was a cardinal of the Circle."

A woman among the viewers hissed, and others muttered dark curses that made Pheresa glance at them uneasily.

"I was not told," she said. "Verence died while hunting. There were no deathbed secrets passed between us."

"He named you successor. He placed the crown of princess on your head," Bokune said as though unable to keep quiet. "He told you then."

"He did not."

"She is not lying," Kanth said, eyeing her closely. "She is desperate and distrustful of us. But she does not know."

Pheresa looked at him in revulsion. She could not get used to their ability to wander through her thoughts at will, and without her knowledge.

"Tell her," Kanth ordered.

Reluctantly Bokune obeyed this time. "Valege was the spiritual adviser of the king."

"Which king?" Pheresa asked.

He snarled at her and did not answer.

"Which king?" she repeated.

"Donan," Kanth replied, while resentment shimmered black and hot in Bokune's eyes.

Bokune had not known the answer, she realized. He was simply a bully and a poorly educated lout, using intimidation as a shield.

She nodded graciously to Kanth. "Ah, yes, King Donan," she said. "Of the fourth dynasty in the cycle of—"

"It does not matter!" Bokune shouted. "The promise was sworn, and you must keep it!"

"In battle was King Donan defeated," Kanth said quietly to Pheresa, taking up the tale. "He lay on the field, pinned to the ground by a spear, and moaned to the gods for mercy. Valege prayed for him, and such was his devotion to his king that he could not let Donan die. And so he took into himself Donan's blood and gave it back to him, making a spell that Donan might live. And the king arose, a healed man, and turned the tide of battle in Mandria's favor. Thereafter, he swore a soul promise to repay Valege."

"A soul promise," Pheresa whispered. She had heard of

such things only in legend, and never had she come across this tale before, not in bard song nor in the old literature.

"He owed Valege nothing less for the gift of his life," Kanth continued. "He urged Valege to take gold and riches, but in the first of his prophecies Valege predicted a day when there would be schism within the Church of the Circle, when priest would turn against priest. He foretold the coming heresy of one called Tomias and the evil of the Reform. He warned of the afflictions that would befall us. For such tragedy did he ask the king's help. Not for himself. But for those of us to come. And so Donan promised, binding himself and all those who would rule after him, to repay the debt whenever it was called in."

Kanth stopped speaking, and a little hush fell over the chamber. Pheresa found herself shivering. *Was it true?* she wondered. She had no special gift of looking into people's hearts for truth or lies. *How,* she asked herself, *could a king of Mandria swear himself across generations?* No, she refused to believe something so far-fetched.

"To this day we observe the Rite of Blood," Bokune said harshly. "As you will. You know how the soul promise has been broken. Since the days of Tomias, we have cried out for help, and always we have been denied. Verence was the worst. He repudiated us, ordered us hunted like vermin, and put bounties on our heads. Royal agents still pay the peasants for each one of us they kill or maim."

"Verence had good reason to be angry with Sebeins," Pheresa said. "You turned his son into—"

"Gavril found his own path of destruction," Bokune said quickly. "Blame that not on us."

"This is not the way old favors are honored, Pheresa of Mandria," Kanth said. "We call in our debt now. You will repay it."

"I am barely on my throne," she said, and as she spoke wondered what kind of chaos was prevailing now in her absence. Her resentment boiled anew; but she forced it down, knowing she must not indulge in that emotion at present if she was to have any chance with these people. "What chance have I to consider clemency when you abduct and abase me?"

"You see?" Bokune broke in angrily. "She insults us with these games. She knows the situation. She knows what we want. Kolahl told her before he was killed. She refused him then and caused his death. Since that time, she has refused every plea for mercy, ignored every attempt to gain her sympathy."

"No, I—"

"You have been queen for a year!" he snarled. "And you have remained our enemy. You will not change, not unless you are initiated."

"Sebeins, hear me!" Pheresa said imperiously. "You violate the laws of this realm. You practice unholy beliefs and do unclean things. Were you to renounce your ways and seek penance, you might be pardoned for all you have done."

Angry murmurs surrounded her. Both Kanth and Bokune looked thunderous, and she realized she'd erred.

"It is not pardon we seek!" Kanth said, his voice razor-sharp. "It is freedom! When you were named the king's successor, we felt new hope that a change was possible. Everyone marveled at your beauty and kind nature. People spoke of your soft heart, of your generous spirit, and we believed you would show us those qualities, too. But always you have refused to listen and resisted our attempts to reason with you."

"Invading my dreams, abducting me, attempting to corrupt my soul?" she retorted. "Of course I have resisted."

"We no longer ask, Pheresa of Mandria," Kanth went on. "We have brought you here to grant our demands. You will rescind the death sentences for all Sebeins. You will allow us to mingle freely among the people of Mandria. You will grant us the opportunity to worship openly without fear of arrest and torture. You will end our persecution from the Reformed Church. You will allow us to resanctify our places of worship and welcome any who wish to join our ways."

The scope of what he was asking made her blink. "You are blasphemers and heretics. You challenge the very—"

"See? We have wasted time," Bokune said. "She seeks to delay us, nothing else. Her mind and heart are closed to our pleas, as they have always been."

"We can endure no more," Kanth said to her. "Our patience has ended, and I warn you that all the Sebein sects have now united, giving us the power to bring far more harm to Mandria than today's mist of death."

She frowned. "What mist of death? That red fog in the church?"

He bared his teeth in an expression that was not a smile. "Did your majesty not see how all who walked through it and breathed it fell?"

"I breathed it," she said in bewilderment. "Yet I am alive."

"That is because we countered the spell for you and the others who partook of the sacramental salt."

She remembered the excessive bitterness of the herbs and felt a cold chill run through her. Had that truly protected her from death? she wondered, and recalled how close she'd come to spitting it out. That tiny act of obedience and submission to the rite, was it all that had saved her? And had everyone else in the cathedral perished? Swiftly she checked the emotions swelling into her throat.

"Yes, we can bring death to many now," Kanth went on, his single eye alight with zeal. "We do not like to threaten. We want to be left alone, permitted to practice our religion in peace. But we are desperate and cornered. We will do what is necessary to save ourselves."

"You ask too much. I cannot—"

"She means she *will* not," Bokune broke in. "She is queen with unlimited power, and even now, held as our prisoner, she dares to revile us."

"I have said nothing that is not true," Pheresa said coldly. "You are heretics in the eyes of the Reformed Church, and you demand a leniency that the church and the citizens of Mandria will not allow me to grant."

"Where the queen leads," Kanth said, curling his twisted mouth into a grotesque smile, "her people must follow. Do not pretend your majesty lacks the power to change the minds of clergy and people. We know better."

"When we initiate you," Bokune said harshly, "you will obey our commands, for henceforth shall you be one of us."

Her heart began to pound, and her mouth was suddenly so dry she found it difficult to swallow. "I will not be coerced. I repudiate you all in the name of Thod and Tomias the Reformer!" She held up her Circle in defiance. "I believe in the sanctity of the—"

"We know your beliefs," Kanth said. He stepped back among the viewers. "Bokune," he commanded, "give the queen her weapon and her slippers. Let the rite commence."

And the others chanted in unison, "Let it commence!"

Pheresa still did not entirely understand why they were giving her the means to perhaps win her escape, but she did not argue when one of Bokune's assistants brought the items and dropped them at her feet. Bending down, she quickly slid on her slippers, grabbed the dagger, and unsheathed it. The bronze blade, wrought from beautiful Saelutian workmanship, was glowing with a pale radiance that warned her evil magic was already in play.

"Take no reliance from your foreign weapon," Bokune said to her, making her whirl to face him. "What works against Nonkind does not work against us."

"I warn you that I have drunk from the Chalice of Eternal Life!" she cried, seeing some of the Sebeins flinch. She lifted the glowing dagger high. Its hilt felt warm and reassuring in her hand. "The miracle of the Chalice's goodness restored me to health, and daily am I a witness to its beneficent powers. Seek not to pour your evil into me, for I would rather take my life than submit to your—"

Bokune spoke words she did not understand, and she found herself silenced, her body shuddering from whatever he cast against her. Her hands felt suddenly boneless, and she almost dropped the dagger. Swaying on her feet, she hastily shoved the weapon into her pocket for safekeeping and found herself turning to face Bokune of his volition, not hers.

The Sebein's dark eyes captured hers and held them before she could remember to look away. She felt herself being mesmerized, and there was nothing she could do to stop it. Around her the viewers began to chant in unison, uttering words she did not comprehend, words of darkness and force that stirred the fetid air and made wind to blow here underground, where no natural breeze could reach.

She blinked slowly, and perhaps for the duration of a few heartbeats she fell unconscious, for when her eyelids lifted she found Bokune grasping her shoulders with fingers like steel. Her body felt as though it were floating, as if did he not hold on to her, she would drift away. He kept talking to her, his dark eyes shining brighter and brighter as he wove the spell through her mind and body.

"The Rite of Blood," Kanth intoned over the background of chanting voices, "is one of our oldest, and most sacred, rituals. From the beginning it has been used to mark all who become one with us."

No! Pheresa screamed, but only in a remote corner of her mind. That part of her could still feel, think, and try to resist. Although she was not paralyzed this time, a strange lassitude held her. She had become two entities—the Pheresa being drawn into a place where all kinds of strange images and thoughts swirled through her mind, whispers echoed in her hearing, emotions alien to her rose and fell within her breast—and the Pheresa who cowered and cringed, quoting holy Writ in her mind to sustain her courage.

Gracious Thod, preserve and strengthen me, she prayed fervently. *Let me die rather than serve this element of darkness.* Her hand groped furtively at her side as she sought the dagger in her pocket. The thought of taking her own life horrified her, but to become the mindless puppet of these blasphemers would not be living. It would be slavery, or worse. She would not submit to such a fate.

But although her hand trembled and twitched at her side, she could not command it sufficiently to grasp her weapon. Inside, she wanted to scream with frustration.

Bokune released his grip on her shoulder, and she swayed. The shadowy chamber of death with its chanting figures receded from her as though she were spinning in a place that didn't exist at all.

She blinked, and again time must have elapsed without her awareness, for when she opened her eyes she had extended her left arm to Bokune. His small knife glinted in the firelight as he cut the inside of her wrist with swift expertise. She hardly felt the pain. It was a fleeting sting of sensation, nothing more.

Her blood spurted in a thin stream from the small cut, and Bokune quickly put his lips to her flesh, sucking her life with greedy, smacking sounds.

She moaned in fear, but although she managed to place her free hand on his head, she could not find the strength to push him away. It was obscene, the way he drank of her. Her head began to swim, and she warned herself that if she fainted, she was surely lost.

Kanth appeared at her side, holding a small bowl of dark metal cupped in his hands. His blind eye reflected the firelight as his drawn, misshapen mouth twisted into a smile.

"You see?" he said eagerly. "Our way is not so frightening, not so harsh as you expected. When Bokune is finished taking most of your life, you will drink the potion in this cup. Then he will cut his wrist and feed you with his blood. You will be reborn as Sebein, and you will serve our cause willingly, O queen."

She could imagine nothing—save perhaps dealing with Nonkind—more repulsive. Bokune abruptly straightened and cut himself, mashing their wrists together so that their blood mingled. Magic pervaded his flesh and being, spreading into her, tingling through her skin. Her heart pounded harder and harder.

"Quick," Bokune gasped. "Give her the potion."

Kanth pressed the rim of the bowl to her lips. The liquid contents smelled tangy and bitter. Clamping her mouth tight, she refused to drink.

A tremendous pressure weighed more and more heavily upon her. She tried so hard to resist it that perspiration streamed into her eyes, stinging them. Her body was shaking, and her heart thudded so violently she feared she would swoon.

"Drink," Kanth commanded.

"*Drink!*" Bokune commanded.

The force of Sebein will bent hers, crushed it until she gasped in surrender. As her lips parted, Kanth was quick to tilt the bowl. The potion filled her mouth, tasting so foul she gagged and spat it out.

"Xabrath damn you!" Bokune swore. He uttered something that made her feel as though she'd been struck, and pressed his bleeding wrist to her mouth. "Take my blood!"

She twisted her face away. Again he spoke that curse, and she rocked from the impact of it. Her will was crumpling. She felt pain inside her head, a piercing tearing pain, as though her very mind were being torn asunder. He was too strong, she realized in despair. She'd underestimated the extent of his powers, and she could not go on fighting him.

Revered Thod, she prayed, *in thy mercy and by the grace of the most holy Chalice, have pity on me.*

That's when she felt something change.

Bokune suddenly choked and staggered to one side. He seemed to be in pain, and she felt the crushing pressure lift from her.

"No!" Kanth said angrily. "Don't lose control of her now. You have her at the very edge of completeness. Maintain your control!"

Bokune struggled to pull himself upright.

The pressure on Pheresa returned, although not as strong as before. Kanth tightened his arm around her and again tried to force her to drink. There was little of the potion remaining in the bowl, but Pheresa twisted her head just in time, and the liquid spilled across her cheek.

Kanth was swearing, but that and the sound of the chanting died away in her hearing. She was wrapped in silence, and with it came a sensation of coldness, as though she were being submerged in icy water.

She remembered the day she'd lain dying in the ruined palace of Nether's kings, remembered the metallic taste of a cup being pressed to her numb lips, remembered that first feeble sip of water so cold and pure it sent a shock jolting to the top of her skull. And the eld poison had been quenched in the miracle of the Chalice's life-giving force.

Now, she felt so strange and peculiar that she wondered if the Chalice's mystery was acting on her behalf once more. She had claimed it would in an effort to bluff Bokune, but per-haps the miracle was still alive inside her after all. It was as though some residue of the Chalice's restorative power re-mained in her body, for the fire of Bokune's magic began to cool and die. Her senses revived from the dreamy state that had fogged them. Relief filled her, and she rejoiced that her prayers had been answered by a merciful Thod.

Then she was jerked to one side, so violently she nearly lost her footing. With a snarl Bokune smeared his bloody wrist across her mouth.

She kept her lips shut and tasted none of his foulness. He screamed at her, but although she saw his bloody mouth open, she heard none of what he was saying. His curses and magic no longer struck her like blows. His hand, the nails rimmed with dirt, clamped harder on her wrist. Taking the bowl from Kanth, he licked it dry before lifting her cut to his lips.

Pheresa, however, had no intention of letting him drink more of her blood. She was not going to become a puppet of this evil cult. She was not going to be tainted into serving this demented creature. Thod had given her a slim chance, and she meant to use it. Angrily she searched for her pocket amid the folds of her skirt.

But when Bokune's lips touched her wrist, it was not to drink. Instead, he spat a tiny amount of potion into her wound. She felt the spell revive inside her, as though flames had been kindled in her flesh. Crying out in pain, Pheresa drew forth the glowing white dagger of Aldana and plunged it deep into Bokune's side.

His eyes opened wide with astonishment. He stared at her with disbelief, and black mist poured from his mouth. When Pheresa pulled out her dagger, the blood that gushed from his side was black as well. She twisted her arm free and retreated from him. He took a step toward her, his face contorted with agony, then he crumpled to the ground.

Someone was screaming, the sound distorted as Pheresa's hearing returned.

"You'll not escape us!" Kanth was shouting. "You will be cursed, you and all of Mandria. The wrath of Valege will be called down on you. The bones of the dead will rise in accusation. Merciless, evil woman! What right have you to turn against us, to dishonor the soul promise of your ancestor? When your people cry out in affliction, you will know you are to blame, for we shall make the very ground of Mandria accursed and barren. You, Pheresa, will be the bringer of doom to your realm, for in revenge we shall make it a foul place where no man can live."

He grabbed at her, but Pheresa spun and slashed him with her blade. He fell back, and she scrambled away.

The viewers rushed her in a mob; but she struck quick and mean with her dagger, drawing blood while she shouted, "Get back from me in the name of Thod most holy! By the power of the Chalice of Eternal Life I condemn your evil and take no part of it. Your curse I throw back at you, and may it afflict you tenfold!"

Reluctantly, snarling oaths and muttering words of magic that made the walls rumble, the viewers parted before her. Their fury and hatred were almost palpable. Trembling, Pheresa held the glowing dagger high for all of them to see, pressed her bleeding wrist hard against her stomach, and ran for the nearest passageway.

Just as she reached it, they closed ranks behind her like a pack of wolves. A man gripped her hair from behind, but Pheresa turned on him and savagely drove him back with her dagger.

Then she was free and running for her life through the shadowy tunnel. This was not the passage that led back to her cell. She had no idea where it led, whether to escape or a dead end. The Sebeins pursuing her could have closed on her easily, for she kept stumbling, and her breath was rasping in her ears, but each time one of them gained on her, she cried out "Chalice!" and the person would fall back.

All they had to do, she realized, was chase her until her strength gave out. Her arm was still bleeding. The front of her gown was already soaked dark, and little spots had started to dance in front of her eyes. She knew she had scant time left, and impulsively darted down a side passage that was narrow and unlit.

In moments the torchlight from the larger passageway no longer illuminated her path. Blinded by the darkness, she bumped into a curve in the wall. The smell of damp dirt was strong here, and she was afraid she'd trapped herself. Stumbling to a walk, she groped her way forward.

Past the curve, she felt the tunnel narrow until she could scarcely squeeze through it. Her head bumped the ceiling, sending little trickles of dirt down the back of her neck. She ducked low for a few more steps before a little sigh escaped her, and she dropped wearily to her knees.

Unable to rise, she prayed that the Sebeins had not noticed her bolting into this dead end. Perhaps she could hide for a short while in the dark until they went by, then double back.

In the larger tunnel shouts were called back and forth. They sounded too close. Holding her breath, Pheresa listened, her heart thudding so hard it hurt her ribs.

Soon, however, the voices grew fainter, and she let out her breath in relief. Tearing the hem of her gown, she tried to bind her wrist, but her fingers were clumsy, and she knew when she knotted the strip of cloth that it was not tight enough to save her.

Carefully, she ventured back the way she'd come, easing around the curve in hopes that no one was lying in wait for her. The passage seemed empty, but before she could hurry along it, she fell again, too weak and dizzy to continue. This time she could not get up. There was a roaring in her ears now that had nothing to do with spells or miracles. Over it, she heard new shouts, along with the sounds of running footsteps and the clash of weapons. Chiding herself for not having hidden longer, she tried in terror to retreat, but could not move.

The darkness pressed close around her, and she was cold, so very, very cold, sprawled here helplessly on the ground.

She could feel her life pumping out of her, her heart thudding as it betrayed her, then she knew nothing more.

Chapter Ten

The sentry at the river landing stood with feet planted on the stone jetty, adamantly shaking his head. Wiry and weather-beaten, with one gnarled hand gripping his pike, he squinted at Talmor in suspicion.

"There's been no one come this way," he said. "An' so I've told ye twice. No boat traffic, no soldiers. Naught suspicious all afternoon, except what's standin' afore me now."

Behind Talmor, Sir Pem and Sir Bujean—the latter's presence commandeered when Sir Pem discovered he could not dissuade Talmor from coming back to Savroix-en-Charva—stirred nervously in the small boat, making its narrow prow swing away from the jetty before it was righted. Sir Pem even cleared his throat in warning.

Talmor ignored him. The sun was dropping low, turning the distant harbor into hues of crimson and copper. Here on the river, where it curled tight against the base of the city walls, the damp air held a cool bite, and the shadows lengthened along the jetty, where a handful of skiffs were moored. Behind the sentry, steps led up to a gate set in the massive town walls towering overhead. Another sentry stood before the gate, the butt of his pike planted firmly on the ground. More sentries gazed down at them from the crenellations.

Frustration beat inside Talmor, making him clench and unclench his fist at his side. His sense of urgency had only grown stronger through the last couple of hours. He remained convinced that Pheresa must be somewhere in the catacombs if she had not already been smuggled out of the town, but with the cathedral closed to all until the priests pronounced the magic spell safely dissipated, Talmor did not know how to find a way into the tunnels. If the guardsmen with him knew, they weren't telling, and Sir Pem would not agree to take him inside the town. Thus far, their search along the banks of the river had accomplished nothing. And standing here in this bobbing rowboat, trying to question a recalcitrant sentry, was doing Pheresa no good at all.

"Aye, I know what yer about," the sentry said irritably, pointing a finger at him. "Ye can't fool me with your cloaks and hoods."

Sir Pem clutched Talmor's arm, but Talmor shook him off, and said, "I only want to know—"

"Well, I know a spy for the ward captain when I see one," the sentry went on as though Talmor had not spoken. "Askin' this and that. I tell ye straight: Ye won't catch me failin' my duty. Damne, ye foul slink, be off! An' no more of yer sly questions."

"Let's go," Sir Pem growled.

"Wait!" Talmor called to the sentry, but the man turned his back and walked away along the jetty.

Talmor had no choice but to sit down in the rowboat and fume while Sir Bujean dug his oars into the water and rowed them away. Because of Sir Pem's concerns about keeping Talmor's identity a secret, they'd employed no oarsman on the outing. Bujean had not complained about doing menial work, but there was a sour, resentful look on his face as he pulled the oars.

"Now, that's all," Sir Pem said, low and angry. "We've humored you long enough, m'lord. Time to be heading back to barracks."

"No," Talmor snapped. He twisted around to catch Bujean's eye and motioned for him to go downstream. "I'm not giving up."

"Ah, morde," Sir Pem muttered. "Lord Nejel's going to have my head for this. The ruined church, he said. Not down here on the river."

The mighty Charva ran slow and wide here, where its mouth met the sea. Its course veered away from the walls, leaving flat mud banks overgrown with marshy reeds. Scowling, his eyes squinting against the low glare of sunlight spangling the surface of the water, Talmor tried to think of what to do next. Once darkness fell, Sir Pem would make him give up and return to the palace. *And Pheresa would be lost,* he thought hopelessly. His instincts kept telling him that his beloved was in mortal danger. He did not know why—for Nejel's theory that she would be ransomed made sense—but Talmor felt that the queen's time was running out.

Clenching his fist atop his knee, he vowed not to fail her.

"How far?" Sir Bujean asked, steering them a bit with one oar while he let the river do his work.

"Far enough," Sir Pem spoke up. "M'lord, we must turn back. We can't float all the way to the harbor. It's been closed, and if you're planning to ask questions along the wharves, well, that's impossible. Besides, Lord Nejel never said we could venture so—"

"I do not answer to the commander," Talmor said impatiently.

"But I do," Sir Pem retorted.

The river was curving again past an enormous stone buttress supporting the town wall.

"What's directly ahead?" Talmor asked.

"Thieves' camp, most likely," Sir Pem muttered. "And if we float into the midst of that, we've every chance of having our boat confiscated and our throats slit before we can jump overboard. Bujean, take us back."

The other knight grumbled something under his breath but dug his oars deep with a grunt.

At that moment, Talmor saw a furtive movement among the reeds on the bank and pointed. "Over there!"

"What?"

Talmor was leaning forward eagerly, his keen eyes watching the slight rustlings within the reeds and bushy catjuys. "To the bank," he said softly. "Make haste!"

Bujean angled them over to land. Talmor sprang from the boat, heedless of Sir Pem's protest, and went scrambling through slippery mud and reeds to pounce on his quarry. His hand closed on a grimy tunic of coarse linsey. The occupant of this garment proved to be a scrawny child, probably male, who twisted and spat in Talmor's grasp like a feral cat.

"Hold still!" Talmor said, breathless from the tussle. The child only squirmed more violently, flailing and kicking until his ragged tunic ripped and he landed on all fours. He tried to scramble away, but Talmor planted a boot on his back and pinned him flat.

The boy yelled a stream of curses, but when Talmor drew a small coin from his purse and dropped it in the mud in front of the boy's nose, the yelling stopped immediately. Quick as thought, the boy clutched the coin tightly in his fist. One wary eye rolled back to peer up at Talmor, standing over him.

"What's it, eh?" the boy said.

Talmor's foot mashed him a little harder into the mud. "Information. Do you know where the tunnels come out along the river?"

"Naught!"

Talmor pulled out another coin and held it where the boy could see it, but this one he did not drop. "'Tis said the thieves of Savroix know all the hidden ways underground."

"Ain't no thief!"

"What are you doing here outside the walls?" Talmor asked harshly, fighting back a cough. "Don't you know the city gates are shut?"

The boy stared at him, but said nothing. He was older, Talmor guessed, than his size implied, but woefully underfed, crawling with lice, and covered with grimy mud. His weasyn's face, narrow and distrustful, scowled, while the quick shift of his eyes warned Talmor that he was calculating deceit as natural to him as breathing.

"The tunnels," Talmor persisted, holding up the little coin while the boy watched it avidly. "Where do they come out?"

"Yer like don't want no tunnels, eh?" the boy said. "Fell in from flooding. Useless—"

He broke off with a grunt as Talmor stamped harder on him. "No lies," Talmor said grimly. "Goods are smuggled in and out of the city without assessment every day. Which means the tunnels are intact."

"Well, but them be guarded," the boy said. "Don't want them, no. Get yer throat slit fast and no questions afterwards."

"I don't want the smuggler tunnels," Talmor said, trying to keep both his temper and patience. "I want the catacombs."

The boy looked astonished. "Old church tunnels? Where they bring out the dead for robbin' and such? Morde, but I never took ye for a grave monger."

"Call it a new line of work," Talmor said grimly. "Where?"

"Naught. Ye don't want that. Filthy work, bringin' 'em out. Leave that to Scolly's gang. Quick and good. Don't charge much for the service and pops 'em back where they belong right away."

Talmor bent down and gripped the boy by the scruff of his neck, hoisting him on his feet and shaking him the way a dog would a rat. "If you won't tell me where to find these tunnels, then by Thod, you'll show me. Come on!"

But this threat seemed to alarm the boy greatly. "Ain't goin' there!" he gasped, white-faced. "No, I ain't. Up the cut, past the stink hole, and under the old trees."

"Show me," Talmor said, but with a cry the boy twisted free and raced away.

Talmor watched him vanish among the tall, winter-dead fronds of the catjuys, then even their rustling stopped as the boy went to ground. A flock of birds skimmed the surface of the river, crying shrilly. The shadows lengthened and darkened to indigo. Sighing, he splashed back out to the boat and climbed in.

Sir Pem sat there, squinting at him quizzically. "That was a pack of lies, if I ever heard any."

"We'll try it," Talmor said, although he was inclined to agree with Sir Pem. The boy was the type to tell him anything in order to get away. "It's the last place we have to search."

"The *last*," Sir Pem told him sternly. "Then we go back."

Talmor ignored him, not wanting to argue. "Bujean, if you please."

They found the cut by its smell, for it seemed that here was where the townsfolk emptied their refuse and channeled their privy wastes. Rotting garbage and dead animals lay piled in a jumbled heap along the narrow bank. Halfway up the walls, Talmor saw a row of wooden trapdoors, each with a long stain extending down the stones where the rubbish was thrown. The smell was overwhelming, the kind that permeated clothing and skin, burned the nostrils, and settled on the tongue.

Sir Pem swore to himself, while Talmor pressed a fold of his cloak to his nose and mouth.

"We ain't going into that," Sir Pem said, eyeing the filthy water with revulsion.

"Forward," Talmor ordered.

"But—"

"Hurry!"

The rowboat slid over into the channel of the cut. As they slid along, the bank separating this narrow branch of the river from the main course rose higher than their heads. More than once, they found the water so choked with rubbish that Sir Bujean had to clear it aside with an oar before he could row onward.

Then at last they were past the stink hole and mercifully upwind of it. All three of them gasped in relief. Sir Pem said something Talmor didn't hear, for he was too busy wiping clammy sweat from his face and resisting the temptation to rest his head on his knees. His throat still burned with every swallow, although he no longer had to cough each time he spoke. Yet he was very tired, having to push himself to keep going, and he refused to surrender to the steady ache in his chest.

She is relying on me, he told himself, forcing himself to straighten. *I have to find her.*

"Getting too dark to see," Sir Pem muttered, and Talmor forced himself to concentrate on the task at hand.

For a moment there was no sound save the rhythmic clunk and creak of the oars in their oarlocks. Twilight deepened rapidly now, for the trees growing thickly alongside the water hung over the river from both sides.

"Trees, the boy said," Sir Pem grumbled. "Damne, where *aren't* there trees?"

Ahead, the cut curved sharply to the right. The bank had eroded into an overhang, and a tree of enormous girth and spreading canopy grew there, its branches knobby with swelling buds, its roots dangling and partially exposed. And Talmor glimpsed a darker shadow than the rest there beneath the roots.

"Slow!" he said, leaning forward. "Look yon, under the roots. See?"

"Aye," Sir Pem said after a moment. "Like a small cave mouth. Could be an animal's den."

"Or a beggar's hole," Sir Bujean suggested.

"Or the entrance to one of the tunnels. Get closer."

As Bujean maneuvered the rowboat beneath the overhang, swearing as the boat's bottom snagged and scraped on something, Talmor squinted up at the city walls in an effort to get his bearings. He thought he glimpsed the roofline of the cathedral's bell tower, which would make this the right location. His heart quickened in excitement.

"Quickly," he said.

Sir Pem's hand closed on his shoulder. "Slowly," he warned. "That boy could be sending us straight to perdition."

Talmor wasn't listening. He picked up the bundle of torches lying at his feet and held one out. "Your strikebox, please, Sir Pem."

The knight lit one of the torches and tucked the others through his belt while Talmor scrambled out of the boat onto the narrow, slippery slope leading up into the mouth of the tunnel. He crouched there, roots fingering his hair, and peered inside cautiously.

It was too dark for him to see anything. He could smell dampness and dirt, but nothing else. Swiftly, stifling his urgency, he studied and fingered the ground but found no footprints in the gloom. A few weeds grew in the crumbling dirt, but none were broken. No one had gone this way recently. He did not know whether to feel hopeful, or worried lest this prove to be yet another dead end.

"You know," Sir Pem said, joining Talmor's side, "there's rumored to be at least a league's worth of tunnels dug beneath the town. We can't—"

"We must," Talmor said grimly, going in. "We're the only ones—"

"That ain't true!" Sir Pem said, right on his heels. "All kinds of men are searching. The commander explained that to you when—"

Talmor sighed. "We're the only ones her majesty can trust."

"All her guardsmen are true to the rattle! You think you're the only one who can protect her, but you ain't."

Halting, Talmor spun around to face him. "Had I been permitted to remain at her majesty's side today, as she wished, she would be safe now, or I would be dead. How can the palace guards say the same, since her well-being was left to them, and they failed her?" When he saw Sir Pem's eyes fill with bleak regret and shame, Talmor held his gaze a moment longer to make his point. "Sir Bujean!" he called softly. "Come on."

"I told him to stay and guard the boat," Sir Pem said.

"We need him," Talmor insisted, and so Bujean tied the boat and climbed into the tunnel at a half crouch, his hand gripping his sword hilt.

Together they ventured deeper into the passage, which was not quite tall enough for them to stand erect. The walls were dirt, with no shoring or support timbers. Talmor had the uneasy feeling that the passage could collapse on him at any moment.

Sir Pem moved to the lead, holding the torch aloft, while Sir Bujean brought up the rear. Kept protected in the middle, Talmor wanted to urge Pem to go faster but held his tongue.

There was a time to act recklessly and a time to show good sense and caution.

When they came to a fork in the tunnel, Sir Pem stopped. "Which?"

Talmor frowned, holding down his worry. No one needed to say that they could easily become lost in this maze, perhaps never to find their way out. "To the right," he said. "We'll head in the direction of the church as best we can."

Sir Pem took the right tunnel, while Sir Bujean paused to leave a mark on the wall. Several more times they came to branching passages. Talmor tried to choose the ones that were the largest and most obviously traveled, providing they kept going in the general direction he wanted. He found himself sweating beneath his hood and impatiently pushed it back. At the moment he almost wished himself to be a *sorcerel,* with special powers to guide him. Instead, he had nothing save instinct and hope. And the farther they went, the more impossible it became to hold back his doubts.

The first torch expired, and Sir Pem lit the second in silence. He'd brought only four torches altogether, and with a qualm Talmor eyed the remaining two brands thrust through his belt.

Time passed while they walked steadily, pausing only for Bujean to make his marks. Talmor felt like an ant, closed in on all sides by dirt, and could not stop imagining the immense weight of the buildings pressing down from above. They did not speak, and he listened for any whisper of sound, however faint or distant, while his nerves stretched tighter.

The second torch began to sputter and die.

"We turn back," Sir Pem said. "We've two torches left. We can't get out of here without them."

Talmor had known that argument was coming. He quietly rested his hand on his sword hilt and faced the two knights. "I will not quit now."

"In Thod's name, m'lord, have sense! You've done all a man can do. More! But it's time to—"

"I will not quit!" Talmor shouted. "We must keep going as long as we can."

"We *have*, m'lord. Once the torches go out, and we're trapped here in the dark, what then?" Sir Pem asked.

"That's a coward's question."

The knight stiffened and would have charged Talmor except for Bujean's restraining hand.

"We're wasting time, and precious light," Talmor said. "Come."

"M'lord, if you knew for sure where to find her, I'd follow you. But we've no trail, no certainty!"

Talmor glared at him, knowing Sir Pem made sense, yet unable to surrender the quest. He could never live with himself if he stopped now, not while Pheresa needed him. A wave of exhaustion swept over him, and he braced his back against the soft, damp wall.

"Give me a torch, and I'll go on," he said quietly, trying to suppress a cough. "You and Sir Bujean can turn back."

"We're all leaving," Sir Pem told him.

Talmor shook his head, and, when Sir Pem stepped toward him, drew his sword halfway in warning. "You'll not force me back," he said.

"Pem, leave him," Sir Bujean murmured. "He's mad."

"Aye, I believe it. But if we return without him, what do I report to the commander? We've orders to keep him safe. And he's—"

A faint sound came to Talmor's ears. He held up his hand. "Quiet!"

At once the knights grew still and silent. Talmor strained to listen. "Hear that?" he whispered.

"Aye," Sir Pem replied. "Men, ahead of us." He drew his sword with his free hand, handed his guttering torch to Sir Bujean, and lit the third one. "Coming our way, you think?"

Talmor frowned, listened harder, and finally shook his head. He drew his weapon and crept forward, but Sir Pem shouldered ahead of him as before, while Sir Bujean closed tight on Talmor's heels.

In silence they went forward, following fast to overtake the men they heard. Then Sir Pem stopped abruptly, and Talmor saw why. They had emerged into a tiny chamber, hardly large enough to hold a handful of men. Three tunnels led from it, including the one they'd entered by. Bujean carefully made his mark, while Talmor and Sir Pem listened.

Talmor could hear the marching of booted feet. Although at first the sound had seemed ahead of him, now the men appeared to have doubled back, for they were approaching.

He signaled a warning, but before they could retreat, a tall knight in a white surcoat with interlocking black circles ducked into sight, shot them a look of astonishment, and halted. He was wearing chain mail from head to foot, and his naked sword swept up in hostility.

"You there!" he said with a voice of authority that boomed and echoed in that cramped space. "Name yourselves, and your business here."

Before Talmor could answer, more church knights appeared behind the first. The leader gestured for them to remain in the tunnel, leaving him to confront Talmor's party alone.

Talmor saw that he, Pem, and Bujean were completely outnumbered by at least a squadron. Even worse, they had met up with the very men they most needed to avoid, if Lord Salba's orders were to be followed. It was too late, Talmor realized, to pull up his hood. He saw by the interested flare in the stranger's dark blue eyes that he'd already been recognized.

"What do you here?" the church knight demanded.

"I ask the same question of you," Talmor countered.

"We are searching for the heretics who murdered his eminence, Cardinal Atol, and did grievous harm to his colleagues."

"Your name," Talmor demanded.

"I am the Reverend Sir Perrell of the Order of Saint Mont," the man said proudly.

Behind Talmor, Sir Pem uttered a faint oath. Talmor felt his own spirits sinking. The Mont Legion served as an honor guard for the highest church officials. Its members were fighters as elite and superbly trained as the men in the palace guard. Only now did Talmor notice the insignia of an eagle clutching a circle in its talons embroidered on the left shoulder of each church knight's surcoat. Such men as these, he thought in discouragement, would not be easily fooled.

Sir Perrell sheathed his sword. He was taller than Talmor and almost as broad of shoulder, but while Talmor's build was muscular and compact, this man was rangy and loose-limbed. His lean, sunburned face sported squint lines around the eyes. His nose was beaky and he had a jaw like a rock. Beneath luxuriant auburn hair, his dark blue eyes stared at Talmor with direct assessment.

"And you," he continued in a voice both educated and intelligent, "are Sir Talmor, protector of the queen. You are wandering far from her majesty's side today, sir."

"This is Lord Talmor, Baron of Edriel," Sir Pem announced gruffly. "Queen's protector no longer."

"A promotion," Sir Perrell said, and gave Talmor a tiny salute. "Congratulations. I had not heard the news, but then I have not been at Savroix-en-Charva long."

"Posted from where?" Talmor asked, feeling as though he were dreaming. It was hardly the time or place for social chatter, yet the longer he deflected Sir Perrell from asking questions—or arresting him—the better. "The Klad front?"

Sir Perrell's eyes widened with respect. "You are well-informed, my lord."

Talmor shrugged. "A guess. Your sword is Klad-made."

"So it is. A gift from a respected enemy," Sir Perrell said, and almost smiled. "But now I ask again. What is your business here, my lord?"

"Queen's business."

"Is her majesty sending one heretic to hunt others?"

Talmor bristled, but Sir Pem spoke first: "We have our orders, same as you."

Sir Perrell frowned at them. "The attack occurred in the cathedral," he said. "The catacombs are considered an annex to the same. This is our jurisdiction. There is no need for her majesty's guards to be meddling here."

"Well, maybe the queen sees things differently," Sir Pem defiantly.

"If so, would she not have sent more than three men?"

"Uh—"

"We are enough," Talmor said.

Sir Perrell's gaze looked him over as though unconvinced. "And is it not strange," he continued, "how the palace guards were able to rescue the queen and get her out of the cathedral with such haste that no one witnessed the rescue?"

"We can't help it if you church soldiers are blind as well as slow," Sir Pem lied forthrightly. "Now we've little time to get on, and much to do. If you'll let us pass?"

But Sir Perrell only stared at them thoughtfully. "Not just yet. I would appreciate the truth now, for knights should not lie to each other."

Sir Pem made a faint, strangled noise in his throat, while Sir Bujean just stood there mute and looking guilty.

Talmor saw the church knights exchanging smirks behind their leader. He stepped forward. "Very well. 'Tis a thin tale, is it not?"

"So thin a child could see through it," Sir Perrell agreed.

"We have no authority to be here," Talmor admitted, ignoring Sir Pem's angry hiss. "'Twas my idea, and these men are with me for my protection, little more." He felt a cough coming on and paused to suppress it. "No one," he said hoarsely, "attacks her majesty and gets away with it."

As he spoke, he let his anger and worry color his voice, and saw Sir Perrell's brows knit together. "I have no royal permission to be here," Talmor went on, "but I intend to hunt down the Sebeins until I find—those responsible for—frightening her majesty, for daring to—"

Coughing, he broke off, and pressed the back of his hand to his mouth to hide the blood.

"I see," Sir Perrell said, and his tone held sympathy. "You know what holy Writ says about taking vengeance?"

Talmor nodded.

"No longer her majesty's protector, but still protecting," Sir Perrell said, and nodded. "Are you a heretic?"

"No."

"Take him, and you have to get through us," Sir Pem said fiercely.

Sir Perrell lifted one brow. "I am hunting Sebeins," he said coldly, and shifted his gaze back to Talmor. "You're nearly out of torches."

"Aye."

"We have a map of the catacombs and know our way about, but if you find yourself lost down here without light, it will prove to be an unpleasant way to starve."

"I was just urging Lord Talmor to turn back for that same reason," Sir Pem said.

Talmor could have struck him. Just when all was going well, why couldn't he be quiet?

"That might be best." Sir Perrell gestured to one of his men, who handed over some spare torches. Bujean took them with grudging thanks, while Sir Perrell smiled.

"Vengeance is best left in the hands of those authorized by Tomias," he said, saluting Talmor. "Leave the job to us."

Talmor returned his salute, liking the man's sense of fairness. Of course Talmor had no intention of leaving. Before he could argue, however, he heard faint shouts in the distance, along with a woman's scream.

Recognizing Pheresa's voice, Talmor stiffened. The top of his head went cold, while his vitals burned hot.

Drawing his sword, he plunged into the tunnel heading in her direction, only dimly aware of Sir Pem and Sir Bujean running after him, while the whole contingent of church knights pounded in their wake.

Thod help me, but I am leading them straight to her, Talmor thought in despair, but there was no way to get rid of Sir Perrell and his men now.

She needed him, and he was going to her rescue, the consequences be damned.

Chapter Eleven

Talmor ran so fast that Sir Pem and his torch could barely keep up. Sir Pem kept trying to get in front, but Talmor could see ahead to the end of the passageway, where there was illumination of some kind, and he would not slow down to let the guardsman go first. He was through waiting. He had found Pheresa, and she was in peril. The last time she'd called out for him was in the church, and he'd failed her. This time, he intended for nothing to stop him.

Icy-hot needles jabbed his lungs, and it was as though he ran full tilt into an invisible wall. He went down awkwardly, his sword banging against the side of the tunnel. Lying stunned and winded on the ground, at first he wasn't sure what had happened. His head weighed as much as a catapult stone, and he could feel every breath sawing through his throat. He thought confusedly that he'd been spell hit, but he sensed no magic around him.

"Let us by!" ordered a voice.

Sir Pem rolled Talmor onto his side and hoisted him upright, propping him against the wall while the church knights thundered past with drawn weapons. Then they were gone, as though a whirlwind had buffeted the narrow space.

Talmor blinked at the dancing spots in front of his eyes and focused on Sir Pem's weathered face peering grimly into his. "What—"

He doubled over in a violent coughing fit, the worst yet, and for a moment feared he would never regain his breath. Furious at his weakness, overwhelmed with worry and disappointment, he found himself sinking to the ground on legs that would no longer hold him.

"No!" he whispered in frustration. "Damn this—"

Another paroxysm of coughing wracked him until he thought his chest would cave in.

While Sir Pem held his shoulders, supporting him, Sir Bujean shifted the burning torch nervously about so that shadows bounced at them from all directions. They made Talmor dizzy.

"Merciful Tomias, Pem," Sir Bujean said in a low voice, "is he dying on us?"

"Could be, the young fool," Sir Pem replied gruffly, his hands gentle as he wiped blood and sweat from Talmor's face. "There, that's over, m'lord. You lie there quiet and catch your breath."

Talmor managed to grab Sir Pem's wrist. "Help me up."

"Better rest."

But Talmor heard the clashing noise of battle joined, and he believed the church knights had found Pheresa's captors. He forced himself to sit up, blinking to focus his wavery vision. "Be all right . . . if I don't . . . run," he whispered, and every word burned his raw throat.

Sir Pem drew a deep breath. "Lord Talmor," he said, speaking slowly and carefully, "you are very ill. No, m'lord, listen to me. We've followed you patiently all afternoon, but if you don't stop now, 'twill be the death of you. Sit quietly and rest while we figure a way to carry you out of here."

Anger boiled up so intensely in Talmor that he felt tiny flames dancing in his palm. Uncurling his fingers, he revealed the fire flickering on his skin. Sir Pem drew back from him with a gasp, and Sir Bujean swore as he swiftly drew a Circle. The fear and horror in their faces ordinarily would have shamed Talmor, but at the moment he cared not what they saw.

"Thod smite you!" he said hoarsely. "You're sworn to the queen's benefit, not mine. Go to her aid now, or I'll burn your very bones. Go!"

White-faced, Sir Pem glared at him but turned and ran in the direction the church knights had gone. Sir Bujean fled in his wake.

The fire was flaming in Talmor's hand, growing intensely hot. Frustration and rage and despair built inside him until he could no longer hold them, then he cried out and threw blazing flames down the tunnel toward the river. An explosion rocked the passage, sending dirt pattering down atop him from the ceiling.

Knocked over, he lay there a moment with his ears ringing from the noise. When he righted himself, he smelled scorched dirt and saw little flickers of fire dancing on the ground. After a short time they went out, and darkness closed around him. The air cooled down. Talmor sat with his back propped against the wall, feeling its dampness soak slowly through his tunic, and listened to the oaths, screams, and sword clashes in the distance. Like an old warhorse running across pasture when it heard battle trumpets, he yearned to be in the thick of the fray. He should be there, he told himself fretfully. He could not just bide at his ease while she needed him.

And so he pushed away from the wall's support. Even doing that felt as though someone had plunged a sword through his chest. Resting a moment, he pressed his hand to his breastbone while he struggled not to cough.

When the pain diminished, he called forth Sanude's teachings from his youth. He'd learned, through much effort and many difficult lessons, how to control the fire most of the time. He threw that same control over the pain in a net and bundled it into one throbbing point of agony that made him shudder. Then he mastered that, holding the pain at a distance. He knew he would pay for this later, once the pain was released, but at the moment it did not matter.

Finally, he was able to lift his sword from the dirt and gain his feet. The effort left him drenched in sweat, but he managed not to collapse. Slowly, leaning against the wall, Talmor took a few cautious steps. He had no illumination save the distant torchlight coming from the end of the passageway, but it was enough for him to grope his way forward. As he walked, he slowly straightened and pulled his shoulders erect. *I can do this,* he told himself. *I will not fall again.*

Although he longed to hurry, he dared not. Every breath was a small victory. Every step another. There was a time, when he was younger and stronger, when he could have banished the pain entirely from his awareness and moved as though uninjured, but no longer, not since he'd lost his arm. Surviving the Nonkind venom had altered him, robbed him of a portion of that special vitality he'd been born with, a vitality that kept him strong and fast and helped him to heal quickly from injury. But it had not destroyed him, he thought grimly, nor would the Sebein mist.

Ahead, the sounds of battle had ended. He wondered if Sir Perrell and his men were the victors and if so, had they gained the queen's rescue. It was bitter indeed, knowing he had already missed whatever action had taken place. But he vowed he would get there, for no one was leaving him behind, not as long as Pheresa needed him.

Voices in the darkness . . . Pheresa came swimming back to awareness. Someone was touching her face and speaking with an urgency that disturbed her, when all she wanted was to remain safely hidden in the dark. Vaguely she felt hands shift her on the cold ground, then there was a painful constriction around her arm, far too tight, before she was lifted into the air and carried.

So many voices . . . far too much noise. Irritated, she tried to turn her head away, and found her cheek mashed against cloth, chain mail, and stalwart muscles. She opened her eyes, squinting against torchlight too bright and colors all blending crazily together, and realized she was being cradled by a powerful set of arms.

"Talmor!" she murmured in glad relief, and snuggled closer to his chest.

"Did she speak?"

"Yes. She's coming to."

The second voice that spoke made Talmor's chest rumble beneath her cheek, but it was not Talmor's voice she heard. Frowning, she blinked and focused, and found herself gazing not into Talmor's golden eyes but instead a pair of indigo-blue ones set in an unfamiliar face and attractive enough in a hawkish, sunburned way. The man regarded her somberly, a faint crease between his brows, before his firm mouth curved into a slight smile.

She wanted to smile back, but he was no one she recognized, and he wore the white-and-black surcoat of a church soldier. It was hard to think, for her wits were still muddled, and her arm ached from whatever was binding it so tightly. Tensely, she looked away from him and saw that she was back in the chamber of death. There were the iron pots where fires still burned. There were the shelves of moldering skeletons. There was the table where she'd lain, trussed like a sacrificial offering. But Bokune's body no longer lay sprawled on the ground, and she wondered if he'd survived his wounds or if his people had dragged his body away.

Instead of being surrounded by black-robed Sebeins, she found herself in the midst of a squadron of church soldiers—large, burly warriors clutching bloodied swords in their fists, their eyes blazing with righteousness and battle lust as they stood over the prisoners they'd taken.

She took no comfort from the sight of these knights, for fear of having exchanged one set of captors for another.

"Be at ease, your majesty," the blue-eyed man said to her. His voice was calm and steady, intended to soothe. "You are safe now. No further harm will come to you."

She frowned at him, her fingers unconsciously tugging at the tourniquet on her arm, and shook her head mutely.

Unasked, he set her down on the table, releasing his hold

on her cautiously as though he thought she might topple over. When he loosened the tourniquet, pain shot up her arm, and she caught her breath sharply.

"We must get your majesty care, and swiftly," he murmured. "This remedy works only for a time, and I know it is painful. Forgive me, but it's necessary."

She did not know what to say to him. Her mind was racing through conjectures and questions. Why had the church soldiers come to her aid instead of her guards? Was she a prisoner or not? Where was Talmor, and what must they have done to him to keep him away?

"Does your majesty feel faint?"

She forced herself to meet those dark blue eyes. Gavril's eyes had been of a similar color, she remembered, but whereas the prince had been a vain, arrogant, self-centered bully, this man looked intelligent, capable, and honest. She could not help but warm to him.

This time she did smile, wanly, as she held out her right hand. "'Tis thanks I owe you and your men," she said now. "You have freed me from the Sebeins and their evil, and I am grateful."

"Your majesty." He knelt before her and kissed her ring of state. "'Tis my honor to serve. Men!"

With a clash of arms against armor, they knelt and saluted her, then stood once more. They did not cheer her name, as her guards would have done, but they were showing her the proper respect. Pheresa relaxed a fraction and shifted her gaze back to their leader. By now she'd noticed that the men were all Montites. Products of wealthy, highborn families, the men belonging to the Order of Saint Mont generally guarded cardinals and bishops. Not for them austere barracks, sentry duty, and hard campaigns. They lived in well-appointed quarters, with servants, skilled cooks, and excellent wine cellars among their privileges. They were not even required to be celibate, unlike some of the more extreme orders, and many of them married and kept families.

"Your name, sir?" she whispered.

"I am the Reverend Sir Perrell de Gide, your majesty."

She could not stop a small intake of breath. The Gides were illustrious indeed. The duc controlled the largest duchy in her realm, and must be Sir Perrell's grandfather. Cardinal Ardminsil was an uncle. Sir Perrell's elder brother, Count Reamon, had served the royal court for a time as Minister of Trade, unless Lervan had ended that appointment. Two of Sir Perrell's sisters—acclaimed beauties who were dazzling the court when Pheresa had been a shy maiden first trying to win Gavril's attention—had married well. Although the Gides were a powerful, ambitious family, to her knowledge they had no treasonous leanings. Relaxing slightly, she looked on Sir Perrell with more favor.

"Your majesty," he said, "I am astonished to find you here. We thought . . . that is, we were told your majesty was safe. Had we known you were in such danger, we would have come to your aid sooner."

She said nothing.

He gestured at the sullen group of prisoners huddled on the ground. Several of them were women, she noticed, and neither Bokune nor Kanth was with them. "We came here searching for Sebein heretics," Sir Perrell said. "These wretches will go to the stake for daring to defile the holy sanctum with magic. They are traitors and murderers, every one."

She drew in a grief-stricken breath. "Were all who assembled in the church today slain?"

He looked shocked. "How came your majesty by such an idea?"

"They said—"

"No indeed! If you were told this lie, 'twas a monstrous cruelty. No, your majesty. Only a few perished, including Cardinal Atol and some of the men who rushed to your majesty's aid."

"But the mist . . . the Sebeins said it was deadly."

"For some, yes. For others, less so."

"But so many people in the—"

"The mist did not spread through the entire sanctum. Only the area directly surrounding your majesty."

She thought about the lies she'd been told, and her heart

hardened against the Sebeins for their cruelty. "Then casualties were few?"

"That's my belief, your majesty. I was not on duty at the time."

"Thod be thanked," she whispered.

Sir Perrell tilted his head to one side, still regarding her with frank amazement. "Yes. We never—" He abruptly cleared his throat. "That is, we didn't expect . . . we weren't in pursuit of . . . we'd been informed that your majesty was safely back at Savroix."

So he'd already said. She understood now. What confusion must have reigned in the wake of her abduction. She supposed her lord chancellor had issued reassurances in an effort to protect the throne. Yet she had to wonder what would happen to her next. She was in the clutches of the clergy now, no matter how kind and civilized this officer seemed to be. No one loyal to her cause apparently knew where she was. And if these men, obeying the chain of authority, took her to their superiors, could she not easily be made to disappear forever? The blame could be assigned to the Sebeins, and who would ever discover the truth?

Feeling icy cold, she shivered.

"You are ill," Sir Perrell said in renewed concern. He tightened the tourniquet so hard she gasped. "We should delay no longer in getting you out of here. Cortaine! Finish securing those prisoners and let us—"

"They are not all captured," she said uneasily, seeking anything to distract him. "How many escaped?"

Sir Perrell frowned. "We slew some, your majesty."

"But not all?"

"Some escaped us."

"Aye," spoke up his second-in-command, a bullnecked man with hair the color of rust and a nose flattened from too many past breakages. "Ran like rats, the lily-livered—"

"Cortaine," Sir Perrell said in rebuke, and the man fell silent.

"You must get them all," Pheresa insisted. "A tall man,

blind in one eye, scarred across the face, and another, younger and—"

"My men will track them," Sir Perrell said. "Now if I may carry your majesty, we'll—"

She drew back. "But Bokune and Kanth are dangerous. I thought I'd killed Bokune, but he—he may not be mortal. They could be lurking close by, ready to unleash terrible magic against us in retaliation."

The smiles appearing on some of their faces annoyed her. She was not babbling fantasies. She wanted them to take her seriously.

"We are equipped to withstand dark magic," Sir Perrell assured her.

"Possess you powers of your own?"

"No," he said rather curtly. "Your majesty is unwell or would surely otherwise not insult her most loyal servants with such assumptions."

Meeting his stern gaze, she did not apologize, for who was he to dare rebuke her? The measures used by the church to counter magic had long been kept secret. She saw that Sir Perrell was not going to share any such information, not even to reassure her. Thinking the church's stance on this matter foolish, for people knew magic existed no matter how often it was officially denied, Pheresa believed that the dispensation of knowledge in combating it would be useful to all. But she was not going to waste her breath now in arguing the matter.

When the silence stretched out, Sir Perrell stepped closer. "Have I your majesty's permission to carry you?"

"No."

She scooted off the table onto her feet, and the chamber of death dipped and spun around her. Sir Perrell reached instinctively to steady her, but she held up her hand imperiously to ward him off and braced herself against the table.

"Your majesty is weak from loss of blood," he said. "I fear you will swoon if you try to walk."

She did not care. Sir Perrell and his men might have saved her from the Sebeins, but that gave him no special privileges. He'd taken sufficient liberties already while she was unconscious. The queen was no ordinary damsel to be handled by just anyone. Only Talmor would she let carry her. Only Talmor . . . and then she remembered that her dear one would never be able to swing her up in his arms again.

"I shall walk," she said stubbornly.

"It's a long way back to the church offices, and your majesty lacks the strength."

"I shall return to my palace."

"That's even farther—"

"How dare you argue against my wishes?" she said coldly. "You—"

At that moment there was a slight commotion. Swearing, Sir Cortaine drew his sword, and Sir Perrell reached for his weapon, while Pheresa spun around in the certainty that Kanth was attacking. The sudden movement made her dizzy, and she gripped the table in an effort to steady herself, refusing to shut her eyes and praying the chamber would stop tilting soon.

The trouble instead proved to be two men in the green cloaks of her palace guard. Bursting in, wild-eyed and brandishing their weapons, breathless from running, they stumbled to a halt and swore fearsome curses at the church knights.

"Where is she?" one demanded. "What have you done with the lady?"

The church knights rushed them, but Sir Perrell yelled a swift order that stopped battle before it could be joined.

"Let them through," Pheresa said.

Sir Perrell looked as though he wanted to refuse, but he gestured for Cortaine to obey her order.

"Come on then, damne!" the older of the two guardsmen was yelling in bravado. "Answer me if you dare! Where—"

As the knights parted, he caught sight of Pheresa, and fell silent. She saw him start to kneel, but he checked himself and gripped his companion to keep him upright as well.

Pheresa had been feeling glad relief at the sight of her guardsmen, but their reaction bewildered her. She supposed she must look horrifying to their eyes, for stripped of her jew-

els, her hair unbound and tangled, and her gown torn and
soaked with blood, she possessed little majesty. Still, she was
their queen, and even these church knights had shown her
greater respect. Worried that the guards had turned against her
in another coup, she began to imagine all sorts of dire events.

"Your—uh—your ladyship," the older guard said gruffly,
his gaze shifting from her to the church knights and back
again. He was a veteran whose face she recognized, although
at the moment she could not recall his name. He seemed extremely distraught, almost frantic. He'd come running into the
chamber not as though in pursuit of trouble, but as though
fleeing from it. He glanced nervously over his shoulder now
and seemed to have to force himself to concentrate on her.

"Sir Pem reporting, if it please you," he said. "The—uh—
her majesty has been terrible worried about you. Are you
well?"

Pheresa frowned. Either his wits had been addled, or he
was trying to preserve her incognito. "Yes, thank you," she
said. "I am quite well."

"Her majesty is wounded," Sir Perrell said, his blue eyes
alert. "And needs treatment immediately. We will be escorting
her to our infirmary for a physician's care."

"No need for that now," Pheresa said swiftly. "These
guards will escort me. You, Sir Perrell, are relieved of further
concern for my well-being."

Sir Perrell simply shook his head. "Your majesty, you may
be expecting a full contingent of guards behind this pair, but
such is not the case. We came across these men a short time
ago, and they could not truthfully answer what they were
doing here on their own."

Sir Pem bristled. "We told you—"

"You told me lies," Sir Perrell said angrily. "Even Lord
Talmor lied. And he—"

"Talmor!" Pheresa said eagerly. "He's here?"

"Aye, your majesty," Sir Pem said.

"Then where is he?"

The two guardsmen exchanged uneasy looks that puzzled
her.

"Your majesty, believe nothing these men say," Sir Perrell said. "They could be traitors, even ruffian deserters. They are entirely unsuitable for your majesty's escort."

Sir Pem stiffened in affront. "You self-righteous blackguard, I'm no traitor and never will be!"

"Nay," the other man spoke up, "and no deserters neither!"

"Whatever you're up to, you're not on duty," Sir Perrell informed him, and Sir Pem turned red, shutting his mouth with a snap.

"As I said, your majesty," Sir Perrell went on, "an unsuitable escort."

Not for anything did Pheresa intend to let him slander her palace guard. Sir Perrell might actually believe what he was saying, or might just be taking an opportunity to insult them, but from the bottled rage in the two guardsmen's eyes, she knew he was wrong.

"Even were there only one guardsman present, 'twould be sufficient and suitable," she said proudly. "But where is Talmor? Why did you leave him behind? Why does he not come to me here?"

Although her men seemed to take heart from her endorsement, her questions rendered both of them pale. They shuffled their feet, shifty-eyed and nervous. With growing alarm, she wondered if Sir Perrell was right about their being traitors. Had they done something to Talmor?

Sir Pem cast Sir Perrell a dour look. "See here, Montite," he said tersely, "I won't have my honor—"

"What honor?" Sir Perrell broke in. "You knew the queen was missing, and you concealed it. Why not tell us the truth about her majesty's capture in the first place? Church knights and guardsmen could have joined forces and found her before she was tortured at the hands of these heretics. Even if you lied to me, in typical guardsman fashion, I expected better of Lord Talmor."

Sir Pem looked as though he did not know what to say. Pheresa longed to remind Sir Perrell about devious church politics and exactly why she and her men did not trust the warriors of Tomias, but she was concerned about Talmor's absence. Where was he? Why would the men not answer her questions about him? Why did they have to wage this stupid argument? The way their tempers were flaring, they'd draw swords on each other next.

Sir Perrell was raking the guardsmen with a cold blue stare. "Claiming to be searching for Sebeins—"

"And so we were," Sir Pem said hotly. "As for you, you got no right to withhold her majesty from us."

"I am the ranking officer present. Her majesty will go to the church infirmary under our escort."

Sir Pem settled himself into a fighter's stance. "Well, best we get that straightened out—"

"Stop!" Pheresa cried.

Both men turned to look at her.

"Your majesty," Sir Perrell began. "My concern is entirely for your welfare. We—"

She held up her hand to silence him. "I decide. I—"

She broke off what she was about to say because she was feeling more and more peculiar, as though her head might begin to float away from her body. Her wrist was throbbing, and she longed to sit down. At that moment she would have given half her treasury just to be safe in her chamber and cosseted by her ladies-in-waiting.

"I want to go to Savroix," she said fretfully. "I don't want the church infirmary."

"Right." Squaring his shoulders, Sir Pem came forward. "That's orders enough for me."

But at that moment Pheresa sagged, and only Sir Perrell's quick arm around her kept her on her feet. He lifted her onto the table.

She resisted lying down, however, and sat there stubbornly, feeling increasingly tired and wretched.

"Your majesty, let me judge what is best for you," he said softly. "You need attention without further delay. We have the finest physicians, capable of dealing with your wound, while the Rullien priests can negate any lingering effects of the spell cast in the cathedral. Three of the cardinals are already fully recovered, praise Tomias, and you will—"

"No! I want to go to Savroix!"

"Your majesty—"

"The lady refuses your offer, Sir Perrell," said a voice dear to her, strangely hoarse and thin, but a voice she'd been longing to hear.

Her heart swelled with glad relief. Looking up, she saw Talmor striding into the chamber. Tall and broad-shouldered, his bronzed skin and black hair distinctive among the paler Mandrians, he threaded his way through the church knights, who parted for him reluctantly. Garbed in a cloak whose heavy folds concealed his missing arm, for that moment he looked as whole and as formidable as ever.

The sight of him filled her eyes, and she did not heed how ashen and strained his face was. She did not heed that his clothing was splattered with bloodstains and as filthy as her own. His dark curls hung tangled across his brow, and his golden eyes blazed so ferociously that all of her fears dropped away. He had come for her as he always did, and it did not matter that presently he faced a dozen potential foes. She knew that he could prevail.

"Talmor," she breathed out.

His eyes met hers across that grisly chamber, and for the space of a few heartbeats she lost consciousness of anyone save him. Then his gaze shifted to Sir Perrell's.

"We are responsible for the queen," he said, his voice a painful rasp. "Thank you for rescuing her from these pagan dogs."

Sir Perrell was frowning. "You should not have lied to me, my lord."

Talmor did not reply.

"After my courtesy to you, this pretense was unworthy of—"

"A discussion for another time," Talmor broke in. He came over to Pheresa, while Sir Pem and the other guardsman sidled nervously away. His gaze quickly took in her appearance, especially her bloody dress, the bandage on her wrist, and the tourniquet holding her life inside her. A tiny muscle leaped in his jaw.

"It's not too bad," she reassured him to take away the bleak stoniness from his eyes. "They hadn't time to do their intended evil."

He bowed to her, a slight, rather stiff gesture of formality that seemed to leach even more color from his face. "May we escort your majesty to the palace?"

"It would be better if she's taken to our infirmary," Sir Perrell insisted. "None of you seem to understand that she needs attention speedily, and the palace is nearly a league away. I imagine it's in disorder because of today's abrupt change of regime. Let our physicians see to her comfort, for she is weak and in difficulty."

Talmor frowned.

"Come, man," Sir Perrell said irritably. "Show reason. The queen needs care."

Pheresa reached out and gripped Talmor's cloak. "Savroix," she said softly, her eyes full of appeal.

His nod made her sigh in relief. Her head really was floating, and she was grateful that she no longer had to be brave and strong. She had only to rely on Talmor.

"Sir Bujean," he said, sounding far away, "will you assist the queen?"

The thickset, younger guardsman gathered her up tenderly as though she might break and bore her out of there with Sir Pem striding close by. She heard Sir Perrell's voice lifted angrily, and Talmor's reply, but she no longer paid attention. By the time they crossed the chamber, Talmor had caught up with them.

Acting wary and ill at ease, as though they still expected trouble, the guardsmen shot Talmor looks she did not understand. He pointed at one of the tunnels in silence, and after Sir Pem lit a torch, Pheresa was carried through that cool, shadowy passage.

She tried to stay awake, but it was growing harder. When she shivered, they wrapped a cloak around her, but it gave her no warmth. The tourniquet was loosened, while someone swore softly and impatiently, then tightened again, which made her cry.

"Talmor," she murmured.

"I'm here."

Reassured, she let her eyes shut and slept until she heard the buzz of insects, felt the softness of night on her face, and smelled the river. She heard thumps and the rhythmic splash of oars. The men were arguing over something, their voices muted but sharp.

It seemed very odd that they were in a boat, but when she tried to rouse herself she felt Talmor's hand gently stroking her hair back from her brow.

"It's all right," he whispered, and she believed him.

"I'll hold her, m'lord, if you're growing tired," Sir Pem said, his voice hostile and grudging. "In fact, it might be better for all concerned."

She reached out, only half-awake, and found Talmor's hand. His warm fingers curled around her cold ones.

"M'lord?"

"I'll hold her," Talmor said, his voice ragged. "Just hurry."

Pheresa wanted to warn him of Kanth's curse, only that would make him more worried than he was already. She wanted to tell him this was not how she'd planned her coronation night to be. This was to have been their night, their special time for each other, and she could not help but feel disappointment.

Still, she knew there would be other nights and other opportunities to say all that filled her heart. Just now, she was content to remain nestled against his chest, her hand in his, safe from the world and her enemies while he held her. Nothing, she vowed, could ever part them.

Chapter Twelve

Deep underground, in the private, rather ancient chapel usually reserved for the all-night vigils of men before their investiture into knighthood, the Reverend Sir Perrell knelt, stripped to the waist, on the stone floor. A Rullien in a yellow robe, shaven head gleaming in the torchlight, held a scourge upraised, ready to bring it down once more across Perrell's back. Blood dripped from the weighted ends of the ropes, and hot rivulets of blood ran down Perrell's back.

Pressing his hands together, he bowed his head and repeated his prayer of endurance, tensing his muscles against the coming blow.

It cracked against his flesh, making him jerk and grit his teeth to hold back a cry of pain. Sweating, panting, he rode the agony, seeking it to cast him higher toward the perfection of Tomias. But too soon, it faded down to a throbbing ache. He dragged in a breath, frustrated at being unable to attain his goal. At that moment, when he most needed the solace of spiritual union with Tomias, he could not concentrate. Instead, he kept recalling long, unbound tresses of glorious hair, a face of physical perfection, a voice low and musical that fell sweetly on the ear.

Although he'd heard much about the queen's legendary beauty, nothing had prepared him for the impact of actually meeting her. She was the most feminine lady he'd ever met, and until then he'd always given his mother that honor. Gracious, even while seriously injured and frightened, Queen Pheresa had exhibited extraordinary courage and resilience, forever winning Perrell's admiration.

She was, in fact, a queen. A special woman, unforgettable in every way. That he'd met her, been able to do her a service, even held her briefly in his arms had completely unsettled him. And although he'd already planned tonight's penance, his encounter with the queen had rendered his devotions useless. He could not govern himself.

"Again?" the Rullien asked softly.

Perrell nodded.

"No, Sir Perrell! Enough, surely this is enough," Brother Span said nervously. Hovering at the foot of the stone stairs that spiraled far above them, the little monk hitched up his robes with a worried look. "I beg you to stop. You won't be fit for duty in the morning."

Perrell ignored him. "Again," he ordered the Rullien. "I have not yet found union."

In silence, the yellow-robed priest moved up behind him, swinging the scourge back and forth so that the weights whistled faintly through the air. Making an effort to clear his mind completely this time, Perrell folded his hands together and braced himself.

"Halt!" cried out a voice from the stairs above. It echoed down through the stone chamber, and at once the Rullien threw the bloodied scourge on the ground.

Wide-eyed, Brother Span darted over to stand beside Perrell. A small, thin man with an ill-shaved tonsure, he fidgeted as though he wanted to bolt, his gaze shifting from Perrell to the men descending the spiraling stairs.

"I told you this was the wrong location," he said wretchedly, wringing his soft, fine-boned hands. "Merciful Tomias, how will I explain my part in unlocking this chapel for such a use?"

Ignoring his moaning, Perrell stood up. His squire came
forth from the shadows to sponge blood deftly from his back
and hand him a tunic. Perrell put it on, wincing slightly from
the effort, and faced the men approaching him.

The one in front he recognized as Father Fisiere, assistant
to Cardinal Theloi. Rather plump within his white robes,
Fisiere was middle-aged, with the face of a dissolute boy. His
jowls quivered slightly as he halted in front of Perrell. His
brown eyes were frowning with censure as he took in the
silent Rullien, the bloody scourge lying on the floor, Perrell's
tight face, and Brother Span's guilty fidgetings. Although
flagellation was not strictly forbidden, the practice was
presently out of favor with church authorities.

Perrell, who had ambitions of rising far higher than a mere
battle officer, would have preferred his private devotions to
remain unknown to his superiors, but now that he'd been discovered, he refused to apologize or explain. He met Father
Fisiere's gaze without evasion.

Fisiere was the first to glance away. "His eminence has
sent for you."

"My uncle?"

Fisiere's brows drew together, and he flashed Perrell a
look of evident displeasure for cleverly being reminded that
Perrell was related to Ardminsil. "No," he said quietly. "Cardinal Theloi wishes to see you. Come at once."

Without waiting for Perrell's response, he turned and
started back up the stairs with his small entourage trailing behind him. Perrell snapped his fingers at his squire, who
loosely fastened his belt around him. Without speaking, Perrell ascended the stairs in Fisiere's wake.

Halfway up, Father Fisiere glanced back. "There is no
need for your companions to await your return," he said
coldly.

Perrell nodded, and when they all reached the passage at
the top of the stairs, he dismissed his squire and Brother Span,
and slipped the Rullien his payment. Tucking the slim purse
into his sleeve, the yellow-robed priest vanished silently into
the shadows.

The walk to Cardinal Theloi's apartments was accomplished without a word. Although surprised by the summons, especially when Theloi was said to be so ill, Perrell asked none of the questions circling his mind. He knew how to hold the discipline of his rigorous training, which was to obey without question, to remain silent unless addressed directly, to serve and protect to the death. Besides, he had been expecting some acknowledgment of his part in saving the queen's life, just not this promptly.

Theloi lived in regal state befitting a prince of the church. Perrell was conducted through an antechamber, reception room, study, and at last into the lord cardinal's bedchamber. Dominated by a massive, heavily carved bed, the posts rising like pillars to support a thick canopy and silk hangings embroidered with Theloi's crest, the room was lit by a cluster of fat white candles near the bedside. Shadows obscured much of the remainder of the room. Perrell could only guess at the wealth of the many furnishings as he crossed thick rugs and knelt with his fist pressed to his heart.

"Sir Perrell, rise and approach me."

Perrell obeyed. The cardinal was lying propped high on a stack of pillows, robed in ecclesiastical yellow, a small silk cap on his head. His face looked pinched and white, but there was nothing feeble in his cold green eyes. They bored through Perrell while Father Fisiere and the others retreated from the room and shut the heavy doors quietly.

"You *fool!*" Theloi said.

Perrell's head snapped up in shock. Just in time he stopped himself from speaking.

Theloi leaned forward, stabbing the air with his thin forefinger. "You had her in your clutches, and you released her. Our one chance to regain power over the queen, and you let her go. I was assured that you possessed some scant measure of intelligence. What happened to it?"

The cardinal's tone was as biting as the scourge had been. Taken aback, Perrell could think of nothing to say except the truth. "It was my intention to bring her majesty to the church infirmary, but she desired to return to Savroix."

"Bah! She was ill, desperately so, hardly conscious."

"Her guards and protector—"

"Two fools, plus a crippled heretic who should be in church custody. And you, Montite, gave her up without a fight."

Warmth was creeping up Perrell's throat. He met the cardinal's glare steadily. "There was nothing to fight about," he said in a firm voice. "The queen made her decision, and I obeyed it."

"And did you not wonder what she was doing there in the catacombs, when the palace edict proclaimed her elsewhere?"

"Of course! But I—"

"And did you never think that these three men in the catacombs might be traitors themselves?"

"Yes, but she knew them and wished to go with them. I did recognize her protector."

"He is *not* her protector!" Theloi raged, then gulped and leaned back on his pillows. He shut his eyes and breathed heavily for a few moments while Perrell wondered if he should call for the cardinal's servants. Theloi opened his eyes. "Minion, familiar, mesmerizer . . . as yet I know not exactly what that creature is, but he has undoubtedly bewitched her."

Perrell thought of when Lord Talmor had strode into the queen's presence. She'd indeed stared at the man as though entranced. There had been a special light in her eyes, a softening of her features, a radiant glow to her skin that spoke of a woman in love. But was not love, Perrell thought to himself, a kind of enchantment?

"I fear that under his influence the queen will fall into apostasy," Theloi said.

Startled, Perrell frowned. "Surely not, your eminence. She was vehemently opposed to the Sebeins and urged me to hunt down all that escaped us."

"Sebeins are one thing," Theloi muttered tiredly, his thin hand clenching on the bedclothes. "Lord Talmor is another. You could have destroyed him and brought the queen secretly away. Did that not occur to you?"

"No, your eminence," Perrell said in a clear, cold voice. "The thought of treason did not occur to me."

"You owe service to the church before the queen!"

"I pay proper coin to each."

Theloi sent him a sharp look, but Perrell met it steadily. After a moment, Theloi's mouth curled in a vestige of a smile.

"You do not intimidate easily, Sir Perrell."

"No, your eminence."

"Nor have I flustered you."

"Not seriously."

Theloi barked out a brief laugh, then coughed and hastily swallowed something in a tall silver goblet. Whatever the substance was, it brightened his eyes noticeably and put two pink spots of color in his pale cheeks.

"You intrigue me, Sir Perrell," he said at last, and his voice was thin and so low Perrell could barely hear it. "I wonder if you would be useful, after all."

"I am here to serve."

"Are you? It seems to me that you think too much, instead of following your orders. It seems to me that perhaps your loyalties are divided."

The warmth was a little hotter around Perrell's throat, constricting it. He dared not speak.

"Has she muddled your mind, Sir Perrell? Has she captured your heart, inflamed your entrails, melted your common sense? Has she besotted you with her beautiful brown eyes?"

"No."

"Really? Is that why you ran to a Rullien for flagellation as soon as you went off duty?"

Startled, Perrell wondered how he knew. Did he keep spies in the very walls? Or had the Rullien told him?

"Answer my question, reverend commander!"

"No," Perrell said tersely. "It was not for that reason."

"I find it hard to believe you are impervious to the queen's charms, if you are a man at all."

"I didn't say I was impervious," Perrell tried to explain, well aware that Theloi was testing him. "Just not besotted.

The lady is extremely beautiful, but I am not in the habit of sighing and penning lines of poetry to faces fair."

"Your part in winning the campaign against the Kladites earned you a post here, but you can draw on that no longer," Theloi said harshly. "You begin here anew, from a fresh slate. And today, you did the church no service. You failed to catch the Sebein leaders. You found the queen alone and unprotected and let her go. We could have turned the tide of power forever in this realm, but it's too late now to rectify your mistake."

"Your eminence, I—"

"How dare you interrupt me!"

Perrell shut his mouth with a snap. Inside, he was afire with the indignity of being dressed down like a raw recruit. But he was also horrified at himself for breaching discipline. Normally he was adept at managing his temper.

"If you are appalled by how freely I speak regarding wresting power from the queen, then you are unworthy of the insignia you wear or your oath to the glory of Tomias," Theloi went on, his tone cutting. "She is a borderline heretic, and as such, extremely dangerous to the future of the church and the souls of her subjects. Something was done to her years ago in Nether, something kept a dark secret indeed. It changed her from a pleasant, comely maiden into a woman of clawing ambition, power-mad, and driven to question every precept of the Reform. She claims to have been cured by the Chalice of Eternal Life, but that is self-deluded arrogance. No such miracle could have possibly occurred, especially when it happened away from the aegis of the church."

Frowning, he swept his hands back and forth across the coverlet. "And no such miracle would have turned her into a scheming liar, an adulteress, and a coward who fled her palace when the barbarians invaded. Many men are so dazzled by her beauty that they cannot see her devious heart. This morning, when she slew Lervan before one and all, was she arrested for treason or murder? Here was a man on the very brink of being crowned Mandria's king, and she plunged a dagger into him without mercy. Yet the fools cheered her and crowned her for it. I could almost say they deserve her reign!"

Perrell swallowed, and even that slight movement made Theloi look at him sharply.

"Be very clear, Sir Perrell, as to what the lines of treason are. We have entered a time when nothing is as simple as it was once. Webs of lies are spun from the palace, and we must take care not to be caught in them. It would have been better for all of Mandria had the queen perished tonight."

Perrell stiffened, and for a moment his mind revolved blankly. Was the cardinal actually implying that he should have murdered the queen in the catacombs? Shocked, he stood frozen at attention.

"I am told by Ardminsil that you are an ambitious man," Theloi said, reclaiming his attention.

"Yes, your eminence."

"Until now, you've risen by virtue of a warrior's courage and a strong arm. It was my hope, from all accounts of you, that you had the wit and intelligence to survive court intrigue. It was my hope that you could seize chances when they were given to you. Thus far, you are off to a poor beginning."

Perrell clenched his jaw. "Lord eminence, had I taken her majesty prisoner, without orders, you might have found a way to benefit the realm, but I would have been thrown in the dungeons as a traitor for acting on my own initiative."

"And if you had such orders?"

Silence fell over the chamber. Perrell's heart was thudding. His tongue felt stuck to the roof of his mouth.

Sneering, Theloi gestured curtly. "Go away and think. When next I send for you, be prepared to give me an answer. Go!"

Saluting, Perrell wheeled about smartly and left the chamber. He encountered Father Fisiere lurking near the door as though he'd been eavesdropping, but Perrell hardly gave the man a glance. Woodenly, his spine stiff, he marched out and made his way back to his quarters.

His mind was reeling. He hardly knew where he was as he returned the salute of the barracks sentry, avoided his usual companions, and shut himself in his quarters with his servants dismissed. There, in the dark, he sat with fists clenched and muscles tight. To have murdered the queen tonight, in cold blood . . . morde, the thought of it made his heart race anew and his knees go weak.

Is treason a relative issue, he asked himself. *Does it depend only on the side a man chooses? If Theloi is right, and the queen is a secret heretic, then is the church not justified in opposing her?*

Oppose her, aye, he thought hastily. *But not . . . Have I come this far,* he asked himself, *in order to be made a murderous assassin?*

Perrell remembered his night's vigil before his investiture as a knight, and how excited and proud he'd been. Barely sixteen, he'd knelt on the hard stone floor, shivering as the winter night stretched on, believing himself to be a shining torch for Tomias. His spirit had been aflame with fervent piety. And on the following day, hollow with fatigue and hunger, he'd been knighted, pledging his service and making his choice of order. The whole world had seemed as bright as sunshine glittering on new snow, and he'd known such zeal and enthusiasm that he could have run from one end of the realm to the other, shouting aloud.

He thought of the windswept plains and barren prairies of Klad, with long days of patrol to guard the border from raids. The sun was grueling, and even the winds blew hot, drying a man's skin to tatters and parching his throat in constant thirst. He'd fought and killed, riding home at the end of battle splattered with blood and coated in dust, his muscles aching with the satisfaction of a hard day's work well-done. He'd fought in the name of Tomias, serving the realm, protecting traveling clergy, and guarding trade routes that funneled gold into church coffers. He'd known his service was honest and worthy.

Now he thought about long fair hair shining in the torchlight, an oval face, and the dark sweep of lashes. He thought of a lady lying half-conscious in his arms, a lady who for a brief moment had clung to him and pressed her face to his chest in trust.

She had been brave and gracious. Even in obvious pain,

clearly frightened, she had not failed to express gratitude to his men for rescuing her. She had given him her hand in thanks. He'd felt honored and proud for having served her, and tonight he'd expected praise, not censure, from his eminence.

Perrell felt as though he'd been twisted and hung upside down. What was he to answer, when the cardinal next sent for him? The Gides had supported the crown for generations, with not a traitor among them. Yet was not the church the supreme authority? Perrell had sworn a solemn oath to obey Tomias, and Cardinal Theloi was the voice of Tomias in this world.

Slowly, Perrell ran his fingers through his auburn hair and gripped it in torment. *What in Thod's name am I to do?*

Chapter Thirteen

The sound of a door quietly opening and closing in the adjoining room brought Talmor's attention away from the window, where he'd been staring bleakly out at the falling rain. Thunder rumbled, and although it was but midmorning, the sky remained black.

Which matched Talmor's mood, for he was tired indeed of his fancy prison and ready to do anything to escape it.

For the past week, since rescuing the queen, he'd not left this pair of rooms. Oh, they were fine quarters indeed, with carved wooden panels on the walls, beautiful tapestries, expensive furnishings of marquetry and costly woods, all the luxuries a man could want. The bedchamber was large enough to hold a canopied bed hung with draperies, wooden chests that contained all the fine new clothes awarded to him by various tailors, cobblers, glovers, and furriers eager to gain his patronage. A case held his sword—cleaned and oiled—and his chain mail—freshly polished. He now owned more possessions than he had ever had in his life, and he'd received so many offers of wares from merchants that Pears was threatening to hire a steward to manage all the transactions.

The adjoining sitting room was furnished with ornate chairs for the reception of friends, not that they came. Its tall window overlooked one of the lesser gardens and took in the morning sun, when any shone.

Oh, very pretty quarters, Talmor thought with a snort. At least they were now, not that he cared much. They'd been bare and cold until Pears arrived and demanded better on behalf of his master. But whether luxurious or austere, the rooms had guards posted at the door, and Talmor could not go forth. He might as well sit rotting in a dungeon with shackles on his feet, for all the freedom he was permitted.

" 'Tis for your own protection," Lord Nejel had said during his single, uneasy visit two days ago.

The commander had roamed about the small sitting room, refusing to sit down on the pretext that he had inspection to conduct shortly. Not once had he met Talmor's gaze. And he'd kept his distance, starting each time Talmor moved.

Nervously pulling his gauntlets through his hands, he stood at the window, and said, "It won't be for long, just until the—er—rumors settle down. The men don't know whether to hail you as a hero or fear you. I've hushed up the wildest barracks talk, of course, but precautions seemed a good idea."

"I want to see her majesty."

"She's improving steadily. No worry there," Nejel said with false heartiness. "The physicians agree that all she needs is rest. I'm told there's to be a huge mass held in thanksgiving for her return to health."

"I want to see her."

"My dear baron," Lord Nejel said, shooting a lightning glance over his shoulder, "it's all a question of whether her majesty wants to see *you.* Nine-tenths of a courtier's life is waiting. I wouldn't like it myself. Well, I must be about my duties."

Since then, no one else had come, and Talmor's patience was at an end. Having spent his entire adult life in a rush of duties and hard work, this enforced idleness was maddening. And every time he thought about how the palace officials had lied about Pheresa's abduction in the first place, he wondered

what inventions they'd come up with now regarding her state
of health. She could have bled to death, could be lying on the
very threshold of Beyond, for all he knew.

Oh, it was not quite that dire, Talmor forced himself to
admit. Pears had been able to glean snippets of information
from Oola, one of the queen's servingwomen, but for a man
in love anxious to see his lady such news as "Her majesty's
color is better" or "Her majesty's appetite has improved" was
nothing at all.

It had to be Pears who'd entered the sitting room. Talmor
could hear him walking about, and since the squire did not report immediately to him Talmor guessed his mission had been
a failure. Tightening his mouth, Talmor jerked open the door.

Pears, dressed neatly in the Edriel colors of ebony and
fawn, was busy poking up the fire on the hearth. Small and
wiry, with a boyish, deceptively unlined face beneath a thatch
of graying hair, the squire had served Talmor most of his life,
was privy to Talmor's darkest secrets, and had remained faithful despite them. It was thanks to his care that Talmor hadn't
died at Thirst Hold last winter. All through this difficult week,
he'd been tirelessly patient, keeping Talmor in bed until he re-
gained his strength, entertaining him with a soft stream of
chatter, sharing all the gossip of the palace, and diligently pre-
venting him from speaking until his throat mended.

"Well?" Talmor demanded now.

Turning to face his master, Pears withdrew the folded
piece of parchment from his sleeve and shook his head.

"Morde!" Talmor took the message he'd written to Pheresa
and flung it on the fire. "Who is behind this conspiracy to
keep me from her? I—"

A knock on the door silenced him. In an instant his fury
was gone, and hope rose in its place. Unable to keep still, he
strode over to the rain-streaked window and strove to master
his impatience while Pears answered the door.

Voices murmured, then Pears said, "M'lord? The lord
chancellor is without."

Surprised, Talmor spun around just as Lord Salba separated himself from his entourage in the passageway and came

over the threshold alone. He nodded briefly to the guards on duty at the door before beaming a smile at Talmor.

"My dear baron!" he said in his hearty, genial fashion while advancing into the room. "How delightful to see you so well recovered. It has been far too long since last we met."

Feeling honored indeed to receive a visit from the lord chancellor himself, Talmor smiled back.

Salba's brown eyes were alert and twinkling beneath jutting brows. Garbed in silk velvet, his heavy chain of office glinting across his chest, he took his time in appraising the room's appointments and even longer in studying Talmor. There was no nervousness in his manner, no evasive shift of his gaze. If he'd heard the rumors that called Talmor a *sorcerel,* he did not behave as though he believed them.

"Lord Salba, you are most welcome," Talmor said eagerly, certain he could persuade the man to put an end to his confinement. "Please be seated."

"Thank you." Settling his bulk, Salba waved away the refreshments Pears brought in. The squire left the tray on a table and retreated swiftly from sight. "Well," the chancellor said, "when last we met outside the cathedral, I was a trifle preoccupied. May I now congratulate you on your new title? It is a splendid rise for you."

"I was honored by the queen's generosity," Talmor said, impatient with such banal remarks. "Lord Salba, I have—"

"What does your father say regarding your new position?"

"I doubt he knows."

"Oh, surely he's been informed. Did you not send word to him?"

Talmor found his temper growing prickly. "My father and I do not—correspond," he said.

"Estranged, are you?"

It was easier for Talmor just to nod than enter into explanations he did not want to make. In fact, he was not officially acknowledged by Lord Juroc as a son, and he was sure his father would be infuriated that Talmor had revealed the connection to anyone.

The silence stretched out and grew awkward. Talmor

caught Salba staring at his empty sleeve. He stiffened with involuntary affront, but Salba gave him no apology.

"Pity," he murmured.

At that moment, Talmor sensed a wave of strong emotion in the older man and inadvertently soulgazed him. Salba, he discovered, felt no regret about the crippling; nay, the lord chancellor was wishing intently that Talmor had died at Thirst.

Shaken by this glimpse of enmity inside a man he'd always considered an ally, Talmor swiftly ended the contact and sank blindly into a chair.

"You do not look entirely well as yet, baron," Lord Salba remarked, frowning at him. "Have some of this wine."

Trying to drag his wits together, Talmor refused the cup Lord Salba offered him from the tray. He wanted to demand to know why Salba had turned against him, but of course the answer was obvious. Sir Pem and Sir Bujean had seen him summon fire; nay, he'd threatened them with it. And they'd included that information in their report. Why in Thod's name, Talmor asked himself for the countless time, had he been so stupid?

"Lord Talmor, you really do look pale," Salba said. "Should I come at another time?"

"No. There's nothing wrong."

"You reassure me," Lord Salba said, still eyeing him dubiously. "The physician has reported that you are speedily and satisfactorily regaining your health. Far quicker, in fact, than he expected."

"I mend quickly."

"And the bleeding in your throat? It no longer troubles you? Praise to Thod. We rejoice in this news."

"Thank you," Talmor said tonelessly and could bear no more idle talk. "How long am I to be kept prisoner?"

"Prisoner?" Lord Salba raised his heavy brows. "What has given you such a notion?"

"I am confined to these rooms. There are guards posted at my door, and—"

"My dear baron, you misunderstand. You are not imprisoned. There is no mistreatment. These measures are for your protection."

"So Lord Nejel said. Protection against what?"

"Come, come! You are not a stupid man, Lord Talmor. You understand perfectly."

"Yes, that I was brought into a bare, unheated room and left to live or die according to Thod's mercy," Talmor said furiously. "Locked in without even a cup of water to ease my suffering."

Lord Salba's bland gaze wandered about the room. "I see a warm fire burning on the hearth. I see superb furnishings. What is lacking that you require?"

"I have such things *now*," Talmor said through his teeth, loathing the pretense that Salba seemed determined to maintain. "Now because the queen is better and has no doubt inquired after me. Or perhaps she has even been gracious enough to issue orders regarding my comfort. But I am not allowed to see her. I am not allowed to write to her. I am kept here, caged, like something to be ashamed of. How long will this go on?"

Salba stared at him a long moment without expression. This time, Talmor could not tell what the man was thinking. "I am sorry you are still so unwell," he said eventually in the evasive way of a trained diplomat. "Perhaps it is your illness that leads you to imagine these things."

"I am refused contact with the queen," Talmor said bitterly. "Yet she knows of—she knows my secrets."

"I assure you that the queen is receiving no visitors as yet. Her recovery is slow. Oh, fear not. She makes excellent progress, but she was much shaken by her ordeal, as you must realize. And she is still confined to bed, under orders to rest. I myself have spoken to her only once."

Talmor bowed his head, curling his fist atop his knee. Was it truth or lie? He could not tell.

Sighing, Lord Salba drew a scroll of papers from his wide sleeve. "I can see that you are tiring, so I will get to the business of my visit. The realm is indebted to you for the service you have performed on behalf of her majesty," he read aloud from a document. "Therewith, it has been decreed that you shall receive the deeds for additional lands and their revenues."

Surprised, Talmor could only stare at him.

Salba smiled slightly. "I am also authorized to give you a warrant that grants you an increased percentage of the duty assessments collected on all goods passing along the eastern trade route."

He paused, regarding Talmor from beneath his brows, and added dryly, "No doubt a new, even more prestigious, title than baron would impress the court, but I have persuaded her majesty that lands and wealth are more substantial rewards by far. I hope you will agree."

"Thank you."

Lord Salba frowned. "You seem a trifle . . . underwhelmed, Lord Talmor."

"I'm stunned," Talmor admitted honestly. Belated realization was beginning to sink through him. The papers Lord Salba was holding must make him an extremely wealthy man indeed. He remembered how he used to while away hours of tiresome sentry duty dreaming of such rewards, and now that it had happened he felt hollow and remote.

"I expected nothing," he said. "I thought only of her."

"Of course. But once again you have done what was deemed impossible. How you knew where to find her majesty . . . by what—er—unusual means you sought her . . . well, does it matter now? You have saved Queen Pheresa and her throne. She, and all those loyal to her, are most grateful."

Talmor frowned. Lord Salba was hinting that he'd used magic to find Pheresa, and, if the lord chancellor believed that, then the entire court did as well. While he had the queen's favor, apparently no one was going to arrest him for wielding magic. Perhaps the report had been expunged or altered in the records of the palace guard, but the rumor would stick to him forever.

In the past, when the talk circulating around him grew too suspicious, he'd always broken his hire and moved on. It was easy enough for a knight to find work at one hold or another.

But no longer could he vanish to evade talk. This time, he had to find a way to brave the whispers and uneasy glances. Perhaps, with the queen's love and his wealth to console him, he could do it.

He looked over the deeds and warrants Lord Salba handed to him, his numb sense of unreality growing as he saw just how generous they were. He was beyond wealthy, he realized. He practically held the keys to the entire eastern trade. The bounty and riches that could pour into his coffers from such a position staggered him. It would be necessary to hire stewards to oversee his affairs. He would need assessors and collection agents. He now owned an estate and could afford to enlarge his rooms here within the palace, or even build a new villa or fortress of his own. He could advance loans to the royal treasury, thus helping Pheresa rebuild what the Vvordsmen had destroyed. He could do so much . . .

But then his speculations stopped, for he saw that it was too much, far too generous.

Suspiciously he looked up. "Exactly what are you trying to buy, Lord Salba?"

The smile that had been playing across the lord chancellor's face vanished, and from that instant Salba's brown eyes became as hard as stones. "That is a most unpleasant and ungracious remark."

Talmor shrugged. "I am only a warrior and a bastard, half a barbarian, in fact. I lack a diplomat's manners, so you will have to speak plainly to me."

"Sarcasm ill becomes you, baron."

"I've said only what is true. Now answer me. What are you buying with this largesse?"

"You seem to understand already."

"But I insist you explain. Does not the queen need some of these revenues to rebuild her depleted treasury?"

"With proper management, the treasury will be rebuilt. You are kind, Lord Talmor, to concern yourself with these . . . larger issues of state, but I assure you there is no need."

The snub was delivered in a gentle, even gracious tone of voice, but Talmor stiffened just the same. Did the man think he intended to meddle in affairs of state, even try to rule from behind the throne? Was that what this was about?

Lord Salba leaned forward, his usual air of mild affability gone. "It would be better if you were to visit your new estates for a time, Lord Talmor."

"How long?"

"Long enough for her majesty to gain a firm grasp on her realm. Long enough for unpleasant rumors to die down and become forgotten. Long enough for her to complete the official period of mourning suitable for a widow."

Talmor snorted. "What hypocrisy is this? She will not mourn Lervan!"

"Give her time, baron. She requires it desperately, for this realm is in serious need of repair. A coronation and a few celebratory feasts are not enough to mend all that has broken in the last year. Lervan's grab for the throne and his death have made a messy business, which must be cleared up. And there is the matter of Lindier's trial, which will stir up considerable controversy. The queen needs friends around her right now. Loyal friends and strong allies."

"Do you think me neither?" Talmor retorted.

"I think you will prevent her from gaining the support of those of value."

It felt like being walloped by a mace. Rather breathless, Talmor slumped back in his chair. Although he'd been expecting something like this, a part of him was yelling a refusal, not wanting to accept it.

"If the queen wants me near her," he said defiantly, "not even you have the power to send me away."

"True. But if you go willingly to help her majesty, then there need be no confrontation between us, no contention that will hearten her enemies."

Talmor frowned. "Aye, she has too many enemies. What of them? Who is to protect her? Who can—"

"She will be closely guarded from now on," Salba assured him. "What happened at the coronation will not be repeated."

"But I—"

"Lord Talmor, I greatly regret that you are not still her

majesty's protector. No man has ever filled the post with as much diligence and competence as you. But change comes to us all, whether we wish it or not. You can no longer guard her majesty. And you should not be her companion . . . at this time. Later, perhaps, when her position is more secure and certain things have been forgotten . . ."

"No one will forget," Talmor said bitterly, shoving himself to his feet and pacing across the small room. "I was acquitted of all charges at my trial in Thirst, but no one here seems willing to remember *that*."

"You are an ambitious man, and you've been given generous means to make yourself powerful as well as rich. I suggest you avail yourself of these opportunities."

"Away from court."

"Yes."

"Away from her."

"Yes."

Talmor shook his head. "I cannot go. She is my life."

"Come, come," Lord Salba said impatiently. "Put aside this romantic twaddle and think of the lady."

"I do think of her!"

"Do you?" Salba asked sharply. "Or is it mainly yourself, and your feelings, that concern you?"

"I—"

"You love her, yes. So you have indicated. That gives you the power to ruin her. Do you not understand that?"

"She is queen. She holds the power."

"You can bring about her downfall."

"Impossible—"

"Heed me!" Salba said urgently. "You were accused of wielding magic at Thirst Hold and even stood trial. The queen took an enormous risk there by defending you."

"I was exonerated. I survived trial by spell-fire. All the charges against me were dropped. That should be the end of the matter."

"How can it end when you continue to wield magic and bring peril to yourself and others?"

Talmor hesitated, but desperation drove him on. "On the

day of coronation, when I was driven from the cathedral," he said, "church knights forced me into an inquisition chamber."

"What?" Salba exclaimed, looking astonished. "How can this be?"

"It happened shortly before you approached me on your way to take the seal of state to the palace. I was—the Inquisitor did something to me. I—I don't know what." Talmor's voice thickened. "But he said I was no *sorcerel,* and they let me go."

"So that is why Theloi has dropped the charges of heresy against you," Salba said. "Ah, yes. I had wondered."

Talmor waited, but it seemed that Salba was not going to offer him sympathy.

Instead, the chancellor said, "So you can fool the priests. Which means you probably fooled those trying you at Thirst, including her majesty."

"No!" Talmor said furiously. "That is not—"

"Come, baron. The guards accompanying you in the catacombs saw you conjure fire from thin air. They are competent men, neither idiots nor drunkards. And they've talked. Your title, of course, protects you from the accusations of common knights, even an officer of the guard. They cannot lay charges, and indeed they will not. But the scandal remains, and such scandal cannot be permitted to touch her majesty. I should not have to explain this to you. As a man of intelligence, you know the situation."

With a little exclamation under his breath Talmor swung away and stood gazing blindly out the rain-streaked window. Bitterness welled up in him so sharply he had to close his eyes against it.

Salba's hand settled gently on his shoulder, making him flinch.

"My boy," the lord chancellor said softly, "I love her as much as you do. I would serve her cause to my last breath. But she must survive this and keep Mandria's throne secure if we are to continue as a great and prosperous realm. And she must be able to quell more enemies than a few vicious Sebeins. Danger faces us on our borders as well as from within."

"That's why I must be close to her," Talmor said raggedly. "To help her. To guard her—"

"No. Not now. You have rescued her from formidable danger, but if you stay, you will destroy all that the people love about her. She is still seen as the Lady of the Chalice and admired for her beauty and piety. But Lervan's lies and slander did her much harm. There is also the loss of her child and heir to explain."

"Thod's bones, do not dare to hurt her there," Talmor said so fiercely Lord Salba blinked and backed up. "She's endured enough. She nearly died with the child, and her grief for it still runs deep. Leave her be!"

Lord Salba cleared his throat carefully. "And now she has killed Lervan—"

"In self-defense!"

"Rather than accept his attempt to divorce her."

"Rather than let him kill her first and steal her throne."

"Yes, yes," Lord Salba said patiently, "but these points I'm raising are ones her majesty's opponents will put forth. You must surely understand that there are proprieties involved. Your companionship can serve only to confirm Lervan's lies. We do not want to give the church grounds for laying accusations against her, questioning her piety or morality."

"More hypocrisy!" Talmor growled. "King Verence kept two mistresses and let his court lead the most abandoned—"

"Queen Pheresa cannot follow in his footsteps. She is not yet sufficiently secure to do as she pleases. And don't bother to mention Lervan's excesses, baron. I'm well aware of double standards and unfairness."

An uncomfortable silence fell between them. Talmor was staring at the floor, his face hot, his ears roaring. "I have not lain with her, if that's what you're asking," he said at last. He looked up defiantly. "But if we wish to be together, neither you, nor the church, nor all the officials of Mandria will stop us."

"That is why I am appealing to your decency and common sense," Salba replied.

It hurt, as though something inside his chest was being

torn asunder. Talmor's jaw worked a moment before he could bring himself to answer. "I see."

"I am sorry, but it is for the best."

"How long?"

"A few weeks, perhaps months. Let's say by Selwinmas."

"That's nearly a year!"

"And is that too great a price to pay for her security?" Salba asked coldly. "For the security of the realm?"

Unable to consider it, Talmor moved away from him. They'd never had any time to themselves, never a real chance. And now . . . when the worst should be over . . . this was not fair.

He sighed, reining in his self-pity. Life had never been fair; he knew that all too well.

Lord Salba waited calmly, refusing to relent an inch.

"The coronation was supposed to end her risks," Talmor said bitterly, his voice starting to hoarsen from so much conversation. "It was supposed to be the end of strife, marking a finish of her difficulties. She's been hoping for a new beginning."

"Life is never so simple, never that tidy."

Slowly Talmor met his gaze. "Does the queen know you're here, what you're asking?"

"Her signature is on this writ of permission for you to withdraw from court."

The hurt stabbed deep. Nodding, Talmor reminded himself that she must be sovereign first and his love second. But, morde, this was hard.

"I'll stay away until Selwinmas," he said. "And then on my return, will I—"

"Once you withdraw from court," Lord Salba said firmly, "you must not return until the queen sends for you. That could be as soon as Selwinmas. But there are no guarantees. Everything will depend on the political situation as it unfolds through the summer."

"So I could be exiled forever," Talmor said bleakly.

"Not an exile. You are inspecting your estates, which have been long neglected and need putting in order. When the queen requests your presence, then you'll be sent for." Lord Salba peered at him very hard from beneath his jutting brows. "Come, baron! This is not a tragedy. It is a temporary sacrifice for your sovereign. You have given an arm in her service. You nearly gave your life last week. What is an absence of a few weeks or months compared to that?"

Talmor said nothing.

"Have I your agreement on this?" Salba pressed him. "Have I your word that you will abide by this understanding and not seek to undermine her majesty's position with spies and covert messages, as you've been doing the past few days?"

Talmor flushed hot and could not help but glance at the fire, where his thwarted message had long ago burned to ashes.

"Well?" Salba persisted.

"Yes."

"Your word, Lord Talmor."

"I swear it, on my honor," Talmor said angrily.

"That's settled, then," Lord Salba said in satisfaction, clapping his hands together. "I have a meeting to attend shortly. Will you excuse me, baron? Enjoy your rustication. I think you will find it most interesting."

"Will I?" Talmor muttered.

"And isn't Edriel fairly close to your father's estates? You might find it worthwhile to be reconciled with him. Officially, Lord Juroc's one of your vassals now, so you can summon him to swear an oath of allegiance."

Talmor's brows knotted, but Lord Salba was already departing with the demeanor of a man who has achieved exactly what he wanted.

Swearing as the door closed in his wake, Talmor kicked a stool so savagely across the room it smashed into the wall. Pears hurried in from the bedchamber, saw his stormy face, and asked, "Shall I fetch water, m'lord?"

"No!" Talmor shouted. "Just leave me!"

"But—"

"Get out!"

Hurt flashed across Pears's face before he ducked his head and retreated. Talmor grimaced, already sorry for taking out his temper on the squire, but he did not call Pears back to apologize.

The deeds lay on the table where the lord chancellor had left them. In sudden fury, Talmor crumpled them to fling them on the fire.

But at the last moment he stopped and held them in his fist, seething and torn. He knew that the wily chancellor had found his points of weakness and greed, as well as how to manipulate them. Yet the deeds hadn't really been necessary, for Talmor would always sacrifice himself for Pheresa's welfare.

After struggling with himself, Talmor finally put the papers down. "Damn you," he whispered bleakly, seeing no way out for himself or Pheresa. "Damn you to Beyond!"

PART II

Chapter Fourteen

Watching guards escort the last condemned traitor to the execution block, Pheresa stood in the shadows beneath a pavilion. It was night, and although torches blazed on all sides, their light failed to hold back an oppressive darkness. A crowd of onlookers, massed silently in the gloom, stood opposite to her. She could distinguish no individual among them. Behind her, always just at the periphery of her vision, hovered a cloaked figure she could not identify yet seemed to know. His presence made her profoundly uneasy, but she did not confront him. She was too concerned with watching the prisoner—her father—mount the wooden steps to the platform.

She could not breathe. She wanted to halt this grisly business. But she could utter no sound. She could not signal reprieve. A band of pain was tightening around her heart, for never had she felt more powerless.

The proceedings paused to allow the prisoner his opportunity to speak, but the duc said nothing. A drum began to pound, and he knelt at the chopping block, stretching his neck across the groove.

Pheresa swallowed hard, wanting to avert her eyes, but couldn't.

The executioner swung the ax high overhead, the blade flashing in the torchlight as it came down.

Lindier's head thudded on the planks and went rolling off the platform toward her. In horror she watched it come, and knew that even if she ran it would follow her. Clenching her fists against her chest, she wanted to scream. When the head bumped to a halt against the hem of her skirts, shudders ran through her. She could not look down at her father's face.

Appearing beside her, Lord Salba said, "Your majesty must pick it up. Pick it up."

"No!" she cried.

"You must."

Reluctantly, she bent and lifted the head by its long black curls. The face was not her father's, but instead . . .

"Talmor!" she screamed.

Pheresa jerked awake, still screaming, and found herself sitting in her canopied bed of state with her hands stretched out before her. It was a dream, she realized, breathing hard. Only a horrible dream. She hadn't killed him. She hadn't killed *him*.

Pressing her hands to her face, she began to cry.

Candles were lit, and attendants came running. They brought her water to drink, and Oola bathed her face and hands with a damp cloth while Lady Carolie—her hair in braids and pillow creases on her pretty face—patted Pheresa's shoulder and murmured reassurances.

"Oh, these terrible dreams," she said. "You are worried about tomorrow, but it will soon be over. Try to lie back and sleep."

Pheresa shook her head, feeling wretched and alone despite the people around her. She missed Talmor dreadfully, and the weeks since she'd last gazed on his beloved face seemed an eternity. Banished to his estates by her order, did he hate her for it? Many times she'd picked up her pen to write to him and explain, but how could she? Would she tell him of her cowardice, her weak will, her selfishness? Would she blame Lord Salba's opposition, the unrest among her nobles, the enmity of the church?

Nay, she feared that were she to let herself write to him, she would pour forth all her yearning and misery. Dear Thod, how she missed him, just seeing him daily and exchanging a quick smile, just hearing his voice. The simple pleasure of knowing him to be in the same room had been a former luxury that she craved now.

Fool to let him go. Fool to heed the advice poured into her ears that urged her to send him far away. And yet, was he not safer apart from her? The palace remained in turmoil during the interminable trials for the nobles and officials accused of treason. It was a time of seething passions, lies, and wild accusations. Endless sifting of evidence and testimony was required to separate truth and fact from petty backstabbing, bribed witness, and falsified accounts. Certainly this was no place for a man accused—however falsely—of heresy.

So said her thoughts, every day. But at night, her heart cried for him.

Meanwhile, she'd had the trials to preside over—numerous accounts of wrongdoing and deceit. She had listened to the pleadings and defenses of the accused men until she felt numbed by it all. Some simply confessed and begged for mercy; others used facile arguments to state their case. Two men had been found blameless and released. The rest, including her father, were condemned to be executed on the morrow.

She had remained ruthless and strong throughout the whole ordeal, but the prospect of witnessing multiple beheadings made her quail. She wished she could spend the morrow in the seclusion of her privy chamber.

Yet she rejected such temptation, scorning the coward's easy path. It was her duty, her moral obligation to watch the outcome—however brutal—of the judgment.

"Enough, Carolie," she said, pushing away the sachet of fragrant herbs the lady was wafting beneath her nose. "I need none of that."

Lady Carolie curtsied. "Some warm milk perhaps, or a posset? I make an excellent one."

"Yes, make it," Pheresa said to get rid of her.

As Lady Carolie hurried across the vast chamber of state, Lord Avlon stepped out of the shadows to open the door for her. Lady Carolie nodded to him and hurried out, and he retreated back into the gloom.

The sight of him made Pheresa sigh and press her hands to her burning eyes.

Avlon had been chosen as one of her protectors, and this month he was on night duty. Wellborn, educated, and polished in manner, his presence should have relieved some of her unease, but despite his competence, the man had a cold and satirical eye, and his drawling voice held a deprecating edge. Pheresa could not fault his service, but she disliked his manner. Nor did she care for her day protector, Sir Lorne. She could not see either of them on duty without thinking of Talmor.

And to be reminded of Talmor—who should have been here soothing away her nightmares and holding her close but was not—to be reminded of his absence was to feel that perpetual dull ache suddenly pierce and jab.

She wept again, clutching her pillow because she could not hold him. Oola shooed the others away and sat with her, humming in the candlelight and gently brushing her hair.

Lord Salba was so focused on the welfare of the realm that he overlooked the welfare of a woman and man in love, Pheresa thought bitterly. Had these past weeks not been a sufficient parting? After all, it seemed that Salba's plan was working. People no longer mentioned Talmor. He'd been forgotten. It was time, she decided, to summon him back to Savroix.

She would make the court acknowledge his worth and see what a good and valiant man he was. She would give him her father's command over a quarter of Mandria's army, for he was unsuited for the idleness of court life. And if Lord Salba dared protest, she might dismiss him to tend his own estates for a while.

At dawn, she arose and dressed in a gown of blue silk with quilted sleeves studded with sapphires. Her hair was coiled smoothly on her neck. And although her face was pale and drawn, with dark smudges beneath her sleepless eyes, she had finished her prayers and composed herself. Now she sat alone in her privy chamber, writing a letter to Talmor. Its phrasing was very formal, as it would be seen and handled by numerous people on its way to him. She made sure it gave no hint of her feelings but merely requested his return.

Outside her windows the light was strengthening, and her candles were no longer needed. She heard no sound save the faint hissing of flame mingled with the steady scratching of her pen across the parchment. A letter to her father had already been composed, sanded, and sealed. It lay ready for delivery to the dungeons, and the writing of it had been difficult, for what was there to say?

She could not write to him of her disappointment. She did not wish to repeat the accusations or express the anger and bitterness she felt at his betrayal. She wanted to offer him comfort in his final hours, yet believed doing so would make her a hypocrite. In the end, she had composed a short missive, very formal and stiff, with a brief quotation of Writ. It was not satisfactory, but she could do no more with it, and very much doubted that Lindier would even read it.

Writing to Talmor was proving equally difficult, although not from a shortage of anything to say. Rather, her heart was so full she longed to pour forth all her feelings for him, yet she dared not express them in a letter such as this.

More than ever, she yearned to hold him, to rest her head against his deep chest and feel loved and secure. Blushingly, she longed for his kisses and far more. It had been too long since she'd slept in a man's arms, and never had she lain with a man who loved her.

She wanted that, and she had no more patience for waiting.

A soft tap on the door interrupted her thoughts, and her pen blotted. Putting it down with a grimace, she listened to Lord Avlon's query and someone's murmured reply.

The door opened, and a man wearing her mother's livery entered.

Irritation came quickly to Pheresa these days. She glared at the fellow. "I am not to be disturbed. Begone!"

He bowed low, wringing his hands. "Most gracious majesty, forgive the intrusion. I am sent with a request from the Princess Dianthelle for audience with your majesty."

"Go away."

He retreated hastily. "At once, your majesty. Forgive me, your majesty. I will tell her highness—"

"Wait." Pheresa sat frowning as her reluctance warred with a sense of obligation. She had no desire to confront her mother, yet she knew this was one audience she could not refuse. Indeed, she'd been expecting the request for days and wondered why it had come so late.

Better to get the interview over with quickly, Pheresa thought with a sigh. "Bring her highness to me within the hour."

It seemed, however, that the princess was waiting out in the passageway, for scarcely had Pheresa resumed writing than a page was at the door announcing her highness.

Dianthelle, sister to King Verence, swept inside the privy chamber with all the regality of her birth and station. Pale-haired, gowned in rustling black silk, and wearing oval Sae-lutian pearls, each as big as Pheresa's thumb, she looked as beautiful as ever, as though age could neither wither nor dull her complexion. Her magnificent eyes swept the room, took note of Lord Avlon standing just inside the door with watchful attention, and focused their formidable gaze on Pheresa.

Impassively, Pheresa remained sitting.

Advancing halfway across the room, the princess curtsied deeply in the most formal obeisance possible.

A little surprised by such a display of respect, yet also pleased, Pheresa laid aside her pen. "Mama," she said in acknowledgment.

Rising, Dianthelle approached. "Thank you for letting me bring my petition to you."

"Of course."

"Your majesty has been employing a brilliant political strategy, allowing the trial to be conducted to satisfy your supporters. But they have gained the convictions they sought. Let that be enough. Your majesty will, of course, grant Lindier a full pardon."

Pheresa's brows drew together. "He confessed his part in the plot. His involvement was heavy."

"Oh, yes, a confession," Dianthelle said airily with a shrug. "Well, it was expected of him as a sign of penitence. And that is surely sufficient."

Pheresa said nothing.

"This man is a decorated marechal, a duc, the father of a queen!" Dianthelle went on. "He has been publicly humiliated, imprisoned, and reviled with the wildest accusations. Through it all, he has conducted himself magnificently and borne his hardships without complaint. It is time to let him go."

"Let him go? A confessed traitor?" Pheresa said in astonishment. "I think not."

"Very well. Banish him from court if you must carry vindictiveness so far. Exile him for a year. Then it will be forgotten."

"I do not lightly forget treason."

"Strategy, not treason," Dianthelle corrected. "Nothing more. Had you lost to Lervan that day, you would be the one on trial. Do not forget that, Pheresa. Political fortunes shift swiftly and are never sure."

Pheresa lifted her chin. "Mine is."

Dianthelle's eyes widened, and a slow flush crept up her throat into her cheeks. Her expression hardened. "You little—"

"Be careful!" Pheresa said swiftly. "Remember that you address the queen!"

On the other side of the room, Lord Avlon had taken a step forward with his hand on his sword hilt. Pheresa glanced at him with a quick shake of her head, and he retreated.

Dianthelle noticed him, and her pale, slender hands clutched her Circle with whitened knuckles. "I am of royal blood," she whispered. "My grandfather, father, and brother were all kings. Would you threaten me?"

"Madam, you forget yourself," Pheresa said. "Perhaps you are ill."

Drawing an audible breath, the princess retreated half a step before stopping. Her gaze would no longer meet Pheresa's, and it was as though, Pheresa thought, she'd finally been forced to acknowledge her daughter's supremacy. Dianthelle's posture and expression might be rigidly controlled, but fury and jealousy raged plainly in her eyes. Dianthelle's ambitions to rule Mandria were quite impossible by the laws of succession and had only frustrated this brilliant, forceful woman who believed her will should override all others.

"My apologies to your majesty," Dianthelle whispered at last, and clearly it cost her a great deal to do so. "I did not come here to argue or to insult you, but to plead for your mercy. He is your father."

"That alone cannot excuse his actions."

"He made a mistake! What man does not on occasion? It is time to grant his release."

"Has he asked you to petition me?"

"What need of that?" Dianthelle asked blankly. "I know my duty as a wife. I have come to smooth this rift between father and daughter."

Far more than a rift, Pheresa thought in anguish. Her mother made it sound as though they'd had a minor argument that could be patched with an exchange of smiles. *But she brings me no apology,* Pheresa thought. *She assures me of no contrition in my father's heart.*

Pheresa hoped for a reason to spare him. A part of her still longed to gain her father's gratitude if she couldn't have his affection. This cheap desire to buy him shamed her. Although she knew she would never be able to forgive herself for letting him die, her conscience would not permit her to overlook his serious transgressions. She'd been wrestling with these torments throughout his trial.

Dianthelle—as arrogant as ever—apparently believed that she had only to state her wishes for Pheresa to accede to them. Clearly she saw nothing wrong with the duc's actions to usurp his daughter. The princess was no more contrite than her husband. It made Pheresa wonder if her mother had also been a part of the plot.

In fierce revulsion, she banished that suspicion. Dianthelle had used her as a political pawn, had always criticized her, and even for a time disowned her. She had been a cruel, indifferent mother in many respects, but that did not make her a traitor. Pheresa warned herself not to mistake contempt and dislike for betrayal. Her mother might employ spies, might scheme and maneuver, but she was too clever to put herself in the dungeons.

"You sit here, as cold as stone," Dianthelle said, "and you make no reply. How can you—who as a girl wept over the dying flowers in the garden—withstand my plea? How can you ignore the reality of what will happen in a few hours? The executioner is going to cut off your father's head unless you issue his pardon immediately. Do you not understand?"

Realizing she had underestimated her mother's astuteness, Pheresa tensed. Here was the appeal to sentiment, and Pheresa found her resolve crumbling, exactly as she'd feared it would.

"He is a condemned traitor," Pheresa said in a choked voice, knowing she was reaching for the weakest argument. "If I pardon him, must I not pardon the others?"

"Why? The father of the queen matters more than anyone else. Let those other fools perish if you want your revenge, but don't make an example of his grace."

"And what will be said if I spare him?" Pheresa asked.

"Said?" Her mother's brows rose. "What do you care what is said? Act like a queen and exert your will. Sparing the life of one man shows your compassion."

"It shows my bias and favoritism!" Pheresa retorted. "His was the worst betrayal, yet I am to overlook it because he sired me?"

"Yes."

"And if he goes free, what is to stop him from committing treason again?" Pheresa asked. "He is not sorry for what he has done. He will be working another plot as fast as he can fund it."

"Lervan was a foolish puppet, but your father did not pull

his strings. If you do not realize that by now, then you are blind. You have not caught the real traitors, Pheresa. Don't suppose that you have settled the trouble."

"Who are they?"

Dianthelle shrugged. "I know nothing. But your father did very little save—"

"—give the army to Lervan's support. Against me."

"What of it? He chose the wrong side. It was a gamble that failed. Is that worthy of death?"

"Yes."

Dianthelle flushed. "Had Lervan been crowned instead of you, your father would be a hero, and you would be sitting in the dungeon."

"So you've said before. But the right of succession was mine, not Lervan's. That is the difference."

"Fie on your little distinctions! How you cling to tiny details, wanting certainty every time. Because you cannot bear to take risks yourself, you despise those with the courage to leap for larger opportunities. Well, there are no absolutes, Pheresa. You're naive if you believe otherwise."

Pheresa lifted her chin. "I believe that if I am to keep my throne, I must stamp out my enemies, not ignore them. Not give them opportunity to strike at me again. If I have not found them all, the hunt will continue."

"Patricide is an ugly stain on a person's conscience," Dianthelle said. "You no longer sleep at night, do you? The whole court knows of your nightmares and poor appetite. You're growing thin and losing your pretty looks. Soon you'll be a skinny hag, draped in jewels, with no true admirer but yourself. Oh, yes, you are queen. But an unloved queen. A queen alone. You killed your child, then your husband. Now you intend to kill your father. Can you live with such acts? I doubt it. Guilt will eat at you until you are an empty, bitter shell of a woman. You will have to buy your friends, and it's not pleasant to live with only toadies for companions. For who will honestly love you, when you kill all those who do?"

Tears swam across Pheresa's eyes, blurring her vision. Her mother was like an assassin, so beautiful and accomplished, yet quick to strike with poisoned words. Sickened and hurt, Pheresa forced back her tears.

"You have the queen's permission to withdraw," she commanded.

Dianthelle looked surprised. "Pheresa, you cannot refuse to let your father live. You must—"

"Withdraw!" Pheresa gestured for help. "Lord Avlon, her highness is leaving."

The protector came forward, but Dianthelle ignored him. "Yes, your majesty," she said with scorn. "Put me out like an unwanted dog, but you know I am right. You will live with this crime for the rest of your life, and deservedly so!"

She swept out into the passageway, where Pheresa glimpsed courtiers hanging about, gawking in blatant curiosity. No doubt the news that Dianthelle had asked for a pardon and been refused would spread through the palace like wildfire, for the princess was unlikely to hold her tongue.

A sense of loathing swept Pheresa. She rose to her feet, too furious to sit still. Damn her mother for having backed her into a corner. Damn her mother's arrogance and spiteful tongue. Damn her for knowing exactly how to find the deepest vulnerabilities and stab them.

Clerks, pages, and some of the cabinet ministers were now pouring into the room, already vying for the queen's attention.

Pheresa struggled to master her violent emotions. They must not see her disordered by this encounter, she told herself. She dared not look weak, not today, not now.

Lord Salba's young clerk came hurrying up to her. Always untidy-looking, with his shaggy hair and ink stains, he held out a letter to her in disregard of protocol. "Your majesty, it's important that you read this without delay. The envoy from—"

"It does not please the queen to read anything at present."

With that, Pheresa swept out through her private door, leaving the men to exchange astonished looks and think whatever they pleased. So distraught was she, so desperate to get herself away to regain her composure, that she failed to notice the clerk's quick glance at her desk, or see him pocket her unfinished missive to Talmor.

Down her private passageway she hurried, only no soli-
tude would await her in her chambers. There was nowhere she
could go to be entirely alone from servants and attendants.
Even here in this passage, she had Lord Avlon following her.

Suddenly she did not care. Halting halfway to her chambers, she waved him back, pressed her face to the paneled
wall, and wept.

Chapter Fifteen

It was almost like her dream, except that sunlight shone brightly on the execution platform. Shaded under a canopy, Pheresa sat surrounded by those of her ministers of state and courtiers in closest favor. The rest of the court gathered to one side, acting generally subdued and solemn. Now and then, Pheresa's gaze swept over them. Were they thanking Thod that the hand of vengeance had not tapped their shoulders, she wondered, or were they here simply for the spectacle?

Her companions watched her, so obviously trying to measure her mood in order to say the right things. With no desire to be amused, she ignored most of the chatter.

She was very tired, and just wanted this day to end. It was her hope that the executions would mark the finish of the dreadful chain of events that had begun with her flight to upland Mandria. Since then, she'd faced too much betrayal and hardship. Her abduction and the fear that it might recur, plus the dangerous snares left in the palace by the escaped Lady Hedrina, kept Pheresa constantly on edge. Refusing to rely solely on her protectors, she continued her thinsword practice and slept with her dagger beneath her pillow. Fatigue and strain made her irritable, impatient, and too ready to snap. She missed Talmor's companionship with an ache that never diminished. And now, thanks to her mother, she sat here on an occasion when she had to appear at her most composed and merciless, and felt nothing save doubt and dread.

She gripped her Circle so hard it pressed into her palm. *I must be strong,* she told herself once again.

The execution block had been placed on a low wooden platform built near the ruined wing of the palace. Charred timbers and broken windows remained as a potent reminder of the night the Vvordsmen had looted and burned part of the palace. Pheresa wanted no one in Mandria to forget how Lervan had surrendered to the invaders and paid them tribute to spare his life. Here, before this testament to his cowardice, would his supporters die.

Drumrolls announced the start of the proceedings. A hush fell over the crowd; heads turned in the direction of the prisoners' walk. Green-cloaked guardsmen escorted the first condemned man into sight. Lord Fillem was pale and shivering, barely able to hold himself upright.

As he was led onto the platform, he turned to Pheresa and held out his hands beseechingly. "Mercy, O queen!" he called out. "Please show your kindness. Please don't take my head!"

Inwardly she flinched, but pressed the thin edge of her Circle painfully into her palm and let nothing show on her face. Despising Fillem's cowardice, and well aware of how greedily he'd robbed the royal treasury, she ignored his pleas. The guards pulled him back from the railing and forced him to kneel at the block, while he wailed and babbled prayers.

The blade flashed down, keen and swift, and it was over.

Pheresa swallowed hard. A cold sweat had broken out beneath her gown. Her hands were trembling, but she held them rigidly in her lap and pretended to ignore the swift, appraising looks cast her way.

The next prisoner was led out. Unlike Fillem, he preserved his dignity and spoke briefly to his family, calling on Thod to have mercy on his soul.

And on it went, ten men put to death in solemn progression. Although it was a lovely day in early summer, with the air warm and the sun not too hot, she found herself wishing it had been winter, or at least raining. Blood now coated the block and puddled on the platform. She could smell it every time the wind shifted, and she fought off nausea with determination.

Some lady's corpulent lapdog prowled about, sniffing and licking, until it was chased away. A few onlookers retired discreetly. One was a pregnant lady who grew so overcome she nearly swooned. Another was a trembling, ashen-faced widow of one of the condemned, who was escorted away by friends. Most, however, stayed to the finish with avid anticipation.

Pheresa supposed some of them had wagers laid as to whether she would pardon her father at the last moment.

She could still do it, she told herself. All she had to do was raise her hand to stop the proceedings.

Lord Salba, standing at her side, bent down to murmur in her ear, "It will soon be over, your majesty. Courage for a little longer."

She gazed up at him.

His brown eyes were kind, yet implacable. "Do not forget," he murmured.

Dropping her gaze, she went back to fingering her Circle. No, she thought, she could not forget. Lindier's wrongs were serious indeed, no matter what her mother said. He'd done more than simply give his portion of the army to Lervan. It was thanks to the duc's refusal to take the Vvordsmen raids seriously that Mandria's army had not been positioned at key coastal defense points. It was on the duc's advice that Lervan chose to surrender rather than fight. Such actions and decisions might have been dismissed as incompetence rather than treason, had there not been Gantese gold discovered in the duc's coffers. Even more damning, he refused to say how he'd come by it.

That was, of course, not the only hint of a Gantese connection in the matter. Lady Hedrina was now believed to have been a Gantese *sorcerelle,* for she'd vanished from Savroix through no visible means of escape and had not been seen in the town or surrounding countryside or roads since. Magic had clouded her room, sealing it from entry until priests finally succeeded in countering the spell. The first guards who entered, however, perished. The agent who opened her clothes chest had his hands burned so terribly they had to be amputated to save his life. The fountain in Pheresa's private garden was found to contain poisoned water, and the mist and spray from it proved to be as corrosive as darsteed venom. One of Pheresa's ladies-in-waiting had rearranged the objects on the queen's desk and was seriously disfigured when a wooden pen box exploded.

And there was worse, far worse, although much of that information had been suppressed at the trials, for it was deemed too incendiary for public knowledge. The investigative agents had gleaned hints that the plot against Pheresa stretched back into the past, all the way to King Verence's death. It was probable that Verence had been assassinated by means of dark magic. Gantese magic. If that were true, the foundations of the throne stood on shaky legs indeed.

At that point, on Salba's urging, she had stopped the investigations. To dig further was to head toward implication of church involvement. Layers of intrigue around Lervan had been peeled away, exposing Lindier, Fillem, and many others, and beyond them the trail led to Cardinal Theloi, a spider at the center of a vast web. Yet nothing could be proven against his eminence. Any possible witnesses tended to disappear; no tangible evidence could be procured. There were only frightened whispers, as elusive as smoke.

His eminence was present as one of the spectators. Guarded by church knights, surrounded by an entourage of ecclesiastical officials, and greeted by Roncel, who knelt obsequiously to kiss his ring, Theloi's presence meant officially that he'd come in support of the crown. Yet not once had he looked in the queen's direction. Nor had he come over to pay her his respects.

She loathed his bold self-confidence, blamed him for Talmor's exile, and despised him for having played a part in Ver-

ence's untimely demise. It was hard to watch him receiving ac-
colades and obeisance while unable to order his arrest. Yet she
was not secure enough, according to Salba, to challenge directly so powerful an enemy as the head of the Circle of Cardinals. Were an open schism to separate the crown and
church—the realm's two most vital institutions—Salba believed that Mandria could not survive. And so she was forced
to play a deadly, dangerous game of pretense, giving no hint of
what she'd discovered lest assassination strike her as well.
Pragmatism aside, she felt a coward and a hypocrite for keeping silent, but she understood that to bring Theloi to the fate he
deserved would take a long, long time. She must be patient.
Someday, she vowed, she would see him stripped of his jewels and fine robes, kneeling at the block like the villain he was.

As though he sensed her thoughts, the cardinal turned his
gaze on her. Since surviving the attack in the cathedral, Theloi's gray hair had whitened, and he'd grown so thin and frail
he looked as though a puff of wind might topple him, but his
green eyes remained as cold and sharp as ever. She met his
gaze with equal coldness, careful to keep her expression otherwise neutral.

"Let him not feel threatened," Salba had warned her, "or
he will strike in desperation. Better that we should keep and
watch the enemy we know than have new and unknown ones
take his place. He may not be the final knot in this thread. Let
us unravel it cautiously, a little at a time."

With Salba's advice fixed in her mind, she nevertheless
felt fresh anger smoldering in her heart for having to sit in
silent complicity with his evil deeds, while other men—his
puppets—went to their deaths in his stead.

A murmur swept through the onlookers, and Lord Salba
stiffened at her side. "The duc comes," he warned her.

She thought herself prepared, but she wasn't. In that moment, she grew suddenly flustered, her heart racing, her hands
slippery and damp.

The Duc du Lindier came limping up between his grim-
faced guards. He was attired in a tunic of vivid blue, his cloak
trimmed with a band of velvet, and he wore a gold chain stud-

ded with diamonds that winked and flashed like fire in the
sunshine. The order of marechals he usually wore at his throat
had been stripped from him. Bareheaded, he carried himself
like a prince and nodded graciously to those whom he passed.
According to the report, he had exhibited marked agitation
that morning, refusing breakfast and yelling curses at his servant. However, he had agreed to receive an unnamed priest,
who came to take his confession. The visit had lasted a long
while, and afterwards the duc had been calm, as though finally reconciled to his fate.

He looked calm now, almost unconcerned, Pheresa
thought. He might have been strolling up to join the queen at
a garden party.

Pheresa's heart raced and lurched. This was the man who
had come to the nuncery school when she finished her educa-
tion and escorted her straight to Savroix to begin her bid to
become Prince Gavril's betrothed. This was the first man to
dance with her. This was the man who had once carried her on
his shoulder when she was four years old, and they had
laughed together and eaten cake before he handed her over to
a servant. This was the man who had gone forth to war in
gleaming armor, astride a magnificent charger, with crowds
cheering in his wake. He had been the most acclaimed warrior
of Mandria, the realm's greatest general, and a trusted adviser
to King Verence. Once he had been handsome, virile, and
strong, but now it had been years since he'd ridden onto a battlefield, and his many glories were old. He was running to fat,
his face dissipated.

He flashed her a look of hatred before he climbed onto the
platform, and the grief in her heart stopped burning and instead grew cold and quiescent. Pheresa knew she would never
understand why she had disappointed him so much or why he
had valued Lervan over her. Had she not risen to be the highest in the land? When she was just a naive and foolish maiden,
she used to believe there was some fault inside herself, some
inadequacy that her father could not accept. Now, as she
watched him walking to his death, she understood that the
lack had been in *him* to treat her so.

I should hate him, she thought, while the duc uttered his final words to the crowd. She could not hear what he was saying for the roaring in her ears. Her pulse throbbed beneath the scar on her wrist, a scar concealed by a wide bracelet of gold and rubies. Her wrist began to ache, and she rubbed it, displeased by the unwanted reminder of the Sebeins.

Then Lady Carolie gasped aloud, and several of Pheresa's attendants cried out in consternation.

Lord Salba moved closer to Pheresa's side, and Sir Lorne, with his sword half-drawn, uttered a loud imprecation to Thod. Boos and hisses rose from the crowd, drowning out the rest of the duc's remarks.

"Cut out his tongue! Foul blasphemer!" someone shouted.

Astonished by their reactions, Pheresa realized she'd heard none of what her father said.

"Do not heed him, your majesty," Lord Salba was saying. He looked pale and shaken, and Lady Carolie was weeping as she dropped to her knees and pressed her face against Pheresa's skirts.

"Don't listen! Don't listen!" she cried. "My dear, sweet lady, it cannot happen. Tomias will not let it."

Bewildered, Pheresa tore her gaze away from the platform where the guards were shoving her father to his knees. She looked at Salba in appeal.

He bent down to her at once.

"What did he say?" she whispered.

The lord chancellor's mouth clamped tight, and his brown eyes looked deeply distressed. "Did your majesty not hear?" he asked.

"No."

Surprise flashed across his face. "What is this? How could your majesty have failed to . . ." He let his voice trail off, then recovered himself with a visible effort. "Forgive me. I am undone by this."

"What did he say?"

Now the others were staring at her, all except Lady Carolie, who was still weeping.

"She did not hear? The queen did not hear? How is it possible?" they whispered among themselves.

"Forgive me, your majesty," Lord Salba said with a sigh, and made a swift sign of the Circle. "I cannot repeat it, for it was most blasphemous."

"He cursed your majesty!" Lady Carolie wailed. "How could he do such an evil thing?"

Everyone in the cardinal's entourage as well as the crowd standing beyond the canopy was looking Pheresa's way. Murmurs spread through the crowd, and Theloi himself came to her.

He shot her a puzzled glance before announcing loudly, "The revered grace of Tomias has protected your majesty by shutting your ears. In Thod's name, let not such a dire utterance come true."

He lifted his hand to pronounce a quick benediction over her, and Pheresa bowed her head to receive it. Still, her mind was less on prayer than the curious questions still racing through it.

As soon as Theloi turned away, she plucked at Salba's sleeve.

"But what did he say?" she whispered. "I must know."

"I dare not repeat it. 'Twas the worst blasphemy I have ever heard, and no ordinary curse. He was taught to say such terrible words. He could not know them otherwise."

"If I know not what he said, then I have no defense against it."

Salba frowned. "Dear queen, I fear that if I repeat the curse, I will somehow strengthen its power."

The chancellor's grim distress and sudden exhibition of superstition frightened her.

"I command you to tell me," she insisted.

He sent her an imploring look. "Please, majesty. If Thod has closed your majesty's ears, why should I defy his will?"

"I will not live fearing the unknown," she said. "Tell me the gist if you dare not repeat the words."

As Lord Salba reached up to clutch his chain of office, she saw that his hands were shaking. His frown deepened, and he cleared his throat. "It was against your majesty's life, and the lives of your children to come."

Hurt, she leaned back with tears in her eyes. How could her father hold her in such contempt or nurse so deep a grievance? But he was her enemy, she told herself. Thod alone knew why, but he was her enemy and lashing out.

After a moment she lifted her Circle. "I live in Thod's grace and protection," she announced, and patted the weeping Lady Carolie on her pretty head. "Pay no heed," she said. "'Tis the poison in Lindier's soul that has come forth, nothing more."

Lady Carolie pressed her lips to Pheresa's hand in a fervent kiss. "How good your majesty is," she cried. "That you can forgive such evil wickedness."

"Death to the traitor!" came a yell from the crowd.

Others took up the cry. "Death! Death! Death to Lindier!"

He was still kneeling with his head on the block. The executioner had not yet raised his ax and was ignoring the shouting crowd as he stared in her direction. Anger spurted through Pheresa, and she wondered if Dianthelle had bribed the man to wait for the queen's signal of clemency.

It had been Pheresa's intention to sit beneath the canopy during her father's execution, exactly as she had with the others'. But Lindier's curse—yet more treason—ensured that she could no longer treat him the same.

She rose to her feet, making the crowd gasp and turn to stare at her.

"No, your majesty! Do not pardon him!" a man shouted, but Pheresa gave no sign that she heard.

Among the jostling onlookers she saw her mother, standing white-faced in that severe black gown. Staring at Pheresa with naked hope, Dianthelle raised her hands in appeal and sent a tremulous smile toward her daughter.

Seeing such relief and joy in the princess filled Pheresa with revulsion. In that moment, she no longer feared her mother. No longer wanted to please her or earn even a moment's admiration. The princess was deluding herself to her husband's wrongdoing. That he had just publicly cursed the queen and her future progeny, and in so doing blighted the realm of Mandria along with her, only condemned him more, yet Dianthelle clearly had not stopped hoping for his deliverance. If she did not share his guilt, Pheresa thought with pity, then the woman was ill and needed care.

Pheresa stepped out from beneath the canopy into the sunshine. Her gaze moved away from her mother's intent face, back across the crowd, to her father. His eyes were shut, and his face looked so pale against the dark, stained wood, it was as though he were already dead.

It relieved Pheresa that he would not look at her.

Turning her stare on the executioner, Pheresa did nothing else. She had only to raise her hand to indicate mercy, but she stood straight-backed and motionless, her hands at her sides.

After a moment, the crowd took up the chant again: "Death! Death! Death!"

The executioner raised his ax. Pheresa felt a tremor pass through her, but she steeled herself not to look away. *Endure it,* she told herself. *And know you do this not out of a petty desire for revenge but because Lindier has earned death with his actions.*

The blade flashed down, and the duc's head thudded on the wooden planks exactly as it had in her dream.

A roar went up from the crowd. Dianthelle fainted, and her entourage carried her away.

Pheresa felt supremely calm. She felt as though she'd lived a hundred years in the past few moments. When she walked back to her throne beneath the canopy, people watched her in wide-eyed silence. Lady Carolie was still weeping, her gaze awash with sympathy and compassion, as though she could not bear to witness what this ordeal had cost Pheresa.

"Bring me wine," Pheresa ordered, and a servant hurried to fill her cup. She drank deeply but felt no better. Why, she wondered, had she felt driven since girlhood to become queen? Why had she wanted this?

But she could show no remorse in public, no low spirits. One could not grieve for a traitor.

A scream startled her, and as she turned around, more

screams and yells arose. The people who had pressed close to the platform in macabre curiosity were now shoving each other in a frenzy to get away. Guards were drawing their swords, and Sir Lorne planted himself in front of Pheresa so that she could see nothing.

"Your majesty must withdraw now," he said. "Please, go indoors."

"What is it?" she asked, craning her neck to see past him. "What is happening?"

"Your safety first," he said.

But she pushed past him and emerged from beneath the canopy just as the fleeing crowd revealed the platform to her.

Her father's headless corpse, which should have been sprawled on the planks, was rising jerkily to its feet and groping blindly about. Blood stained the blue tunic, and a cloud of black mist was boiling from the headless neck.

Pheresa stood frozen with shock, her widening gaze unable to look away. She could not believe what she was seeing, for surely it was impossible. This was Mandria, lower Mandria, where such things could not happen. Had she stood in Nether, or anywhere north of the Charva River, she would have already been taking action. But perhaps this was only another nightmare. Perhaps she'd gone mad and could no longer distinguish dreams from reality. Perhaps the curse was already descending.

But, no matter how impossible, she knew this *was* real.

The corpse lurched forward, but was stopped by the railing. Again it tried to advance, mindlessly unable to cope with the simple barrier in its way.

Through her mind raced other, equally horrific memories, of the soultaker sucking the life from Gavril and how his corpse had reanimated itself thereafter in the fight that had nearly cost Faldain his life. She had seen part of the great battle that raged on the fields outside Grov, with armies of shambling, rotting corpses fighting Mandrian and Netheran warriors. And she knew that somehow, the long arm of Gantese evil had reached all the way here, to the very heart of Mandria, to strike at her.

This creature might have once been her father, but was now something unclean and loathsome, and infinitely dangerous. At that moment, the terrible stench of the grave reached her nostrils.

"Nonkind!" she screamed, and reached in her pocket for her salt purse.

As though it somehow heard or sensed her, the headless corpse turned in her direction and came stumbling off the rear of the platform. More people scattered, screaming, and just as the guards rushed to confront the creature, the executioner awoke from his terror and cleaved through its shoulder with his ax. Staggering, Lindier went down on one knee, and the executioner struck again.

Although in pieces, the monster tried to crawl in Pheresa's direction. Behind it, on the platform, the head grotesquely rolled over as though turned by an invisible hand. Horrified, she gasped aloud, fearing that now the head would roll toward her as it had in her nightmare.

The guards gathered to hack Lindier's body to bloody pieces, but she uttered a wordless cry of protest.

"Salt it!" she called out, impatient with their ignorance. "It's Nonkind. Salt it!"

Holding aloft her salt purse, she stepped forward, but again Sir Lorne blocked her path.

He was white-faced, his jaw clenched with determination, his eyes darting frantically. "In Thod's name, majesty, no closer! Come away *now!*"

Frustrated, she thrust the salt purse at Sir Lorne. "Take this and fling the salt over the body, or nothing is of any use, no matter how much they mutilate him."

Her protector only looked at her without comprehension, but before she could explain, Lord Nejel came rushing up, grabbed the purse from her hand, and dumped salt on both the hacked body and head. Only then did the monster lie still.

A hush fell over the garden, broken only by the sound of a woman's hysterical weeping. The executioner had ripped off his hood to be sick. Guardsmen retreated, grimly wiping their blades clean.

Pheresa took a shaky step back, and suddenly she could not draw a full breath. She shuddered, closing her eyes for an instant, and found herself sitting down, with people babbling around her in frightened, almost hysterical voices.

"Be quiet, all of you," she said, and waved away a cup of wine. Her head was aching. She wanted to run from here as fast as her legs would take her. She wanted to throw up. She wanted to cry.

But a corner of her mind was filling with a strange sort of relief. The duc had been coerced by Nonkind, she thought. His evil had not been entirely of his own will. And his final curse had been directed under the control of some Believer, rather than stemming from actual, personal hatred of her, his only daughter.

Tears slipped down her cheeks, and she found herself pressing her hands to her trembling lips. A blur of white passed before her. When she blinked her vision clear, she saw Cardinal Theloi bending over her. At once she tensed.

His face was as pale as his robes, and although he was breathing a trifle fast, his voice remained calm, as he said, "Your majesty, be assured that the evil has been driven forth, to return no more. His grace will be taken by our Rulliens and prepared suitably for burial so that he can't rise again. We shall pray for his pitiable soul, that it may be permitted to reach Beyond."

She stared at Theloi in surprise at such kindness and compassion. Despite her flow of tears, she managed to nod her gratitude and even placed her hand in his.

His clasp was feather light and so icy cold it made her shiver. "We shall see his grace put at peace," he said, and withdrew.

Dabbing at her tears with a handkerchief provided by the Duchesse du Meringare, Pheresa watched Theloi walk away. He might be her enemy politically, she thought in astonishment, but he was still an official of the church, and as such, his purpose was to deliver Thod's solace to those in need. She had, in her scramble to survive and thwart him, forgotten that.

"Your majesty?" Lord Salba said in a worried voice.

Recalled to her surroundings, she looked up. Her hand continued to tingle from Theloi's touch, and she curled it into a tight fist.

"Come, your majesty," Lord Salba said with gruff solicitude. "Are you well enough to walk, or shall I arrange for you to be carried?"

"I can walk," she replied, but her voice did not sound like her own.

"Then let Sir Lorne see you safely back to your chambers. Other surprises could be lurking out here in the palace grounds. Go and rest, while Lord Nejel and I see to this matter."

She rose, surrounded on all sides by solicitation, and let them care for her. But even once she was back inside the palace, she could not rid herself of that last sight of her father's bloody corpse, so mutilated and horrific. Was it not enough that she'd been cursed by the Sebeins, she thought, pacing up and down despite the efforts of her ladies-in-waiting to make her lie abed or at least sit, but that now she had been cursed by Nonkind as well?

For generations, lower Mandria had lived securely protected by the Charva River, because Nonkind could not cross it. But somehow, the evil was finding a way past the old protections. And Mandria, so prejudiced against magic, had few defenses against it.

Shooing away her ladies-in-waiting, she bolted herself in her little prayer room and knelt, clutching her Circle tightly. Her hands still could feel the coldness of Theloi's grasp, and she felt as though her fingers might never be warm again. "Oh, great and almighty Thod, have mercy on us," she prayed aloud. "Draw nigh to protect us from the evil that is coming."

And then she wept.

Chapter Sixteen

The following morning she met with her privy council as usual; however, even as Lord Salba rose to his feet to begin courteous inquiries about her health, Pheresa lifted her hand to cut him off.

"The queen thanks her council for assembling today, but we shall not conduct our usual meeting."

"Your majesty?"

"I have reached several decisions, which I wish to announce. This is for your information, and not an invitation for discussion. Our meeting this morning will be brief."

Pausing, she glanced down the row of attentive faces. For once, they were all staring at her with keen interest. Lord Salba eyed her warily as though uncertain of what she had to say. She was sure he would not like it.

Drawing a deep breath, she began: "Yesterday has proven that Nonkind can infiltrate lowland Mandria and this palace."

Clune coughed irritably as he leaned forward. "Naught but fears and superstitions. Your majesty, this—"

"Do not interrupt," Pheresa said. "This is not a discussion."

He sat back, his face a trifle pink. The others shifted uneasily in their seats.

"The palace guards are not sufficiently trained to handle this kind of foe," she continued. "Commander Nejel and his officers will henceforth drill the men to deal with forces of magic."

More protests broke out, but she ignored them. "Lord Salba, please send a request to the reverend general of the church soldiers, asking for assistance in this matter. No doubt they will have found a spirit of cooperation since yesterday, but if not, then chevards from upland holds should be brought to Savroix without delay."

Salba's brows kept climbing higher, but he nodded without a word.

Roncel, holder of the second most powerful duchy in the kingdom, an ambitious man with numerous progeny, and one who'd never forgiven Pheresa for winning over his daughter to become Prince Gavril's betrothed, now dared to speak up with one of his usual sneers. "A most industrious plan, your majesty, but surely an overreaction to—"

She turned on him with a contempt she didn't conceal. "Overreaction? Has your grace ever fought Nonkind?"

"Well, no, your majesty, if they exist at all."

"Then you need not comment on what you fail to understand." As he flushed and sputtered, she swung her attention back to the others. "This most tragic and unholy possession of Lindier is but the second warning. The first was my abduction."

"Say you the Sebeins and Gantese work together now?" Clune barked.

"I am saying that twice in the last few weeks we have been attacked with magic, and twice we have been woefully unprepared. Let us not repeat that mistake, my lords. I doubt we'll be as fortunate in the third strike."

The men exchanged dubious glances, but she was not finished. "Furthermore, I shall be dismissing my present protectors from their posts as soon as replacements from upland holds can be sent to me."

Thin, dark-haired Lord Meaclan looked up from the notes he was busily scribbling. "Does your majesty no longer trust the palace guards?"

"I trust them implicitly," she replied. "But when I ordered Sir Lorne to throw salt on Lindier's corpse yesterday he failed to obey my order."

"That alone is grounds for his dismissal," Lord Bennoit growled.

She glanced at him. "I have found a tendency among Mandrian men-at-arms to freeze when confronted by Nonkind for the first time. That, as the warriors among you know, is usually a fatal mistake in battle."

A few of them nodded. The rest were exchanging scowls.

"More importantly," she went on, "Sir Lorne failed to act because he did not understand the order."

"Not his business to understand," Clune said. "Supposed to obey, without question."

"Agreed. But he did not know the simplest and first rule of combating Nonkind, which is that salt is a principle defense." She took a moment to look at them each in turn, making sure she had their full attention. "Unlike some of you, I have seen Nonkind several times. Never have I forgotten watching Prince Gavril being slain and possessed by a soultaker. It is not an easy death, my lords."

They flinched collectively, and a few clutched their Circles. It was a subject no one at court liked to remember, and for years King Verence had forbidden anyone to discuss his son's tragic death. But Pheresa no longer intended to keep the details hidden. She wanted to shock them in order to drive home her point.

"Have any of you ever seen a soultaker? No? It is a loathsome creature, my lords, that you could never forget. It enters a body through the neck and sucks the life and soul away until nothing is left but the empty husk, a corpse ready to be possessed by the evil the soultaker carries."

"That's heresy," Lord Bennoit whispered.

"It is deliberately a heretical act," she said. "The purest evil, and the means by which most Nonkind are created. The

Gantese armies carry soultakers with them into battle and release them among the fallen, to collect as many victims for their side as possible. It is how they can turn the tide of a battle that at first seems to be going against them."

"But how, your majesty, could such a thing be brought here, if that is truly what happened to your father?" Roncel asked.

She raked him with an impatient glance. "Who was the priest who visited his grace yesterday morning?"

Again they looked startled and uneasy.

"Surely your majesty does not suspect a member of the clergy!" Lord Bennoit said in outrage. "That's—"

"Who was the priest?" she repeated impatiently.

"No one knows," Lord Salba answered.

"Exactly! An unnamed man, wearing the robes of a cleric, was admitted to the prisoner." She leaned forward, her eyes blazing with anger. "Almost certainly that individual was a Gantese agent, disguised, and carrying a soultaker with him."

"Great mercy of Thod!" Lord Bennoit burst out, wide-eyed. "That's—that's the foulest, most dishonorable act—"

"You see why the guards must be retrained?" she broke in. "You see why we can no longer be complacent, believing ourselves safe from the evil that has plagued upland Mandria and Nether for years? The dark forces are spreading, my lords, and we must take steps to combat them before they sweep over us all."

They sat, staring at her in silence, and she saw how old most of them were. They were afraid of new ideas, wary of change, unable to believe that the world as they knew it could ever be different. She saw that convincing them, even after yesterday's horrific demonstration, would be like trying to shift an enormous boulder without tools, team, or fulcrum.

At that moment she was filled with a sense of frustration so strong she wanted to shout at them. Instead, she said calmly, "The Circle of Cardinals can aid us if they will break their band of secrecy regarding the old ways of defense against magic, but if not, a request can be sent to King Faldain, asking him to loan us of one of his battle *sorcerels*—"

They all jumped to their feet, protesting vociferously. Bennoit was holding his Circle aloft and sputtering passages of Writ. Roncel was trying to outshout Clune, who pounded the table. Meaclan, her minister of finance, clutched a sheaf of papers to his chest and stared at Pheresa as though she'd lost her wits, while Salba murmured something into his ear.

She sat quietly, letting them rage and sputter, and at the first lull, said, "Heretical or not, against Writ or not, we have our survival to think of. Mandria is ripe for attack. In the past year she's been raided from the west and east, and this state of affairs will continue unless we take the offensive. We have grown complacent and weak, and our worst flaw is that as yet we will not admit how vulnerable we are."

"Your majesty!" Roncel cried. "We have the finest standing army of any—"

"Is it not shameful," she said, ignoring him, "that barbarian hordes can raid our villages and burn our homes while demanding tribute from *us,* the foremost realm in the land?"

"We deploy the armies in defense of our villages, your majesty," Lord Bennoit assured her. "We do what we can."

"The army is spread too thin. While it defends the coast, Klad attacks our borders. The army rushes back and forth, like a mouse toyed with by a cat, and all the while we ignore every dire warning that a great evil is coming upon us. The greatest evil, perhaps, that Mandria has ever faced. Will you have us do nothing until hurlhounds and Believers overrun the palace?"

"Your majesty would lead us into apostasy!" Bennoit shouted, while Clune and Roncel both stood red-faced, apparently too incensed to speak. "*Sorcerels* in Mandria. Great Thod! Who would agree to such—"

"No doubt Cardinal Theloi will protest some of these intended measures," she said, carefully avoiding Lord Salba's fulminating eye. "And I havé reason to think King Faldain will refuse his aid, as he has before. As for Saelutia—"

"Foreign dogs," Clune muttered furiously. "That we should turn to foreign dogs . . . bah!"

"The wielding of magic is forbidden," Roncel said flatly.

"Your majesty's suggestion that we drop the sacred principles of our faith and use the forces of darkness ourselves is most—"

She lifted her hand to silence him, and he stopped with visible reluctance. They glared at each other a moment.

"Let no man here misunderstand the queen," Meaclan spoke up quickly. "Our churchmen know how to combat magic without employing it themselves. They will, of course, be consulted, as her majesty has said. The Circle of Cardinals will be asked to deliberate the matter and give her majesty advice. Naturally, we all wish to put our trust in the church soldiers before we seek foreign aid. But let us not forget that other realms do contend against the darkness daily and have means at their disposal that we might foolishly overlook."

"Hear, hear," Lord Salba agreed loudly.

The other men turned to him as he walked over to stand beside Pheresa. "Your majesty's concerns are valid," he said. "The need for swift action is clear. But let us not act so hastily that we—"

"Thank you, lord chancellor," she broke in, causing his brows to knot. She swept the group with a glance. "I have given you my decisions and called the council here, not to deliberate and vote on suggestions, but instead to inform you of what is to come. No doubt Mandria's enemies think her vulnerable because she is now ruled by a woman, but Mandria will not be found weak. She will not be caught unprepared again. And she will not permit invasion, either by barbarians or by Believers. That is all."

The men advanced on her, all talking at once, but Pheresa did not listen. Nodding to them, she walked out.

In the afternoon she sent for Lord Nejel, subjecting that miserable commander to a blistering reprimand and informing him of how she expected his men to improve their recent performance. Nejel, very red-faced and stiff, having lost his customary sleek self-assurance, promised compliance in every way and even agreed to accept training from the church knights should they deign to share their secret knowledge.

Dismissed at last, he saluted her and rushed out, nearly

bowling over Lord Salba, who was waiting for his private appointment.

The lord chancellor walked in with an astute roll of his eyes at the ruffled commander and bowed deeply to Pheresa. "I see that your majesty has made her new policies clear to the guardsmen. A bit unusual, is it not, for the queen to be so direct?"

"Come and sit with me, lord chancellor," she said, gesturing at a chair. She had no intention of letting him chide her for overriding the usual chain of protocol. "Please enjoy some of these refreshments."

A servant had left a tray of wine and sugared fruit, but although the latter was one of Lord Salba's favorite treats, today he grimaced at the offering and took nothing.

Pheresa rearranged her embroidered skirts in a feminine trick calculated to irritate him.

When she looked up, she saw him staring at her with complete comprehension of what she was trying to do. Involuntarily she smiled, and he smiled back before his expression sobered.

He leaned back in his chair, making it creak beneath his weight, and steepled his fingers. "Alas, your majesty. Alas. You have set the council on its ear, and the whole court is buzzing with what you mean to do. I shudder to think what Cardinal Theloi is going to say."

"I do not much care."

"You had better," he warned her. "I have advised your majesty not to provoke him unnecessarily, especially not now."

"Thod's bones!" she cried, slapping the arms of her chair. "I care not one jot about provoking the wretched man. My father was rendered Nonkind and would have slain me in my own garden. Surely I have justification for action."

"Yes, of course. No one questions that," Salba replied. "But your majesty dares go too far, too quickly."

"I'll go much farther if I must," she said grimly. "I am tired of being underestimated, threatened, and attacked. If Gant wants war, I shall bring them war. If the Vvordsmen dare to come back for tribute, I shall give them steel to eat. Mandria is mine, and I'll do whatever is necessary to keep it."

"So you have awakened at last," he said softly.

"I have grown up." She glared at him. "I grew up at Thirst."

"When you lost your child?"

"Yes. And when I failed to persuade my chevards to wage civil war for me. And when I saw a good man fight hurl-hounds and nearly die for it because he knew not how to combat Nonkind." She paused, frowning over her memories. She knew Salba had deliberately called them forth in her mind to distract her, but she drew strength these days from the difficulties of her past and could not be softened. "And perhaps I grew up most," she continued after a pause, "when I fought a soultaker alone in my bedchamber and killed it."

Salba's mouth fell open. "Thod above!"

"Didn't your spies tell you about that?"

He shook his head, still staring at her in shock. "Your majesty forgets I was not in office at that time and lacked my—er—usual resources."

She let silence fall between them for a few moments, giving him time to adjust, then with a piercing look, she asked, "Why did your clerk steal my letter to Lord Talmor yesterday morning?"

Lord Salba shot to his feet. "What is this?" he almost roared. "I know of no such—"

"Was he not acting under your instructions?"

Beneath his ginger hair Salba's face turned dark, and his eyes blazed. "Your majesty," he said through his teeth, "this accusation is most—"

"It has been your determined intention to part Lord Talmor from me, to keep us separated permanently," she went on calmly, plucking a bit of lint from her sleeve. "You have intercepted all my letters, have you not?"

"No!"

She did not believe him. "Just as you have intercepted all his letters to me?"

"Your majesty, I have the man's word not to write to you at all. To my knowledge, he's kept it."

"I see," she said coldly, and her tone of voice made Salba swallow hurriedly.

"Your majesty knows I think it ill-advised for Edriel to be at court in the present circumstances. Nor do I recommend that you recall him to Savroix under any pretext. Not yet, while suspicions against him remain so strong. But I give you my word that I have not meddled with your majesty's correspondence."

"Nevertheless, your clerk took it. My servingwoman saw him."

"Not on my orders." Wrath kindled anew in Lord Salba's eyes. "By Thod, that little varlet will regret selling his offices to another's spies. I'll see the truth wrung from him before this day is out."

"Very well," she said with a nod. "And you need not look so alarmed, for the letter contained nothing that can be turned against me."

"Is your majesty certain of that?"

"It was an order for Lord Talmor's recall to court, barely a sentence long." She shot him a resentful look. "No endearments."

Lord Salba sighed and sank back in his chair. "Thod is merciful."

"I am not foolish enough to betray myself in correspondence likely to be read."

"I am grateful the queen sees the necessity for caution in some areas of her life, although I very much regret when she does not guard her tongue more closely in council."

"Is that a reprimand?"

"Merely a regret, your majesty. Today's remarks have given the queen's enemies new fodder for mischief."

She shrugged. "I have more to worry about than trouble-making courtiers."

"Alas, I concur, although I wish it were not so."

She paused a moment to smooth her hands across her lap. "I have reached another decision, one I do not as yet wish to share with the council without consulting you first."

He straightened warily. "Yes?"

"I have been thinking of other ways to strengthen my position, and I realize I must marry soon."

A smile spread across Lord Salba's face. "Now this, your majesty, is news most welcome. We in your council are in full agreement, if I may be permitted to say so, although we had anticipated that your majesty would require a little more time."

She gestured impatiently, in no mood to put up with the peculiar and delicate shyness of old men regarding such things. "If Lindier's curse is to be thwarted—"

"Your majesty!"

She glared at him. "If his curse is to be thwarted, I must set about getting an heir without delay. The succession should be secured."

"Er, yes. I have, naturally, been giving the situation much thought, and it seems to me that among the noble families one or two suitable young lords can be—"

"No."

His thick brows rose. "Does your majesty have a particular individual in mind?"

"I do."

"Ah. Then with whom am I to begin negotiations?"

"Edriel."

"Ed—ah, no, your majesty. Surely not."

Her chin lifted dangerously. Beneath her skirts, her foot began to tap. "What mean you by this protest?"

"Your majesty, the baron is not a suitable candidate under any circumstances."

"I love him. I intend to marry him . . . if he agrees," she added under her breath, and thought, *even if he does not*.

"Your majesty—"

"Oh, stop gabbling 'your majesty' and see that it's done. I have no interest in your protests or objections. 'Tis my will."

Lord Salba sighed heavily. "Forgive me, for I do not mean to cross your majesty's will. But there are certain laws of the realm to which even a sovereign must submit. And, regarding whom a sovereign may or may not wed, the laws are very stringent indeed."

"A pox on these laws! I have stated my wish. It's up to you to see it accomplished."

"Before King Evareau and Verence, we were ruled by tyrants," Salba said coldly. "Does your majesty intend to take Mandria back to governance by whim instead of law?"

She glared at him, feeling light-headed with anger. "I'm no despot. How dare you!"

Salba said nothing, and it was she who looked away first. "What is the legal objection?" she asked. "The circumstances of his birth?"

"For a start. He is lowborn."

"He is a baron, and the son of a chevard."

"He is lowborn," Salba repeated stubbornly. "His present qualifications render him eligible to seek the hand of a younger daughter of a chevard or baron, but he cannot do better. And most certainly he is as far beneath your majesty's estate as a peasant is to a lord."

"You're a snob, lord chancellor."

"I am a realist, your majesty. The man, however handsome, will not do. The people would never accept him. Your nobles would never accept him."

"'Tis a consort I want, nothing more. He will not rule, and certainly my opponents will not choose him to depose me."

Salba met her stormy gaze and simply shook his head.

She left her chair, obliging him to rise also, and, fuming, began to pace up and down. "I have done enough," she said. "I married to please the king, taking to my bed a cousin of suitable bloodlines, and look what that brought me. Disaster. I won't repeat such a mistake."

"Your majesty, were you anyone else you could indeed, as a widow, marry to please yourself. But you are queen and, as such, must marry for the sake of the realm. You know this duty. No matter how much you protest, such is the way of our laws and traditions. You pledged to uphold them."

Stung by that reminder, she faced him, breathing hard. "Shall I be blunt, Lord Salba? I want Talmor in my bed. No one else."

"Your majesty cannot bear a child of mixed blood and ask

the realm to accept him as future sovereign," Salba replied with equal bluntness. "Marry a man of suitable lineage and bear his children. Sport with this Lord Talmor all your majesty pleases, discreetly, but bear in mind that public duty and private pleasure must remain separate."

She felt as though she'd been dipped in burning oil. For a moment she could not speak, then the anger poured from her. "Oh, this is fine advice indeed, Lord Salba. How obliging of you to grant me permission to commit adultery."

He turned red beneath her scorn, but did not look away. "The queen must marry suitably. There is no other choice."

"And if I choose not to wed at all?"

"That, too, is your majesty's choice. But there will be trouble eventually. I fear it will endanger you, whereas if you have children, you will—"

"Enough!" she cried, unwilling to listen. "What if I marry him morganatically? That would make us lawfully and morally wed, but Talmor would not be presented publicly, would not be crowned, and would have no say in any official matters. 'Tis possible under the law, is it not?"

The chancellor sighed. "Yes."

"Good! Then that ends the objections."

"As far as marriage is concerned. It does not solve the problem of succession."

She frowned at him. "Explain."

"Any issue of such a union cannot inherit the throne. Your majesty would have a husband, but Lord Talmor's children could not succeed you."

A burning sense of unfairness smote her. She wanted to scream at such a stupid law, and yet her own good sense restrained her. Of course she understood why such a system had been created, but it was maddening that she could not find a solution to this problem. She wanted an honorable union with the man she loved. She did not want another marriage of deceit and hypocrisy.

"The responsibilities of the monarchy are often onerous indeed." The soft compassion in Lord Salba's voice irked her. "While I admire your majesty's integrity and desire to take the honorable course, I must insist that any union with Lord Talmor is quite impossible. If your majesty forces the issue, if you force him on your subjects, he will cost you your throne." Before she could speak, he held up his hand swiftly. "I say that not as a threat, but as a warning. I pray you will heed it."

Her eyes were burning. She could not bring herself to look at him. She could not speak. What else, she wondered bleakly, had she expected Salba to say? When he believed it was too dangerous for Talmor to attend her court, how could she expect him to approve marriage?

"I am deeply sorry," Salba said. "Your majesty sought my opinion."

"I seek your help," she whispered.

"I fear I cannot do the impossible. Were Lord Talmor an ordinary man, a union with him would be ill-advised but permissible. But he is not."

Bitterness welled up inside her. She bowed her head.

"I am grieved for you both. I find him an admirable and honorable knight. He understands where duty leads your majesty, and he is sensible enough to accept it."

Goaded too far, she cried out, "Well, I do not accept it! What do I care if Mandria has no heir to follow me? I shall take my happiness as I please and live my life as I wish."

"Then you condemn your realm to political chaos. And you expose yourself to the very danger you wish to prevent."

There was nothing she could say. She knew he was right, and she hated him for it.

After a moment, Lord Salba bowed to her. "I will see that the council begins selecting some potential suitors for your majesty's consideration."

"You may be damned, lord chancellor."

"Yes, your majesty. If I have the queen's permission to depart?"

"Yes," she snapped. "Please go."

Bowing again, he left her.

Furiously, she grabbed up a cup of wine to throw it. But instead her fingers tightened around it until they were white and aching, and she did not give way to the childish urge for a tantrum. She realized she'd become a prisoner of the very duties, obligations, and responsibilities that she'd once embraced so fervently. Queen, aye, but also servant, and doomed to another loveless union. Had she never known Talmor, had she never loved him, she could have borne it. But now . . . knowing there was something better if only she could find a way to grasp it . . . no, she could not endure the touch of a man who did not cherish her. To be a royal broodmare, straining in the dark to conceive a child without joy . . . Thod forgive her, but how could she bring herself again to such shame and humiliation?

Slowly, aching with bitterness, her eyes stinging with unshed tears, she put down the cup and resumed pacing, hugging herself as she raged with longing and passion for the man she wanted so desperately and could not have.

Chapter Seventeen

Summer heat sweltered in this miserable back street where tall, narrow houses on rotting timber foundations propped each other up, slop jars were emptied from windows without regard for passersby, and scrawny mongrels, children, and rats scampered in all directions before the horsemen riding slowly along.

Slacking the reins as his horse pulled at the bit and slung its head at flies, Sir Perrell eased himself slightly in the saddle with a wince. His flogged back felt sore and sweaty beneath the weight of his padded undertunic and chain mail. It was midafternoon, and he was thirsty, but the stench of the street kept him from reaching for the waterskin tied to his saddle. After a yet another week of this thankless, clearly futile search through the most miserable slums of Savroix-en-Charva, he almost wished himself back on the Klad border. Instead of guarding the church's elite, he'd drawn permanent duty Sebein hunting. Clearly, Cardinal Theloi meant to punish him harshly for his mistakes.

The street had narrowed into little more than a winding pig trail that forced the men to ride single file. Uneasy at being hemmed in, especially when he was on the trail of Sebeins, Perrell reined up, obliging his small squad of knights to halt behind him.

Ahead he could see the charred ruins where one of the tall houses had burned down. Ax scars had gouged the door of another dwelling. He realized he'd reached the quarter of the town where the Vvordsmen had pillaged last year.

Sir Cortaine edged up alongside him, his flattened profile rendered even uglier by helmet and nose plate. "Looks to be the right place, doesn't it?"

"It does," Perrell agreed. He gave his second-in-command a nod, and the man dismounted quickly, along with about half their small force.

Sir Cortaine drew his sword with silent care, gathered his men with one fierce look, and headed down the side of the building toward the rear. A few moments later, Perrell heard a shout and the sound of splintering wood as the door was kicked open and Cortaine's knights charged into the house, yelling as though they were on a battlefield. A handful of men shot out the front door like rats off a sinking ship, only to be caught by Perrell and the rest of his knights.

Easily subdued, the captives lined up as ordered, shuffling their feet and scratching their fleas. Sir Tolard examined them quickly, peering into their eyes and peeling back their upper lips.

"None," he reported over his shoulder to Perrell.

Sighing, Perrell gestured. "Let them go."

The men fled, and by then a slovenly woman with a baby at her breast and a naked toddler clinging to her skirts appeared in the doorway, watching the knights with dull eyes. Perrell could see fleas hopping on the child's bare skin. The baby was speckled with bites, and flies that she did not bother to brush away kept swarming its tiny face.

Revolted, he was tempted to order her thrown off the wharf into the harbor waters just to see her and her brood cleaned.

Sir Cortaine appeared, shoving the woman impatiently out of his way. "Revered sir!" he called. "You'd better come have a look."

Eagerly, Perrell strode past the woman into a squalid entry crammed with a staircase of rickety wood steps that led almost straight up. The place stank of urine, rotted meat, and smoke.

The latter scent made his nostrils flare, for beneath the ashy smell of simple woodsmoke he thought he detected something else recently burned.

"Aye," Sir Cortaine said, watching him with the glimmer of a smile. "You smell it, too. This way."

He led Perrell upstairs, and although Perrell was doubtful the creaking staircase could support both his and Cortaine's weight at the same time, he followed close on his second's heels, keeping next to the wall. Cortaine turned onto a landing and led him along a scruffy, poorly lit passage with three doors. He pointed at the last one.

Hearing some of his men's voices inside, Perrell ducked through the low, slightly canted doorway and glanced around at the room.

It was larger than he'd expected, square in dimension, and illuminated by a single narrow window. An iron pot, very rusted, held char and ashes from a recent fire. Next to it stood a crude, three-legged table where Perrell saw the stub of an Element candle, a bronze blade from a ceremonial knife missing its haft, the pelt of a small animal, and a short stone jar.

Excitement kindled inside him, and he moved quickly to the center of the room, already taking note of the shabby blankets piled in one corner of the otherwise bare room along with a discarded food pouch, pair of sandals, and a pile of blood-stained bandages that smelled foul.

"They were here, revered sir," Cortain said. "And not long gone, by the look of the place."

Bending, Perrell held his palm over the ashes in the iron pot. A faint suggestion of warmth radiated from them. With his dagger blade he very gently stirred the ashes, taking care not to breathe directly over them.

As the others backed prudently away, Sir Cortaine sneezed. "Aye, Sebein magic's been burned in here," he said.

Perrell nodded. "The trail gets warmer all the time."

Abruptly he pulled his dagger from the ashes, suddenly conscious that he'd been stirring them faster and faster without being aware of it.

A little prickle of unease moved up his spine. Backing away from the pot, he stopped one of the men from gathering up the ceremonial items.

"They've left us a trap," he said in warning.

His knights froze in place, their eyes glistening alertly.

Sir Cortaine moistened his thick lips. "In the fire pot or on the table?" he asked quietly.

Concentrating, Perrell let his thoughts drift through the four levels of understanding, and closed his mind to the sudden torrent of dissonant voices, spirits, and emotions left behind by the Sebein occupants. He had been trained as a sensitive, and he was very skilled at sifting through the atmosphere that filled a dwelling after people had been in it for more than a few hours. Sebeins, of course, knew that sensitives could track them, and as a result they often obscured their trail with overlapping thoughts, wild outbursts of emotion, and spells . . . if they had time.

These had left hastily, and their work was sloppy . . . except for the trap. His gaze shifted past the fire pot to the table. Taking his time, although he could feel the force of the trap growing and knew it would spring at any moment, he focused his gaze on each object individually.

"The blankets," he said suddenly, whirling around to draw his sword just as a formless shape of mist rose from the corner and flew at them.

His men scrambled to join him in a circle, each man facing outward and holding his sword aloft.

"In the name of Tomias, the Circle admits you not!" Perrell shouted. The words were rote, a simple formality to focus his tone of voice into commands of power.

For an instant he thought he'd been too slow. The spell-shape swooped right over him, blocking out the light, sucking the very daylight from the room. In another moment it would engulf him in black, deadly mist. Once he breathed it in, he would die.

Just as the mist touched his face with pervading cold, Perrell spoke with a power that made the air in the room crack. His men shouted with him in unison, and Perrell plunged his sword deep into the spellshape.

It burst into flame, then ashes, vanishing as though it had never been. A sour, charred stench lingered in the air for a moment.

Perrell staggered slightly and caught his balance, drawing in a deep breath of relief. His men broke apart with grins and booming laughs, scattering to resume their search.

"Sweet saints," Sir Cortaine said in hearty admiration, "what I'd give to be able to do that, revered sir."

"I was a fool to spring that snare, stirring in the ashes like a novice," Perrell said brusquely, sheathing his sword. "You'd think by now I'd know better."

Sir Cortaine glanced at the cracked ceiling with a shrug. "I didn't notice, and that should tell us both there was a compulsion spell left in here."

Frowning, Perrell quickly turned and stepped out into the passageway. Although it was dark, grimy, and squalid, the air there seemed cleaner, safer.

"Board up this room," he ordered. "It's still unsafe."

"Aye, revered sir. Have you enough to trail the fiends this time?"

"Perhaps," Perrell said vaguely. He looked about, casting a little to see if he sensed anything lingering out here, and turned to face one of the two remaining doors.

Just as he did so, one of his men staggered out through it backwards, clutching his sword close to his stomach and looking pale.

Sir Cortaine started forward in concern. "Rafie? What's—"

"Don't touch him!" Perrell said in sharp warning.

Sir Cortaine snatched back his meaty hand from Rafie's shoulder.

"What's in there?" Perrell asked tensely. "Be careful. Look, but don't step inside!"

His second-in-command eased up to the threshold and

peered in, only to jerk back with an oath. He hastily drew a
Circle.

By now, Perrell's heart was hammering. There was something wrong about this house, he realized. Too few men had
run out of it. That slattern downstairs with the children had
been too dull-eyed, as though drugged or enspelled. He told
himself the entire dwelling could be a trap, and he and his
men had been inside it too long.

But he could not keep from stepping up to the doorway
and looking inside the room for himself.

"Sweet mercy of Tomias," Sir Cortaine was whispering.

And Perrell saw a family of five—parents and young children—sprawled on the floor where death had felled them.
They were already bloating, and flies buzzed on their faces
and staring eyes. He looked at their weird pallor, their black
protruding tongues. He saw the telltale pustules and the
rivulets of dried blood that had run from their ears and noses.
A pouch fashioned from closely wrought metal links, like extremely fine chain mail, lay on the floor like a gauntlet cast
down in challenge.

His heart felt as though Thod's hand had reached forth and
squeezed the life from it.

"Is that a—"

"Yes!" Perrell said, suddenly regaining his wits. He backed
into the passageway, swallowing hard. Although he'd never
seen a plague pouch before, he recognized it all too clearly.
"Cortaine, get the men out of here."

"Aye, revered sir!"

"Touch nothing. Leave all the evidence."

"But, sir, the—"

"Leave it!" Perrell said hoarsely, trying not to sound pan-
icked.

"Aye, revered sir. I'll get them out. Men!" Cortaine bellowed.

"And mark the front door," Perrell continued. "This house
and everything in it will have to be burned. Move!"

Sir Cortaine roared again, and they all went clattering
down the rickety steps in a closely bunched group. Outside,

the woman had disappeared. No other residents could be found. Sir Tolard grimly daubed a large muddy X on the front door.

"Leave two men on guard," Perrell ordered, and Sir Cortaine grimly made his choices. "This whole street will have to be searched and every house entered."

"Aye, revered sir. And then burned."

Perrell frowned, again throttling down his sense of revulsion and fear. At the moment all he could think about was rushing back to barracks, burning every stitch of clothing he was wearing, and plunging himself into incense smoke and prayer. He realized he'd almost forgotten about the Sebein trail he was supposed to pick up. Well, he'd lost it now. His concentration was shattered, and no doubt that was exactly what the creatures had intended.

Mounting his horse, he led his men out of the slums and across the bustling city. Hard to believe that the sun had not yet set and that men and merchants were still going about their business. In the harbor, a ship under Saelutian sail was coming in, her pennants streaming in the wind. Atop a garden wall a slim youth was fingering out the reedy notes of a new pipe, playing ragged wisps of sprightly dance tunes. Cartloads of merchant wares rolled by, heading for one of the guild halls to be unloaded, sorted, and priced. *Such a prosperous town,* Perrell thought, kicking his horse to a faster trot as he pressed through the thronging streets.

But if what he'd just seen was any indication, it could soon be a town of death. For if the Sebeins had unleashed plague on the populace, there was little indeed that could be done to stop it.

Far to the east in the sprawling barony of Edriel, Talmor and a party of twenty armed men were riding homeward from an inspection of his southernmost customs house on the great trade road running from the Gulf of Mandria all the way northward to Grov in Nether. He was in charge of four customs houses now, and revenues poured into them daily from the almost constant caravans of merchants traveling back and forth. And although he employed agents of business and assessors, and although the queen's collector came through regularly with armed escort to take away the royal share of revenues, Talmor thought it beneficial for him to make unexpected, unannounced visits from time to time, just to keep everyone honest.

Of course, there was much more to his new barony than just customs houses and guard posts. Edriel encompassed rolling pastureland and uncut forest. Part of it bordered Klad directly, and an army-manned fortress was located there. And there were two additional holds as well, Templan and Kauf, helping to guard the line. Templan Hold, the southernmost outpost that guarded sea as well as border, belonged to Chevard Juroc, Talmor's father. It was the place where he'd been born and reared until he was driven out, never to return. Thus far, since his return to the region, Talmor had not visited there, nor did he intend to. It was the duty of Lords Juroc and Feteusil to visit *him* as his vassals, and Talmor had not yet granted any audiences. In fact, so quiet had been his coming, with so little fanfare and so little pomp, that he doubted more than a third of the people on his estates even knew of his residence.

He was not in the mood for throwing banquets and getting acquainted. Exile was exile, however appealing the package it came in. When he'd agreed to Lord Salba's terms and departed Savroix, he'd done so thinking the queen would soon relent and call him back. He knew Pheresa well, knew how dependent she could be on the few individuals she trusted. She would want him at her side, for had she not been telling him so and insisting on keeping him close when he would have left her service in the winter?

But as spring turned into summer, she did not send for him. After each foray of exploration across his lands, he returned home eagerly, anticipating a royal messenger waiting to summon him back to Savroix. Always he was disappointed, until he no longer rode up to the stone walls of his villa with any quickening sense of hope at all.

He could have sulked and brooded about it, but he'd not been made for idleness. And there was much to do here, a lifetime of work. For the past forty years, this prosperous little fiefdom had belonged to the crown, the warrants of deed and ownership reverting to royal ownership when the last baron died without issue. The villages had gone on through season after season much as before. A steward and a few servants had maintained the large villa. The fields were harvested, and the chevards ran their holds as they pleased. Now and then a royal agent would ride through on inspection; but after revenues were collected, the place was left to its own devices.

Graft, naturally, had flourished under such loose management. Without a master, the peasants had grown surly and rebellious. The chevards were arrogant, and Talmor remembered all too clearly how his father used to snort whenever the king levied him for armed men. Lord Juroc might send a handful of knights, or he might ignore the request altogether. After all, there was no baron as intermediary to force him to comply. And King Verence had seldom remembered or bothered disciplining an unruly chevard in the provinces so far from Savroix.

The steward of the house lived like a little king and treated the place as his own abode. He had dowried his daughters from the sale of furnishings and wines, and pocketed any revenue he could get his greedy hands on.

He was the first man to be dismissed, and a goggle-eyed Lutel had been installed in his place despite Pears's mutterings that the boy was too young for such a responsible post. But Talmor had eyed the musty, ill-maintained banquet hall, cracked floors, peeling woodwork, faded squares on the walls that betrayed where missing tapestries had once hung, and knew this dormant, slumbering household needed youth and zeal to come alive. And so Lutel, bursting with pride in his steward's collar of hammered silver, darted here, there, and everywhere all day long, inspecting household inventories, cellars, stables, and granaries. He counted linens and watched as his assistant, who could write, tabulated the inventories. He reported at first daily, then weekly to Talmor of his findings and his changes, and grew in height and confidence with boundless enthusiasm.

Pears seemed content, grumbling less than usual, once he'd helped Lutel whip the household servants into order. Talmor believed his old squire was happy to be back in the countryside near his birthplace. For that matter, Talmor had hoped he would feel at home here as well, but he did not. Although he was tempted to seek out old hunting courses or fishing streams, he never did.

His past did not really beckon. Happy childhood memories were scarce and best, he believed, left alone. He was reluctant to see his father, and now that he lived less than a day's ride from Templan Hold, he found himself avoiding such a meeting in every way possible.

That's why, a fortnight past, when a courier from Lord Juroc had ridden in with a tersely worded request for audience in order to swear allegiance to his new liege lord, Talmor had fled on an inspection of the customs houses.

Now, he was heading home, but avoiding even the road and winding through the forest to delay his return. He knew that he would have to send a reply to Lord Juroc, granting permission for the visit. He dreaded doing so more than he could say.

The discordant blat of a hunting horn jolted him from his morose thoughts and made him rein up sharply in a clearing. Around him, his men also halted, looking in all directions.

Sir Nedwin, his new protector, a stocky young man with a wide grin, snub nose, and easygoing temper, swung his horse closer to Talmor's and loosened his sword in its scabbard. "Hark at them horns," he said. "I count four at least."

Talmor frowned. He'd heard only three, wailing over the forest. In the distance came a rumble, indicating that the hunt was galloping their way.

" 'Tis a big party," Pears said quietly, his eyes getting bigger as he watched first the forest, then Talmor's face. "And moving fast."

"They're after a stag, to be running so," Sir Nedwin announced. "Morde, he must be taking them on a proper chase. A boar would turn and fight them."

Talmor heard the suppressed excitement in his men's voices, but his irritation grew. "Whoever's hunting here is poaching," he said flatly.

Sir Meine, his master-at-arms, stiffened at once, as though recalled to business. "What's your order, m'lord?"

"We stop them," Talmor said. "This forest is teeming with game. Had they asked, I'd let them hunt, but no man will rob me and dance away."

From the corners of his vision, he saw his hire-lances exchange quick grins and ready their weapons with an eagerness he pretended not to notice. He knew he walked a fine line these days between imposing order on his unruly lands and turning into a surly, unfair tyrant. But it was one thing for a man to hunt game needed for the feeding of his family and another to run a stag with all the arrogance of a lord.

"Sir Meine," Talmor said sharply, "make sure the men understand this is not a war."

"Aye, m'lord," the master-at-arms said with a quick salute. "They're keen, but we'll shed no blood."

An arrow came whizzing past the head of Talmor's horse, causing it to rear. Unprepared, he was nearly unseated. Had he been astride Canae, he could have quickly pulled that well-trained warhorse back to order, but this mount was new and barely tried, a fleet-footed, nervous courser of a hot, Kladite bloodline. Riding it was like perching atop a keg of old Lord Albain's saltpeter with a torch blazing nearby. The wretched animal was always ready to buck on the least pretext, and now fell to with a will, ducking its head between its forefeet and pitching its hindquarters high.

Another arrow hurtled by, far too close, but Talmor could spare it no attention. He was too busy staying in the saddle, his feet braced deep in the stirrups, his hand hauling on the reins in a futile attempt to lift the horse's head. Just in time did he duck his head to avoid cracking it on a tree branch, a moment that threw him off-balance again.

He swore, clutching the horse's mane and pushing himself upright just in time to avoid having his mouth smashed by the brute's rearing neck. Someone was whooping lustily, advising him to spur harder, and grimly Talmor vowed that he'd have that man at attention in his study as soon as he'd seen this horse sold for meat.

Above all things, he was determined not to be pitched off in the dirt in front of his knights. They were new to his service, as yet untried, good-natured since he paid them generous wages, but not truly loyal to him. It was bad enough that often these days he rode a courser instead of a warhorse. Bad enough that he'd procured himself a protector on Pears's insistence when by rights he should be able to handle himself against any attack. Bad enough that only yesterday, when startled, he'd momentarily forgotten his hard months of practice and tried to reach for his weapon with a hand he no longer had.

Morde, he thought grimly, giving up trying to calm his horse and spurring it instead so that it squealed and bucked harder, *don't plow the ground with your nose, or they'll never respect you.*

He hauled back on the reins, spurring without mercy, and the animal reared up, shaking its head and mane. Just when he thought he was finally regaining control over the horse, an enormous stag with spreading antlers came bounding into the midst of the clearing.

It was a magnificent animal, mature and wise with all the tricks of the forest. Blood was streaming from its shoulder, and an arrow—badly shot—wobbled there. Close by in the undergrowth came the ferocious baying of dogs, and another blat of a hunting horn.

An arrow thudded into a tree less than an arm's length from Pears.

Talmor's temper snapped. He rose in his stirrups, forgetting that he was not on an experienced battle horse. "Men!" he roared. "To arms!"

They yelled with him, charging past the quivering stag that bounded aside and vanished. Talmor led his men straight at the hunting party as it galloped into sight.

Seeing a dozen men, perhaps more, Talmor took little trouble to count them. His experienced eye had immediately noticed that they were not warriors and wore no armor. Indeed, they seemed to be armed with nothing but bows and daggers. Bending low, he spurred his horse through the pack of dogs that scattered, yelping, out of his way. His terrified horse, snorting and walleyed, took the bit in its teeth and tried again to bolt with him.

But by now, Talmor had reached the leader of the hunting party, a bulky-shouldered man garbed in hunting leather and sporting a thick brown beard. Dropping his reins, Talmor drew his sword and swung at the man.

He saw his target's eyes popping in terror and heard a frantic yell as the man ducked. Talmor thwacked him hard across the back with the flat of his sword and sent him tumbling off his horse like a big, fleshy ball.

Howls and jeering laughter mingled as his men followed suit, unseating most of the hunters in the first onslaught. Perhaps three men escaped, and with quick glances over their shoulders, galloped away with no attempt to help their fallen comrades.

Talmor circled the leader, who by now had risen to his feet. The man staggered a little as he tried to gain his balance and face Talmor.

"Whoreson!" he roared, flinging down his bow and extending his arms wide. "Bandit! By what right do you come attacking decent men on their own lands, eh?"

"By the right of Edriel, who owns this land and that stag," Talmor replied.

His nettled horse pranced too close, swinging sideways, and in that moment's opportunity the bearded man sprang at Talmor, gripping a fold of his cloak and yanking hard.

It was his right side, where his balance was weakest. And yet, had his horse not shied, Talmor might have been able to fend off his attacker. Instead, swearing furiously, he toppled out of the saddle and hit the ground hard on his side. He had less than a moment to whoop and wheeze for breath before his sword was kicked from his fingers. A boot toe landed hard in his ribs, making him grunt as he was rolled over, and a heavy foot planted itself on his chest.

Talmor found himself flat on his back, pinned by the fat provincial, who was holding a dagger and uttering a profane stream of curses.

It was only then that Talmor recognized the voice as one from his nightmares. He found himself staring up into the black, furious eyes of his half brother, Etyne. The brother who'd so tormented him and driven him over the edge of terror he'd nearly not come back again. The brother he'd burned in self-defense and been exiled for.

No! his mind shouted, but there was no denying it. This was Etyne, as bad-tempered and as dangerous as ever, and—once more—holding the upper hand.

Chapter Eighteen

It seemed that Etyne recognized Talmor at the same time, for he stopped the stream of insults and stared down at Talmor with his mouth gaping open.

"You!" he said.

In that instant of shared recognition, Talmor felt a confused tangle of emotions and saw his brother's astonishment tempered by a swift flicker of hatred. But then a grin spread across Etyne's coarse, bearded face, and he began to laugh, full and deep from his belly, while he ground his boot harder into Talmor's chest.

"So you've come back, eh?" he said, and laughed again.

It was a mean laugh, full of cruelty.

"I have," Talmor gasped, still trying to catch his breath.

"Well, you're not welcome, you damned whelp. And I'll teach you to interfere with my—"

A sword tip suddenly plunged a whisker's breadth from Etyne's throat, and Sir Nedwin said grimly, "Let him up."

Etyne froze, his eyes rolling to get a look at the man behind the sword.

"Let him up," Sir Nedwin repeated, and pressed the sword closer.

Etyne flinched with a yelp, and Talmor seized that moment to push free. Rolling to his feet, shedding leaves and bits of twigs from his cloak, he stepped out of Etyne's reach.

Pears hurried over and retrieved his sword for him. Talmor sheathed it grimly, furious at this meeting, mortified that he'd been unseated and pinned as though they were still children, with Etyne the huge bully and he the scrawny underdog. *Morde and damnation,* he thought with his face on fire. He'd wanted Etyne to slink into his hall as nothing more than a provincial vassal's son, while he sat watching from the full splendor of his new rank and authority. *But nothing's changed,* he thought, struggling to find some remaining shreds of dignity while Pears brushed him off. He felt as though the intervening years had never existed at all. He felt nine years old again, locked in the mute rage of helpless frustration, while Etyne smirked and hurt him.

But Etyne the man was dabbing at his throat and trying to back away from Sir Nedwin's sword. "He's cut me!" he yelled. "Call off your surly knave, Talmor! What barbarians do you bring, that slit a man's throat with no provocation?"

"Shut up!" Sir Nedwin gave Etyne a rough shove. "You keep your tongue and your place."

Etyne fell silent, glancing around, and for the first time seemed to notice Talmor's armed men ringing the clearing and his own companions standing subdued and uneasy. The dogs milled about, whining and uncertain.

Sir Nedwin glanced at Talmor. "All well with you, m'lord?"

All but my dignity and pride, Talmor thought. He nodded, and Sir Nedwin turned his attention back to Etyne. As yet neither Nedwin nor the rest of Talmor's men had put away their weapons. Talmor frowned, but gave no order for them to do so.

"Might have known the great oaf would turn up, damn 'im," Pears muttered. "And poachin' as bold as ye please. Time ye taught him a new lesson, m'lord."

"Not just yet," Talmor said.

Sir Meine came up to Talmor and saluted. "M'lord? What shall we do with these poachers?"

"Poachers!" Etyne blustered before Talmor could reply. "Why, gentle sirs, you're mistaken. I don't see why strangers should meddle, but—"

"We're the baron's men, you fool," Sir Meine said shortly. "And guarding the baron's land. Name yourself, for as far as I'm concerned, *you're* the meddling stranger here."

Etyne turned pale behind his beard. His eyes flickered over them. "Black and fawn . . . Edriel's colors. Morde! Is the baron now in residence?"

Chuckles broke out among Talmor's men. Grinning, Sir Nedwin shot Talmor a look of inquiry, and Talmor—seeing a chance to sport with Etyne—nodded slightly.

"Aye!" Sir Nedwin called out merrily. "The baron is indeed in residence, and not the sort who takes kindly to neighbors coursing his game. Maybe we can hang you for his pleasure."

More laughter rang out, while Etyne's men shifted nervously.

"No, no!" Etyne said, holding up his hands. "You mistake everything, good sirs! We're not poachers. Not at all! I am Etyne de Barant, the son of Lord Juroc of Templan Hold. These are my guests and friends. Talmor here can vouch for me, and I—why, I have standing permission from the baron to hunt his lands at will."

"Do you now?" Talmor asked, while his knights grinned and nudged each other. "I wasn't aware that you and Lord Juroc had as yet paid your respects to Edriel, much less gained the boon of free hunting and sport."

"We haven't. That is, we haven't met the man. I was referring to an old custom, an old privilege of long standing."

Talmor had read all the old deeds and familiarized himself with the customs, old grants, and privileges of the area as soon as he arrived. He said now, "That privilege was extended to chevards in winters of harsh necessity, and not, I think, to their sons' desire for idle sport."

Etyne's face flamed. Glowering, he said sullenly, "Then I'll beg the baron's pardon, when I meet him. As for you, Talmor, what brings you here? I heard you were in the palace guard, although how you got in that elite force, considering your origins—"

"Take care!" Sir Nedwin warned him.

Etyne left the insult hanging and satisfied himself with sending Talmor the old superior smirk that used to infuriate him so.

But Talmor was too surprised to pay much heed to Etyne's insults. Struck by the fact that news of his appointment as queen's protector had never reached this corner of the realm, he realized Juroc had not known—or perhaps not cared—about his unwanted son's achievements, after all. Swallowing that bitter pill, Talmor reminded himself that Lord Juroc would soon be forced to hear far bigger news about his youngest, whether he liked it or not.

"Blind lout, ain't he?" Pears said loudly. "Our big Lord Etyne can't see what's plain before him."

Etyne scowled at the squire, but then shot Talmor a shrewd glance. "You're wearing Edriel colors, too. Gone into the baron's service, have you?"

"That's one way of putting it," Talmor replied.

"Well, no matter how you lied your way into the guards, losing that arm put you right back out again, didn't it? I like you this way. I wonder if it hurt." He stared at Talmor avidly, licking his lips. "I'll wager it did."

Talmor frowned, wanting desperately to look away from the sick malice in Etyne's eyes, yet knowing that if he dropped his gaze first, it was to lose. He hated how swiftly he and Etyne had fallen back into the stupid games of childhood, games that were so petty and counted so much.

"And you know what Father's always said about hirelances who move too much from master to master, eh?" Etyne went on. "Still, I suppose so far you've managed to do all right for yourself, although word is that Edriel's an upstart with no lineage behind him at all." Etyne cast a look around and loosed his mean laugh. "Coming here with hire-lances and bastard boys to do his bidding. I suppose he can't do better."

Pears growled, and Sir Nedwin stiffened. Sir Meine, who had sheathed his sword sometime ago, again reached for the hilt.

"You'd better guard that tongue," Talmor warned Etyne. "These men aren't used to it."

"Oh, I never mean what I say." Etyne's black eyes gleamed with malice. "Not that I've spoken falsely now, have I?"

Pears edged closer to Talmor. "Tell him, m'lord, and shut him up. Why not tell him?"

"No," Talmor said through his teeth, and Pears shot him a frustrated look.

"And see here, Talmor," Etyne blustered, "you don't need to run and tell your new master about today's little encounter, eh?"

"Why should I keep silent about your privileges?"

Etyne scowled but kept his tone cajoling. "Oh, to avoid silly misunderstandings. The fellow's new here, fresh from court. He probably doesn't understand our provincial ways. He might take offense. And that would set him and Father off on the wrong footing, eh? What harm will it do to keep quiet? The stag got away, after all."

"The baron," Talmor said, remembering how as a child Etyne always forced him to swear not to tell their father about the torments, "has ways of finding out everything."

"Not easy to work for, eh?" Etyne nodded sagely, like he knew what he was talking about. "Well, you'll soon learn how to manage. You were always fairly stupid, but I suppose you've had some of that beaten out of you as a knight, eh?"

Talmor's men had long since stopped smiling. Watching their anger grow, Talmor deemed it time to change the subject. "How fares Lord Juroc?"

"Poorly. His health's foul, but he won't admit it's time for him to step down as chevard and let me run the hold." Etyne jabbed a thick finger in Talmor's direction. "And don't think of riding by to see him, for he won't have *you* on the prem-

ises. You may want to show off your finery, but he's not forgiven you, nor will he ever!"

"I have no intention of visiting the hold," Talmor said
coolly. "If Lord Juroc sees me, it will be here."

Etyne sneered. "He'll come for the baron, but he won't
come for *you*. Not once has he spoken your name since you
left. He's not relented, if that's what you're hoping for."

Talmor felt as though his face had been carved from wood.
"I have no hopes where any of you are concerned."

"Good. At least you've learned that much in all your time
away. Now, are we free to go?"

Talmor gestured, and Sir Meine ordered the men to stand
back. Etyne's companions rushed to gather their horses and
dogs. Puffing as he heaved his bulk into the saddle, Etyne
glowered down at Talmor.

He beckoned, and reluctantly Talmor went to stand by his
stirrup. Etyne leaned down, and said quite softly, "I'll warn
you once, here and now, not to come onto my land, for I won't
forget this day. I haven't forgotten anything."

Talmor looked up right into his eyes. "Did you grow that
beard to hide the scars I gave you?"

"Damn you!" Etyne lashed at him with his bow, but Talmor dodged, and it whistled harmlessly through the air.

Swearing, Sir Nedwin came at a run, but Etyne was already wheeling his horse around. He and his men galloped
away.

"What a surly knave!" Sir Nedwin said, staring after them.
"Forgive me, m'lord. I didn't think he'd dare strike at you
again."

"Is that really your brother?" Sir Meine asked.

"Half brother!" Pears said adamantly, and spat for emphasis. "And no kin our lord will claim!"

"Well, he's the biggest fool I've seen in many a year," Sir
Meine said frankly. "Doesn't he know his own half brother is
the baron? Can't he tell an escort when he sees it? Doesn't he
recognize a protector at work or fathom why a man would
travel with a squire?"

Talmor thought of all the things he could tell them about

Etyne, and how that twisted, malicious cunning and shrewd-ness made up for a lack of intelligence. Etyne paid attention to what he wished to and ignored—or destroyed—anything that did not fit his ideas.

He'd tried to destroy Talmor when they were children, but eventually he'd paid a terrible price for it. Talmor curled his hand into a thoughtful fist. He'd expected Etyne to fear him still, but he did not. Which meant that either his brother thought he possessed something that made him impervious to Talmor's curse, or he'd forgotten about being burned.

Either theory was alarming, for Talmor feared Etyne would try to renew the old feud. And the results might be equally, if not more, disastrous. He found himself thinking of setting that woolly beard on fire, or perhaps letting tiny flames dance on Etyne's skin until he howled and writhed. Shuddering, Talmor hastily shoved the temptation away. He would not become what his brother was, someone who enjoyed torturing others. Morde, he did not know why he even thought such things.

"Why didn't you tell him?" Pears insisted, as they mounted up and headed on their way. "I wanted to see him learn that you're a baron now and must command his respect."

"I'll never have his respect." Talmor sighed. "Besides, he'd only run with the news straight to Lord Juroc. And my father would never come to me then."

Compassion filled Pears's face. "Aye," he said softly. "Do ye think the chevard will walk out without givin' ye his oath?"

It was what Talmor feared. He wondered about the public humiliation of such a scene and whether his father's temper and infamous capacity to hold grudges would drive him to commit so grave an offense. Talmor dreaded what was to come. He'd never forgotten his father's thunderous roar as he was driven off Barant land forever, and he wished—with a streak of cowardice he could not quite master—that he could avoid the coming reunion at all costs. Yet he was baron, and by law he must eventually demand and receive the chevard's oath or see Lord Juroc broken.

And Lord Salba thought I would enjoy an opportunity to reconcile with my father, Talmor thought derisively. It was more likely to start a war.

Sir Perrell—clad in fresh white surcoat over a polished hauberk, the emblematic black circles interlocked across his chest and embroidered with the symbol of his order, sword clean and shining in its scabbard, helmet carried correctly beneath his left arm—strode down the long, silent passageway once more to Cardinal Theloi's apartments.

In the past few days since discovering evidence of plague, Perrell and his men had been busy indeed. The affliction was spreading rapidly through the poorer sections of Savroix-en-Charva. The port had been closed, and travelers by road were being turned back at the city gates. No one could use the road between town and palace without a signed warrant, and even then Perrell had been stopped at a checkpoint, leaving his horse and companions behind while he journeyed the rest of the way to the palace by boat.

It was believed the air on the river had cleansing powers. Even so, at the landing, he'd had to stand in the cloying smoke of incense for quite a while until he was permitted through guarded gates into the wing of the palace where Cardinal Theloi resided.

Now, Perrell strode along impatiently behind the cleric escorting him to Theloi's chambers. His mind was on a hundred details still undone, for his order was exiting the town at dawn, assigned to escort the cardinals, cathedral bishop, and other high-ranking church officials who were scattering across the realm to safer towns and monasteries for the duration of the summer. But he could not help but recall the last summons he'd received from Theloi and the questions his eminence had put to him.

Is this the night that I'll be ordered to murder the queen? he asked himself, and felt a chill sink through his body.

Theloi had warned him to be ready with his answer. Despite prayer and much searching of his conscience, Perrell had no idea whether he would obey the order or refuse it. He was an officer, trained to follow orders. If the Circle of Cardinals believed her majesty to be a secret heretic and a danger to herself and others, then their decision must be obeyed. And yet . . . she was the queen and crowned sovereign, and Perrell believed in the Thod-anointed sanctity of her majesty's right to sit on the throne.

Dreading what was to come, Perrell told himself to stop being a fool. He must follow orders. An officer could do nothing less. An officer's conscience was the same as his duty; and part of his duty was to believe in the chain of command, to follow it, to obey it without hesitation. If he could no longer do that, then he would have to break his oaths and withdraw from the knighthood. The prospect made him sweat.

A door opened before him, and he was ushered into a small, oppressively furnished sitting room. Cardinal Theloi sat in a chair near the unlit hearth. Lamps burned around him.

Snapping to attention, Perrell stood stiff and unmoving as the cardinal's servant crossed the room to give his master a cup of wine. Nothing was offered to Perrell.

Theloi said not a word of greeting to Perrell. His green eyes glittered beneath heavy lids. His thin, pale face might have been carved from stone, and his free hand toyed with the diamond-studded Circle hanging around his neck so that the jewels flashed and burned in their settings.

"The queen and her court were informed about the plague this afternoon," Theloi said, as soon as the servant left. "A decision has been made to close Savroix and move her majesty and the court to Aversuel."

Perrell remained at attention, not daring to speak. He told himself he was perspiring because the room was so hot and stuffy. But his heartbeat had quickened, and he felt oddly short of breath.

"I am putting you in charge of her majesty's armed escort," Theloi went on.

"Yes, lord eminence."

"I believe you were assigned to escort Cardinal Ardminsil northward, but his safety is secondary to her majesty's."

"Of course."

"Ardminsil has protested most strongly. It seems he finds you a capable officer and can feel safe only in your charge."

There was a hint of amused mockery in Theloi's voice. Perrell dared let his gaze meet the cardinal's but said nothing.

"Be at ease, reverend commander."

Perrell relaxed his stance slightly.

"Do you recall our previous conversation?"

"Yes, lord eminence."

"Have you found enough courage to take chances?"

Perrell felt a trickle of perspiration run down his temple. He resisted the desire to wipe it away. "I am a reverend commander and knight of Saint Mont. If I lacked the qualities you question, my lord, I would not be here."

"Ah." Theloi leaned back in his chair and steepled his fingers together. "The last time we talked you seemed unsure. I'm glad to see you have found answers for me."

Perrell swallowed hard. "I have."

"Good. About the queen . . . you will guarantee her absolute safety on the journey. Should any danger befall the royal caravan, you and your men are to spare no effort on her majesty's behalf. And if anything happens to the queen, I expect you to be too dead to report to me about it."

"Of—of course, lord eminence."

Theloi leaned forward, and the movement was like the ripple of muscle beneath a crouching cat's velvet fur. "Are you prepared to commit what some would call treason? For the sake of this realm, for the future of Mandria, will your sword shed royal blood?"

Braced as he was for that question, still Perrell felt stunned as though he'd taken a harsh blow to the head. He fought to keep his wits clear.

"If by that your eminence means would I take advantage of an attack on her royal majesty to slay her, then myself, my answer is . . . no."

Theloi laughed. "A Gide to your core, sir! I expected nothing less than honor at any price."

Perrell stood there, flushing, and could barely restrain his growing annoyance. "My record and reputation speak for themselves, my lord. I—"

"Will you surrender your oaths to your order? Will you surrender your place in the holy knighthood? Will you obey me in that?"

Bewildered by the questions, Perrell felt like a schoolboy in an unexpected examination. Assassinations, possible ambush of the queen, surrendering his oath and order . . . it was as though Theloi was trying to confuse him completely.

"Well?" Theloi demanded.

"Lord eminence, what do you want of me?"

"An answer! Yes or no?"

"Then, yes, lord eminence," Perrell said reluctantly. "I would obey my orders to the degree of surrendering my knighthood oath." He met Theloi's gaze. "But not my allegiance to Tomias. For nothing will I forswear my soul."

"Have I the word of a Montite officer on that?"

"Yes, my lord."

"Excellent." Theloi leaned back, and his frail body relaxed beneath the white robes. Picking up his cup, he drank deeply of its contents and even smiled, without mockery this time. "It seems that at last I have chosen well for Mandria. It is a profound relief to not mentor a fool. Your integrity is a credit to you and your family. I think you will probably serve my purpose capably. At least, you are the best tool to hand."

Perrell's sense of bewilderment had not abated, but he held his tongue. Although he felt a slight measure of relief in having pleased Theloi somehow, he did not like to be doubted or tested. His annoyance over that remained.

"Do not look so troubled, sir," Cardinal Theloi said. "To my knowledge no attack is planned against the queen when she departs. *If* she can be persuaded to go. I hear that she is resisting abandoning Savroix most strenuously."

"She had better go," Perrell said shortly. "The plague is spreading very fast."

"Salba will persuade her if anyone can. She has a woman's propensity to obsess over unimportant details while ignoring what is most critical. She is stubborn to a fault. But the peo-

ple love her more than ever, and the treason trials strengthened her political base. Therefore, we must deal with the sovereign we have and seek new ways in which to manage her.
And that is where I have decided to put you to use, Sir Perrell."

Perrell forced himself to pay attention. Perhaps, given the
rumor that the queen intended to dismiss her protectors, he
was going to be assigned to serve her in that capacity. It
would, he thought, be interesting work.

"The queen," Theloi was saying, "must marry and produce
heirs quickly in order to prove to her now-anxious subjects
that the Duc du Lindier's curse has no validity. Her womb was
slow to quicken while she was wed to Lervan, and the late
miscarriage may have rendered her barren. She wants to
demonstrate otherwise."

Perrell blinked at such intimate details.

"My sources," Theloi continued, "inform me that she is
willing to take a new husband. Unfortunately, her choice is of
the caliber one can only expect from a foolish, headstrong
young woman. Entirely unsuitable in every way."

"The heretic," Perrell guessed.

"Exactly. For once Lord Salba and I are in complete accord
and unified against such a stupid notion."

Remembering how radiantly the queen had stared at Lord
Talmor in the catacombs, Perrell understood that her emo-
tions had clearly blinded her to the man's impure blood and
tainted upbringing. She had even been heard to claim that
Lord Talmor had saved her life that night, when in fact it was
Perrell and his men who had actually rescued her from the
Sebeins.

But women in love, as Perrell knew from observing his sisters, could be extremely willful, self-deluded, and resistant to
common sense. "How can she seriously contemplate him?" he
asked.

Theloi shook his head. "How are you at wooing pretty
women, reverend commander?"

Surprised, Perrell scrambled to find his tongue. "Out of
practice."

"Why haven't you taken another wife, since your first died?"

"I did not enjoy marriage."

"Oh, come, sir! I find that difficult to believe. By all accounts the lady was a pretty little thing. What could there be to dislike?"

Perrell set his teeth. There were few things he hated more than prying, personal questions. He had found his short marriage to be intensely frustrating and humiliating, and when Araith had died in childbirth he'd been relieved to be rid of her.

"For an ambitious man, Sir Perrell, you are strangely reticent about some matters," the cardinal said. "Shall I answer the question for you? Your father and hers arranged the match in order to seal an exchange of land. She came to you a very young wife, perhaps too young, and was wedded straight from her nuncery school. No doubt she arrived in your bed entirely ignorant of wifely duties. And was she not cold, perhaps even afraid of you? That could sour a marriage quickly, could it not?"

Perrell's stomach was burning. He forced himself to endure Theloi's little theories. The man, he thought angrily, had obviously pried old rumors from Uncle Ardminsil, who loved to gossip. Theloi's information was entirely wrong, but Perrell had no intention of clarifying the errors.

Araith had come from the nuncery already deflowered, as wild as the wind, and indifferent as to whom she bedded. Stableboy or steward or guest were all alike to her. And Perrell's duties and long absences only contributed to the problem. He, so committed to duty, honor, and honesty, had liked her not, nor enjoyed her open flirting with any man in his household. It had hurt his pride to be cuckolded so quickly. He found her sly, as ready to lie as to laugh, a thief who rifled his purse rather than ask for money. Nor had the difference in their ages helped, for along with her tantrums and sulking, she had the slim, small-breasted body of an immature girl and was not to his taste at all.

"The child would have made a difference," he said through

his teeth, repeating the lie he had told his father at the funeral.
"Had they both lived, motherhood would have steadied her."

"No doubt," Theloi said dryly. "But we come back to my
question. Why not marry again? You are intelligent enough to
know that not all women are nervous, silly little idiots."

Perrell thought, *The queen! Does he truly mean to set me
forth as a candidate for her hand?*

"How fare you with courtiers?" Theloi was asking. "Have
you winning manners? Any polish of address? Or have your
years as a soldier so roughened you that you cannot be witty
and flirtatious?"

Perrell's frown deepened. "I am a Gide," he said with involuntary arrogance. "I can hold my own with any courtier
and walk at ease in any palace. I was not raised a bumpkin,
lord eminence."

"Therefore, you will woo the queen."

The very idea of it sent Perrell's mind reeling. "I can try—"

"You must do more than try! You have said you find her
comely."

"Well, yes, lord eminence, but—"

"She favors warriors. Her first infatuation was with Faldain of Nether; her second has been with this heretic bastard
Talmor. You are strong, muscular, possessed of sufficient
looks to win a woman's admiration. Come, sir! Do my compliments not swell your vanity? Have you no confidence?
Where is your ambition?"

Perrell's eyes narrowed. "How far does your eminence
mean me to go? Am I to distract her majesty from thoughts of
the heretic so that she can be persuaded to marry the man chosen for her, or do I pursue her for myself?"

Theloi stared at him with glittering cold eyes. "Ah, now I
see evidence of the famous Gide ambition. Your father
courted Princess Dianthelle and lost her to Lindier. Can you
do better?"

Perrell drew a sharp breath. His family and lineage were
impeccable enough for him to reach for the throne, if he had
enough courage and cunning . . . exactly as the cardinal had
been saying. Excitement swelled Perrell, and he found that he

wanted this very much indeed. He thought of the queen, whom he'd held briefly in his arms. Even bedraggled and injured, she had been beautiful, every inch of her curved and womanly. He allowed himself to think of her as a woman, not as his sovereign, and that was pleasing, too.

"And so, while Lord Salba annoys the queen by arguing against her choice, you will gain her friendship and her love," Theloi said coolly, as though the matter would be simple. "And from there—"

"A woman already in love is not easily won," Perrell said.

"I leave that to you. Meanwhile, I shall—"

"How far will you leave matters to me?" Perrell asked, daring to interrupt. "How much time have I?"

"Little. Events must move quickly."

"She has not forgotten Lord Talmor, and if she's attempting to gain approval for him—"

"She'll never get it," Theloi said with a gesture. "Never."

"The more resistance the council raises against Lord Talmor, the more she'll want him."

"Then what will you do about that?" Theloi asked.

"The best way to gain an advantage over a rival is to remove him from the contest."

"Lord Salba has already done so, and to little effect. She pines over the knave all the more."

"Of course she does," Perrell said. "The more he is forbidden to her, the more she desires him. No, lord eminence, the removal of Lord Talmor must be permanent."

Theloi's cold green eyes locked on his. "As I have said, I leave that entirely up to you."

"He is a baron. His death will bring an investigation."

"I can squelch that," Theloi said impatiently. "Meanwhile, you, reverend commander, are sworn to stamp out heresy wherever you find it. As far as I'm concerned you can kill him in the road like a dog. But for the queen's sake, perhaps you should be more discreet."

Perrell nodded, already turning over ideas in his mind.

"Make certain, however, that the queen never suspects you," Theloi said in warning. "You must win her trust quickly, while I attempt to persuade the Privy Council of your suit-ability."

"If I became one of her majesty's protectors—"

"No, we will not use that route," Theloi said sharply. "There must be a marriage, unassailable, and an heir safely born. Then, reverend commander"—and his cold eyes bored deep into Perrell—"well, let us not plan too far into the future. We have enough to do at present."

Perrell felt the air leave his lungs. He stared at Theloi in fresh concern, not liking the suspicions awakening inside him.

"You will do your duty and follow your orders," Theloi said coldly, as though sensing his doubts. "You are pledged to obey me to the end of your life, sir, even if publicly you re-nounce your order in order to marry the queen."

Perrell nodded.

The cardinal rose to his feet. "You will never escape my will. You will never possess power of your own. You will exist only to shift the political fortunes of the throne *as I de-sire them to be shifted.* That will be your sole purpose if I set you so high. Do you understand?"

"Yes, I understand, lord eminence."

"You will be in a position to fix the fortunes of your fam-ily forever if you succeed in all that I ask. Do you under-stand?"

Just as I can see my entire family destroyed and ruined if I disobey or fail, Perrell thought. "Yes, lord eminence."

"Now, because of the affection I hold for your father and uncles, I shall permit you a choice. Refuse this opportunity, and I shall not hold you to me. You can be posted back on the Kladite border, or perhaps a Netheran patrol instead. And I will trust you to remain forever quiet about what we've dis-cussed tonight."

Would he? Perrell wondered cynically. Or would he order a swift death? It was so easy for an arrow to go astray in bat-tle. Frowning, Perrell found his hands curling into fists at his side. Carefully, he forced them open.

"Or will you seize both risk and opportunity? In time, the

queen will probably give you command over her armies, where you can serve Mandria ably. Furthermore, I believe you capable of steadying her majesty's present weakness of faith. You will be in a position to rejoin crown and church as they were meant to be. And one day, you will father a king."

Theloi stretched out his hand. "What say you, Sir Perrell? What is your choice?"

Perrell dropped to his knees before the cardinal. His heart was beating fast, and his mouth was dry. "I choose to obey your wishes, lord eminence," he said as Theloi smiled. "I will serve you, to the end of my life." He drew the sign of the Circle, then kissed Theloi's ring. "In the name of Tomias do I so swear."

"Swear fully."

Thod help me, Perrell thought, and closed his heart to doubt. "In the name of Tomias will I so serve. Without question. Without hesitation. In all things giving obedience, as I have sworn so to do."

"Then go," Theloi said to him genially, making a swift sign of blessing. "Escort the queen to safety and rid us forever of the heretic. And in all you do, may Tomias grant you success."

Chapter Nineteen

The summer palace, Aversuel, perched on a precipice in the Ildeau Mountains. In contrast to sultry Savroix, the air here was cool and invigorating, the views magnificent. A lake of crystal blue waters surrounded by forests of ash, yewn, linden, and holly was located just north of the palace, and served as the headwaters for the small, swift Aver River, which came gushing down through a series of gorges and ravines to shoot past the edge of the palace grounds in a breathtaking waterfall.

Originally a hunting lodge, the palace had been expanded over the years so that it rambled in a maze of odd-shaped rooms and passages. Pheresa had never liked it, despite its lovely setting, for it was dark and cavelike inside, depressingly masculine, with endless hunting trophies hanging on the walls, animals hides serving as rugs on the stone floors, and so many displays of weapons that she might as well be living in an arsenal.

Verence, an avid huntsman, had adored Aversuel and often dismissed his court at Savroix as early as midspring in order to come here. Pheresa, who occasionally went hawking, but had scant interest in sport, found it dull indeed.

Moreover, news took longer to reach her in the mountains, at a time when she felt most in need of quick reports and plentiful information. Because of the plague, the queen's progress across the realm scheduled for the summer had been canceled. Trade negotiations with Nold were not going well because of competition from Nether, and, although no pestilence had been reported in upland Mandria, the dwarf clans remained aloof and fearful of contact. To avoid plague, no Saelutian ships would venture into lowland Mandrian harbors, and the prices of goods were rising. Lord Meaclan wanted to levy new taxes to pay for Lervan's debts, the coronation, and her depleted treasury. Since her armies were being deployed to the west, the infamous Klad chieftain Bara Tang was threatening to cause new trouble in the east, and the chevards of the border holds wanted support.

Still, Bara Tang was a lesser problem than King Mux, who was demanding the tribute Lervan had promised him. Pheresa had recently sent her army instead of gold, with orders to attack without parley. Today, messengers had arrived to report the outcome of the battle, and she received them in her throne room.

"We took the barbarians by complete surprise, your majesty," one of the messengers boasted. "They tried to rally, but Marechal Ormont's cavalry struck so decisive a blow they did not counterattack. Our valiant infantry chased them off the very beaches. If only we could have had ships ready to smash their longboats, they would have been annihilated."

"A great Mandrian victory," the second messenger chimed in, grinning. "Our losses were few, and theirs many."

"And good riddance!" Lady Carolie declared with such ferocity that Pheresa smiled.

"Splendid news," she declared. "This pleases me well, and I shall send Marechal Ormont my highest commendation."

The messengers bowed to her, and throughout the throne room the courtiers applauded. Still smiling, Pheresa bestowed rewards on the messengers, who swaggered out beneath the admiring eyes of blushing ladies and hero-worshiping little pages.

"Oh, majesty," Lady Carolie said, "may we celebrate this victory?"

"And what would please you?" Pheresa asked indulgently, already knowing the answer.

"A ball, your majesty. With dancing and feasting and more dancing!"

Pheresa's smile dimmed, and her heart felt pinched with envy. Pretty Lady Carolie, always so cheerful, so ready to flirt with her husband or any handsome man, loved entertainments. But without Talmor present, Pheresa found the other men in her court dull fellows, especially Alain de Camin, the latest suitor to pester her. He was five years her junior, callow, conceited, and a dead bore. She did not want to dance; more importantly, she did not want to watch others dancing and making merry.

But she checked the refusal that came to her lips, for she was aware that her court needed cheering in this summer of plague and uncertainty.

"A ball it shall be," she proclaimed.

Lady Carolie clapped her hands in delight. Courtiers exchanged amazed smiles, and even the dour old Duchesse du Meringare brightened. A pleased murmur of anticipation ran through the room.

"A ball *and* a banquet feast," Pheresa declared. "To celebrate our victory. Soon we shall drive these skull folk from our shores forever!"

Amidst the laughter, applause, and sudden excited buzzing of plans that filled the room, Lord Salba, who'd been busily conversing with Lord Meaclan, paused to send her a solemn look. Pheresa pretended to ignore it. She understood perfectly that this battle would provoke terrible reprisals from the Vvordsmen and perhaps launch a full-scale war, but she refused to pay tribute even temporarily to buy a measure of time. She refused to negotiate for new terms with Mux, whom she considered a common bandit.

Coming to her side, Lord Salba bowed, and murmured, "Perhaps too much jubilation is a trifle premature, your majesty?"

She frowned at him. Because of his efforts in driving Talmor from court, she no longer held her lord chancellor in much favor. He was necessary, for she relied on his political astuteness, but he'd made her private life a misery. With each passing day, she missed Talmor more than ever, and she blamed Salba for it.

"The people need cheering," she replied shortly. "And if my marechals would advise me on developing a cohesive set of tactics to rid us truly of these skull folk instead of fighting piecemeal according to individual strategies, we could smash Mux's forces for good."

Salba raised his heavy brows. "And if your majesty would choose a replacement for Lindier capable of leading these marechals, the army might be restored to its former glory and efficiency."

Frowning, she curled frustrated fists in her lap. She wanted to give Talmor that position, and Salba kept blocking his nomination, saying the Privy Council would never agree to award him so much power.

"Is your majesty free now for today's lesson?" Sir Georges du Maltie murmured politely.

His interruption was a relief, for she was weary of quarreling with Lord Salba. Glancing around, Pheresa saw no one of much importance still waiting to address her. Beckoning to her chamberlain, she told him that her audience was at an end for the day.

As the announcement was made, she rose to her feet. At once her courtiers made obeisance to her, and the musicians ceased to play their soft music. She left the room with her ladies and Sir Georges in attendance. A few men sneered at him as usual and would have probably turned their backs to snub him had Pheresa not been present. She eyed such bigoted fools with impatience.

Sir Georges du Maltie had come to her service recently. Middle-aged, rangy, and as tall as his younger brother Thum, this stolid uplander possessed the du Maltie freckles, but his hair was brown instead of red. Pheresa remembered Lord Thum, now minister of state in Nether, with affection as a highly intelligent, well-favored young man. His brother was not as polished in address, not as quick of wit, but Sir Georges's character seemed steady and self-assured. His hazel eyes were direct and honest, and Pheresa had liked his blunt, no-nonsense manner from the moment of his arrival. Not inclined to vanity, Sir Georges knew exactly why he'd been summoned to court. He put on no airs, attempted to impress no one, and if sometimes he looked wide-eyed at the resplendent clothing and furnishings around him he kept to his simple ways, spoke in his uplander accent without apology, and wore his unfashionable clothing without embarrassment.

Lord Avlon—reputedly furious—had been dismissed as the queen's night protector, and Sir Georges was appointed in his stead. On the very first evening he came on duty, he'd sprinkled salt on the windowsills and thresholds of Pheresa's bedchamber, filled a large basin with more salt by her bedside, examined her magicked dagger with a nod of cautious approval, and took up a stance outside her door with his drawn sword resting across his arm. He did not smirk at her, or roll his eyes at her fears when he thought she was not looking, and never questioned that somehow Nonkind were infiltrating lowland Mandria.

Pheresa found his presence to be a tremendous relief. Although her sleep remained troubled by Sebein nightmares, for the first time since Talmor's departure she felt that her safety was in competent hands.

Each afternoon, the uplander gave Pheresa's lessons with dagger and thinsword. Garbed in leggings and a long tunic split like a hauberk to allow her freedom of movement, she feinted and parried, stumbling to learn footwork, while her ladies-in-waiting watched from a safe distance beneath a shady canopy. Plying their needles, hiding their shocked disapproval, they gossiped and yawned while Sir Georges patiently called out instruction and encouragement to the queen.

The lessons lasted roughly an hour, sometimes less if she were called away by Lord Salba to deal with dispatches. Most of the time, at the end of her fighting lesson, she found Sir Perrell waiting with her groom and a saddled courser to escort her for a ride through the forest.

Although wary of him, she'd found such outings left her invigorated and refreshed from the problems of governance. Moreover, Sir Perrell's conversation held her interest, for he did not waste time flattering her.

The fact that he'd treated her guardsmen and his knights the same during their journey to Aversuel, dividing duties equally between them, had commended him initially to her favor. Rather than foment trouble by crowding his men into the palace barracks, the reverend commander had instead established a separate camp for the church knights on the shores of the lake. The guards manned the palace, and the church knights patrolled the forest and roads. Thus far, it had worked well.

She'd grown to admire the reverend commander's efficiency, quiet manners, cleanly habits and appearance, and unobtrusive piety.

Nor had she forgotten Sir Perrell's part in her rescue from the catacombs. Were there more reverend commanders of his integrity and worth, she thought, the army of the church would be vastly improved.

This afternoon, emerging from behind the screen where she'd exchanged her tunic for more proper riding attire, Pheresa thanked Sir Georges graciously for her lesson and hurried to greet Sir Perrell, who bowed to her with one of his rather serious smiles.

In the sunlight, his thick auburn hair shone and glinted with hues ranging from gold to copper to chestnut. It fascinated her, for never had she seen its equal, and her younger ladies-in-waiting declared themselves to be jealous of such glorious hair.

But his gaze never failed to unsettle her. She avoided it now as she and her ladies-in-waiting were assisted onto their horses, and the queen's party headed into the forest. Blue eyes were rare in Mandria, and light blue eyes were always suspect, for they usually indicated eldin blood. Although Sir Per-

rell's were dark, nearly a sapphire blue, Pheresa hated any re-
minders of Gavril, who'd possessed such eyes as well and
symbolized the most horrid period of her life.

She could not help wishing, despite the excellence of Sir
Perrell's company, that it was another man who accompanied
her on these gentle outings, a man with unruly black curls, a
man whose skin turned a dark bronze in summertime, a man
with golden eyes like sunlight in honey.

"We have good news this day," she said, stroking the neck
of her gray mare. "A victory against the Vvordsmen."

"So I heard," Sir Perrell said. "Congratulations, your
majesty."

Something in his tone made her frown. "You consider this
no victory?" she asked sharply. "Do you share Lord Salba's
opinion in believing this aggression will cause us further trouble?"

"If the Vvordsmen have been routed and no tribute paid,
then that is a decisive victory, your majesty."

Her pleasure in delivering the news had cooled. "I'm glad
you think so."

His gaze flicked to meet hers as though he understood why
her tone had turned impatient. "The summer is but half-gone,"
he said. "They have time to rally and retaliate before winter
closes the seas."

"You're another pessimist. Why not believe we have discouraged them?"

"False hopes are worse than none. They are fierce warriors, and they seem driven."

"Driven? How?"

"In meeting any foe it's critical to understand why a man
is fighting and what he is fighting for. If it's only a simple
raid for horses or food or women, then his motivation is
weak, and that man can be discouraged. But if he is fighting
for defense of his home, his heart is fierce, and he will not
give up."

"The Vvordsmen are raiders and thieves," she said dismis-
sively. "They come to pillage, not defend their hearths. As
long as we meekly hand them whatever gold they demand,

they have every reason to return. But when we give them steel instead of gold, and death instead of acquiescence, then they will leave us in peace."

"But is your majesty so sure tribute is all they want?"

Pheresa grew thoughtful. She found his questions unusual and intriguing. "What think you?"

Sir Perrell shrugged. "I would have to see and fight them to be sure of my guess, but I sense desperation behind their attacks. Yes, I realize that since they sacked the palace and treasury they have demanded gold, but what have they taken more than anything else?"

She frowned. "Captives for slaves."

"Well, yes, but they go after food, majesty. They always raid villages that have just brought in large catches of fish."

Startled, Pheresa thought over the reports she'd read. "I believe you are right."

"Consider, majesty, how late they start raiding each year. They wait until early or midsummer, when the villages have smoked ample stores of fish. They like the gold, but 'tis food they need."

It made sense. Pheresa felt her worry grow. "If they are hungry, they'll—"

"If they are *starving*, majesty, they will not be driven back until the last man is dead. And why should they brave the rough seas, risk the dangers, and throw themselves on our swords if they are not driven to it?"

"Perhaps they are lazy rather than hungry," she countered. "They might prefer to steal food rather than catch it for themselves."

"Perhaps," he agreed mildly. "Your majesty will soon know if they continue to return."

He moved his horse ahead of hers as the trail narrowed and grew steep. In single file they pressed through a stretch where the wild laurels, blooming pink and fragrant, nearly engulfed the trail. So interlaced were the branches that the groom had to hold them aside for Pheresa to pass. As usual, the forest teemed with game. She saw deer aplenty and also vixlets scuttling to cover. A hill mouse, so fat from acorns, seeds, and berries that it waddled rather than ran, moved behind a fallen log and peered out with beady, fearless eyes.

Past the laurels, they emerged into a small clearing where the late-afternoon sunlight fell on a dazzling carpet of color. Tiny wildflowers of scarlet covered the ground. Bees droned everywhere, so laden with pollen they could barely fly. The ladies-in-waiting called out in delight.

It was so enchanting that Pheresa sighed with pleasure. Throwing Sir Perrell a smile, she laughingly accepted the bouquet that Lady Carolie had already picked for her.

It pleased her to dismount for a short time and walk through the flowers. Sir Perrell escorted her, saying little, and Pheresa was content to savor the beauty of the place. *If only I could walk here with Talmor,* she thought, and felt her momentary happiness fade. She sighed aloud.

"Tired, majesty?" Sir Perrell asked her. "Perhaps your sword lessons are too fatiguing in combination with your ride."

She shook her head. Her body felt strong and vigorous. She'd never been healthier. It was only her heart that felt weary and lost, besieged by the unyielding disapproval that surrounded the man she loved. Of course, she could have Talmor, if she sent for him in secret, if she loved him in secret as though ashamed of him. But she wanted him openly, proudly, honorably. Why did that have to be impossible?

Suddenly the clearing lost its enchantment. The strange little scarlet flowers were starting to close as the sun dipped lower behind the trees.

"It pleases the queen to depart," she announced abruptly.

At once her ladies stopped picking bouquets and headed obediently to where the horses were cropping grass at the edge of the trees. Sir Perrell, however, hesitated.

Squinting into the sun, so that lines crinkled at the corners of his vivid eyes, he said with unusual awkwardness, "Your majesty, I must ask—that is—I must inform you that I won't be able to escort you tomorrow. I hope today has pleased you sufficiently to balance any disappointment."

"What mean you?" she asked. "Have you been reassigned?"

"No. It's just that I must investigate a certain matter in a nearby village."

"Sebeins," she said at once, her instincts prickling. "Have they been sighted here?"

"No, your majesty. Not exactly."

Dread sank through her. "Plague?"

He evaded her gaze. "I will not trouble your majesty with theories until I have determined the exact problem."

"It's plague," she said. "Why must you church knights be so secretive? How close to Aversuel does it come?"

"A half day's ride from here, to the south."

"That's very close!"

"Do not be alarmed," he said, holding out his hand. "'Tis why I prefer to know the situation before I speak much of it. People will panic if they hear this news."

She glanced at her ladies, happily chattering among themselves, and nodded. "I do not wish to be deprived of your company. Can your men not deal with the matter?"

Her question seemed to please him. "No. I—I have special training for this sort of thing. I am needed."

"How long will you be away?"

"Perhaps a fortnight."

"That long?" she asked, startled. "I thought you said the trouble was nearby."

"Yes, your majesty, but they leave trails that must be followed. Even if my return is sooner, I must see to increased vigilance from our patrols to guard your majesty's safety."

She studied him, curious as to why he seemed so ill at ease. Something was troubling him, something he did not wish to tell her. And why, she wondered, had he chosen a flower-strewn meadow instead of her own audience chamber to inform her of his departure?

Is he in love with me?

She wondered suddenly about the daily rides, the special places he found to show her, his shy smiles and sudden, awkward silences, the way he stood now, with broad shoulders a little crooked against the sky, his auburn head lowered, and his gaze brooding into the distance. Was he sulking a little, she wondered, because his duty called him away from her? Was he missing her company already?

She almost smiled, but then did not, for she suddenly felt deeply sorry for him. In the past, she had known what it was like to love unrequited, to extend heart and hope and be rejected.

Poor Sir Perrell, she thought, wondering how to be kind to him without encouraging emotions she could not return.

"Thank you for telling me," she said aloud, and began walking toward the others, so that he was obliged to follow. "I shall look forward to a report of your success."

"Your majesty," he said.

She glanced back over her shoulder. "Yes, Sir Perrell?"

"Be careful while I am away, and do not go riding."

"But I have formed the habit, and it pleases me to continue," she said. "I have Sir Georges or Sir Lorne, as well as the grooms. I can attach extra guardsmen to the party if necessary."

"Your majesty, with reports of Sebeins so close by . . . I do not wish to alarm you, but I urge you to take the greatest precautions."

"They will not dictate my daily routine! Already they have disrupted too many of this summer's plans."

"Please, your majesty's safety is paramount."

"What else have you not told me?" she asked with quick suspicion. "So much concern cannot spring from a single report. What else has happened?"

Frowning, he said, "I have told your majesty all I can."

Which she considered no answer at all.

Annoyed, she climbed onto her mare. Although she'd intended to ask his advice about the shadowy watchers she saw frequently in her dreams, watchers she feared were Sebeins, she changed her mind.

Sir Perrell was a minion of Cardinal Theloi's, she reminded herself, and as such, not to be completely trusted. No matter how much she liked him, she was certain he spied on her and reported back to the old spider.

Jerking the reins through her hands, she told herself she would do better to confide in Sir Georges du Maltie if she chose to tell anyone, and rode away without speaking to Sir Perrell again.

Chapter Twenty

A still summer's night . . . Pheresa tossed and turned restlessly. She was dreaming about a cradle draped with the royal
crest. It was a handsome cradle, magnificently carved, fit for
a tiny prince. But when she looked over the side at the infant
within, she saw the tiny form convulsing. Blood soaked the
bedding, and the baby was screaming. A man stood nearby
watching. Robed in black, his face hidden by a cowled hood,
he did nothing to help the child. The wails grew louder and
louder, and Pheresa cried out. She rushed to lift the baby, but
as she gathered it into her arms, it jerked one last time and
died.

Horrified, she shuddered awake, and lay sobbing. "Just a
dream," she whispered aloud. "Just a terrible dream."

"Only a dream, Pheresa of Mandria?" asked a soft voice
that made her scramble back against the carved head of her
bed. Someone drew open the bed hangings, allowing a shaft
of moonlight to spill into the dark confines of her bed. She
saw a robed silhouette standing there, staring at her.
"Dream?" the voice repeated. "Or prophecy?"

Terrified, she jerked in rapid breaths and could not seem to move. She did not know whether this was reality or another nightmare. All else was quiet and shadow. From the next room she could hear delicate snores from her ladies-in-waiting. Verine sat slumped over in a chair by the door, oblivious to the intruder. And her protector?

"Here," her visitor said as though he could read her thoughts. "But of no use to you."

As he spoke, he stepped aside and pointed.

Craning her neck, Pheresa caught a glimpse of a shadow lying on the floor. Sir Georges was either dead, drugged, or spell hit, she realized. There was no one else to help her, and this Sebein watcher had stepped out of her dreams into her chamber, exactly as Kolahl had done years ago. Her heart began to thud painfully fast.

"Did you enjoy the dream?" the Sebein whispered, gloating. "I thought it would interest you to see the future your Gantese enemies have planned for you."

Pheresa felt icy cold. Frantically, she groped beneath her pillow for her dagger, but could not find it. "My—my father's curse will never come true," she said defiantly.

"I have come to finish the Rite of Blood," the Sebein said, "and when you are ours we can protect you from such curses. Your children will be our children. Your—"

"Get away from me!" she screamed. Lunging at the bedside table, she grabbed a handful of salt and flung it at him.

But he dodged and grabbed her by the arm, pulling her toward him despite her flailing struggles. When she saw moonlight glinting on his knife blade, she strove with all her might to break free.

His strength outmatched hers, however, and when she tried to scream for help he pressed a hand over her mouth. And all the while he was whispering in her ear, uttering terrible words she did not understand that made her feel dizzy and ill. He was, she feared, enspelling her.

He laughed, his breath puffing hot against her ear. "Did you think you would escape Bokune so easily? Did you think you would not pay the price we have demanded for generations?"

She bit his finger so hard she drew blood. It spurted, bitter and hot, into her mouth, while he yelled in pain and struck her with his fist.

Stunned from the blow, she landed facedown on the bed, and groggily tried to stay conscious.

"May Chaos and Xabrath damn you," he muttered. "I come to offer you immortality, and still you resist."

Her head was clearing a little. She gripped the rumpled bedclothes and inched her way forward, hoping this time to find her dagger. It had not killed him the last time, for whatever Bokune was, he was not a man, but there was enough power in the dagger's magicked blade to hurt him enough even for her to break free. That was all she needed, just a chance to run, until she could rouse the palace and find help.

Desperately, she ran her hands through the blankets and dug beneath the pillows. Just as her fingers touched the hilt of the dagger, however, Bokune grabbed her legs and pulled her back.

She lunged desperately for the weapon, and her hand just missed closing on it as he flipped her onto her back and pinned her. She arched in his hold, kicking and struggling with all her might, but he laughed at her.

"Not this time," he said. "I know your tricks, and by now you should know exactly who and what I am, if the priests have finally told you. Have they, Pheresa of Mandria?"

"No," she gasped, and dragged in enough breath to scream.

"Don't bother to cry for help," he said. "No one can hear you. In a moment you shall be pulled into my dream, into a place where no one can save you. The Rite will be completed as it was destined to be."

"You can't," she said. "My blood will poison you as it did before. The Chalice and my faith protect me."

His small knife nicked her wrist, and she cried out more in fear than in pain. "Not this time," he said. "I am prepared now. I am stronger."

As he lifted her bleeding wrist to his mouth, Pheresa kicked him in the midsection as hard as she could.

With a grunt, he went staggering away from the bed. Rolling over, she scrambled for the dagger and got it. When she pulled it forth, its blade was glowing a brilliant white, which filled her chamber with radiance.

Bokune was still hunched over, moaning and gasping. He lifted his forearm as though to shield his eyes from the light, and snarled something.

Warned only by instinct, Pheresa held the dagger with both hands before her face and ducked. The spell hit her shoulder, and although it was only a glancing blow, she felt herself go tumbling off the bed and onto the floor, landing with an impact that jarred her entire body. Unable to move, dizzy and sick, she uttered a little moaning sob in the back of her throat.

As though from far away, she heard Bokune's footsteps thudding toward her.

There was bright light shining around her, so bright her dazzled eyes streamed with tears. Blinking, she turned her gaze toward the dagger, which still lay in her loosely curled hand. With all her remaining willpower she tightened her grip around it, and something warm and alive inside the hilt tingled against her flesh, rousing her.

Bokune yanked her upright. While she swayed and stumbled, he shook her roughly, snarling things that made the air crackle and pop around their heads. His words were like verbal slaps. She flinched in pain each time he spoke, but she did not drop her weapon.

The dagger was still glowing in her fist, keeping her conscious and feeding her will to fight. Through the confusion in her mind, she dimly recalled one of Sir Georges's lessons and let herself slump against Bokune.

He staggered to catch her and prop her against the bed. An unlit candle went rolling off the small table and clattered on the floor.

"Stand up!" he said. "Do not faint. You are not bleeding that much."

With her free hand Pheresa gripped the salt basin and threw its contents in his face. As he hissed and writhed, lifting both hands to his eyes, she plunged the dagger into his chest.

Knocking her aside, he wheeled blindly and went stumbling away. Verine jerked awake as though released from a spell, jumped to her feet, and screamed.

Pheresa stood illuminated by the pale white light of the dagger, the weapon held aloft in her hand, her golden hair streaming loose on her shoulders, salt and blood staining her nightgown.

Across the room, Bokune blundered into furniture, shoving it furiously out of his way. As she watched him, Pheresa's heart went like thunder in her chest, threatening to burst. As long as he stayed between her and the door, she could not escape. Verine was still screaming, and now Pheresa also shouted for help.

Sir Georges, moaning and clutching his head, sat up on the rug.

"Georges!" she shrieked. "Get him!"

The protector staggered to his feet and sent her a dazed look before swinging his broadsword down across Bokune's back.

With a hoarse, guttural cry, the Sebein fell to his knees. Blood gurgled in his throat, and Verine threw herself at the door connecting to the next chamber, pounding on it with her fists and screaming for help.

"Majesty," Sir Georges said in a thin, breathless voice. Swaying, he held out his hand. "Your dagger."

When she ran to him to hand over her weapon, the dagger seemed to twist in her grasp, and she could not release it.

Afraid, she tried to fling it away, but Sir Georges caught her wrist.

"Quick!" he said. "Drive it hard through his throat. Both hands. Thrust straight through."

Her courage faltered, but at that moment Bokune, who was still hunched on his knees despite the terrible gash in his back, began to straighten. A black mist was spreading around him.

Sketching a Circle, Sir Georges retreated. "Too late," he said. "Thod help us now."

Pheresa realized this was the only chance they had. Just as Bokune started to his feet, she struck with all her might. His own movement carried him onto the blade, helping her drive it into the base of his throat and up toward his jaw, exactly as Sir Georges had instructed her.

Bokune's eyes flared open wide. When he opened his mouth, more blood and black mist spilled from his jaws. They should have drenched her arms, but the dagger's light shielded her, and she felt not even a splatter.

His face caved in as though the very bones were crumbling, then he collapsed in a small heap of ashes and dust at her feet.

Pheresa stood there, panting hard for breath, unable to believe what she'd just witnessed. The radiance slowly dimmed from the blade until only moonlight illuminated her bedchamber. The hilt was no longer warm and alive in her hand. It was only an inanimate weapon, and she could release it if she chose.

Her fingers opened, and she dropped it, stepping back.

She and Sir Georges exchanged a single, wordless glance. Again, he sketched the sign of the Circle. She wanted to do the same, but she was trembling so much she could not command her limbs.

There came the scrape of a strikebox, and flame suddenly created a harsh light that made Pheresa squint and blink. Verine was lighting the lamps and candles, her face drawn with fright.

"My lady!" she cried, rushing to clutch Pheresa. "Oh, my dear queen, are you all right?"

Slowly Pheresa realized that she was, despite the cut on her wrist. Sir Georges swiftly bound it for her, although already the bleeding was slowing. In the darkness or in his haste, Bokune had missed making the deep cut he so obviously intended.

"Forgive me, your majesty," Sir Georges said hoarsely, still looking shaken. He ran bloody fingers through his hair, ruffling it in all directions. "I don't know what happened. I could see the creature, hear him, but I couldn't move until you fought him. How did he get in?"

"Sebeins have terrible ways of magic," she whispered, and heard a voice call out a belated query in the next room. "Verine!" she said sharply. "Go and rouse the guards. The spell must have affected them, too."

"Yes, majesty."

"Send also for a physician, but do not let my ladies enter. They should not see this." As she spoke, she gestured at the disordered room, the bed slashed and torn, the overturned tables, the salt lying in mounds on the floor, and the heap of ashes and immoral filth that had been Bokune. "Go!"

The servant hurried out, weeping and pressing the hem of her overskirt to her face. Pheresa herself slammed the door in the curious faces of her ladies and bolted it.

Sir Georges stared at her in consternation. "Majesty?"

Pheresa wasn't listening. Instead, she was thinking rapidly and more clearly than she had in a long time. She foresaw endless questions, speculations, worry, and quibbling as her advisers debated what should be done. The church knights would come and examine the room. They would take away the evidence and keep their secrets. She knew she would be hemmed in even more closely than before, scrutinized and watched at every moment, never left alone. But despite all that, she would not be one jot safer. Right now, before the guards arrived, was her only chance to act.

She turned to Sir Georges. "Talmor must come to me."

"Majesty?"

"Lord Talmor of Edriel. I want you to fetch him right away, this instant."

"But I can't leave you—"

"You're the only one I trust to get through. I can't send a letter. It would be intercepted. But this meddling is at an end. I won't be stopped, not this time. Swear to me that you'll bring him."

"Yes," the man said in bewilderment. "If your majesty wishes it, I'll fetch the man, but what if another Sebein gets in?"

"They won't try again, at least not right away," she said with a confidence she did not feel. What she was saying was probably foolish, but she did not care. Even Sir Georges, for all his experience, could not withstand the Sebein spells, and she did not trust the church knights enough to ask them for protection. Only Talmor's advice could she rely on now.

Hurrying to her desk, she yanked out a pen and a scrap of parchment, and hastily scribbled out a pass.

"This will get you through any checkpoint on the roads," she said, handing it over. "Tell no one your business if you can help it. When you reach Edriel, speak to no one save the baron. Tell him all that transpired tonight and say that I need him to come to me without delay."

"But, majesty, how will you—"

"Oh, hurry!" she said, hearing the sound of booted feet. "They're coming. Don't let anyone stop you." Running to the servants' door, she flung it open and handed him a lamp to light the dark passageway beyond. Go, Sir Georges! Hurry! And Thod be with you."

He sent her a last, worried look and ducked into the passageway just as her chamber door was flung open and guards rushed in. Lord Avlon was leading them, with Sir Lorne at his shoulder.

"Majesty! What has happened?"

"Sebeins!" she cried, pointing at Bokune's black robe lying on the floor. "They enspelled my attendants and sought to abduct me from my chamber. Sir Georges has gone in pursuit. You must find them and drive them from the palace! And bid Sir Perrell to come here at once."

For once Lord Avlon was all business, with no mockery or sarcasm evident. He exchanged a sharp look with Sir Lorne, who stationed himself at once beside Pheresa.

"I'm coming on duty as of now," he said. "The uplander's an amateur, deserting your majesty this way. Don't know nothing."

"We'll find these demons, your majesty," Lord Avlon said. Saluting Pheresa, he spun on his heel and strode out, barking orders to the other men.

After that, Pheresa's ladies and attendants rushed in to escort her away to different chambers. Half of them were hysterical and crying. The others were staring at Pheresa wide-eyed and shaken, as though unsure of how she had survived. With the excitement over, cold shock was setting in, and Pheresa wanted to huddle next to a warm fire and cry.

She held back her tears, however, aware this was not the time for public hysterics. After the previous Sebein attack, she'd succumbed to her injury with the result that Lord Salba and her Privy Council had seized the reins of government and exceeded their authority far too much. She had no intention of letting that happen again.

Accordingly, she sat in calm submission during the careful examination of the physicians. After that, a gray-haired church knight named Sir Barthol came. Pheresa, belatedly recalling that Sir Perrell was away on his mission, gave Sir Barthol permission to question her. He did so carefully, his voice gentle but his eyes probing and observant. He asked if the Sebein had touched her. If he had placed any substance on her skin or in her mouth. He requested the physician to unbind Pheresa's wrist so that he could examine the small wound.

She sighed. It was the same procedure as before, as though these examiners were trained to ask questions by rote.

"He gave me no poison," she said impatiently.

Sir Barthol regarded her gravely. "Perhaps. We cannot be too careful with your majesty's safety."

Then why didn't you guard my dreams? Pheresa wanted to shout at him, but she held her tongue. This was not the man, any more than Sir Perrell had been, to confide in.

She was exhausted now, her nerves shredded, and all she wanted to do was lie down in peace and sleep. But she knew that there could be no peace, no easy slumber for her, until Talmor was here. She prayed that he would disregard whatever had been said to keep him so long from her side.

Please, oh Thod, she prayed fervently. *Please let him come to me soon.*

•   •   •

At daybreak, the sound of galloping hooves caught Sir Perrell's attention. Bare-chested and clad only in leggings and boots, he straightened from the leather bucket of icy mountain stream water and dried himself with a towel handed over by his squire.

A rider in a white surcoat with black circles came thundering into camp and reined up sharply before him, dismounting with a salute.

"What have you to report?" Perrell asked.

"We've caught a man on the road, a traveler alone, with nothing to explain himself. All he has is this." The sentry handed over a scrap of parchment.

Perrell took it with a frown and recognized the queen's agitated writing. "A pass, signed by her majesty's hand."

"Yes, sir."

"Who is he?"

"He won't say, sir. We haven't tried to beat it out of him yet."

"Don't," Perrell said. He was thinking rapidly, and felt a quickening of his pulse. "Whither is he bound?"

"He won't say, but he was heading east when we caught him."

"Let him go."

The sentry frowned in bewilderment. "Sir?"

"Let him go. And give him back his pass," Perrell said, handing over the parchment.

"Do we follow him?"

"No, I know where he's going. Release him at once!"

The sentry saluted and rode away.

Nodding to himself, and feeling anticipation rushing through his veins, Perrell turned around for his tunic. Sir Cortaine was there instead of his squire to hand it to him. Their eyes met briefly.

"So the queen's finally gotten a messenger through all the guards and spies around her," Cortaine said softly. "Why let the varlet go?"

"He's going to do our job for us," Perrell replied. "There's no need for us to ride all the way to Edriel now. The baron will come to us."

Cortaine scowled. "So you're back to dancing attendance on her majesty?"

"No," Perrell said. "It's best if she still thinks me very busy chasing Sebeins. I don't want her to know I am in the vicinity at all when her baron falls afoul of a Sebein ambush and is slain."

"And who better than us Sebein hunters to know how to stage such an attack, eh?" Cortaine said with a chuckle.

Perrell frowned at the tunic he was unconsciously crushing between his hands. He felt none of Cortaine's amusement, only a grim determination to end this as quickly as possible. "Who indeed?" he echoed coldly.

Chapter Twenty-one

A cloudless sky, hazy from heat, arched over the jousting field at Edriel. No breeze stirred to cool the spectators gathering on the grassy slope overlooking the field, but no one seemed to mind. People reclined on their elbows in the grass beneath small awnings, fanning themselves and drinking the ale and water generously supplied from the baron's kegs. Pennons hung limply from poles, and a thin cloud of dust could be seen along the road leading up to the villa as more people from neighboring towns and villages continued to arrive. But the chevard of Templan Hold was not among them.

Lord Feteusil of Kauf Hold had arrived early this morning with much fanfare and pomp. A bearded man clad in splendid garments and sweating profusely from the heat, Chevard Feteusil had brought fifty knights of his fighting force. Their lances, painted white, shone in the sunlight as they rode in well-drilled formation, wheeling through the portcullis into the bailey of the fortress end of the villa and dismounting in unison.

Watching from his tower window, Talmor had been impressed. But although tempted to hurry down to the bailey to greet his guests, he restrained himself. It would be better, he'd decided, to keep strictly to the formalities required by this occasion. And so he allowed Lutel, as steward of the household, to appear on the steps in greeting, welcoming Lord Feteusil, his lady wife, and bevy of assorted children indoors.

Now, with the noonday sun blazing down, Talmor looked once more out the tower window at the emptying road and sighed. Somehow, despite all his care, his father must have heard the truth of his identity and refused to come. It was time for the festivities to begin, and thus far not a single knight or lord from Templan Hold was in evidence.

Scorched with humiliation, Talmor bowed his head. His father's stance could not be more plain, and now Talmor would have to deal with that defiance by either forcing Lord Juroc to accept him as liege or divesting him of his title and holdings.

"Damn," he said aloud.

"M'lord?" Pears said softly. "Time for the speeches."

Knowing there was nothing he could do about his recalcitrant father today, Talmor pushed regret, bitter disappointment, and anger aside to be dealt with later. He had to get through his first speech as baron, and there were the official ceremonies to endure before jousting could begin.

"Aye," Pears said, fussing with the folds in Talmor's cloak, draped over his right shoulder to conceal his missing arm, "ye look fine today, as fine a lord as any in Mandria. And now there's none from Templan to unsettle ye, damn 'em, so put aside yer worries and enjoy the day."

Talmor frowned at him, finding scant comfort in what Pears obviously meant as reassurance. "None from Templan," he echoed darkly. "Which means war for us next week."

"Never mind that now," Pears said, brushing lint from his master's tunic of black linen. "I figured ye was just pining to compete."

Talmor sighed again. "Aye," he admitted. "I miss it sorely."

"No good wishing for what's gone forever," Pears said, tidying up so busily he avoided the sharp glance Talmor shot at him.

Refusing to dwell on his squire's homilies, Talmor headed down the long, spiraling staircase, with Sir Nedwin at his heels.

Outdoors, Canae was waiting for him. Saddled and brushed to a sheen, the warhorse snorted at the sight of him and eagerly shook a long mane braided with ribbons. Talmor eyed these with scorn and gestured for the groom to remove them. From the corner of his eye he saw Pears and Sir Nedwin exchanging looks, their faces contorted with the effort not to grin.

Sir Meine was standing at attention in the bailey yard. When Talmor rode into sight, an order rang out, and his knights crashed their swords against their shields in unison.

Talmor rode down their line to inspect them, and approved of what he saw. In their short time in his service, they were already responding well to the rigorous drills he insisted on, becoming bonded into a proper fighting unit worthy of his flag.

"Very good, Sir Meine," he said.

The master-at-arms puffed out his chest. "All's ready, my lord!"

With a nod, Talmor rode out beneath the portcullis gate and down the hill to the jousting ground, his knights following in escort. A lusty cheer rose from the crowd as he came into sight, with people jumping to their feet to wave at him.

A little surprised by their enthusiasm, Talmor lifted his hand in return, while the cynical part of him reflected on what a few weeks of good management, firm discipline, and generous supplies of free ale, food, and entertainment could accomplish. Beneath him, Canae began to prance, tossing his head eagerly and pulling at the bit.

"Ah, you know the joust, don't you, old fellow?" Talmor murmured to him, stroking his neck. Stifling a fresh pang of regret at not getting to compete, Talmor impulsively pandered to the crowd by making Canae rear and leap forward in a battle cavort.

The crowd loved it and yelled for more, but Talmor felt he had showed off enough and rode forward to the viewing stand that had been erected for today's purpose. Fashioned of wood and equipped with a few benches and a canopy to cast shade, it commanded the best view of the field.

Dismounting before it, Talmor climbed the steps and stood before the assembly. He waited nervously for the people to grow quiet. After a lifetime of trying to stay in the background and attract as little attention to himself as possible, Talmor was finding it hard to change.

When the cheers faded at last, he spoke to the crowd, bidding his distinguished guests welcome. Three wealthy merchants and their assorted entourages sat between Lord Feteusil's party and the empty seats where Lord Juroc and his family should have been. Talmor mentioned the merchants with a few remarks of appreciation that made them smile and bow to him, and he referred briefly to his plans for populace and villages. However, his years of close observation of royal panoply had taught him to keep official remarks short. And if his tone was rather gruff, no one seemed to mind.

When he finished he was cheered again. He sat with a sense of profound relief. His master-at-arms, protector, and steward stood at attention behind his chair, making a thin entourage where friends, family, and hangers-on should have been gathered. As the Edriel knights positioned their matched bay horses in a double line leading up to where Talmor sat, a buzz of anticipation rose from the crowd. Talmor signaled for the herald to call for the pledge of vassals.

Although Templan Hold held precedence over Kauf, since Lord Juroc was absent, the name of Lord Feteusil was called first. Feteusil stepped out of the crowd, a vivid figure in his bright blue tunic and crimson leggings. Puffing and red-faced from the heat, he walked past the long line of knights and knelt a little self-consciously at the steps to Talmor's viewing stand.

"Baron of Edriel," Feteusil said loudly according to rote, "I, Feteusil, Chevard of Kauf, do hereby pledge my service and loyalty to thee as vassal to liege and claim thee as lord over me, my men-at-arms, and all that I own. I will serve thee unto death. So do I swear."

Talmor, his throat choked at hearing the pledge, held forth

his sword. It took all his strength to extend the heavy weapon fully with one hand and hold it steady, but he had practiced hard to manage it and was rewarded by seeing Feteusil's quick look of respect as the man came up the steps to him.

"Lord Feteusil," Talmor said, remembering to project his voice loud and clearly across the silence, "I do accept your pledge and loyalty as my vassal with thanks."

Drawing his own sword, Feteusil briefly slid it beneath Talmor's blade before lowering it. Their eyes met, Feteusil's gaze suddenly wide and nervous as he now observed Talmor close-up.

Do I look a proper baron to him? Talmor wondered.

Certainly Lord Feteusil's attire outshone his somber tunic of black with the cloak of fawn linen draped with false casualness over his right shoulder. Talmor wore no jewels save a chain studded with amber and topazes. His hands were bare of rings other than his signet. In contrast, Lord Feteusil was festooned in possibly all the jewels he owned, even sporting a rather foreign-looking earring in one ear.

Giving the man a nod, Talmor laid his sword across his knees and gestured.

"Your presence is most appreciated, Lord Feteusil," he said, forcing his tone to sound friendly, although his nerves were tight. "And beyond the obvious reasons."

"Er, Juroc does seem to be late."

It was a limp joke at best, but both of them, Talmor realized, were trying. He gestured again. "Come, my lord, and sit with me. We'll watch the joust together and get acquainted. I will wager three dreits to one that my men beat yours today. What say you?"

Feteusil grinned. "Aye, I'll take that wager, baron. I'll back my men any day, so I will." Then he hesitated and glanced around. "Er, are we done with official business?"

Frowning, Talmor beckoned to the herald and consulted with the man briefly before turning back to Feteusil with a shrug. "I was to make another speech, but it seems pointless in the—"

The sound of a distant trumpet made him break off. He

rose involuntarily to his feet, looking southward at a cloud of dust now growing visible over a distant rise and hearing the faint drumming of galloping hooves. He found that he was holding his breath. So his father was coming after all. He wasn't sure he felt any relief.

A lone rider on horseback came into sight, galloping off the road and across the grassy field to rein up sharply where Talmor's men stopped him. Garbed in Templan livery, the varlet bent down from his saddle to speak urgently to the herald, who then approached Talmor.

"Compliments of Lord Juroc, my lord," the herald said softly. "He and his party will arrive shortly with apologies. A cast shoe and a lame horse are at fault."

Perhaps, Talmor thought. Annoyance pricked him. He knew his father's strict insistence on punctuality. Had he really desired to arrive at the proper hour, Lord Juroc would have started his journey in ample time to allow for any minor mishaps. This tardiness was a deliberate slight, and although Talmor knew he should be relieved that the chevard was coming at all, he found himself in no mood to show his father any favors.

"Very well," he said. "We shall await the men of Templan Hold. Let the jugglers come back to entertain the crowd."

Lord Feteusil looked nervous again. "Perhaps I'd better move. No point in taking my ease until Lord Juroc has—"

"Bide where you are," Talmor said.

Lord Feteusil rose to his feet. "No, really, my lord baron. When you meet the fellow you'll understand. I should withdraw, for Lord Juroc has precedence over me and will surely be affronted to kneel before us both."

Talmor glanced at the rotund chevard. "Lord Juroc is late," he said firmly, "and has precedence over no one in such circumstances. You have done me honor today by coming eagerly as a vassal should, and I return that honor to you. Sit and take your ease beside me, for that is my pleasure."

Feteusil mopped his brow but sat as gingerly as a man ready to leap for his life. He fidgeted like a man with fleas, while Talmor felt as though he himself had been carved of stone.

They waited as Lord Juroc's large party wended its way

into sight and came rather slowly up the road. Although he tried to remind himself that this was his father's first time to pledge fealty to Edriel in forty years, Talmor knew there was no excuse for such petty defiance as this deliberate tardiness. He told himself that it wasn't personal, that to his knowledge his father was not resisting *him* but simply the re-creation of the barony by her majesty's desire; but it made no difference.

With every passing moment his temper grew hotter, his impatience more sharp.

The Templan procession halted at a distance and began to mill about in disorder as men dismounted, women were assisted down from wagons or palfreys, and children scattered in all directions with the hunting dogs. Watching with building amazement and displeasure, Talmor wondered if his father had decided to bring the entire hold with him, for the old chevard was escorted by at least seventy knights, if not more. The pennons were tangled, but eventually Talmor could see that all three of his half brothers were also present, along with what looked to be their wives and children.

His mouth went dry. Although he longed for wine, he dared not call for it. This was an occasion where he would need a very clear head. After his encounter with Etyne the other day, he hardly knew what would occur as these men realized the truth and discovered they were to kneel to him. He wished suddenly that he had not chosen to make this a public spectacle. He should have had the sense to meet Juroc in private.

Lord Feteusil was still fidgeting and wiping his brow. "Damne, but it's hot," he complained, glancing around as though for wine. "Great Thod, but if they don't get on with things, we'll run out of daylight before the jousting's scarcely begun."

Talmor forced a smile to his stiff lips. "Oh, there'll be ample time for you to lose your wager."

Feteusil laughed so loudly that Lord Juroc glanced toward the viewing stand and seemed to realize for the first time that he was holding up the proceedings. He lifted his hand in a vague wave and turned back to his arguing sons.

Behind Talmor, Sir Meine was beginning to mutter beneath his mustache.

Talmor glanced over his shoulder. "Get them to hurry, can you, Sir Meine?"

"At once, my lord."

Gripping his sword hilt, disapproval fierce in every line, the master-at-arms went striding down the line of the now-restive Edriel knights and confronted Lord Juroc's still-disorganized party. With several curt gestures and a voice that barked audibly even at that distance, Sir Meine clearly got their attention.

Lord Juroc swore at him, but Etyne broke away from the others and came striding toward the viewing stand. Talmor stiffened involuntarily, but his men were well trained.

Two knights sprang to bar Etyne's way, pushing him back. Etyne cursed them, his beard bristling with ill temper, before he went marching back to his father, who scowled but otherwise ignored him.

"Like a mummer's performance, ain't it?" Lord Feteusil said with a chuckle, then glanced at Talmor's grim face and coughed hastily. "Uh, er, well, that is, they're being damned rude to you, baron. I don't know why, except Juroc's rude to everyone. The older and sicker he gets, the worse his temper. But, morde! You'd think he'd remember his place today."

"Perhaps he does," Talmor said dryly. "Perhaps that is precisely Lord Juroc's problem."

Feteusil made a jittery reply, which Talmor barely heard. He forced himself to lounge back in his chair, with his hand resting quietly on his naked sword. Inside the empty sleeve, however, his scar was throbbing and itching and burning. He could feel jagged spurts of temper stabbing him. An hour ago, Lord Juroc's behavior could have been overlooked. A half hour ago, it might have been forgiven. Now, it was reprehensible and as deliberate an insult as the chevard could make without roaring a challenge.

At last Lord Juroc seemed to be ready. The disorder sorted itself out, and there stood the old man, stooped as though the weight of his sword was too much for him, with his three sons lined up at his heels.

The herald glanced at Talmor, who nodded. Pacing forward and holding up his hands for quiet from the restive crowd, the herald bawled out Lord Juroc's name with such pent-up impatience that several people laughed.

Perspiration trickled down Talmor's face. He wanted to flee from here and never return. This day had become a farce, and he was crawling with mortification.

Lord Juroc limped forward. Talmor saw that the past thirteen years had not been kind to his father. Juroc's black hair was now gray and thin, hanging loosely on his shoulders. His fierce face, carved by sun and the elements, was weathered and creased. His features no longer looked formidable but simply old and stubborn. As Juroc halted at the steps where he was to kneel, Etyne looked up at Talmor, and his black eyes widened above his beard.

"You!" he said in a choked voice and gripped Juroc's shoulder. "Father, halt!"

"Have done, fool!" Juroc whispered loudly. "Be silent and help me kneel."

"In Thod's name, you'll not bow to *him*. Look, Father, at who sits before you!"

Lord Juroc lifted his gaze to meet Talmor's. There was no recognition in his eyes at first, nothing but pain and impatience. Etyne whispered fiercely in his ear, and Juroc blinked. A trace of what he'd been once leaped to life in his face. His mouth opened.

"What is this?" he asked loudly. "Talmor? What in Thod's name are you doing standing in for the baron?"

Talmor sat like stone, so filled with wrath that the heat was coiling alive and almost uncontrollable in his palm. Could Juroc not even believe him capable of advancement? He clenched his fist, stiff with the effort of holding himself in check. If he could not control himself, if he could not force the flames to subside, then he was finished, for he would be torn to pieces and salted as a heretic if he unleashed fire here and now.

"Talmor?" Lord Juroc called louder.

Sir Meine shoved his way past Etyne. "That's Lord Talmor, Baron of Edriel!" he said angrily. "And high time you

men of Templan show the baron proper respect and give him
your fealty as you've come to do, or by Thod I'll see you put
out of here!"

Lord Juroc's craggy face darkened with equal temper.
"You'll put no Templan man in his place, sirrah!" he barked
in the voice that used to flay Talmor and every other member
of his army or household who displeased him. "Stand aside
and cease to interfere!"

Looking like he might explode, Sir Meine glanced at Talmor for orders.

Talmor could not move, could not speak a single word to
quell the situation. He sat as though chained to his chair and
dared not lose his concentration. He felt as though the flames
inside him were boiling him in his own skin. He was shaking
and rigid with the effort of holding the fire, the pain growing
more and more intense until he wanted to scream. Yet as he
met his father's eyes he held on. Even if the fire consumed
him and drove him mad, he was not going to surrender to it
this time, not even as far as throwing it into the grass and setting the jousting field on fire.

"Damne, it must be the hottest day of the summer," Lord
Feteusil remarked, pulling off his velvet cap and fanning with
it. "What we need is a good rain, to settle the dust and break
this infernal heat."

"Father," Etyne said at Juroc's side, "come away and put
an end to this nonsense. He can't be the baron. He's toying
with us, pulling a joke at our expense. He—"

"Silence!" Juroc roared, and Etyne's protest died unfinished.
Juroc turned to glare at all of his sons before facing Talmor
again. A rigid muscle was twitching in his jaw, and his dark eyes
met Talmor's with such fury that Talmor felt the flames inside
him abruptly die out as though they'd been doused.

Stunned, at first unable to grasp what had happened, Talmor blinked in bewilderment. Meanwhile, his father slowly,
painfully lowered himself to his knees.

A lump filled Talmor's throat. Involuntarily soulgazing his
father, he saw past the fury filling Juroc's mind to intense bewilderment, along with humiliation, regret, and hatred.

Stung by that barrage of emotions, Talmor averted his gaze and wished he could jump to his feet and run. Instead, he held himself in his chair, sweating and sick at heart. Whatever he'd expected from today's meeting, it had not been this.

"I, Juroc, Chevard of Templan, do hereby pledge my fealty to thee, Baron Edriel, as vassal to—to liege." Juroc paused a moment before continuing while Etyne, Porhal, and Amic stood rigid and stunned behind him. "I swear to thee," the old man's voice quavered momentarily before he strengthened it and went on more loudly, "that thou shalt be lord over me, my men-at-arms, and all that I own. In the sight of Thod, so do I swear."

Talmor swallowed hard. His heart was pounding so violently he barely heard the formal words. After Juroc climbed to his feet with Porhal's help, the old man came forward up the steps.

Talmor extended his broadsword, conscious of Etyne's black eyes glittering at him, while Juroc fumbled to draw his own weapon and slide it under his.

Their eyes met, father's and son's. Talmor could no longer read anything in his father's face, for Juroc had himself at last under control.

Rising to his feet, Talmor found that he was now taller than his father, broader of shoulder, deeper through the chest. Of all his brothers, he saw that he resembled his father the most in build and strength. His fighting prowess and lithe grace were Juroc's legacies.

There had been a time when Talmor knew nothing but the fervent desire to please this man and earn his love, even if it was just a scant nod of approval. It was not the illegitimacy Juroc had hated, for in his view what man did not have several natural-born sons scattered around? No, it had been the Saelutian blood, the blood of sorcery. It had been the fact that Juroc had let himself fall under the lustful enchantment of a woman of foreign blood, who left him with a son cursed in ways forbidden under Writ. And now, as they stood face-to-face after years apart, Talmor saw that the fury that Juroc had turned against him thirteen years ago was the same fury he showed now, only muted, tamped down beneath rigid self-control.

What it had cost Juroc to utter that allegiance oath, Talmor did not want to guess. He only knew that he wished to Thod he were not forced to accept it, for it was as falsely said and as falsely meant as any lie could be. And to pretend that he believed it was to stand accomplice to that lie and hypocrisy.

The herald cleared his throat softly, and Talmor realized that every eye was focused on him. He had to speak.

"Lord Juroc," Talmor said, rendering his voice as clear and as strong as before, "I do accept your pledge of fealty as my vassal." His golden eyes bored into his father's black ones. "And will hold you to it . . . until death."

A murmur rose among the crowd. Lord Feteusil's mouth opened, and his eyes bulged a little.

Juroc's face turned a mottled red, and behind him Etyne began muttering and swearing beneath his breath.

Amic elbowed his older brother. "Quiet," he whispered. "In Thod's name, stay quiet. Family matters belong within the family."

Etyne turned on him, but before he could speak, Lord Juroc held up his hand for Talmor's attention.

"My sons are knights, free-sworn in my service," he announced. "That is uncommon these days, but our custom at Templan. Let them also pledge their fealty to you, baron."

Without waiting for Talmor's response, he turned around and walked past his sons, gesturing for them to take his place on the steps. His dark eyes were glittering with malice, as though he hated all his sons equally this day. Watching him, Talmor understood at last that this was a man who could never take pride in his children. Juroc was too spiteful, competitive, aye, and even too insecure to want any of his sons to succeed. For he obviously did not want them to surpass him, to accomplish more than he had done, even to emulate his past deeds, talent, or strength.

It saddened Talmor to see through the old man, and he wished he hadn't wasted so many years yearning for the approval Juroc would not give him. His father, Talmor saw at last, had nothing to give any of them, save the poison that festered in his soul.

"Etyne," the old man said in a voice that brooked no defiance, "you are eldest. Bow to the baron and fear him not. I am sure he will be a liege to you unlike any you expected."

Talmor winced, expecting Etyne to walk away.

"Well? Go on!" Juroc ordered Etyne. "Don't keep the baron waiting."

Etyne's expression was hidden behind that thick beard. But his eyes were snapping with fury. "I am free-sworn!" he shouted. "I—"

But Juroc gave him a look that was like a blow. Abruptly falling silent, Etyne came forward and dropped to his knees before Talmor. He mumbled the pledge, running the words disrespectfully together, and he angrily slapped his blade beneath Talmor's with such force he nearly knocked the sword from Talmor's hand.

Swearing softly, Sir Nedwin started forward, but Talmor glanced at him with a shake of his head, and Sir Nedwin subsided with a mutter.

Porhal's turn came next. A slighter, less forceful copy of Etyne, he knelt, his eyes resentful and his clean-shaven jowls quivering with whatever emotions he was trying to master. He, too, mumbled the pledge while Juroc looked on with scorn. His sword slid so briefly beneath Talmor's the two blades barely touched. Without meeting Talmor's eyes, he turned away.

And then Amic knelt. Amic had been the dreamy one, who'd preferred studies to combat. He'd once hoped to enter the priesthood, but clearly, Talmor thought, Juroc had denied him that career. While Etyne had been the bully and Porhal the coward, it was sometimes Amic who would protest the torture Etyne put Talmor through. Amic, who came after dark to untie Talmor on the occasion Etyne tried, unsuccessfully, to hang his little brother. Amic, who occasionally slipped Talmor a crust of bread or a pippin to keep him from starving when Etyne stole his supper.

Today, Amic looked thin and tired. His face held the disillusionment of a life surrendered to the will of others. He alone of his brothers met Talmor's gaze, but his eyes were so bleak and empty that it was Talmor who looked away first.

Amic did not rush through his oath. He spoke it clearly and audibly. But his tone was so flat it was as though a dead man uttered the words. When he finished, he arose and put his blade against Talmor's with a tiny, chilling smile that meant absolutely nothing, and turned away.

So puzzled was Talmor that he nearly called after Amic, but just in time he checked the impulse. Sheathing his sword, Talmor spoke the formal speech he had rehearsed for this part of the ceremony while Etyne strode away from him with deliberate rudeness, and the others hovered near their father.

When the trumpets sounded a fanfare signaling the opening of the joust, Talmor called after his father: "Lord Juroc, you and your sons are welcome to join Lord Feteusil and myself. Come, and bide in the shade. Have some wine or ale, if you like."

"Ah, ale!" Lord Feteusil said eagerly, and clapped his hands at the servant finally coming forward with a tray of refreshments.

Juroc turned as jerkily as a puppet on strings. With every sign of reluctance he came back, ducking under the canopy and seating himself on the bench to Talmor's left. Porhal joined him, but Amic murmured something about competing in the joust and melted away into the crowd milling about in search of better seats to watch the field.

Conscious of his father's presence, Talmor turned to Lord Feteusil and invited him to bring his wife and children into the shade. While the chevard bowed merrily and dashed off to collect his family, Lord Juroc glowered in silence.

Talmor forced himself to keep chatting to the old man with courtly address, pretending they were strangers newly met. "I see my—I see that your sons have brought their wives," he said. "Let the ladies join us, if they please. I would be honored to make their acquaintance."

"Porhal," Juroc snarled, and Porhal hastened away like a kicked cat.

Temporarily alone except for Sir Nedwin, who was keeping a wary eye on them, Talmor and Juroc faced each other.

Talmor found himself choked with things he'd longed to say for many years. "My lord—"

"You've had your laugh at our expense," Juroc interrupted him.

"No one is laughing," Talmor said. "Least of all myself."

"I deny the connection," Juroc said furiously, rolling his eye at Sir Nedwin. "I shall always deny it. Nothing has changed! I'll claim you not, no matter how high you rise."

Talmor found himself smiling involuntarily. "Clearly," he replied with scorn. "Morde, put aside your fear. I want nothing from—"

"My fear? My *fear?*" Juroc said, rising to his feet. "How dare you!" As he spoke, he lunged at Talmor as though intending to grip his sword arm, but although Talmor twisted quickly, Juroc's hand knocked aside the cloak and closed on empty sleeve.

Looking stunned, he stared openmouthed at Talmor, whose face was burning. He did not know why he felt so furiously ashamed, but at that moment he would have rather died than have his father know he was a cripple.

"Unhand his lordship!" Sir Nedwin said fiercely. "Unhand him now!"

Juroc dropped the sleeve as though burned. Talmor straightened himself, trying to master his harsh breathing and thumping heart by tucking his rumpled sleeve back into his belt. He waited for Juroc to say something, anything, but his father kept silent.

And when Talmor's gaze flashed up, he found his father staring at him with raw consternation.

Hope awakened in Talmor. He rushed to that softening like a moth to flame. "I lost it in battle, protecting the queen," he said.

Juroc snorted. "So you get a barony in exchange for an arm. That tells me how you came here, reviving an expired title. She's soft, like all women, and no fit ruler for this realm."

Talmor jumped to his feet. "You'll not insult her majesty. Not in my presence, you—"

"I'll do as I please! And I'll take no orders from the likes of you." Juroc stabbed a finger into Talmor's chest. "We of Templan were tricked into coming today, and we've capered to your command, but don't expect to see us again."

Talmor forgot his desire for reconciliation. "I'll see you on any day I demand your presence at arms. You may not intend to keep your oath, but it was spoken aloud before witnesses. And in the name of Thod and the queen you'll do as you're told, or I'll see you broken from Templan Hold and your warrant of deed destroyed."

Juroc blinked, and for a moment there was only silence between them. Talmor eased out his breath, surprised at having lashed out so sharply. It was as though his father had spoken, he thought in shame. He had never expected to hear himself imitate Juroc so perfectly.

"So it's like that, is it?" Juroc said at last. He remained as unyielding as the day he'd beaten Talmor and driven him from Templan Hold forever.

Talmor met his gaze with eyes as stony as the old man's, and there was no going back. "Aye," he replied. "It's like that."

Chapter Twenty-two

The joust was over; the prize had been awarded to a dusty, blood- and sweat-stained victor; Amic had broken his arm in the contest; the banquet had roared late into the night with merriment; the Templan party was the first to depart when the festivities closed the following day; the merchant princes lingered with flattering reluctance to go.

Gray-faced from lack of sleep, his scar aching, Talmor bade farewell to the last of his guests with a sense of profound relief. A thunderstorm blackened the horizon, and distant flashes of lightning made him edgy and restless. He felt a hot desire to ride into the midst of the storm and throw fire to rival the lightning, but instead he retreated to his chambers in the tower.

The plastered walls and curved ceiling seemed light and exotic after his years at Savroix, with its heavy use of dark woods and tapestries. Talmor's quarters were so sparsely furnished they seemed as austere and plain as barracks living. He needed a bed, a writing table, a chair, and a chest to hold his clothing. Beyond that, he was not interested.

At the moment, he saw none of it. Pacing back and forth

while rain splattered the, windows, he tried to drive thoughts of his father and half brothers from his mind. They were provincial barbarians, and he hoped to Thod he never had them under his roof again. The woman he'd thought was Amic's wife turned out to be Lord Juroc's young mistress, and Talmor had discovered that at least two of the children scampering about like small savages were his half siblings. They all ate and drank like gluttons, and Porhal's wife stole bed linens and spoons.

At their departure, Juroc limped out to his horse without a word of farewell, trailed by his family. Only Etyne paused to speak to Talmor. Red-faced, his eyes glittering with hostility, he glanced impatiently at Sir Nedwin, who was hovering close by, and stepped even closer.

"You threatened Father," he said, his voice hoarse from his efforts to keep it low. "You damned mongrel, you have no right—"

"I have every right," Talmor broke in coldly.

Etyne's powerful fists clenched, but when Sir Nedwin reached for his weapon, he subsided. "Someday," he said, "you'll be without your protector. You'll be all alone."

Talmor met his eyes, frowning at the mad hatred shimmering in them. "It won't make any difference."

"Father taught us never to rely on one battle skill," Etyne said. "And an arrow flies quicker than fire. There'll come a time, Talmor. When you least expect it, I'll get you."

Now, standing with his palm pressed against the cold window glass, Talmor shrugged off thoughts of his half brother. He'd heard bully threats before. Most of them came to nothing.

More than ever, he yearned to be leagues away from here, no longer exiled from a pair of lovely brown eyes and a voice like low music whenever she spoke. According to the news he'd heard yesterday, the queen was now in residence at Aversuel, only fifteen leagues away. If he changed horses often, Talmor thought, he could be there in what . . . two days?

For a moment he seemed to hear her voice saying something soft and indistinguishable, then he blinked hard and realized it was only the wind lashing outside. He told himself he had to stop pining like this for the impossible. She wasn't going to send for him. Pheresa was a pragmatist, and so was he. Somehow, he had to get past this sense of waiting and start building a life for himself here. The joust was a beginning. He must plan another festivity for Aelintide, but he would not invite the inhabitants of Templan Hold. Meanwhile, the merchants had brought disturbing news of a Klad raider named Bara Tang, once again on the move and stirring up trouble. *I'd like a good battle,* Talmor thought grimly.

As the tired old barracks joke went, there was nothing like a good round of bloodshed to make a man feel reborn.

I shall relearn the lance, Talmor decided. It would mean brutal hours of training, and of course the physical risk would be tremendous since he could not hold a shield for protection, but it was something to do. Anything, he thought bitterly, to keep himself from thinking about her.

Outside, lightning raked at the tower, while thunder boomed loudly enough to rattle the windows. Talmor yanked them open and stood there, daring another bolt to strike him. Rain gusted inside, soaking him and blowing papers off the writing table until Pears came running in and fought to slam the window shut.

"Are ye mad?" he asked. "Look at ye now. Wet through, and—"

"Leave me," Talmor said in a voice he did not recognize. He felt the storm's fury pulling at him, stirring the fire, and although it was tempting to let it go, he held it close and tight, using the pressure and building pain to punish himself.

"M'lord," Pears said worriedly, "I think ye ought to—"

"Leave me!" Talmor shouted. "See that I'm not disturbed."

Going to the door, Pears hesitated. "They're not worth it," he said. "Yer brothers ain't worth nothing compared to ye, and they know it, damn 'em."

Talmor turned to stare at him, and the gray-haired squire nodded earnestly.

"They're just jealous, always have been. Yer the best of 'em. Nay, yer something they can't even compare to. That's why they hate ye."

Astonished by the squire's outburst, Talmor could only stare at Pears. He felt a sudden rush of gratitude and affection for this man who had served him faithfully for so long and who still believed in him despite everything.

"Thank you," he said finally.

Pears gave him an awkward nod, smiling a little. "Now why don't ye come down and sup with the household? 'Twill be quiet enough, with the guests gone at last, merciful Thod. Come along. It's no good, brooding alone up here."

And although he had no wish for company, Talmor felt some of the anger and torment ease inside him. He went downstairs, obedient to Pears's cajoling, and broke bread with his servants and knights. They seemed bashful and awkward around him at first, but by the end of the evening there were smiles and laughter. And the sour wretchedness left in the wake of Lord Juroc's visit was wiped clean.

Sometime in the night, Talmor was roused by a hand shaking his shoulder. A voice said urgently, "M'lord! M'lord, wake up!"

He opened his eyes in confusion, thinking for a moment they were under attack, and reached for his sword that wasn't there. "What?"

The candle flame made him squint, but he recognized Pears silhouetted behind it.

Irritably Talmor sat up. "After all these years, you know better than to rouse me this way. I might have stabbed you."

"Barons don't sleep with their weapons," Pears said, yawning. "There's a messenger come, m'lord. Says he's from the queen."

Shortly thereafter, Talmor was dressed and hastening downstairs, where he found a man travel-stained and weary, unshaven, with bleary, bloodshot eyes. The messenger was gobbling food, but at Talmor's entrance, he shot to attention.

Despite his evident exhaustion, the man moved like a fighter, Talmor noted. To his knowledge, he'd never seen the knight before, but there was something familiar about his freckled face and reddish brown hair. He wore the queen's colors on his surcoat.

"Your name," Talmor demanded eagerly. "What brings you here?"

"Queen's business. I'm Sir Georges du Maltie, one of her majesty's protectors."

"Du Maltie!" Talmor said in surprise. "Then you're—"

"—an uplander?" Sir Georges broke in. "Aye, I am, and proud of it."

"I was going to say that you must be related to Thum du Maltie."

Sir Georges grinned. "My younger brother, and right proud we are of how he's turned out."

Talmor did not return the smile. His acquaintance with Sir Thum had been brief and far from pleasant, for it had been Sir Thum who ordered him put through trial by spell-fire at Thirst Hold.

"Her majesty sent me to you in all haste," Sir Georges went on, handing over a grubby piece of parchment.

Expecting a message, Talmor was disappointed to find it was nothing more than a pass, scrawled in Pheresa's hand and much smeared and blotted.

"They've been blocking her majesty's letters all summer, keeping her hemmed close for her protection, so they say, but—"

"Who?" Talmor demanded in bewilderment. "Who keeps her prisoner and where?"

"Nay, she's not imprisoned," Sir Georges said. "She resides at Aversuel still, but is hard-pressed. A Sebein broke into her room four nights past and attacked her."

Talmor felt his insides knot, but he fought to keep calm. "She is well? She was not hurt?"

"Nay, not hurt. She put up a good fight, our lady." Sir Georges grinned. "She's been working hard at her swordplay, and learning fast."

"Never mind her swordplay! Tell me what happened."

"We killed the foul pagan thing," Sir Georges said proudly. "Me and the queen together. Aye, it took us both, and never did her majesty lose her courage. But she was shook, just the same, and sent me straight to you. And I was to bid you to come to her at once with all—"

"Why didn't you say so immediately?" Talmor spun away from him and gestured to Sir Nedwin. "Pass the word to Sir Meine. I'll want men saddled and ready to travel right away. Lutel, see that we have provisions. Pears, fetch my sword and chain mail. Sir Nedwin, I'll want—"

"No!" Sir Georges said in consternation. "She wants your lordship to come in secret, not leading an army. You're not to come openly to the palace, but—"

"We'll arrange that later," Talmor told him.

"But—"

"Thod's bones, man, am I to ride to Aversuel with no one but you?"

Sir Georges rubbed his face and shrugged. "Forgive me, my lord. I'm not thinking clear."

"No, you're dead on your feet."

By now, Pears had come running with Talmor's mail and sword belt. Hooking the latter over his shoulder, Talmor headed for the door. "Can you ride with us, Sir Georges, or need you stay behind and rest? Catch up with us on the road."

Sir Georges grabbed a hunk of cold meat off the tray and came after him. "I'll ride now, if it's all the same, my lord."

Torches were flaring outside on the steps and illuminating the stableyard, where sleepy grooms were standing at the heads of saddled horses. Knights, roused by Sir Meine's orders, came at a run, yawning but ready to mount up and ride.

Talmor ran his eye over them in approval and paused while Pears yanked his mail shirt over his head and squatted to fit on his spurs.

"You move out as fast as a warrior," Sir Georges said in admiration.

Talmor swung into his saddle and paused to pull his cloak

across his shoulders. He'd learned to buckle it with one hand although in his haste he found himself fumbling with the strap. Finished, he gathered his reins and stared down at Sir Georges standing by his stirrup.

"I *am* a warrior," he replied and beckoned impatiently. "Someone get this man a fresh horse. Let's ride!"

Chapter Twenty-three

Watched more closely than ever, with an anxiety that no one bothered to conceal, Pheresa left her audience room for a walk around the Aversuel parapets. Gone were her daily fighting lessons, for Sir Georges had not returned. She did not know whether he'd managed to get through the patrols and sentries, whether he'd survived the plague now sweeping through villages to the west and south, whether he'd reached Edriel at all. Gone, too, were her daily rides through the forest, for Sir Perrell came and went at all hours so that she saw him only by chance, and then briefly.

She felt tense and on edge from a sense of growing anticipation as though this summer of uncertainty, secrets, and isolation could not continue much longer without something dreadful happening. The plague was spreading closer, and her subjects were dying from it no matter what the physicians did or how many prayers were said.

Today, the Privy Council had discussed whether her majesty should depart Aversuel for some region where the plague had not yet struck. Adamantly opposed to this, Pheresa argued that if the plague were of the Sebeins' making, it would strike wherever she took residence. It angered her that the church refused to send forth more priests to hunt the Sebeins, for she knew they must possess the knowledge of how to countermand the evil spell of plague. Why wouldn't they use it?

At the end of her walk—a hot, boring exercise—she was resting in her chambers when Oola entered with an air of suppressed excitement and a rigidly blank face. Gazing around, the woman hesitated before approaching Pheresa's bedside.

"May I brush your majesty's hair?" she murmured.

"Leave her be, Oola!" one of the ladies-in-waiting called out in vexation. "Her majesty will fall asleep if you don't chatter to her."

"Forgive me, majesty," Oola whispered, moving closer. "May I brush your hair?"

As she spoke, she reached out with an odd, almost furtive look on her face. Suspicious, even a little alarmed by her behavior, Pheresa caught her wrist to stop her.

Oola pressed something into Pheresa's palm, curtsied, and retreated. Pheresa rolled over to turn her back to her ladies and uncurled her palm.

She held a scrap of cloth with the Edriel crest embroidered on it. With a leap, her heart began to race. Joy and relief and the desire to burst into tears consumed her. She gulped, pressed her fingers to her lips to keep silent, then kissed the little piece of cloth.

Talmor had come, she thought, wanting to laugh aloud. She must find a way to meet him without delay.

There had been plenty of time to plan her strategy. Feeling like a young maiden planning an illicit rendezvous, Pheresa called for sweets. When those were brought, she called for wine. When that was brought, she called for a literature scroll. When that was brought, she declared herself bored with such amusements and expressed the desire to bathe.

Looking astonished by so odd an activity in the middle of the day, her ladies arose to take their places for the formal disrobing of the queen. Pheresa, who on state occasions was required to wear a great many jewels and layers of clothing, thought she would die of impatience through the ceremonial removal of each article from her person. With due ceremony, each item was carried away in turn by a designated lady-in-waiting. Such protocol had to be endured, Pheresa reminded herself, or her ladies—some of whom had gained their places in her court through fierce lobbying and stratagems—would be affronted. More delays might result.

Finally, when she was clad only in thin linen underclothes and a robe, all blissfully cool on this warm day, she dismissed her ladies and, choosing only Oola, Verine, and Lady Carolie to assist her, entered her bathing chamber, now filled with steaming, scented water. Pheresa paused, a little affronted. Had she truly intended to bathe, she would have preferred cool, rather than hot, water. But it did not matter now.

"Bolt the door," Pheresa commanded.

Oola obeyed, while Verine and Lady Carolie stared.

"Quickly," Pheresa said, holding out her arms. "Carolie, give me your gown. I'll keep my own slippers. Yours pinch too much."

Lady Carolie's eyes grew even bigger. "Majesty," she said with a surprised giggle, "what mean you to do?"

"What think you?" Pheresa asked impatiently, snapping her fingers to make them all hurry. She could not understand why they dawdled so.

"Does your majesty intend to wear my stomacher and the padding?"

Pheresa barely glanced at her. "I think not. Yours won't fit me."

Lady Carolie's pretty face turned pink. "No underlacings? Oh, majesty! Such daring! Have you taken a lover? Who is he? Sir Perrell? I saw him smile at your majesty from afar this morning. Oh, I'll bet my new earrings 'tis he."

Taken aback, Pheresa almost reprimanded her. Of course, Lady Carolie was a product of King Verence's court, which had been infamous for its wild banquets, licentious behavior, and shameless flirtations. Frivolous of mind, but always loyal, Lady Carolie meant no harm, and Pheresa realized that she now had a plausible excuse for her behavior. She should have thought of it herself, only it hadn't occurred to her. She had never taken a lover except her worthless husband, and the idea of being thought suddenly willing to loosen her strict morals left her much discomfited.

"Never you mind who it is, m'lady," Oola said reprovingly to Lady Carolie, who giggled and whirled around the room the way she used to as a girl. Oola undressed her despite her capering, while Pheresa shrugged off her robe and flung it around Carolie's shoulders.

"Am I to impersonate your majesty?" Carolie asked in a loud whisper. "I'm rather good at it, aren't I?"

"Yes," Pheresa replied, holding her breath until Verine finished lacing up her borrowed gown. "All you have to do is enjoy the bath, splash about once in a while, and command anyone who inquires at the door to 'go away.'" Feeling unfettered in half the garments she usually wore, Pheresa stepped into her slippers without waiting for help. "And, yes, Carolie, you must get into the water."

"All of me? But why?"

"Because I bathe entirely immersed," Pheresa replied. "No one will believe you are me unless you're wet. And don't let anyone see your face."

Lady Carolie—of the sponge and basin school of cleanliness—peered dubiously at the pool of water and dipped her toe into it with a little grimace. "Yes, your majesty," she said with a sigh, then laughed and skipped over to kiss Pheresa's hands.

"I hope he pleases you," she said with a wicked grin. "Sir Perrell! Oh, morde, I cannot stand it! Of course he's been in love with you since we arrived, but I didn't think you'd noticed. The reverend commander is quite the handsomest man at Aversuel. That marvelous auburn hair, how it shines in the sunlight. Don't you long to run your hands through it? And his eyes make me shiver, for I vow they are every bit as blue as the lake. I could swoon with envy, for 'tis said"—and she bent close to whisper in Pheresa's ear—"that there is no lover quite like a church knight."

Pheresa's cheeks were burning at Lady Carolie's teasing,

but again she spoke no reprimand. How would Talmor look?
she wondered. Was he keeping well? Was he still as handsome
as ever? Would his golden eyes smile at her when they saw
each other, or would he remain serious? But, no, she must remember to keep her mind on essential matters, for she anx-
iously desired his advice on so many things, such as how to
stop the Sebeins, and how to guard her dreams, and how
to . . .

"Smile!" Carolie called after her. "Your majesty is looking
far too serious about this. Oh, dear. We should have anointed
you with perfume to drive his senses mad. And put rouge on
your breasts and—"

"Will your ladyship *hush!*" Verine scolded, and Lady Carolie giggled more than ever.

The thought of Talmor even looking at her breasts overwhelmed Pheresa, and suddenly she felt so nervous that she
couldn't breathe. Had he missed her? Had he thought of her
as much as she'd thought of him? What would he think of her
in a ridiculous gown that was too short and insufficiently fitted? Lady Carolie always did wear her bodices cut too low.
Pheresa told herself that she should have taken the time to put
on the underlacings. Even worse, she didn't have her jewels.
Her hair was not—

"Come, majesty," Oola whispered, and led Pheresa
through the servant door into a narrow, dusty passage.

They tiptoed through the maze of servant back stairs and
hidden corridors until Pheresa was completely lost. At last,
she was led into a paneled room with the shutters closed so
that only a few bars of sunlight trickled through. It smelled
musty from disuse.

Halting, she strove to order her thoughts. A less romantic
meeting place she could not imagine, and told herself she was
glad of it, for there was much business to discuss. She intended to get right to it.

The door opened, and three men entered, all of them bowing to her. One was Sir Georges du Maltie. One she did not
recognize. One was Talmor.

Her breath caught in her throat, and all the ideas and questions she'd been debating dropped forgotten from her mind. She saw no one but her dear Talmor. He stepped forward into a thin shaft of sunlight, and although his face was unsmiling, his golden eyes locked on hers with such warmth in them, such gladness, that she felt the blood rush to her face. Perhaps she said his name. She did not know what she did.

He glanced at the others. "Leave us," he commanded. "Even you, Sir Nedwin."

The two protectors and Oola went out, closing the door behind them. No sooner had it shut than Pheresa was flinging herself into Talmor's embrace.

"I thought I would have more pride than this," she murmured against his lips, kissing him frantically. "Dear Talmor, I have been lost without you."

"Pheresa," he said in a low voice, kissing her back. His arm tightened around her, and his lips stole the breath and life from her so that she knew only him, and could not think or care about anything else.

Although she'd yearned for him daily, she found now that she wanted him with an urgency that inflamed her. Her skin was on fire. Her pulse was pounding so hard and fast she could not breathe between his kisses. Dizzy, she entwined her arms around his neck in order to keep from swooning.

Abruptly, he pushed her away, holding her at arm's length while he panted for air. "Not here," he said hoarsely.

Embarrassment roared through her, burning her cheeks. She was trembling, unable to hide what she thought and craved. Her gaze went to his, revealing all her desire, and she saw him turn pale and swallow hard.

"Not here," he whispered again. "It's not private enough. Not . . . safe."

She trusted his instincts and judgment completely. "Where? I'm watched constantly, even in my most private apartments."

He blinked rapidly as though trying to clear his head, and put his cloak around her. "There's a way out of the palace . . . very dark and dirty."

"I don't care. Anywhere," she said and blushed again.

Smiling, he kissed the tip of her nose. "Come."

They hurried along more passageways, and steep, unlit staircases that spiraled down into musty, foul-smelling places where water covered the ground and seeped through the walls. She followed him in total trust, leaving a worried Oola behind, and cared not what she risked as long as Talmor's hand held hers.

I've been a fool, she thought, blissfully happy while she ducked to creep under a thick cobweb. *I swore that I'd no longer listen to any judgment save my own, yet all I've done since being crowned is let Salba persuade me against this man. The traditions are wrong. The laws are wrong. All history is wrong. Talmor alone is right. I should have never let Salba send him away.*

But she resisted the impulse to ask Talmor to turn back right now. There would be time later for her to announce him to her court as her choice. Today, this afternoon, these very hours, belonged to them alone. And the illicitness of an adventure with him, slipping away where no one could find her, filled her with excitement.

At long last, they crept outside into the daylight. Blinking and squinting, Pheresa tried to look around to get her bearings, but saw little save that she was in a narrow ravine choked with brush and boulders. Behind her, the passage trickled water from inside the palace. Sir Georges grimly set the rusted iron grate back across the opening, and Pheresa shivered at the thought of how easy it really was to get in and out of her fortress. If the Sebeins chose to read the minds of her sentries and learned of such ways, they could pour into Aversuel, and who would stop them?

"No," Talmor said quietly, seeing her look, "your palace is not sufficiently secure."

Wearing the hood of Talmor's cloak over her head, although no one patrolling the walls could see them down here, Pheresa was put in front of his saddle and borne away into the forest. As soon as they reached a safe distance from the palace, Talmor spurred his steed to a canter.

She put her arms around his torso and clung hard, pressing

her cheek to his chest and feeling safe. His heart beat strongly beneath her cheek, and she longed to press her heart to his, to feel her skin against his, to experience their blood pounding in the dance of man with woman. She blushed again, her whole body hot with the force of her feelings, and kept her face pressed out of sight lest the protectors see how wanton she'd become.

Then the men drew rein and conferred in hushed voices while Pheresa straightened and looked around. They were deep in the forest, much deeper than Sir Perrell had ever escorted her. Here, even the wild ferns did not grow, and there was certainly no laurel. Trees with pale smooth bark greened with moss grew in tall formation on all sides. And how quiet it was, she thought, how hushed and shadowy.

"I've never been here before," she said in wonder.

The men exchanged glances. Sir Georges was looking worried and nervous. "There's little time, and we've used too much of it," he said. "If she's missed—"

"Join Sir Meine and the men. Keep watch for church knight patrols," Talmor said.

The two protectors wheeled their horses and rode into the trees out of sight. Talmor turned his horse in the opposite direction and took Pheresa deeper into the forest.

She drank in every line of his handsome, sun-bronzed face. There were deeper lines carved on either side of his mouth than she remembered. He looked tired.

"Did you miss me?" she asked, tracing the line of his jaw with her fingertips.

Talmor smiled at her with such warmth she forgot to breathe. "Every moment," he replied, then frowned. "Your majesty, Sir Georges has been telling me of the troubles here. Why—"

"No," she said. "Not that. Not now."

Talmor sighed and averted his face, frowning into the distance. She saw a muscle flexing in his jaw and wondered what he would do if she kissed it.

"Your majesty," he said, "I—"

"Say my name," she murmured. "The way you did before."

"Pheresa."

It thrilled her to hear him speak it. *I am grown as silly as Carolie,* she thought, and did not care. Smiling, she caressed his cheek. "Talmor, I have longed for you so very much. I was a fool to listen to Salba."

"No, you were right. He's a wise man."

"He is cruel!" she cried. "He would part us forever, and I love you too much to permit that."

"Your throne comes first."

"Not today."

Talmor's arm tightened around her. "You must be sure," he said in a low voice. "You must not be rushed into something you don't—"

"I want this with all my heart."

"As queen—"

"Right now, I'm not a queen." She turned his face to hers. "Look at me as a woman. Do I not please you?"

He moaned. "Oh, Thod, yes!"

"Then let us have what we both want. Now, Talmor. Please."

He swallowed, his breathing quickening audibly. She felt herself trembling, and could not believe how bold she'd suddenly become. Yet she was caught in a wild spiral of emotion that she did not want to govern. All summer she'd been bound to prudent thoughts and prudent conduct, and she was tired of both, tired of living constricted and confined and bored and lonely. For what good was it to own the world if she had no one with whom to share her heart?

Moments later, Talmor drew rein beneath a gigantic tree that looked as old as the mountains. So wide did its canopy spread that no other seedlings or undergrowth crowded its base. The mossy ground looked soft and inviting. Sunlight dappled through the swaying leaves across them. After tying his horse, Talmor pulled Pheresa close to kiss her so deeply and profoundly that when he stopped she sagged against him without strength.

"Talmor," she whispered, trembling. "My love . . ."

"I can't be gentle," he warned her. "I can't—"

"I don't want you to be," she told him, and lifted his hand to her low-cut bodice. Beneath his feather-light touch, her flesh quickened, and she drew in her breath audibly. "You have my permission, dearest."

Together, in that strange, mossy gold light, they sank down upon the cloak he spread for them and undressed each other. Her skin looked very pale in outdoor light. Slowly, rather shyly, she revealed herself to him. The admiration in his eyes made her feel more womanly and beautiful than ever before. In turn, she found herself blushing rosy as she stared at his body. How perfect he was, she thought, how magnificent. Even his missing arm could not mar his physical splendor. She had never gazed on a nude man in daylight before, and she felt entranced by the ripple of his chest and abdominal muscles, the strong spring and flex between his hipbone and ribs, the shifting grace of sinew, flesh, and bone as he tossed aside clothing. The sight of his masculinity made her stomach tighten, and she found herself breathing short and fast.

His muscles were like bands of steel, yet when he gathered her against him it was with such care, such near reverence that she clutched his head and pressed him tighter to her.

How skilled was his touch. His hand skimmed over places that made her moan, and he unfastened her hair so that it fell around them in a veil of golden silk. She ran her hands across his chest, realizing she knew nothing of how to please him in return, and was ashamed and frustrated by her ignorance. But as he pressed her back, she found herself sinking into a place where nothing mattered save his lips and touch. His flesh felt very hot to her shy fingers as though he burned with fire, and she felt heat of her own spreading into her thighs and belly. Her body seemed to have become something she did not know, molten and pliant, unable to obey her had she been capable of commanding it. But it was Talmor who commanded her now, Talmor she responded to with quick-drawn breaths and tremors and a building urgency that almost frightened her.

His ardor flattered her, for it was like nothing she'd known with Lervan. After initial surprise she threw all memories of Lervan away as something cheap, to be forgotten. For here was love as she'd always hoped to find it, love as genuine and real as all she'd known before was false. And, despite his warning, Talmor was a gentle lover, giving her time to be at ease with him, treating her as though she were delicate, as though—and she blushed all over—as though she had never been bedded before. Yet, despite all that Talmor gave to her, despite his patience and care, she realized how strong he really was. And in the midst of her most intense pleasure she found that he was no longer restraining himself as he had at first. He did not give as much as he took and took, driving her to what she had not known, until she was shuddering in his grasp, until she could not bear these new sensations, until she arched against him and clung tight while he murmured to her and held her and kissed her into a sweet, hot aftermath.

Together they lay spent, his head between her breasts, his breath puffing warm on her skin, his fingers idly tracing parts of her that shivered and tingled from his touch. She laughed suddenly, low and deep in her throat, and he lifted his head to smile at her.

"What, beloved?" he asked.

She smoothed his unruly hair back from his eyes. "I feel . . . perfect," she said with a sigh.

He laughed, too, with a boyishness she'd never seen in him before and abruptly yanked her up to tickle her until she had to muffle her squeals against his shoulder to keep them from echoing through the forest.

"Hush," he warned her, still laughing. "Hush!"

She tried, but his hand was all mischief now, delighting her as she had never dreamed possible. And when her laughter grew too loud, he silenced her with a kiss that was merry at first, then grew serious and deep. Pleased by his sudden urgency, she kissed him back with all she had to offer. When her body was aching with readiness for his, this time she wanted to weep and laugh alike, for it was as though he had spread magic around her and put her into an enchantment far beyond her imaginings.

And as his hand swept up from her loins to her breasts and down again, their mutual need was stronger and more intense than before. Pheresa realized she had come very close to losing this wonderful, splendid man through her own misguided attempts to govern her realm properly. *I am queen,* she thought, *but more importantly I am a woman. This matters, perhaps more than all the rest.* Had she lost him, given him up as she'd been urged to, it would have been the greatest mistake of her life. She knew that now, knew it to the depths of her soul, and her hands tightened on him as though never to let him go again.

The poignancy of how close they'd come to disaster intensified all her feelings until her thoughts swirled together and melted. There was nothing in her mind and soul but Talmor. She wanted so deeply to please him, to make him understand how much she loved him. And with such sweet willingness did she surrender that he trembled against her, for so was it ordained that man and woman should become one.

"I am yours," she whispered, making a vow of it as her body sang with his. "Forever and always. So do I plight my troth to thee."

He lifted his head to stare into her eyes with a gaze smoldering and primitive. "Mine," he said thickly, and made her so.

Chapter Twenty-four

They sat together, dressed once more and quiet, while the sun dipped low in the sky. Talmor leaned against the tree, and Pheresa snuggled against him with his arm lying heavily across her. She held his hand in her lap, her fingers sliding idly along his.

"I had better get you back," he said.

"I hate to return," she murmured. "I hate to lose this."

He kissed her temple. "We can never lose this afternoon. Until the next time I return, we will—"

"Next time? Return? What mean you?" she asked in surprise, twisting in his grasp to stare at him. "You're going back to the palace with me, and I shall announce our—"

"No," he said very gently, closing his hand over hers. She tried to pull away, but he tightened his grip just enough to stop her. "No, Pheresa."

She stared at him in disbelief and slowly dawning anger. "You mean you agree with them? With Salba? Against *us?*"

"Our affair cannot be made public."

"Affair!" she said angrily. "That cheap word. Ours is no affair, Talmor! I want to marry."

"And you will," he said calmly. "But not yet, and not again to a cur like Lervan."

Pheresa could not believe he was saying this, not after what they'd experienced together. Hurt filled her, and for a moment she almost hated him. She managed to work her hand free of his and hugged herself, shivering.

"You don't want to marry?" she asked in a small voice. "You don't want me?"

"Pheresa."

He reached for her, but she drew back from him, wide-eyed and stiff. "I thought—" Her voice nearly failed her. "How could I have been so mistaken?"

Talmor sighed. "I want you," he said flatly. "I want to throw you across my saddle and take you where no one can ever find you again. I want to hold you against me through this night and into the morrow. I want to wake up every morning and see your face in dawn's light. You are a part of me that I can never surrender."

"Then why?" she asked. "Why not—"

"You know the answer to that. We both do."

Her anger turned instead against her ministers and her court. "Those narrow-minded bigots. What care I for what my people think? I shall force them to accept you."

"No." He shook his head. "You care very deeply what your people think. And acceptance cannot be forced."

"I am queen," she said with determination. "I—"

"And talking foolishly."

"Oh, Talmor!" she cried. "'Tis our happiness, our lives we're throwing away."

"Not true. I'll never forsake you. Send for me, and I will always come, just as I did this time."

Now her tears did spill down her cheeks. She didn't bother to wipe them away, didn't move, didn't speak.

He rubbed her wet cheeks with his thumb, then pulled her close. "I'm sorry. I'm sorry," he murmured, stroking her hair.

"Everything was so wonderful," she said, choking. "And now you want to leave me."

"I do *not* want to leave you. I shall stay until this trouble with the Sebeins is settled somehow, but not openly. I can't live at court as the queen's official lover."

"Not even if I command you?"

Regret and longing filled his eyes.

"It is not fair!" she said, tossing her hair back over her shoulder. "Lervan was a despicable, lying, deceitful, arrogant fool, and you are worth five of him. There's not another man in my realm close to your valor and goodness. You are so—"

"Don't," he said awkwardly.

"But I mean what I say."

"Thank you, but don't deceive yourself. I am not a good man at all."

"That's not true! You are the very best of men, and I would show everyone what you really are."

A strange expression crossed his face. "Too many know already," he said harshly.

She could have bitten her tongue. "I'm sorry. I was not thinking of the fire."

"No. You are kind and sweet, and you always forget the fire. I cannot. And Cardinal Theloi will not. Let me remain a shadow behind you. Do not force the people to look at me, or they will see too much."

Despair was starting to hollow out all the happiness she'd known today. She stared into a future of bleak separations and stolen moments of delight, and knew the separations would far outweigh any time together. She did not think she could bear such a life.

"You sound like Lord Salba, urging me to marry for the good of the realm and take my lover as I can find him," she said bleakly.

"Sensible advice."

"Don't say that! Do you want me to marry another man?"

Talmor's face grew stony. "Eventually you must."

"But is it what you want?"

"No."

"Do you want me to bed another man?"

"No!"

"Why not? It would be for the good of the realm."

He clenched his fist, and his golden eyes grew murderous.

"Could you play a courtier's role, applauding me in processions and ceremonials, knowing I belong to another man?" she asked him with deliberate cruelty. "Could you think of me—"

"I have done it!" he burst out. "Thod's bones, what do you think I endured while you were married to Lervan? You had no eyes for me then, but I—I loved you from the beginning. On your wedding day, I stood by as your protector, watching him smirk and preen, watching you believe his flattery and cheap wit. I thought I would die."

Remorse filled her. "Talmor—"

"On your wedding night, I guarded your chamber door and wanted to kill him." Talmor jumped to his feet. "What do you think I am? Made of stone? How much do you think I can endure?"

"Well, what of me?" She scrambled to her feet and faced him. "How am I to suffer the cold touch of a stranger after I've known your love? I won't do it! I won't bear another man's children when I want yours."

"Oh, Thod, Pheresa, there must be no children!" he said in alarm, wild-eyed. "We dare not—"

"Why not?"

"You know why. I am cursed. Everything I've ever loved or wanted has eventually turned to ashes in my hands. That cannot be passed down to a child!"

Her mouth quivered, and her eyes stung. "You are condemning every last hope. Why must you be so harsh and afraid? Why not believe our children could be normal?"

He winced, and she gasped, putting her hand to her mouth. "Forgive me! I did not mean that."

"And if they were like me?" he asked bitterly. "Strange and accursed? The blood royal must remain pure."

"I've heard that until I'm sick of it. Everyone thinks of me as the queen, but I am a woman, with a heart and feelings and my pride. I am not a crown and scepter, chained forever to duty. I am—"

She couldn't finish, for suddenly she was out of breath and overwhelmed, pressing her hands to her face.

"Oh, my poor love." Talmor gathered her close and held her as she wept against him. "Forgive me."

"What are we to do?" she cried, clutching his tunic front. "What are we to do?"

He stroked her hair and kissed the top of her head with such gentleness it made her cry harder. "I don't know," he replied.

"I love you so much," she said. "I don't want to lose you."

"You haven't lost me," he assured her. "You will never lose me. Never. But now I must get you back. It's late. We've tarried too long."

She clung to him, afraid that she'd never see him again. "Talmor—"

"We'll think of something," he said, walking her toward his horse. "I don't know what."

She let him lift her onto the horse and dried her tears while he climbed into the saddle behind her. When his hand gathered the reins, she rested her fingers atop his.

"Why can't we make the day stop when we wish it?" she asked, with a sigh. "There are so many problems, and we've barely talked."

"We'll meet tomorrow, in that room in the palace where you came today."

"Please, can't we put aside this stealth and secrecy? Come back with me tonight and stay."

"Pheresa, I want to. But you're thinking with your emotions now, and not with good sense."

As she bowed her head, he said, "That's no lover's comment, is it? Forgive me. I'm not very good at this."

No, she thought silently, knowing she forgave him anyway.

"As long as you're in danger, one of us must keep a clear head," he went on. "You were right to send for me in secret, and I can do more if few know I'm here."

"What mean you to try?" she asked, momentarily diverted.

"Sebein hunting."

"Sir Perrell has been doing that for days, with no luck,"

she said impatiently. "And I suspect there's an agent in the palace."

"I'm sure there is. There are always spies and skulkers. You must never be alone."

"I'm not."

"Do they come to your dreams?"

She shuddered in memory of the watchers that haunted her at night. "Yes. Know you some way to keep them out?"

"I wish I did."

"Bokune, the creature who attacked me in my chambers, said that he could take me back through his dream. Is that possible?"

"I'm not sure," Talmor replied, sounding worried. "You should ask a priest."

"I would be told nothing and urged to read Writ for the good of my soul," she retorted with scorn.

"The Sebein cult used to be a part of the Circle. They were priests who became heretics and branched away from the true Writ and teachings."

"Churchmen and their secrets," she said in annoyance. "They could put a stop to the plague if only they—"

"Are you sure?" he asked.

She frowned. "But they know magic! They hide it, shroud it in ritual, and pretend it doesn't exist. It's a great lie, Talmor. They used magic to keep me alive and enspelled when I was poisoned. I know they could put an end to these deaths."

"Perhaps Sebein magic is stronger than church magic."

Alarmed, she drew the sign of the Circle. "I pray you are wrong."

Silence fell between them while the horse picked its way downhill.

"Talmor," she asked at last, "should I ask Sir Perrell how to guard my dreams?"

"Who is that?"

"A reverend commander, and rather nice. Not the usual sort of arrogant zealot. He might answer some questions. I nearly confided in him the other day."

"Can he be trusted?"

"I think so. He's an honest man and a worthy knight of great courage. Don't you remember him? That night I was a prisoner in the catacombs? He was there when you came."

"Oh," Talmor said, his voice suddenly cool. "That one."

"Yes. I wish—" She stopped.

"Go on," he said, nuzzling the back of her head. "What do you wish?"

"I wish *you* could guard my sleep tonight."

"Were I with you, no sleep would you get," he said, and kissed the nape of her neck.

In quick delight, she twisted around to hug him. "Wicked man!" she whispered. "Sneak into the palace with me, and I'll hide you somewhere."

Whatever he might have said was lost, for his horse pricked its ears forward, and Talmor drew rein abruptly. Alert and tense, Pheresa watched in silence as a rider appeared in the trees ahead.

"It's Sir Nedwin," Talmor said. "My protector."

She sat up straighter on the horse's withers, studying the young man who rode up to them. The idea that Talmor had taken a protector of his own pleased her. This man looked stalwart and alert; she liked him on sight.

"The patrols are sweeping the southward trails now, but they'll swing back this way about moonrise," Sir Nedwin said. Although he kept his voice low, Pheresa heard a trace of uplander accent. "Sir Meine has set up camp. And the palace looks to be in an uproar since about the time of sentry changeover."

"Then her majesty has been missed," Talmor said.

"Probably. Sir Georges said she'd better not be gone much longer."

Another rider came out of the trees to join them, and Pheresa saw that it was Pears, Talmor's faithful squire, looking nervous indeed.

"They're on the jump and no mistake," he said, and gave Pheresa a quick bob of his head. "Majesty."

"I hope you're well, Pears," she said graciously, for she and the squire were firm allies. "And I'll wager my earrings that it's the duchesse who's discovered my trick and sounded the alarm."

"The place will be in a panic by now," Pears said. "And if they're turning the palace inside out, searching for her majesty—"

"Yes," Pheresa agreed with a sigh. "I must hurry back."

"Pears," Talmor said, "your horse for the queen."

The squire slid out of his saddle at once, as Pheresa turned to Talmor in surprise. "But I thought—"

"Pears and Sir Nedwin will see you safely back," he told her, and glanced at his protector before she could argue. "Sir Meine should have waited for my orders before going back to camp. We could use him as her majesty's escort right now. Is Sir Georges waiting?"

"Aye, m'lord," Sir Nedwin said crisply. "He said he'd wait for her in the ravine and get her back into the palace. Best we be there before dark."

"Agreed," Talmor said, lifting Pheresa down without dismounting himself.

"Aren't you coming with me?" she asked. "At least as far as—"

"Better we part ways here," he said, sounding suddenly remote. "I've something I want to look into before night falls."

She was furious. Was this the way they were to part? With him as cool as ice, having had his pleasure and ready to dump her the way he would a doxy? With a wordless growl, she whirled away, but Talmor bent down from the saddle and snagged her shoulder.

Pulling her around, he gave her a quick, hard kiss. "Till tomorrow?" he murmured.

Her anger faded, and she kissed him back. "I'll count the hours," she told him, and walked over to the squire's horse.

"Guard her well and see her home safe," Talmor ordered his men. "I'll join you at our camp by moonrise."

Pears helped Pheresa into his saddle, but instead of shortening the stirrups for her, he went over to Talmor. "Best ye take Sir Nedwin, m'lord, wherever yer going."

"Don't be a fool," Talmor said sharply. "'Tis the queen who matters. Now see to her, and quickly!"

"But—"

"I'm just going to the lake," Talmor said.

"But, m'lord, the church knights are camped there."

Talmor stared stonily at Pears.

"Oh," the squire said after a moment. "Aye, I see. But wouldn't it be better if ye waited—"

"I don't want to waste time. I can talk to Sir Perrell and be back to our camp by the time you have the queen safely home."

"Don't like it," Pears muttered. "Those brutes in white ain't to be trusted, damn 'em. Why not swing by camp on the way and take some of the men with you?"

Talmor shot a glance past him at Pheresa, who was watching and listening to every word. Worry knotted her insides. She could not guess what he was really up to, but she feared it would be dangerous.

Apparently Pears thought so, too. He was still gripping Talmor's stirrup. "Best take someone," he insisted stubbornly. "Time's not that precious."

"Very well. I'll get Sir Meine," Talmor said. "Now stop worrying, Pears. You're alarming the queen."

Shivering as dusk closed in, Pheresa watched him go. The locusts had begun their shrill night song. The air smelled dusty there under the lindens and ash trees.

Sighing gustily, Pears stumped over to grip the bridle of Pheresa's horse and lead it toward the palace. He muttered under his breath and kicked the ground with every other step.

"You're an old woman, Pears," Sir Nedwin said cheerfully, riding alongside. "Fussing his lordship to death that way. I wonder why he hasn't dismissed you long ago."

The squire lifted his head. "And who's done for him, bless 'im, since he came out of swaddling cloth? Me, that's who."

"I'll lay odds it's just the polish you keep on his gear that makes him value you," Sir Nedwin said, still teasing, and Pheresa hid her smile.

Pears didn't bother to reply. Plodding steadily along, he

started to mutter again, and after a moment Pheresa heard him say, "Getting careless. Gone off with no mail on, nay, and no men at his back. He won't remember he's not the fighter he used to be."

Her fears came rushing back. "Pears," she said.

"Aye, majesty?"

"I'm safe enough in your company this short distance. Perhaps Sir Nedwin should go after Lord Talmor." She bit her lip as both men stared at her. "Just—just in case some danger should befall him."

"See?" Sir Nedwin said to Pears. "You and your fussing."

"Yes," Pheresa said decisively. "Sir Nedwin, I desire you to go after your master."

The protector bowed to her from the saddle. "Begging your majesty's pardon, but I have my orders."

"Now you have mine."

"Aye, majesty, but if he's told me to guard your safety, then that's what I'll do. We're not far from the ravine now, so be very quiet, both of you."

Astonished that he would dare disobey her, Pheresa opened her mouth, but he held up his hand.

"And the quicker we get your majesty back to the palace, the quicker both Pears and I can catch up with his lordship."

"You impudent—"

With a warning gesture, Sir Nedwin stopped his horse and dismounted, holding his scabbard to keep it quiet. He tied his animal to a bush and gestured for Pears to do the same while he lifted Pheresa down. "Hush now," he whispered. "Not another word. Sound carries strange through these gorges."

She swallowed her ire, aware that despite his deplorable manners the man was right. Remaining silent, she did as he bade her.

Shadows deepened in the ravine, but Sir Nedwin must have had the eyes of a cat. He seemed to have no trouble following the trail down through rocks and brush that snagged at Pheresa's clothing. Pears respectfully kept a grip on her elbow to aid her over the rough spots.

The fierce little squire had long held a place of affection in

her heart because of his devotion to Talmor. She smiled at
Pears in the twilight, and as they came through the bottom of
the ravine and saw the iron grate already shifted out of the
way across the black mouth of the passageway, she briefly
touched the squire's shoulder to convey her thanks.

He bowed to her, smiling rather shyly, and helped her
climb over the rocks up to the passageway.

Sir Georges should have been there, but they saw him not.

"Where's the knave?" Pears muttered under his breath.
"Wandered off, after all his scolding. And no torch left for us
to use either. Come, majesty," he said, leading her forward.
"Hurry."

"I can start in alone," she whispered, but doubtfully. The
tunnel looked pitch-black and its dank air felt clammy on her
face. She did not want to go inside it, and suddenly she realized Sir Georges would not have failed to be here. Something
must be wrong.

She backed up a step.

"Fear not," Pears said. "We'll escort ye all the way."

Ahead, from within the tunnel, she heard footsteps running
their way. She pointed. "We've been discovered. You and Sir
Nedwin had better withdraw, for I don't want either of you de-
tained with questions."

The two men hesitated, exchanging doubtful looks.

"Go on," Pheresa urged them. "I'm well able to handle my
men. And Thod speed you until the morrow, when we meet
again."

Sir Nedwin backed out of the passage, only to utter a
choked cry, reach for his sword, and topple over.

Pears gave Pheresa a shove. "Majesty, run!"

But she was looking at the black-robed Sebeins who surrounded Sir Nedwin's unconscious form. Fear swept through
her, and she clung to Pears's arm.

"Morde!" he swore, drawing his dagger. "Stick close.
Come on!"

"Wait," she said. "My guards are coming—"

At that moment, black-robed figures emerged from inside
the tunnel. They surrounded her before she could even run.

She fought them with her dagger until too many assailants knocked the weapon from her hand. Fighting to protect her, Pears was clubbed to the ground. He lay there, unmoving, blood on his face.

"Pears!" she screamed, then looked up at the walls. "Help! To the queen! Help!"

A dirty rag was shoved in her mouth. The Sebeins pushed her, struggling and stumbling, across the rough ground. After a moment, they paused to secure her gag more firmly, and her hands were swiftly bound.

She wondered why they had not used magic against her as before, then told herself bitterly that there was no need. She'd been captured with humiliating ease, and what good had her guards, escort, or self-defense lessons done her?

"Unwise to leave your palace walls, little queen," a hoarse voice gloated near her ear as she was shoved back up the trail she'd just descended. "Now you are ours, as you were destined to be. And this time, nothing will save you."

Chapter Twenty-five

Bats wheeled and dived after insects in the cool night air. The moon was rising, white and fat, above the mountain lake north of Aversuel. From his vantage point on a rocky knoll, Talmor had a good view of the palace crowning an adjacent hilltop, its lights shining like golden starlight through the trees. He could also see the camp of church knights pitched on the southwest shore of the lake.

Tents were arrayed in tight formation, moth white in the shadows. Burning campfires dotted the dark while men moved about, eating supper, unsaddling horses, polishing weapons and chain mail, studying Writ.

He'd already ridden to the camp checkpoint and been turned away, curtly and arrogantly. The sentries on duty had no interest in his business and would not let him wait until Sir Perrell elected to receive visitors. He was told he could ask for the reverend commander at the palace on the morrow, but he wasn't allowed on camp premises for any reason.

"Be off," the sergeant told him gruffly, and Talmor left.

He wasted no time on annoyance, for from his days as a guardsman he knew well the typical rude arrogance of these knights. Church knights and the palace guard had a long-standing rivalry so fierce that they were seldom allowed to compete against each other in tourneys or jousts because such contests usually devolved into pitched battles with no quarter given. Talmor knew Pears had been right in telling him to come here with an entourage. But even if he'd ridden up with pennons flying and a company of knights at his back, he suspected he would have been turned away—with better manners, perhaps, but the same result.

He glanced at the sky, indigo spangled with starlight. The full moon was beginning to silver the surface of the lake. A waterbird called eerily through the darkness, making him shiver.

Suddenly a queer cold feeling passed through him, leaving him breathless and alarmed. Bracing himself against a tree, he glanced around in the certainty that something was dreadfully wrong. But although he saw and heard nothing amiss, his skin continued to crawl, and he felt . . . he felt . . .

"Pheresa," he whispered.

Then the feeling vanished, leaving him to straighten and wipe perspiration from his brow. She was safe, he told himself, for he'd left her in excellent hands. The premonition, if it had been one at all, was already fading. Usually, if his instincts were truly warning him of danger, the strangeness persisted.

With a shrug he told himself it was time for him to head to the campsite. Certainly he was gaining no ideas or insight from skulking here. He supposed Pears was already busy readying a simple meal, perhaps even cooking some of the fish Sir Nedwin had caught early this morning. And Talmor was ravenous.

The sound of an approaching horse sent him melting expertly into the brush. He waited while a sentry rode by, then made his way through the trees halfway down a hillside to where Canae was tied. He chirruped softly to the big horse, letting it know he was the one approaching. Canae moved in the dark, nuzzling him and champing at the bit.

Climbing into the saddle, Talmor settled himself, calmed

the eager horse, and listened with caution before backing his
mount from the brush and starting down the trail. Moonlight
shone brightly on the steep, twisting path, making him feel
too exposed, so, wherever possible, he forced Canae into
cover.

He took his time, letting the horse walk quietly so that little sound carried.

Pheresa, he thought with a smile. His heart grew warm and
his loins ached for her sweet body beneath his. After years of
waiting, today's union had been a gift he could scarcely believe. She was the most exquisite creature, so beautiful he almost feared to touch her, an endearing mixture of minx and
maid, and willing, so very willing to let him have his way
with her however he wished.

For a short while this afternoon, she had been his lady, exactly as he'd always dreamed her to be, but reality had ended
the dream far too soon.

Although he felt honored by her insistence, marriage did
not matter to him. Being favored at court did not matter to
him. But to know she cared for no other, to lie with her until
each day's dawning . . . aye, he wanted that, craved it with all
his heart.

But he knew the vultures would strike at the Lady of the
Chalice for consorting with a suspected wielder of magic. She
was too beloved, considered too lovely and perfect to be permitted such freedom. And if they could not destroy her, they
would make her life and reign a misery.

That was really why he'd abruptly left her with Pears and
Sir Nedwin. Talmor had lost his courage, knowing that when
they parted at the secret passageway she would cajole him
again. He hadn't been sure he could withstand more of her en-
treaties. Just gazing into her eyes made his insides melt, his
mind fall athwart. He could barely think rationally around her,
much less resist anything she wanted.

And he knew that he wasn't ruthless or cold-blooded
enough to play the games of kings. To say one thing and mean
another. To plan one strategy that hid another. Thod knows
he'd tried this afternoon, for from his years in the palace he

knew how politics, governance, and statecraft worked, but it wasn't in him to lie to Pheresa.

For no matter what he'd tried to say, how could he let her go to another? For realm, for crown, for the good of Mandria . . . Talmor cared not a dreit for any of those things if it meant giving her up. Even now he was jealous from wondering which of her fatuous courtiers would be smiling at her tonight. Who would jest and joke to win her laughter? Who would dare touch her hand in dancing after the supper feast? Who would look too long and too boldly at her beauty?

Grinding his teeth together as he ducked an overhead branch, Talmor told himself to stop being a lovesick fool. He would do whatever she needed him to do, just as he always had. He would say whatever she needed to be told. He would keep silent when she needed that. And, Thod help him, whenever she sent for him, he would fly to her as though swept on wings. Exactly as he had this week. Exactly as he would in the future. For though he would suffer in slow, poisonous misery inside if she eventually married some highborn lout, he would go on loving her and serving her till the end of his days.

He told himself to put his emotions tightly under control and think about how to stop the Sebeins. For years, King Verence's policy of persecution had so harried them that seldom had they been a problem. But something was driving them out of hiding. They were getting very bold, very desperate. Their threats were not idle. The plague worried Talmor, for such a spell was surely so dangerous and complex that the Sebeins might lose control of it entirely. Or, if Pheresa continued to refuse their demands, they might even unleash it on her.

The thought chilled him to his bones.

A twig snapped loud in front of him. Talmor reined up sharply, his heart suddenly thumping. He listened, his hand firm on Canae's reins, and a queer sense of unease passed through him. His mortal soul seemed to creep up around his ears, and he thought of how he had no men, no armor, and one arm too few.

Canae pawed the ground, and Talmor eased his hand forward, allowing the horse to advance a mincing step or two.

"Halt!" called a man's deep voice in challenge. "Name yourself and your business here."

That voice, although hostile, was mortal. Realizing it was only a sentry patrolling the forest, Talmor loosed his pent-up breath. He hoped he had crossed paths with a guardsman this time.

"I'm Edriel," he called out, keeping his tone deliberately calm and assured. "As for my business, I've been—"

"You are far from home."

"Not so far."

"What do you here?"

"I have been summoned to court."

"No decent man travels at night."

"I'm not traveling now," Talmor said. "I'm returning to my camp."

"Why not the palace?"

"The gates have shut for the night. I will go there in the morning."

"Show yourself."

Talmor moved onto the trail where the moonlight shone on him so brightly he almost cast a shadow. He kept his movements slow and nonthreatening and made sure his hand stayed away from his weapons.

The sentry was barely visible, sitting on a ghostly pale horse in the gloom beneath an ash tree. Moonlight gleamed here and there on his mail hauberk, and his surcoat glimmered white.

Another church knight. Disappointed, Talmor swore under his breath. He was tired and hungry, and in no mood to be bullied again.

"I'm Talmor, Baron of Edriel," he said. "By whose authority do you stop and question me?"

"Well met, Lord Talmor," the man said, moving his mount forward to reveal himself in the moonlight. "I am the Reverend Sir Perrell, commander of the church knights assigned to guard her majesty. And the authority by which I stop you is my own."

"Sir Perrell!" Talmor said, brightening. "I have just come from your camp, seeking you."

"Seeking me? Why?"

"To discuss the Sebeins, and to ask—"

"Why should the Sebeins concern you?"

"Why shouldn't they? They threaten the queen and her subjects. She is much worried about the problem."

"The queen has us to deal with the problem."

"And what are you doing about it?" Talmor asked sharply.

Sir Perrell hesitated. "I report to her majesty, my lord, not to you."

"In this, can we not work together?" Talmor asked patiently. "If you are hunting them, tracking them—"

"What of it?" Sir Perrell broke in. "Do you offer abilities in hunting blasphemers of magical powers? Do you admit powers of your own to aid our quest?"

The hair began to prickle on the back of Talmor's neck, and he understood what that tiny premonition at the lake was about. Something was wrong here. The man's belligerence did not match what he remembered of Sir Perrell's manner the last time they met. Nor did it fit with Pheresa's endorsement of him only a short time ago. But men could change, Talmor thought. And men could hide their true natures from lovely women ready to enjoy their charm. The thought of Pheresa trusting this fellow sent jealousy twisting through Talmor.

"I admit no powers," he replied cautiously, checking the shadows for more knights. Sir Perrell was not a sentry, and he was unlikely to be out riding alone. *But I am,* Talmor thought. *Why not him as well?* "I'm sure you meant no insult, nor wished to imply that—"

"Hand over your written summons from the palace," Sir Perrell ordered.

Talmor stiffened. "Do you doubt my word?"

"If you cannot prove you are here on queen's business, then I must detain you for interrogation."

At that, Talmor did move his hand stealthily toward his hilt. He wished with all his heart that he were wearing mail.

But in his vanity today, he'd worn finery instead of armor to meet the queen.

"Your summons," Sir Perrell repeated.

"No," Talmor said. "You have no right to detain me, to doubt my word, or to interrogate me. Back away. Let me pass."

Sir Perrell did not move. "I can question any suspicious activity near her majesty's residence, and I can certainly detain liars."

"Commander, do not forget you're addressing a baron—"

"I am addressing an imposter, for no baron would sneak through the night without entourage and baggage cart," Sir Perrell said. "We know every messenger and courier who travels to and fro from here. None have gone to Edriel."

"You fool—"

But without warning, Sir Perrell drew his sword and charged Talmor.

Caught off guard and furious, Talmor made Canae rear up and strike out with his hooves, giving him time to draw his own sword. He twisted in the saddle, meeting Sir Perrell's blow with a clang of steel. Sparks flew in the gloom.

Sir Perrell fought with deadly determination. Again, Talmor parried, this time blocking a blow that could have split his skull in twain. He struck back, but his blade hit chain mail. Hastily, Talmor ducked as sharp steel whistled past his chest.

Spurring Canae forward past Sir Perrell, Talmor forced the commander to wheel his mount and follow. Sir Perrell gave Talmor no chance to flee into the dark, but instead crowded Canae from behind, his mount biting Canae's rump as the warhorse squealed and kicked.

Busy trying to control Canae with his legs and spurs, for he had no hand to spare for the reins, Talmor managed to turn his horse, but doing so brought him right into the next blow, which struck him across the side.

Had the blade's edge hit him, he would have been cut in half. As it was, perhaps the gods favored him, for the blow was clumsy and did him no harm other than to topple him from the saddle.

Kicking his feet from the stirrups, Talmor twisted with agile skill, rolling over Canae's near side and landing upright with his sword at the ready.

Canae had been trained to stay close by him, but before Talmor could scramble back into the saddle, Sir Perrell was at him again, standing in his stirrups and reaching over Canae to strike at Talmor's head.

Talmor ducked as Canae reared, striking out with his forefeet. But Sir Perrell smote the horse in the throat with the flat of his sword, and Canae shied back, nearly trampling Talmor, who jumped to get out of the horse's way. Now he stood vulnerable, without even Canae's body as shield.

Sir Perrell spurred his horse at Talmor, and with a yell Talmor whirled and sliced his sword tip across his attacker's leg. Sir Perrell shouted in pain and galloped on into the darkness on the other side of the trail.

Gulping in air, Talmor ran for cover, but he wasn't fast enough. Already Sir Perrell was coming back, galloping into him from behind and knocking him off his feet.

Talmor hit the ground with a jolt that snapped his teeth together and skidded on his armless shoulder into the base of a tree. Stunned, he tried to get to his knees, but sank down again. Perhaps that saved his life, for Sir Perrell's horse thundered past as though its rider could not see Talmor lying in the deep shadows beneath the tree.

Relieved, Talmor caught his breath, scrambled unsteadily to his feet and froze in the dark while Sir Perrell made another futile pass.

With mail hauberk glinting in the moonlight, his face a pale blur beneath his coif, the reverend commander called out, "Come forth, coward! Why not face me and confess the truth? Are you not a secret sympathizer with the Sebeins? Have you not come here, hoping to gain audience with the queen to enspell and harm her?"

Rage tightened Talmor's skull, but he held silent and still, striving to regain his breath and give his trembling legs and arm a chance to rest.

"Coward, hiding in the dark," Sir Perrell called. "The

guardsmen like to boast of what a legend you were on the
jousting field and how dangerous you are in battle. Rubbish!
I've met green trainees better able to handle weapons than
you."

Talmor, ignoring taunts that would hardly provoke a
schoolboy, realized that Sir Perrell was moving again, coming
right at him this time.

He did not know how Sir Perrell had sensed where he was
hiding, but that hardly mattered. The tree was large, its roots
knobby and treacherous atop the ground. The hill sloped up
sharply here from the trail, and if he turned his back on Sir
Perrell to climb it . . .

Instead, Talmor threw aside caution and ran straight at the
charging horse. Long hours of work with the lance had taught
him how to wait for the exact moment, and he did not let himself pay heed to the fact that he had neither a horse nor a
lance. He ducked his left shoulder and twisted sideways just
enough to avoid being knocked flat by the animal, and as he
did so gripped Sir Perrell's stirrup. He yanked up as the horse
swept past him and unseated the commander.

It was a move he'd learned neither in knightly training at
arms nor as a guardsman at Savroix. It was dirty, unfair, dishonorable, and risky. He had his brothers to thank for it.

Sir Perrell fell awkwardly, hitting the ground with a grunt
and rolling over twice before climbing unsteadily to his hands
and knees. He'd lost his sword and started groping for it.

Talmor ran at him with the speed and agility that had once
made him so effective on the battlefield. He careened full tilt
into Sir Perrell, knocking the man down, and tumbled over
him in a roll that brought him back on his feet, facing Sir Perrell as the man attempted a second time to rise. Sir Perrell's
wounded leg, Talmor noted coldly, did not support him well.
In the gloom he could not tell how much blood the commander was losing, but he hoped it was a lot.

"Perdition smite you!" Sir Perrell swore at him, out of
breath, managing to recover his sword. "How dare you—"

Talmor wasted no breath in talking. In real combat, there
was no honor. That came later, in the hour of victory or defeat.

He swung at Sir Perrell's head, intending to take it off at the neck, but Sir Perrell ducked, throwing himself sideways. Talmor circled him and struck his back.

The white surcoat, such a good target in the gloom, split as sparks flew off Sir Perrell's mail. Rather than go down under the blow, however, the commander twisted awkwardly and gained his feet. Although he was barely upright and not set, he even managed to parry Talmor's next swing with two-handed strength.

Talmor could not help but be impressed. The man was a good warrior, and tough.

Too tough to grant the slightest quarter, Talmor reminded himself hastily. Although he'd leveled the odds somewhat in unhorsing Sir Perrell, in hand-to-hand combat the commander still held the advantage.

Shaking off momentary light-headedness, Talmor went at his opponent. He had been trained to fight two-handed or with sword and shield. He had no choice but to use the latter method now, swinging high and chopping down as he crouched to make himself less of a target. His legs were burning with fatigue, but he advanced in steady attack, driving Sir Perrell, who was still limping, into a stumbling retreat.

But Sir Perrell was far from finished. Soon he rallied, caught Talmor's blade, and attempted to lock swords. Talmor shifted free, nearly wrenching his shoulder in doing so. Sir Perrell sprang at him, sweeping his sword tip at Talmor's unprotected midsection with such force the weapon whistled through the air.

Steel sliced through Talmor's tunic. He felt his flesh rip like fire with a gush of blood, but it was no mortal cut and not deep enough to spill his entrails. With scarcely a pause, he used the pain to drive himself forward and in midswing changed his attack to Netheran style, aiming low at Sir Perrell's legs, where the man was already vulnerable. If he could lunge low enough in the dark, Talmor hoped to clip one of Sir Perrell's knees or even wound the commander's other leg.

But the shadows and uneven ground hindered him. He could feel blood running down his stomach and soaking into his clothing. As yet, he had not weakened, but he knew from experience that he must fight with all he had in hopes of defeating his foe before blood loss slowed him.

Although the Netheran maneuvers appeared to catch Sir Perrell by surprise, it was only for a moment. Sir Perrell switched his style of fighting from Mandrian to something strange indeed. Very fast, quick jabs and lightning switches back and forth from hand to hand.

This was not broadsword fighting at all, but Kladite knife dance. Talmor knew that style as well, but with only one hand he could not meet it. He wasted no time, but instead gauged the rhythm of Sir Perrell's swings and charged recklessly straight inside the commander's guard. Wearing armor, it was one of the most dangerous moves in hand-to-hand combat. Without armor, it was madness indeed. If he misjudged the slightest bit, or if Sir Perrell countered correctly, Talmor knew he would be impaled on his opponent's steel.

Sir Perrell countered by gashing Talmor's shoulder. He yelled in agony, the splash of sweat and blood hitting his face, but despite that, Sir Perrell's parry was a weak one. Talmor was already smashing past it, aware on some level through pain and battle fury that he was only cut, not stabbed. And he had Sir Perrell this time, his sword tip already in the man's ribs, his momentum strong enough to drive it deep.

Something struck the back of his skull. The night burst into white, blinding blankness. Talmor's knees crumpled, and he lost his grip on his sword as Sir Perrell stumbled back from him, still upright and alive.

It was as though time froze. Talmor seemed to be falling forever and ever. Then he struck the ground, his cheek scraping over pebbles and dirt. He heard himself grunt as his body landed as awkwardly as a dropped armload of firewood.

There were bursts of color exploding through the whiteness in his skull. He would have found them pretty had he not been so perplexed and enraged. He had Sir Perrell defeated, dead. What happened?

Then blackness filled his skull, taking away the white, and in a sudden rush of clarity Talmor heard a hearty voice laughing. "That's finished him, revered sir. If you'd just waited for me, I could have—"

"You've done enough, Sir Cortaine. Thank you," Sir Perrell replied, choking and panting for air.

"So do I throw him in the gorge?"

You damned dirty cheat, Talmor thought. But he never heard Sir Perrell's order, for suddenly everything faded inside him, and there was nothing.

Chapter Twenty-six

Still breathing hard, sweat soaking his padded undertunic and making his mail feel as though it weighed twice as much, Sir Perrell heaved himself into the saddle, with Sir Cortaine boosting him from behind. Pain lanced through Perrell's leg, making him grit his teeth to keep from crying out as Cortaine's big hands fumbled with his foot.

"No," he said hastily. "Not in the stirrup! Let it hang."

"It'll hurt more, revered sir."

"Leave it. Morde! Just let it hang."

Blood had filled his boot, and the cloth Sir Cortaine had stuffed through the sliced leather was doing a sorry job of stopping the flow. Catching his breath, Perrell forced himself to straighten in the saddle. Despite the pain, the injury wasn't serious. No tendons had been severed. He might limp once his leg healed, but he wasn't crippled, Tomias be thanked. As for the scratch to his side, it hardly mattered.

"Let's get back to camp," he said.

"Aye, sir."

Sir Cortaine had already caught Lord Talmor's big brute of a warhorse, admired it for a moment, then stripped off the bri-

dle, slashed his dagger across the saddle, and spooked the
horse into galloping off into the darkness, empty stirrups flap-
ping. Now Cortaine swung astride his own mount, gathered
his reins, and paused to stare down the mountain slope where
he'd tumbled Lord Talmor's body.

"I'd feel better if we'd taken the time to throw him in the
river, revered sir. Come daylight, he could be found too soon.
I can't see how far down he rolled."

"Let him lie," Perrell ordered. " 'Twill serve."

They headed up the trail toward the lake at a slow walk.

As he rode, Perrell bowed his head, for his conscience was
hurting him far more than his wound. There was no honor in
what he'd done tonight, no honor in provoking a man to combat under such conditions. Perrell had thought that a good
rousing fight would be the best way to kill the baron. Better
than simply ambushing him like a cutthroat. Instead, Perrell
felt ashamed of himself. The man had worn no armor, and still
he'd fought bravely. The man possessed but one arm, and still
he'd managed horse and weapon well. So well, in fact, that
had Cortaine not intervened in the nick of time, Perrell knew
he would be dead.

Victory through cheating, he thought in self-disgust. But a
man fought to win at any cost in war, he told himself, and so,
too, was this a war. The war for a woman's heart and hand.
Lord Talmor's body would be found eventually, mauled by
animals with any luck, and his death would be declared an ac-
cident. The queen would grieve, of course, but then she would
forget her dead lover. A new favorite would fill her eyes.

Scowling, Perrell touched his Circle with bloodstained fingers. It was done, he told himself harshly. He would make his
atonement later.

"Doing all right, revered sir?" Sir Cortaine asked.

"Yes."

"He put up quite a fight, eh? Wish I'd seen all of it. Always
heard he was a tough bastard, but no match for you, was he?"

Sir Perrell grimaced in the dark. This was one fight he
didn't want to discuss. "He nearly had me at the end."

"Seemed like it. I did see that," Sir Cortaine said with rel-

ish. "Sweet saints! We weren't allowed to practice that move
in training. What's it called? Leap of Death?"

"Don't know," Perrell said, although he did.

"My old instructor said it was tantamount to suicide and a
mortal sin to use it. But this Talmor being a heretic like he
was, well, now, he probably had no qualms at all."

A heretic, Perrell thought, *who wore a Circle just like mine.*
He'd felt its outline beneath Talmor's clothing when he rolled
him over. What if the rumors weren't true? he wondered.
What if Talmor had no magic in him and was nothing more
than a man of mixed blood caught up in political events too
large for him? Perrell reminded himself hastily that such judgments weren't for him to make. He followed orders and
served Thod. That was surely enough.

"Nay, revered sir," Cortaine was still chattering, "you'd
have handled yourself all right, even if I hadn't come when I
did. Maybe taken a bad wound to your side, but you two were
well matched, and you—"

"Well matched?" Perrell said angrily. "And him a cripple?
Thank you."

"Forgive me, revered sir. I didn't mean—"

"That's enough," Perrell said sharply, and Sir Cortaine fell
silent.

They reached camp soon after, and Perrell went straight to
his tent. His adjutant delivered the nightly report from the
duty officer while a physician set to work on his leg. Stripped
to the waist and sponged off by his squire, Perrell reclined on
his cot, gritting his teeth and grimly watching the moths flut-
ter about the lamp over his head.

A sentry hurried in. "Forgive me, revered sir," he said,
saluting, "but guardsmen from the palace have come. There's
bad news."

Perrell propped himself up on his elbows despite the
physician's attempt to push him down. "Bring them to me."

Moments later Lord Avlon strode in, flanked by two ser-
geants in bright green cloaks. Avlon's heavy jaw, shadowed
tonight with beard stubble, was clamped tight, and his heavy-
lidded eyes were smoldering.

At the sight of Perrell, however, he checked in surprise. "What's happened to you?" he asked.

"Sebeins," Perrell said, wincing as he sat up. From behind the guardsmen, Perrell's young adjutant blinked and shot a startled look at Sir Cortaine, who gave him a swift frown of warning. Pretending not to see the exchange, Perrell kept his gaze on the tense guardsmen.

"Sebeins?" Lord Avlon echoed, looking pale. "Damne, are the fiends everywhere?"

"If you've news to impart, do so," Perrell said impatiently.

The rebuke made Avlon stiffen. "The queen is missing. Since this afternoon."

A jab of intense anger drove Perrell to his feet, despite the physician's attempt to stop him. "What in the name of Tomias do you mean, *since this afternoon?*" he shouted. "Why do you come only *now* to inform me?"

"It was believed her majesty left of her own will. A—er— lover's tryst. Or so her lady-in-waiting told us."

Perrell frowned. The idea of Lord Talmor sporting with the queen twisted a hot poker of anger through his insides. She deserved better, he thought. She was the Lady of the Chalice, the queen, not a scullery maid to be lured out into the forest for an illicit seduction.

With eyes narrowed and his mouth clamped tight, Perrell no longer regretted Lord Talmor's death in the least. "Go on," he said coldly.

Avlon was a seasoned officer of the guards, a nobleman's son, and a man of considerable courage. But at the moment under Perrell's icy gaze, he looked anything but self-assured.

"When it grew dark, and the queen did not return, we broadened our search beyond the palace walls. One of her servants showed us exactly how she left the palace in secret. While examining the area, we found signs of a struggle. A torn scrap of gown, one of her majesty's slippers, and her dagger."

Looking grim, Avlon paused. "The queen is never without that weapon. She keeps it close like a talisman."

Concern spread like frost up Perrell's spine. "Surely there were tracks to follow."

"Aye, but the land is rough, broken with rock and brush, and we lost the tracks in the dark. All we've discovered is her protector, spell hit and unconscious, and two injured men in Edriel colors."

"What have they told you?"

"Nothing. None can be roused as yet. But Sir Georges was surely attacked by Sebeins."

Perrell found his gaze shifting to meet that of Sir Cortaine. The flat-nosed second-in-command wore an expression that gave nothing away, but his eyes glittered in the lamplight. For one wild, impulsive moment Perrell considered accusing Lord Talmor of abducting the queen. He even wondered if he dared delay rescue attempts. Surely Cardinal Theloi would be delighted if the queen perished, but the idea of it sent a queer feeling through Perrell's heart. He knew he could not do it. If her majesty was in danger, he must find her.

"And you've fought them as well today," Lord Avlon went on, nodding at Perrell's wounds. "We fear they've taken her majesty as they did before."

"Clearly," Perrell said. "It seems to me that you've bungled seriously, wasted hours, and botched everything. Small wonder you were dismissed as her majesty's protector. You should have sounded an alarm and informed me the instant the queen was known to have left the safety of the palace. What in the name of Tomias do you expect from me now when her majesty could be leagues away?"

Avlon's face had grown ugly with temper, but he managed to control it. "I don't think they've taken her majesty far. At least not yet."

"Must I drag every piece of information from you?" Perrell demanded impatiently. "Have you more evidence, or is this just a hopeful guess?"

"My commander says it," Avlon growled. "What he bases it on, I do not know. Now, reverend commander, I was sent to ask for your aid. I'll put my men under your command, in exchange for your help, if you'll give it."

"How many men have you brought, Lord Avlon?" he asked.

"Thirty."

"Step outside, and I'll join you in a moment."

"Well, hurry!" Avlon said, and went out.

Perrell gestured to his squire. The man came forward to strap him into a padded undertunic, hauberk, and fresh surcoat. While his weapons were brought, not yet cleaned of Lord Talmor's blood, Perrell pulled on new boots with a wince. He paused a moment, trying to catch his breath.

"Sir Cortaine."

"Revered sir!"

"Ready the men. Divide them into two parties to start a search. Split the guardsmen between them. I'll want Sir Nireau to lead one group. I'll take the other."

With a swift salute, Sir Cortaine ducked out of the tent and hastened off, taking the big-eyed adjutant with him.

The physician was scowling. "If you walk on that leg, you'll start bleeding again. You're in no condition to ride."

"Nothing can excuse me from this duty. I'll take Clamp," Perrell said, grimacing while the squire belted his sword for him. His whole body was starting to stiffen with bruises from the fight, and standing with even part of his weight on his leg made it hurt fiercely. Picking up his gorget and mail coif while his squire fetched his gloves, Perrell accepted the potion handed to him by the physician.

The brew had a complicated herbal name, but the church soldiers called it Clamp, for it could work wonders on pain and had enabled many knights to finish a battle without faltering. However, it was known to be highly addictive, and sensible men took it as seldom as possible. There were many scarred veterans of war who stood in line at the campfires each night to receive their nightly dose. And some who would steal a vial of Clamp from the fingers of a wounded man.

It was also likely to dull the very senses Perrell needed to trace the Sebeins. But, pain could be an even bigger distraction. He tossed back less than half the measure given to him and put the cup down.

Limping from his tent, he found that Sir Cortaine had the men ready, as ordered. A fresh horse was saddled and waiting for Perrell. He got on with help, drawing a sharp breath to keep from yelping. As yet, his few swallows of Clamp hadn't started working.

"You'll have to use the stirrup this time, revered sir," Cortaine said quietly.

Nodding, Perrell held his breath while his foot was eased into the stirrup. It hurt like fire, but he tried to ignore the agony. He had to concentrate now and pray that the mercy of Tomias would guide him swiftly to her majesty's rescue.

"You," he said, pointing to Lord Avlon. "Show me where you lost her tracks. Hurry!"

Soaked to the skin, her wet hair streaming into her eyes, Pheresa cringed on the precarious, water-slick trail next to the thundering waterfall. Moonlight glimmered through the spray drenching her. She kept slipping on the rocks, hampered by the missing slipper, and feared plunging to her death in the gorge below.

One of her Sebein captors pushed her from behind and shouted something she could not hear. She stumbled forward, grabbing any projecting root or stone with her bound hands and tripped often by her wet, bedraggled skirts.

Someone in front of her grabbed her wrists and yanked her forward. She lost her footing and fell, yelping against the gag, but the man dragged her bodily up the last difficult part and stood her upright on a narrow stone ledge. Terrified, she trembled from head to foot.

The waterfall hurtled past her. It was so forceful and loud she felt like screaming. Her captors pushed her forward into the water. It engulfed her in a numbing, hammering torrent before she emerged behind it.

Blinking and sputtering, she found herself in a cave mouth behind the waterfall. Moonlight shone through it, diffused strangely by the rushing water. One of the Sebeins lifted his hand, and a spark of orange light hovered in the air before her, just bright enough for her to see where to walk.

Her captors surrounded her on all sides and pushed her forward. She followed the sparks the way she'd once chased fairlight bugs as a child. The air was cold, and her wet clothes stuck to her skin, making her colder. Although she could not stop shivering, she knew it was as much from fright and dread as actual physical misery. How long, she thought, until Talmor missed Pears and Sir Nedwin and started in search of them? Was either man alive to even tell him what had happened?

He'll come, she told herself, trying to keep her courage alive. *He'll come, and I must hang on somehow until he does.*

Chapter Twenty-seven

Throbbing, clammy, sweaty misery . . . groaning, Talmor came to slowly. He hurt in a thousand places, his head pounding most of all, as though someone meant to hammer a stake through it.

When he tried to move, he found his head weighed more than a catapult stone. The very effort of shifting it made him dizzy, then sick. After that, he lay without moving and hoped the misery would go away.

It eased in time, and he realized he was lying on hard ground that smelled pungently of weeds. Little rocks pressed into his cheek. The locusts were buzzing as loud as the noise in his head.

Where is Pears? he thought fretfully. *Need him.*

Then he heard a furtive patter of feet running toward him. He listened, relieved that Pears was coming for him.

A second set of footsteps. Pears, he thought, and . . . and the other fellow. His thoughts faded.

Someone knelt beside him and gripped his shoulders, lifting him enough to roll him over. He couldn't see clearly, for the starlight overhead was spinning dizzily, but he smiled.

"Pears," he mumbled.

"Pick him up," said a voice he did not know. "We must hurry. There's little time."

Fingers ran over Talmor's body as lightly as a spider. "He's injured, losing blood. He could die."

A hand clamped tight around Talmor's wrist. Its touch was icy cold, like the grave. Alarmed, he tried to pull free, but was too weak.

"There's enough life in him to serve our purpose," the first voice said. "Bring him. And hurry."

Pheresa was led deeper into the cave, eventually coming to a torchlit place with a fire blazing on the stone floor. Brought before a robed man seated on a ledge of stone, she looked around while her wrists were untied, then she jerked the filthy rag from her mouth with relief.

"Welcome, Queen Pheresa," the man said to her.

She had no difficulty in remembering this Sebein with his gray hair and scarred face. His left, blind eye reflected the firelight's dancing flames.

A little snake of dread slithered through her veins, but she made herself stand straight and composed before him. "Kanth," she said.

"You have come to fulfill the soul promise. The old debt will now be repaid."

"No," she said, her voice ringing out through the cave. "I refuse."

The Sebeins around her muttered and stirred, but Kanth's expression did not change.

"Ah," he murmured, "the expected defiance. So despite all we have done to soften your heart, Pheresa of Mandria, you insist on clinging to the falsehood of Writ and the blasphemy of Tomias's Reform."

She was too tired and frightened to play verbal games with him. "You have slaughtered innocent people in an attempt to frighten me. You have haunted my dreams and killed good men. The plague you have sent is despicable. I call you cowards, hiding in shadows, creeping through the darkness. You will not come into the light of day because you *are* the darkness. And I repudiate you in the name of Thod, Tomias, and the sacred Chalice of Eternal Life."

Her voice rang out defiantly, echoing through the cave, but the uproar she expected did not come. The Sebeins watched her unmoved.

Kanth rose to his feet. His scar twisted the left side of his visage, pulling that corner of his mouth into what appeared to be a perpetual smile, but was not.

"So is this your final answer?" he asked. "This ringing declaration of allegiance to the cruelty of the Reformed Church?"

"I will not grant your request. You deserve no mercy after what you have done to my subjects."

"What do you care about your subjects?" he asked. "You've never met these people. They are as ants to you. Peasants, simple people of toil. Their deaths do not matter to you."

She stared at him, too angry to answer.

"You murdered Bokune, who was chosen to lead you through the Rite of Blood." Kanth shook his head. "This has made you our enemy."

"I was never your friend."

"No," he replied regretfully. "I believed and hoped for it, but I was wrong. This is perhaps the only truth you will speak. How do you think you will resist us? How do you think you will stop us from forcing you to share the blood?" He leaned toward her, his sighted eye stony and implacable. "I can stop your heartbeat with a single word. How will you defy my command of your mind?"

She began to tremble with fear, for escape seemed impossible. No one knew where she was. Her magicked dagger was lost. She possessed no tricks that would fool these creatures. Although before Kanth had seemed a reasonable, sensible man, even a possible ally, tonight she sensed only hostility in him. She realized that he was probably far more dangerous than Bokune had been.

"Does the queen fear to speak?" Kanth demanded. "Or are you preparing more lies?"

"Before, you said the Rite of Blood worked only if—if I performed it willingly," she replied. "You told Bokune not to coerce me."

"Bokune was impatient and very young in our ways," Kanth said softly, his one eye glittering. "He was drunk on his power. He *wanted* to force your compliance."

Stiffening, she said quickly, "I do not comply. I will never give up my soul to you. Kill me if you must, but I—"

"Kill you? Now why would we do such a thing?" Kanth broke in. "We want alliance with you. Killing you is not at all to our purpose."

"Then let me go," she insisted, "for I won't give you what you want."

"I think perhaps you will." As he spoke, he gestured to his minions. "Show her what we have found."

The people surrounding her parted on one side. Torchlight flared so brightly that Pheresa was momentarily dazzled. Squinting, she held up her hands to shield her eyes, and when the brilliant light faded to normal levels once more, she blinked at the sight before her.

A man lay on the ground, his hand and feet chained to iron bolts driven through the rock. Blood stained the front of his tunic. More blood glistened on the stone beneath his head. He lay without moving, his eyes shut, and only a slight movement of his chest told her that he lived.

Her heart turned over, and all her courage trickled away. "Talmor," she whispered.

He stirred as though he heard her. His head turned to one side, and his eyes opened momentarily. They were hazy and unfocused, and if they saw her, she could not tell, for he fell unconscious again.

"This was the rescue you were hoping for," Kanth said. "You seem to think this man possesses miraculous powers."

"He does," she replied steadily. "He loves me."

"Yes, we have seen his love of you."

Some of the Sebeins snickered, and Pheresa felt her face

flame hot. Had they been watching while she and Talmor . . . she could not complete the thought. The idea of it infuriated her.

"Such passion," Kanth said, his voice taunting and cruel. "We have waited many weeks, certain you would make a mistake, and today you did. Once more, you stand in our power, and this time you will not escape us."

"Perhaps not," she said, "but I won't help you."

Kanth walked over to Talmor and nudged him with his toe. Talmor moaned but did not fully rouse.

Dreadfully worried about him, Pheresa frowned. What had they done to him? How badly was he hurt?

"Talmor's dreams are closed to us," Kanth said, circling him slowly. "We cannot follow his thoughts as we do yours. But we know of him, just the same."

Her sense of unease grew. She knew she was being toyed with, but she did not know how to stop it.

"He is a fire-mage," Kanth said. "Very rare in this age of nonbelief. The religion you cling to so staunchly condemns such as he to death. Are you aware of that?"

Her lips felt stiff and bloodless. She could not force herself to answer.

"Yes, there is a small fear always in the back of your mind. You worry about him, yet deny that he is in danger. Tell me, would you love him so much, worry about him so much, if you knew *everything* about him?"

"I know enough," she replied.

"Do you know that his power is growing? I can sense it in him, coiled now, ready to be unleashed. He is dangerous. And he will surely go mad."

She didn't want to believe what Kanth was saying, and when she saw a flicker of amused satisfaction in the Sebein's face, she knew he was deceiving her, trying to make her doubt the one man she could always trust.

"This is the choice before you, Pheresa of Mandria," Kanth said. "You will come willingly through the Rite of Blood, or this man will suffer in your stead. I cannot shake your worthless faith and convictions, but I can do him great harm. And he will suffer, Pheresa. He will suffer greatly."

His threat chilled her. Desperation sent a dozen possible ploys through her mind, none of them viable. She did not think she could bear to see Talmor tortured in her stead.

Talmor opened his eyes and stared at her as though trying to tell her something. His golden eyes looked alert and fully conscious now; perhaps, she thought in hope, he had been faking his degree of injury before.

"You forget, Kanth," she said with renewed spirit, "that you cannot drink my blood. I was cured by the restorative powers of the Chalice of Eternal Life, and you will find as Bokune did that your evil will not prevail."

"Oh, dear," he said in soft mockery. "Have I overlooked that? It isn't necessary for you to go through the Rite of Blood to keep the soul promise. You can simply grant us full pardons, allowing us to worship and convert whom we wish."

"I've told you I won't!"

Baring his teeth, Kanth knelt and gripped Talmor's arm. Flickers of lightning shot from his hand across Talmor's body. Twitching and jerking, Talmor choked out a hoarse cry.

When Kanth released him, he continued to shudder and gasp. His face had turned gray.

Horrified by that casual display of torture, Pheresa felt tears running down her cheeks.

"Oh, it hurts him a little, but he's a strong man, well able to endure it," Kanth said airily. "The problem for Talmor is that he walks a precipice edge between his true nature of destructive force and his desire to be acceptable in your naive sight." Kanth gripped Talmor's arm and sent another jolt of lightning through him, making Talmor arch his back and writhe before releasing him. "And the more often I touch him this way, the stronger the fire in him burns."

"No," she said breathlessly. "No, I don't believe you. You're just hurting him."

"I am making him stronger, pushing him toward the fire, increasing its power over him. I can make him crave it until he's obsessed and crazed. I can turn him toward destruction so very easily." And Kanth gave Talmor another jolt.

"Stop!" she cried.

Kanth released Talmor at once. "Do you feel the air getting warmer?" he asked softly. "Do you see how the torches are burning more and more brightly? He is gathering fire. I am making him do it."

"You can't control him," she said, refusing to believe what Kanth claimed. "You're just trying to trick and frighten me into doing what you want. But he's—"

"Let's look through your memories," Kanth said, and shut his eyes a moment. "Ah, when Talmor threw fire at the hurl-hounds, what happened?"

"No!" she said, shaking her head. "No!"

"Did he destroy the Nonkind beast or make it stronger?"

Again she shook her head, pressing her fists to her temples. She refused to believe him.

"He made the hurlhound stronger. Remember, Pheresa! Admit it!"

"I'll admit nothing."

"A fire-mage is no friend to your soft religion. A fire-mage is enemy to Writ's teachings. A fire-mage is part of all that you fear and disavow. I can make him stronger, Pheresa, because he shares that which I worship."

"Liar!" she whispered desperately. "You're trying to claim he is evil, and he's not. He's not!"

"He burned his own brother, Pheresa," Kanth said. "Deliberately. Oh, yes, the evil's there, clawing in him to get out. I can release it for him, help him past the last hurdle and let him become what he was born to be."

Crying out, she ran past Kanth to kneel on the other side of Talmor. Touching his ashen face, she felt his hot skin. It was as though fever raged in his body. He was sweating, his hair plastered to his skull, his tunic soaked through.

"Talmor," she said, caressing his cheek. "Talmor, I believe in you. I will always believe in you."

Her beloved lifted his head, gasping with the effort, and looked at her. For a moment she thought she saw firelight dancing in his amber eyes, but then told herself that was only fanciful imagination, fed by Kanth's evil accusations.

"Don't give in," he whispered to her. "Whatever happens, don't agree. Run to the waterfall."

She frowned, suddenly afraid he meant to do something terrible. She had seen him ill and feverish from Nonkind venom, throwing fire in his delirium. What might he do under Kanth's torture?

"Can't," he whispered, so softly she leaned closer to hear him. "Can't help you. Run to the water."

"Run to the water," Kanth echoed from behind her.

Pheresa faced him angrily. "You fiend! How dare you mock him?"

Kanth gripped Talmor's clenched fist. Although Talmor tried to resist him, Kanth forced open his fingers.

There, dancing on Talmor's palm, were tiny flames.

Pheresa gasped in fear.

"See?" Kanth said. "I tell you no lie. One more push from me, and he will be swallowed by the darkness. But you can save him if you will give me your compliance."

"My word alone will not satisfy you," Pheresa said furiously. "You'll never stop until you control me like a puppet."

"Yes, I shall govern you," Kanth told her arrogantly. "Do not depend too much on the Chalice's protection. It fades in you every day of your life. And when enough of its influence is gone, I shall have your blood, and you shall have mine."

She saw then that he was completely ruthless and quite mad. Talmor was right, she thought. There could be no deal struck with Kanth, no honor upheld. And although she was terrified, she knew that she could not surrender her soul's honor to the Sebeins for an instant, not to save herself, not even to save Talmor.

"Go, Pheresa!" Talmor called out desperately. "You have one chance."

She cast him a grief-stricken look, trying to imprint his dear face on her memory.

"What is this foolish plan?" Kanth asked. "He will destroy me and my followers with fire while you escape? I think not."

Bending down, Kanth gripped Talmor's wrist once more

and stared at her. "He wants to sacrifice himself for you. How touching. How futile."

"You—"

"No more protests," Kanth said. "Whatever he becomes, it is by your decision."

She was shaking in fear. Her heart was crying out, yet she had to face this. No one, she knew, could help her.

"Now, Pheresa!" Kanth said sharply. "Decide now. Are you mine, queen of Mandria, or is he?"

Chapter Twenty-eight

Magic tingled in the night air, giving it the uneasy heaviness of an impending rainstorm. Standing in the bottom of the ravine where the queen had supposedly been abducted, Perrell had no trouble detecting heavy Sebein presence. The problem was, as he limped his way through thornbushes and scrub, that the Sebeins had left their trace too prominently. He could not determine which way they'd gone. Moreover, they'd left a concealment spell behind them, and the longer he and his men crossed back and forth where the protector and squire had been found unconscious, the more confused his mind and senses became.

Perrell retreated to clear his head, with Lord Avlon protesting all the way.

"You aren't giving up!"

Perrell's mouth clamped in a tight line, but he did not bother reassuring the man. Instead, he beckoned to Sir Cortaine. "Clear these guardsmen back."

"Aye, revered sir."

"You can't do that!" Avlon protested. "We've as much right—more, in fact—to search for her majesty, and—"

"It would be best if they were to retreat into that tunnel leading under the palace," Perrell said to his second, as though Avlon hadn't spoken. "Let them light torches and see what additional evidence they can find."

"Afraid we'll steal some of your glory if we remain close?" Avlon asked at his most scathing. "Or are you worried we'll see there's no mystery to church knights after all? I think you're just hoping to find a clear footprint, like the rest of us."

Still ignoring him, Perrell gave Cortaine a nod, and his second-in-command spoke to Avlon: "If you will order your men to search the tunnels, m'lord, 'twould help greatly."

Avlon stood planted in Perrell's path with his fists on his hips. "My men can go, but I'm sticking close. I—"

"Will you be silent?" Perrell snapped, losing all patience. "You asked for my help. Now let me have a chance to provide it."

Without another word, Avlon spun on his heel and moved his men back. Stubbornly, however, he returned alone, climbing atop a boulder to watch Perrell as though hoping to see some kind of performance. By then, Perrell had succeeded in sifting through the eddying layers of the spell of concealment to the myriad emotions lingering in this place. The strongest feelings included joy, terror, agony, and triumph.

He selected terror and focused his senses on it. Shutting his eyes a moment, he sifted carefully through woven tracings of anger, despair, and fear, resisting distraction from the emotions of those around him.

His men knew how to curb their feelings during this kind of search. Lord Avlon, however, proved to be an intense distraction, growing worse all the time as his impatience increased.

Frowning, Perrell forced himself to sift and untangle with infinite, careful patience. Getting this wrong could mean the queen's life.

And then he found the tracing he sought. "Kanth," he murmured, swiftly suppressing elation lest he lose that tenuous connection. He had hunted this Sebein priest for a long while. It would be a triumph finally to catch him.

Turning slowly about in the moonlight, Perrell opened his eyes and found himself staring at the waterfall. Silently he pointed, and his men swiftly spread out, as noiseless as a hunting pride of canars, to hurry toward the river. Perrell limped behind them, keeping his focus, his hand on his sword hilt, his heart starting to thump in anticipation of a good fight.

Over to one side, Sir Cortaine held Avlon gripped by one arm as he quietly but forcefully explained the procedure. "Not a word from you," he growled very softly. "Keep quiet and stay away from the reverend commander, or I'll be wearing your tongue on my belt for a trophy."

Perrell did not hear Avlon's reply. All he knew was that shortly both men caught up with him and tagged at his heels.

As the terrain sloped upward and grew difficult, Cortaine gave Perrell assistance without being asked. Perrell was deeply focused now not only on holding the tracing but also in masking their approach from the Sebeins, and he could spare little attention to where he was walking, especially after tracks were finally found on the muddy slope near the falls. Cortaine guided him gently away from the precipice and over to the safer side of the incline.

Something bumped Perrell's mind. He stopped walking and quickly wove a deception through his thoughts and those of his men. The suspicious moment of connection ceased, and Perrell drew in a breath. He lost concentration just enough to become aware that he was being drenched with spray. Looking ahead, he saw Sir Tolard in the lead. With drawn sword in hand, the knight stood at the edge of the plummeting water. So loud and thunderous was the roar that Perrell could barely hear other sounds. He saw Sir Tolard step through the water, vanishing from sight. The next man followed, and Perrell and Sir Cortaine exchanged looks.

"What is it, a cave behind the falls?" Avlon bellowed in Perrell's ear.

Although his voice was somewhat muffled by the rushing water, Perrell jumped and nearly lost the deception he was using to conceal their presence.

Not even daring to let himself feel any emotions, he shut

his eyes, refocusing his concentration swiftly while Sir Cortaine shoved Avlon away from him. There came sounds of a brief scuffle before all was quiet.

Then Sir Cortaine returned, gently gripping Perrell's elbow and guiding him forward up the narrow, slippery trail. A torrent of water sluiced over him, drenching him to the skin, and he passed through the falls and stood inside the dark cave where his men were waiting.

They had pulled their Circles out atop their surcoats and held their swords ready. The hilt guard of each weapon was shaped in a circle and engraved with the Blessing of Tomias. Drawing his weapon, Perrell lifted the guard reverently to his lips as with his mind he sparked the beginning of the Unison. Whispers of the Blessing filtered through his mind. He drew them into his being in formless prayer, feeling Sir Cortaine's thoughts link to his, and Sir Tolard's, and Sir Gelire's and so on, around the circle of men until the Unison was complete.

Perrell let the deception he'd been holding fade from his thoughts, for he no longer had to shoulder the burden of masking their presence alone. With all his knights joined to his mind in Unison, it was easy now to stay undetected by Sebein thought readers. The Unison could not be sustained for long, of course, but Perrell believed their quarry was close.

He made a gesture that started his men stealthily forward.

Only a scant amount of moonlight filtered through the waterfall to illuminate their way, and within a few steps it faded completely. They all stopped as of one accord, despite Avlon's stumbling bewildered in their midst. As long as he remained within the center of their Unison, even he could not betray them. But Perrell could have done without his hindrance.

Listening, Perrell tried to let his eyes adjust to the darkness.

The darkness of the Sebeins, he thought. *Like vermin, they live in holes and caves and tunnels, shunning the light as they shun all goodness in the world.*

He let the quiet stretch around them and was rewarded at last by hearing a quick murmur of voices up ahead before there was silence again.

One of the voices he recognized as the queen's. His heart leaped, but he swiftly disciplined himself lest Unison be broken.

They edged forward, finding a jutting wall of stone in their way. Peering past it, Perrell saw blazing torchlight ahead. Sebeins stood clustered, shifting and swaying. One of their most infamous leaders, Kanth, stood head and shoulders taller than the rest. His gray hair and blind eye marked him unmistakably.

Perrell saw the queen kneeling on the ground with her hands lifted in supplication. The fervent murmur of her voice rose and ebbed as she turned to touch the face of a man lying chained on the ground.

At first Perrell could not see who it was, but when the queen rose to her feet, he saw that it was Lord Talmor for whom she pleaded.

Shock at seeing the man alive ran through Perrell, and he nearly snapped the Unison. Sir Cortaine gripped his shoulder, but Perrell hardly paid attention. How could the baron be alive? he wondered. Was this some spell concocted by the Sebeins to trick the queen? Or did the baron possess special protections of his own to bring him back from the dead? Was he immortal? Surely otherwise that blow from Cortaine had broken the man's skull. Talmor had not roused when they rolled him over the edge of the trail. He'd not loosed a moan or a whimper.

Perrell realized he was not breathing. He was sitting there in disbelieving shock, letting his discipline unravel.

Having finished what she was saying to Kanth, the queen now knelt again by Lord Talmor. She caressed his face with such gentleness, such tenderness that jealousy ignited in Perrell, and he let the Unison shatter completely.

Kanth whirled in their direction, staring as though he could see where they lurked in the darkness. "We are not alone!" he said loudly.

"Men, get ready to attack," Sir Cortaine whispered.

"No!" Perrell countermanded the order swiftly. Despite their obvious surprise, he kept his gaze locked on what was taking place. Jealousy was raging in his heart, blinding him to good sense. Clearly Lord Talmor was intended to be a victim. *Let him be sacrificed,* Perrell thought savagely, and whispered to his men, "We do nothing. Not yet."

"But, revered sir!" Cortaine whispered urgently. "We—"

"Nothing!"

Avlon pushed forward. "If you won't save her, I will—"

Perrell thrust his sword point against Avlon's side, and the guardsman froze, his breathing audible. "Are you mad?" he whispered. "This is our one chance to save her!"

Part of Perrell wanted to charge forward and yank Pheresa from danger. Another part of him seemed to be hearing a thin, cold voice in the back of his mind, urging him to wait. *If they both die,* he thought, *the path to the throne is open.* Torn and horrified by what he was thinking, he still could not seem to stop himself.

"Are you with them?" Avlon asked in disbelief. "A sympathizer?"

Seeing doubt and suspicion creeping into the faces of his men there in the gloom, Perrell frowned and suddenly wrestled himself under control. He drew a ragged breath, aware that he'd cost them their slim element of surprise.

"Let's go," he commanded, and they charged forward.

Faced with the worst decision of her life, Pheresa knew she could not take the slim chance of escape Talmor was offering her. She could see the strain in her beloved's face. His eyes had darkened to something unrecognizable, so dangerous and angry they frightened her. He was shaking now, his lips skimming back from his teeth in a grimace as he fought to control whatever Kanth had stirred inside him. She could see the sinews popping up in his throat as he writhed on the ground. And the flames were licking up between his clenched fingers, dancing on his skin, shooting up and ebbing low.

Frightened by what she saw, a part of her wanted to turn and flee as he'd bade her, to get far away from whatever he was. But the rest of her that loved him knew this was not his doing, not his fault. Kanth had wrought this evil in him. Pheresa understood that Talmor intended to immolate Kanth and as many of the Sebeins as he could. Once he surrendered control of his fire, she would have only scant moments to flee for her life.

"No, Talmor," she said, caressing his hot face, trying to get him to look at her so that terrible fury would leave his eyes. "Talmor!" she shouted. "You must not unleash evil that I may live. I won't run away. We'll die together."

"Oh, very touching," Kanth said.

She glared at the Sebein. "You want him to lose his soul, but he isn't going to. I won't let him throw it away."

"Your bravery is a farce—"

"No, 'tis my faith I draw on now," she corrected him.

Kanth drew back with a hiss, and for an instant she felt jubilant, believing her words had touched something vulnerable inside him. But instead Kanth whirled to stare into the dark end of the cave.

"We are not alone," he said.

His followers turned. Some reached for knives, and others drew forth pouches made of tightly woven metal links.

Pheresa seized the opportunity to bend over Talmor. "Whatever comes, do not give way," she whispered to him. "I love you. Our souls will go Beyond together if Thod wills it. But do not let Kanth take you into darkness, not for me. Not for any cost."

Talmor said nothing. He was panting, his face running with sweat. At first she did not think he'd heard her at all, but then he twisted his wrist until he was able to grasp the chain binding him. Seeing his knuckles whiten, she believed he was gripping hard to keep from throwing fire. He looked up at her and lifted one corner of his mouth in a tiny, tremulous smile.

Such tenderness surged through her that she almost couldn't smile back. And suddenly she wasn't afraid anymore. At least, not like before. Acceptance filled her, and she found herself growing strangely calm. Her soul was at peace, and all that remained was for her to find the courage to carry through the sacrifice she intended to make.

Whipping around, Kanth glared at her as though sensing
her decision. His lips pulled back from his teeth, and his re-
finement dropped, revealing the savagery beneath. "Fool!" he
shouted at her. "It is not that easy."

As he spoke, he rushed at her. When she saw the ceremonial knife in his hand, Pheresa scrambled back from him with
a scream. She stumbled over Talmor's legs, tripped, and fell
awkwardly.

Kanth plucked her upright on her feet as though she
weighed nothing and put his knife to her throat.

"Pheresa!" Talmor shouted frantically.

She tried to look at him, but Kanth's grip would not let her.
"Remember!" she called out. "Your promise, Talmor. Your
promise!"

"Pathetic little fool," Kanth was spitting at her. "Do you
really think such simplistic beliefs will avail you?"

Crying, she tried to answer, but another voice, familiar and
masculine, spoke first: "In the faith of the Circle do we face
you. In the name of Tomias we refute you. In the force of
Thod we come to destroy you. Let her majesty go!"

Holding Pheresa as a shield, Kanth spun around. She saw
Sir Perrell standing at the head of his knights, pointing a
drawn sword at Kanth. The reverend commander's dark blue
eyes burned with righteous fury, and there was a glow around
him and his men, a glow such as she'd seen emanating only
from magicked weapons in the presence of darkest evil.

Pheresa dragged in her breath in wonder, staring at Perrell
as he advanced on Kanth like an avenger. The other Sebeins
drew back, and although some lifted the metal pouches in
silent threat, it took only a church knight's sword pointed their
way for them to drop the pouches unopened.

"Come no closer!" Kanth commanded, and the power in
his voice made the air tremble. "Heathen defilers of the truth,
do not use the power of the Circle against me! You don't
know the meaning of the words you use. You don't even believe you're using magic."

"We have no magic," Sir Perrell said firmly. "What we use
is far older."

Suffocating in the crook of Kanth's arm, Pheresa prayed with all her might: *I believe in the sanctity of the Chalice of Eternal Life. I believe in Thod the merciful. I believe in the unity of the Circle. I believe . . .*

Kanth shook her so hard her teeth rattled. "Stop it!" he screamed, and slashed at her throat.

Instinctively she twisted and dropped in one of the fighting moves she'd been taught. The knife skimmed the side of her throat, only scratching her. At the same time, Sir Perrell cried out a word of such magical power the stone above their heads cracked. Kanth staggered back as though he'd been struck, and Pheresa broke free of his grasp.

Talmor, who'd been writhing frantically on the ground, burned through the chain securing his arm with a burst of sparks and molten metal. He sat up, and yelled, "Pheresa, get down!"

She ducked just as Talmor threw his dagger, and the blade thudded into Kanth's chest.

The Sebein priest staggered from the blow, but then bared his teeth in a mad grimace of amusement. "Stupid fool!" he said. "Did you not wonder why I left you armed? I have no heart for you to stab."

As he spoke, he reached up to pull the dagger from his chest. But Sir Perrell's sword took off his head from behind.

"In Thod's name, you are destroyed!" he shouted.

Kanth's head, gruesome and slinging gouts of blood, went rolling past Pheresa into the fire. His body swayed and toppled to the ground, twitching until Sir Perrell swiftly staked it.

The other Sebeins tried to flee, but there was nowhere for them to go as the church knights rounded them up swiftly and held them at sword point.

Pheresa hardly dared believe the worst was over. She ran to Talmor, still sitting chained by the ankles, and hugged him in relief. "I knew you could withstand him," she whispered in pride. "Thod be thanked! I—I—was afraid I might falter, but you I never doubted. I—"

"Your majesty?"

It was Sir Perrell standing over her. She glanced up, feel-

ing flushed and giddy and shaken. "Reverend commander,"
she said, scrambling for some composure, "please see that
Lord Talmor is freed at once."

Sir Perrell beckoned to one of his men, the large one with
the broken nose, who sidled up to a scowling Talmor as
though expecting to be attacked. Pheresa could not help but
notice how pale the reverend commander looked. His dark
blue gaze kept shifting from her to Talmor.

"Valiant Sir Perrell, you have come to my rescue just in
time," she said, extending her hand.

He took it, his callused fingers enclosing hers as he knelt
before her.

"'Tis my duty to serve," he said gruffly, then lost his composure. "I beg your majesty's pardon for waiting too long. I
did not act as swiftly as I should have. I have been much at
fault this night."

"What? I find no fault in your actions," she said in surprise. "Come, do not be undone now. Please rise and accept
my thanks. I know not how you subdued that monster. I think
perhaps I witnessed a miracle of faith."

"Verily, it was not."

"Well, I am pleased that you came when you did."

Her praise and compliments did not seem to hearten him,
for he frowned. "Your majesty," he said, "please let me escort
you outside. My men have grim work before them. It is not
fitting that you should watch."

Some of her gladness fell away, for she understood that the
church knights intended to perform executions on the spot.
"No," she agreed quietly, "I do not want to watch."

But although he offered his arm with a courtly bow, she
did not take it. Instead, she glanced over her shoulder at Talmor, now freed of his chains and standing hunched over and
pale. When he saw her gaze, he tried to straighten with a
wincing smile.

Her heart turned over, and she went to him, holding his
arm to steady him. "You silly man," she said softly, for his
ears alone. "Pretending to flex your muscles and look so hale.
It's bed you need, and the attendance of a physician."

His expression tender, he started to reply, but Sir Perrell joined them. The two men glared at each other grimly, like two hostile dogs claiming the same territory.

She could have shaken them both. "Talmor," she said in rebuke, "will you not express your gratitude to Sir Perrell for coming to our aid?"

Talmor scowled. "There is much I want to say to Sir Perrell."

The commander stiffened, his burnished head rising haughtily, his eyes taking on a look of defiance.

When Talmor narrowed his gaze, Pheresa stepped hastily between them. "What is this rivalry I see? Tonight you men worked together to defeat a terrible enemy. You are both valiant warriors, both loyal Mandrians, and both to be praised in our victory. Why can you not be glad of that? Well? What say you?"

"Will you explain to her majesty, or shall I?" Talmor asked Sir Perrell coldly.

"Explain what?" Pheresa asked in exasperation. "You have been fighting each other, haven't you?" She stared at Sir Perrell, from his pale, set face to the leg he was favoring. As for Talmor, he was filthy, his clothing torn and bloody, his face scratched, and the wound on the back of his head still oozing down his neck. When she'd first seen him chained tonight, a prisoner of the Sebeins, she thought they'd inflicted such harm to him. Now she was not so sure.

When neither man answered her, she scowled. "Yes, fighting," she said. "Tearing at each other instead of Sebeins." She did not have to ask them why. As a woman, she understood, and she was suddenly, fiercely angry with them both for being such *fools*.

Without another word, she swept away, gesturing imperiously for Lord Avlon, who for once appeared neither insolent nor mocking, to escort her from the cave.

Talmor and Sir Perrell were left behind to glare at each other. With Pheresa finally out of the way, Talmor longed to draw his sword on the reverend commander and resume battle, but he lacked the strength. His head ached mercilessly, and Kanth's torture had left him feeling prickly and queer as though he could jump out of his skin.

"You cur," Talmor said in a low, furious voice. "The queen trusts and values you, but you are a—"

"Lord baron," Sir Perrell broke in quickly, clearing his throat. His blue eyes shifted from Talmor's, refusing to meet them. "I was in the wrong tonight. I should not have challenged you. I withdraw any insult I said to you and offer my apologies."

Talmor's brows drew together. He waited, but it seemed Sir Perrell had nothing to say beyond this stilted little speech. "Is that all?" he asked.

"All?"

"Yes, all!" Talmor said so loudly some of the knights looked their way. Sir Cortaine was glaring at Talmor with open hostility. Talmor glared back at him before turning his hot gaze on Sir Perrell. "You provoked our fight without cause."

"Agreed," Sir Perrell replied mildly. "I—I misunderstood the situation. I had my mind on other problems, and that colored my judgment."

"Worse, you ended the fight without honor."

Red crept up Sir Perrell's throat. "That happened without my order. Sir Cortaine can be . . . protective."

"Your weak apologies only insult me more," Talmor said in a rage. "The man is your responsibility, and I hold you to blame for his actions as well as your own. I want—"

"Please," Sir Perrell said softly, his gaze darting past Talmor to his men and back again. "I have admitted my wrong. Let that be an end to it. If you challenge me publicly as I deserve, the queen will want to know why. I beg you to keep this between us." He paused, his mouth tightening. "And though I prefer to meet you on any field you name, lord baron, I am precluded from doing so."

"Why?"

"Because you're the queen's favorite. She's made that very clear," Sir Perrell said bitterly. "And to attack the queen's favorite is to attack her majesty. I am bound by duty to withdraw. Again, I offer my apologies. Let this end an unfortunate matter."

Talmor frowned, finding Sir Perrell's tone frosty, but sincere. Yet instinct made Talmor hesitate. He thought back to the sense of unease he'd felt just before Sir Perrell attacked him on the mountain trail. He'd suspected the man of lying then, of pretending suspicion and ire to mask some other purpose. And he sensed a lie now.

To end his doubts, he soulgazed Sir Perrell . . . or attempted to, but it was as though a stone wall protected the reverend commander's mind. Talmor slid past Sir Perrell's thoughts as though they did not exist, and learned nothing. That inflamed his suspicions even more.

For a moment the two men stared at each other very hard.

"This is not finished," Talmor said, very softly indeed.

"So do you intend to tell her? She will order my career destroyed if you ask it," Sir Perrell said stiffly.

It was the worst insult Sir Perrell had given him yet. Affronted, Talmor wondered how a man of such apparent worth, courage, and dedication could rot inside like this. He did not need to soulgaze Sir Perrell to sense his guilt and fear. Talmor knew all about overachievement to compensate for the hidden flaws that could eat away a man's confidence. Whatever Sir Perrell was or had attained, somewhere along the way he'd sold an essential part of himself to get there.

Thus far, Thod be thanked, Talmor had not. He let his gaze wander back to the broken chains lying on the ground, then looked at Kanth's headless body and knew he'd come close tonight to doing so. Too close. If not for Pheresa's faith and courage, he would have been lost.

Clammy coldness sank through him, and he suddenly felt very tired. Too tired to set himself above Sir Perrell and judge him.

"No," Talmor said with a sigh. "I will not carry tales to her majesty. I accept your apologies, and I will not issue challenge."

"Thank you," Sir Perrell said, and extended his hand in truce.

Talmor would not take it. He watched Sir Perrell slowly lower his hand, and he kept his expression hard and unforgiving.

Before walking away, Talmor said swiftly, "If your Cortaine comes at me again, I'll kill him. That, I swear to you."

Leaving Sir Perrell staring after him, he strode out of the cave, ducking through the waterfall and emerging into the waning moonlight. Pheresa was waiting there on the ledge for him.

Lord Avlon had moved farther down the trail, waving and shouting a loud halloo toward the palace.

"I told him to hurry and announce the news of my rescue," Pheresa confessed with laughter in her voice. "Have you and Sir Perrell decided to behave like men of good manners, good morals, and civilized decency?"

"We have an understanding," Talmor said carefully.

"You realize that there will always be men infatuated with the queen," she said more seriously. "You cannot, indeed you must not, fight them all."

"I'll remember," Talmor said, dismissing Sir Perrell from his thoughts. At any moment he knew they were going to be surrounded by jubilant guardsmen, then courtiers, then officials and ministers. And it would all begin anew. But at that moment they were alone, and he did not intend to waste such an opportunity.

Gently, he tilted up her face. In the moon's pale radiance he saw her smile. She said something so soft he could not hear it in the water's roar, but it did not matter. He knew she was safe tonight because she'd had the courage to believe in what was good and right. Even more, she had believed in him with such utter trust that he'd also found the inner strength he needed. She was, he thought gratefully, his savior. He knew he was willing now to go on struggling against his curse, determined to control it no matter what befell him.

And nothing, no law or criticism, could ever break the bond forged between him and Pheresa this night. They would, he thought, find their way.

As for the lady, she never ceased to enchant and amaze him. Smiling down into her shining eyes, Talmor knew he could never love her more than he did at that moment. He pulled her close, and kissed her to tell her so.

DEC 0 9 2016